REVIEW COPY
Not For Sale

Gudrun's Tapestry

Also by Joan Schweighardt
(Permanent Press)

Island

Homebodies

Virtual Silence

Gudrun's Tapestry

Joan Schweighardt

Reno, Nevada

Gudrun's Tapestry

 Beagle Bay Books,
a division of Beagle Bay, Inc.
Reno, Nevada
info@beaglebay.com
Visit our website at: http://www.beaglebay.com

Copyright©2003 by Joan Schweighardt

All rights reserved. No part of this book may be reproduced or transmitted in any form or by any means, electronic or mechanical, including photocopying, recording, or by any informational storage and retrieval system, without permission in writing from the publisher, except for the inclusion of brief quotations in a review.

Cover Design: Doug Andersen
Editing Services: Diane DeChillo

Library of Congress Cataloging-in-Publication Data

Schweighardt, Joan, 1949-
  Gudrun's Tapestry / by Joan Schweighardt.-- 1st ed.
    p. cm.
  ISBN 0-9679591-3-6 (hardcover : alk. paper)
  1. Kriemhild (Legendary character)--Fiction. 2. Attila, d. 453--Fiction. 3. Burgundians--Fiction. 4. Huns--Fiction. I. Title.

PS3569.C568G83 2003
813'.54--dc21
                                                2002155060

Book design by Robin P. Simonds

FIRST EDITION
Printed in the Canada

10 9 8 7 6 5 4 3 2 1

DEDICATION

Gudrun's Tapestry is dedicated to the memory of Jean Egurrola, a wonderful friend and a brave woman who insisted, in her last days, on sticking to her promise to edit the first chapters of an earlier version.

ACKNOWLEDGMENTS

Thanks to Alexis Hurley, Kim Witherspoon and Lorna Tychostup, whose enthusiasm for *Gudrun's Tapestry* kept me in the ring longer than I might have stayed otherwise. Thanks to Arlene Weber, who—long before we became close friends—agreed to accept some strange payment (including a stair bannister) in return for retyping parts of the original manuscript following my computer's demise. Thanks to Jacqueline Church Simonds and Robin Simonds for their support, which went above and beyond taking on this title, and also for being so much fun to work with. And thanks to Adam Mason, Alex Greenberg, Min-Young Kim and Michael Dooley for loving me.

Gudrun's Tapestry

PREFACE

When I was a young girl living at Worms, there was nothing I delighted in more than song. And of all those who lifted their voices in our great hall, there were none who did so as beautifully as my brother Gunner. Were he beside me now, he would rebuke me for the method that I have chosen to relate my story to you. He would insist, instead, on fashioning a melody for my words and singing them to you from beginning to end. He would begin modestly, singing, as he always did, that he had no talent for melodies, but entreating you, nevertheless, to remember his words. And, friend, as there is no bird, no Summer breeze, no sweet stream lapping or soft rain falling that could compete with Gunner for one's attention, have no doubt that you would have remembered them. He would have looked into your eyes while he sang and touched you in a deeper place than he ever touched a man or a woman when he went without his harp.

Though I can never hope to emulate his elegance, let me begin likewise, telling you first that I have no talent either. This thing, this process of setting down one word after the next on parchment, is new to me, and, as a friend once stated, tedious. And in spite of all the pains that I have taken to learn it, I find that I am apprehensive now because I cannot look into your eyes as my brother would have, because I cannot hope to touch you in that holy place where the hearts of all folk are joined together. Still, I would have you remember my words.

The City of Attila

Chapter 1

I fell to my knees at the stream, so eager to drink that I did not think to offer a prayer until afterward, when I was satisfied and my flask was full. I was exhausted. My skin was parched and I was filthy; but according to the map my brothers had given me, I was very near my destination. I left on foot, pulling my tired horse behind me.

I had not had a full night's rest since the terrain had changed. The land was flat here. There were no caves or rocky ledges where I could shelter myself. The forests, so sacred to my people, had long since been replaced by endless grasslands. As I trudged through them, I felt that I had left more than my loved ones behind.

When the sky darkened, I used the single live coal I carried from the previous night's fire to light my torch. I was sure that the light could be seen from some distance. I expected at every moment to hear the thunder of hooves beating on the arid earth. But on and on I walked, seeing no sight other than my own shadow in the gleam of the torch light and hearing no sound but that of my horse plodding along beside me.

When the sun began to rise, I saw that there was a sandy hill ahead, and hoping to see the City of Attila from its summit, I dragged myself on. But the hill was much farther away than it had seemed, and it took most of the day to reach it. And then it was much higher, too, the highest ground that I had seen in days. My horse, who was content to graze on grassy clumps and to watch the marmots who dared to peek out of their holes, made it clear that he had no desire to climb. I had to coax him along, and myself as well, for now I was afraid that I would reach the summit and see nothing but more grasses stretching out to the far horizon. I imagined myself wandering endlessly, seeing no one, coughing and sneezing in response to the invisible blowing dust, until my food ran out and my horse gave way.

I crawled to the top of the hill—and looked down in amazement at the camp of make-shift tents below. In front of one of them a fire burned, and the carcass of an antelope was roasting over it. There were many men about, perhaps two hundred, all on horseback except for the few tending the fire.

It was not until I heard the war cry that I knew for certain that the scene was real and not some trick of my mind. I had been sighted. The entire company was suddenly galloping in my direction, a cloud of dust rising up around them. I forced myself to my feet and spread my arms to show that I carried no weapon. When I saw that the men were making their bows ready, I dropped my head and lifted my arms higher yet—to the heavens—where, I hoped, the gods were watching carefully.

Part of the company surrounded me. The others rode past, over the summit. When they were satisfied that no one was riding behind me, they joined the first group. Upon the command of one of them, they all lowered their bows. I began to breathe again. A murmur went up, and while I waited for it to subside, I studied their horses. Of the two that I could see without moving my head, one looked like the ones the Romans rode—a fine, tall, light-colored steed. The other looked like no animal I had ever seen before. Its legs were short and its head was large and somehow misshapen. Its matted mane hung down over its stout body. Its nose was snubbed and its eyes bulged like a fish's. Its back was curved, as if by the weight of its rider. Yet its thick neck and large chest suggested great strength.

The murmur abated, and the Hun on the horse I'd been scrutinizing cried out a command in his harsh, foreign tongue. I looked up—and noted that he resembled his horse. He was short and stout, large-chested, his head overly large, his neck short and thick, his nose snubbed. The only difference was that while the horse had a long mane and a bushy tail, the Hun's hair was thin, and his beard—if one could call it that—was thinner yet. He seemed to be waiting for me to speak. I stared at the identical scars that ran down the sides of his face—wide, deep mutilations that began beneath his deeply set eyes and ended at his mouth. "I've come to seek Attila," I said.

The Hun, who appeared slightly amused, looked to his companions. A murmur went up again. While they debated, I took the opportunity to scan the other Hun faces, all hideous replicas of the one who had spoken to me. Of course I had known the Huns were strange to look upon. Although I'd been hidden away during the siege, I'd had a description from those who had seen the Huns and survived to tell about them. In fact, there were some among my people who mutilated their own faces after the siege, believing this would make them as fierce as their attackers. Still, none of this had prepared me sufficiently to look upon them with my own eyes. Some wore tunics and breeches, not unlike the ones my own people wore. Others wore garments made entirely of marmot skins. With some on Roman horses and others on Hunnish ones, some dressed like Thuets and others in skins, they looked like no army I had ever seen before. Their confusion over how to respond to me only heightened the impression of disorder.

"Attila!" I cried. My brothers were sure I was mad, and when I heard my shout I thought they must be right.

The startled Huns stared for a moment, then they took up their debate again, their voices louder and more urgent than before. Finally the leader nodded, and the man whose argument he had come to agree with rode to my side and took my horse's reins from my hand. While he started down the hill with the horse, another Hun poked me from behind with his riding whip to indicate that I should follow. Half of the men began the descent with me. The other half stayed on the summit, looking off in the direction from which I had come.

I was brought to the fire, where I reiterated my desire to see Attila. One of the Huns pointed beyond the tents. I followed his finger. There were a few dark clouds converging on the eastern horizon. "Can we ride?" I asked, pointing to my horse. The Hun gestured for me to sit. The meat had been removed from the fire and torn into pieces. The horseless Huns were distributing it among the riders. One of them brought a piece to me, and another brought me a flask of what smelled like Roman wine. I ate the meat—which was tough and bland—and kept my eyes fastened on my horse and the sack that hung from his side. I tasted the wine and, to the amusement of the Huns who were watching, quickly spat it out—for this is what I imagined a woman who had grown up alone in the forest would do.

After the meal, I stood and pointed east. "Take me to the City of Attila," I demanded. Again, my words caused a stir.

Then one of the Huns said something which quieted the others. He gave a series of commands, and one of the listeners slid off his horse and reluctantly offered me the reins.

I hesitated, unsure what to do about the sack. Gathering courage, I led the Hunnish horse past my guards and over to my own horse. I reached for the sack, but a stout Hunnish arm cut me off. "For Attila," I said. The man who had stopped me looked to his fellows. Again there was discussion, and after a moment, a decision. The arm withdrew. I swallowed and removed the sack from one beast and secured it onto the other. Then I mounted the Hunnish horse and settled myself as best I could on its hard wooden saddle. The Hun who was to be my escort came forward. Someone furnished him with a torch, and, also, what sounded like a lecture.

Riding at his side, I considered how easily it had gone. The Huns might have insisted that I stay the night in their camp. Or, they might have made me leave the sack behind. And there was much worse that I could think of, too. If I had felt bold before, I felt even bolder now, and, indeed, quite mad. I was already imagining the expressions that would appear on my brothers' faces when I was home again relating the story.

The comical-looking beast beneath me was as fast as he was strong. He galloped along as if riderless, keeping pace with the Hun's horse and seemingly oblivious to my touch on his reins. I lowered my head onto his thick dirty mane, and, keeping my arms tight around his neck, closed my burning eyes. After a while, the horse's steps became shorter, choppier—so that I knew the terrain had changed. The grasses were higher now, like the ones I had ridden through some days earlier when the trees had first begun to thin. I relaxed and gave way to the muffled sound of the horses' hooves. When I opened my eyes again, I thought to find myself riding beneath the stars with the moon on the rise to the south. To my astonishment, the sky was pink, and it was the sun that was rising. My arms, which were stiff and badly cramped, had kept their vigil all through the night.

My companion laughed heartily when I lifted my head. And thinking that my riding and sleeping on horseback would make a fine story for Attila's ears, I laughed as well. I imagined myself explaining that valkyrias did this all the time. I had trained my mind on the powers I would feign to have for so long that my uncanny slumber made me feel I had actually come to possess them.

Soon enough, the City of Attila appeared on the horizon—a vast tract surrounded by a high wooden palisade. My escort stopped to point it out, and I checked myself for panic. When I was satisfied that I felt none, I nodded, and we began to ride again. Before long we reached the city gates and the men who guarded them. My escort stayed at my side only long enough to deliver his message to the guard who rode to meet us. Then he turned and rode off, taking with him the story which I had hoped to hear repeated to Attila. The gates were pulled open. My new escort led me in.

Activity was everywhere. Clusters of men on horseback were engaged in conversations. Women walked among them carrying baskets or vessels on their heads. They were trailed by small children while older children sat in circles on the ground laughing and teasing one another. Most were Huns, but there were others who were clearly Thuets. And there were some, especially among the children, who appeared to be half and half. The Hun women, like their men, were short and stout. Many were quite fat. Only their lack of facial scars distinguished them from their male counterparts.

Mud and straw huts dotted the landscape. Beyond them, in the distance, was a second wooden palisade, its circumference so great that it appeared to take up half the city. As we approached it, the gates opened. We entered a long tunnel from which I could hear the pounding of feet overhead. There were other smaller tunnels leading off to the left and right, but their doors concealed the chambers they led to.

When we came back out into the daylight, I saw yet another palisade—this one set back on a high grassy mound. Like the city walls and the first inner palisade, it was circular, with wooden towers protruding at intervals. From each tower, guards looked down. "Attila's palace?" I asked my escort, though I knew the answer even before he nodded.

There was as much activity here as there had been within the first palisade, but my gaze fell on the group of men who tarried on their horses nearest Attila's gate. This group was more richly dressed than others I had seen. Many wore arm rings and finger rings. Some even had precious stones sewn into their shoes. It was the most heavily jeweled that my escort seemed to be eyeing as we approached. Thinking this man must be Attila, I took a deep breath and prepared myself to speak the words I had so thoroughly rehearsed. But when he turned toward me, I saw immediately that he could not possibly be Attila. He was not even a Hun. Though his face was as deeply scarred as those of his companions, he was clearly a Thuet. I had felt no emotion seeing the other Thuets in the village, because I took them to be prisoners, men who had been forced into Attila's service. But the jewels and dress on this one indicated that he was pleased to live among the Huns, that he had earned Attila's favor. He glanced at me. If he saw the involuntary look of disdain that crossed my face, his expression did not reflect it. He listened to the words of my escort, then jerked his head to indicate that I should come with him.

To my disappointment, he led me away from Attila's gates, off to the southwest of his palisade, past a good many more huts and through a large open field and very nearly to the far wall of the inner palisade. There were only a few huts ahead of us now, and unlike the others that I had seen, they were spread apart and faced west rather than east. The one the Thuet took me to was the most isolated of all. But it was built up on a small knoll, and I could see the vast stretches of grassland beyond the tops of the inner palisade and the city walls just behind it—a boon for a woman who had never before found herself enclosed within so many fortifications.

The Thuet motioned for me to dismount. My legs were weak, and I had to hold on to the Hunnish beast to get my balance. When I was able, I made a move toward the sheepskin curtain that covered the doorway of the hut, but I hesitated when I heard voices inside. The Thuet heard them too, and in what seemed one motion, he jumped from his horse and threw back the curtain, exposing a young couple. In the Hunnish tongue, he admonished them harshly, his riding crop held threateningly over his head. Holding their garments in front of them, the couple backed out of the hut and bolted. The Thuet lowered his whip and laughed as he watched them flee bare-assed across the open field. Then he turned back to me, his expression fierce again. "Get yourself inside now," he shouted.

I stepped into the hut, and holding the curtain open, watched anxiously as he cut down the sack from the side of my horse. I told myself that I should be pleased to be in the company of one who spoke my language, but my hatred persisted. He threw the sack in carelessly, so that it fell just short of my feet. Then he entered, drawing the sheepskin curtain behind him so that only a little daylight streamed in.

I looked around in the dim light. There was no window, no hearth. A pile of skins were thrown into one corner, and more skins lined the four walls. "I have come to seek an audience with Attila," I said.

He laughed.

"I must see Attila," I reiterated. "I've come a long way—"

His hand sliced through the air. "You are not to leave your hut," he said in a voice that was unnecessarily loud in the tiny space. "A guard will be posted at your door day and night. You are not to attempt to speak to him. You are not to speak to anyone. If you try to escape, you will be killed. Do you understand?"

I did not. His declaration was a contradiction to the ease that had brought me this far. I took a step toward him. "What is your connection to Attila?"

He laughed, then sobered abruptly. "I am Edeco, second in command," he boasted.

"Then let me speak to the man who is first in command," I hissed.

Edeco drew his lips back, exposing his teeth. His hand came up from his side slowly, and I lifted my head, bracing for the impact. But his hand faltered and hung in the space between us, quivering for a moment. Then it dropped. He turned and went out.

I stood where I was, considering our exchange. At first it seemed to me that things had changed now, that my run of fortune had come to an end. But then I realized how tired I was; my sleep on the racing horse had done little to relieve my fatigue. Perhaps it was best that my audience with Attila be delayed.

I took the sack from the earthen floor and hid it beneath the pile of skins. Then I took a skin from the top and spread it out and lay down. I fell asleep almost immediately—and found myself in the forest behind my brothers' hall, walking among the birches.

Someone called out my name, and when I turned, Sigurd was coming up behind me, leading his steed. I ran to him. When I was safe in his embrace, I cried, "Oh, Sigurd, I have been so afraid! I am so glad to have found you. Things will go well enough now. You will not let me face Attila alone, will you?"

He smiled. "I will not," he said. "I'll be at your side every moment, as I have been all along, whether you knew it or not."

I clung to him, my heart almost breaking with emotion. "I have the war sword," I whispered. "I plan to give it to Attila."

"Let him have the cursed thing," Sigurd answered. "For all that it shines like the sun, it brought me nothing but trouble." There was a warm honey-like scent in the air; it seemed to emanate from Sigurd.

"But if the thing is truly cursed," I asked, "how is it that it had no effect on me in all the days that I carried it at my side?"

Sigurd only smiled. "Have you thought by what name you will call yourself here?" he asked.

"Brunhild," I answered.

"It will bring you bad luck to call yourself after someone who loved you so little," Sigurd replied. "Why not call yourself Ildico?"

"Ildico," I repeated, and I recalled that Ildico had been the name of the valkyria who had befriended my mother many years ago, the same woman who had brought my eldest brother into the world.

"Ildico," I said again, but this time I spoke aloud as well as in my dream, and the sound of my voice awakened me.

I remained motionless for a long time. I had dreamed of Sigurd many times since I had regained my health, but always he was at some distance, riding among other men. Or, if he was close, he was silent and oblivious to my presence.

I gave up the notion of falling asleep again and sat up. He was with me; he had said so. No matter what dangers lay ahead, I would be satisfied if sleep would sometimes bring me the sight of Sigurd's face and the feel of his embrace, from which my skin was still tingling. But the dream puzzled me, too. Ildico: I had never thought to call myself that. And why had I told Sigurd that I was afraid when I felt no fear? When my madness lingered and made me bold?

The curtain was drawn aside. A Hun woman entered carrying a bowl of meats and breads, a cup, and a large wooden vessel of wine. She set everything down and left without once looking at me. I got up and rushed to the curtain, but she had already turned the corner of the hut. I saw only the guard who had been posted outside, and the sun, which was low in the western sky. I had slept for some time.

I ate with vigor, in a manner that I would have once scolded my brothers for. I was determined not to touch the wine, but as I had no water left in my flask, I took a sip. It did not taste nearly as bad as it had the last time I had tried it on Burgundian lands. I drank more.

When the curtain opened again not long afterward, it was the Thuet, Edeco. He left the curtain open behind him and sat down across from me. I studied his face and sipped at the wine, which made me feel light-headed and even more impudent. "Have you come to hear me speak?" I asked.

Edeco laughed. "I did not come to clear away your crumbs."

I ignored his sarcasm. "Then I will tell you what I tried to tell you before. I have come a long way, riding for days, to see the face of Attila. I have eaten, I have drunk, I have rested. I would be pleased to be brought to him now."

Edeco threw his head back and laughed so heartily that I was forced to think of Gunner, who also threw his head back when he laughed. Then Edeco's face changed. "Why should he see you?"

"I carry a gift for Attila," I said.

"Attila receives many gifts, most so large that they must be carried in carts pulled by oxen and guarded over by many men."

"Mine is greater."

"Show it to me."

"I've told you about it. I will show it only to Attila."

Edeco jumped to his feet, his blue eyes flashing. As there was only one place in the tiny hut where a person might hide a thing, he went directly to the skins and cast them aside one by one until he had uncovered the sack. Then he turned it upside down and shook it so that its contents—my cloak, the wooden bowl which Guthorm, my dead brother, had once played with, and the straw concealing the war sword—tumbled out. Edeco fell to his knees and tore at the straw until some part of the blade was revealed. Even in the dimming light, it blazed, as if excited by his agitation. He swept the rest of the straw aside hastily. Then, with his eyes swimming in their sockets, he ran his fingers over the hilt, tracing its intricate engravings. He turned to me and saw, no doubt, my self-satisfied smile, and he immediately lifted his hand from the thing. He cocked his head as if considering something. Then he came back to sit in front of me, though his eyes continued to stray toward the sword.

I got up slowly and placed the war sword back in the sack. I gathered up the straw and shoved it in after it. Then I put the sack in the corner and covered it over with some of the skins. As I went to sit again, I found, to my disgust, that Edeco was just replacing my wine cup. His hand was quaking. "A thing of great beauty, is it not?" I asked.

He looked away. In profile, the deep scar across his cheek looked even more hideous. I seemed again to smell the warm honey scent that had come to me earlier in my dream. Sigurd had to be there, invisible but beside me, just as he had said. The notion made me giddy. Edeco turned back so sharply that I wondered if I had unwittingly laughed aloud. "Who are you?" he demanded.

"Ildico." The power of transformation seemed to lie within the word itself. I was glad Sigurd had suggested it.

"Who are your people?"

I looked aside. "I have none."

He took my chin and jerked my head toward him. I was pleased to see my composure reflected in his eyes. "I'm a Thuet!" I sneered.

"I can see that for myself."

"I was separated from my people when I was a child," I went on. "A band of Romans cut us down while we were traveling. They killed my parents and my brothers and would have killed me, too, had I been older. But I suppose they did not feel it necessary to redden their swords with a small child's blood when she would likely starve or be killed by some beast anyway. But as you can see, no beast crossed my path. And I did not starve, either."

Edeco laughed and let go of my chin roughly. "You look half-starved to me."

"Aye, half. I ate roots and berries. I grew. I learned to steal from the Thuet tribes I came across in my travels. I learned to hunt. There was no excess, but there was enough. And so you see me as I am."

Edeco searched my eyes. "If there were other Thuets about, why didn't you show yourself and beg for mercy?"

"When I was younger, I did not because I was afraid. Having seen my people put to death before my eyes, I had no notion of mercy, and I would not have known how to ask for it anyway since I had no language skills then. As I grew older, I did show myself to other Thuets; I stayed with various tribes from time to time. I learned my language and more. But I longed for the way of life I had become accustomed to."

"How did you come by the sword?"

I sighed and glanced at my wine cup, contaminated now by this Thuet who was a Hun. "It is no ordinary sword. You have seen that. It was fashioned by Wodan himself, back in the days when the gods roamed the Earth as freely as people do now."

Edeco's eyes widened. "How can you be certain?"

"The man it once belonged to told me so."

"And what man is that?"

"He was called Sigurd, a Frankish noble. Perhaps you have heard of—"

"I have not. Tell me how you came by the thing."

I stared at him. These matters I had planned to save for Attila's ears. Now I feared that if I told too much to Edeco, Attila would be satisfied to have the story second-hand. But as it was clear that Edeco would not retreat until I answered him, I explained that long ago the gods had lost the sword to a family of dwarves, and that one of these dwarves, wanting the sword for himself, killed his father. To keep his brothers from confronting him, he changed himself into a dragon and took the sword off into the high mountains. Then, years later, one of the dwarf-dragon's brothers, Regan, promised the sword to Sigurd if Sigurd would accompany him into the high mountains and help him to avenge his father's death. I made no mention of the rest of the gold. Nor did I mention the curse.

Edeco heard my words with interest, taking his eyes from mine only long enough to raise the wine cup to his lips now and again. Once, when I hesitated in my discourse to catch my breath, he passed the cup to me. I put my hand up to renounce it but then thought better of it and drank, the shared cup being an emblem of camaraderie. Edeco smiled then, and I was satisfied to think that I might easily deceive him into believing that I had come to the City of Attila as a friend. "And how did you come to steal the sword from the Frank?" Edeco asked.

"I did not steal the sword from Sigurd," I answered. "After he was dead, I stole it from the man who had gotten it from him. Sigurd loved me. He would have wanted me to have it."

Edeco squinted. I sighed. "You see," I explained, spurred by his disbelief to give more details than I might have otherwise, "Sigurd returned from the high mountains with only his horse, the sword, and the heart of the dragon. His companion, the dwarf, changed his mind about giving Sigurd the sword when he saw again what a glorious thing it was. And since the dwarf had bought Sigurd's assistance with the promise of the sword, Sigurd had no choice but to slay Regan.

"I found Sigurd, forlorn because he'd had to kill an old friend, at the foot of the high mountains, not far from the cave where I lived at the time. He was tired, and confused about what he should say to the Franks concerning Regan's death; although Regan was not a Frank, he had lived among them for many years, and the Franks loved him. Sigurd was afraid that they would demand the war sword as his man-price when they learned that Regan was dead. Thus he was only too glad to return to my cave with me until he had settled his mind on the matter. He lingered, and I wrote a rune outside the cave to keep the Franks at bay in case they should be looking for him. This rune-wisdom was taught to me by a peasant woman with whom I stayed for a time and made potent by the gods themselves when they determined that I should become a valkyria."

I hesitated, but Edeco made no comment on my avowed enlightenment. It occurred to me that perhaps being a Thuet who was not a Thuet, he knew nothing of such matters. "We were well matched," I continued, "me a valkyria with the power to alter events and Sigurd the man who slayed the dragon. And thus it happened that our admiration for each other grew into something more. But before Sigurd and the dwarf set off on their quest, Sigurd had betrothed himself to a Burgundian woman for whom he no longer cared. Still, being a Thuet, he did not like to defile his betrothal vows. And so it was that our intimacy only served to confuse him further. Thus he stayed on with me, vacillating, making himself ill with worry.

"At length, he reached the decision which a man of his word must. He would return to the Burgundian woman, to let her know that he was safe, and then he would ride to the Franks and tell them the truth about the dwarf. But until he had the Franks' reaction to this news, his desire was to keep the sword hidden. He decided to leave it with the Burgundians, for safe-keeping. Even then I felt that his decision was less than wise, but I was so in love with Sigurd that I mistook my premonition for envy and made no attempt to stop him from doing what he felt he must.

"He'd been safe enough with me, but my powers are mine, and once he was away from me, I had no means to lay them on him. He saw the Burgundian woman, left the sword with her brothers, and then he went home to inform the Franks of Regan's death. Later he returned, as he felt he had to, to marry the Burgundian. But shortly after their wedding, her brothers began to behave toward him in a manner which was insulting. The elder of the two complained that Sigurd should have offered the war sword to him as part of his sister's bride-price. Sigurd's wife likewise became greedy. It was not enough for her to be married to so great a man, a dragon-slayer . . . . She once heard him call out my name in his sleep. And when he reddened the next morning when she asked, 'Who is Ildico?' she became enraged. She conspired with her brothers against him. But he grew wise to their conspiracy, and one day he rode out to see me, to tell me all this and to ask my advice. I looked into the fire that was burning at the mouth of my cave, and I saw that Sigurd's wife and her brothers were set on killing him, that his life-blood would be spilt as soon as he returned to them. I told him he must never return. But Sigurd's wife was already heavy with their child, and though he had every right now to break his vows to her, he had no mind to give up the child. He wanted to go back, to offer the sword to his wife's brothers in return for his life, and then, once his wife had delivered the child, which he hoped would be a son, to steal the child and the sword and return to me. I begged him to see that it was more than the sword that these folk wanted. They wanted the glory that Sigurd would have attained, had he lived, in retrieving it. They wanted Sigurd dead so that they could say that they were the ones who had gone off into the high mountains . . . .

"When I told him all this, he shook with rage. He could get used to the idea of giving up the war sword. But to know that the brothers would bask in the glory of his acquisition was too much for him. He was set on returning, now to kill the brothers who would do this to him. I begged him not to go. He went. He was killed."

I hung my head and waited. At length, Edeco spoke. "How did you come to learn of his death?"

I lifted my face so that he could see the tears that had sprung to my eyes. "I knew because I knew. I had foreseen the event in the fire, and I saw it again later, on the walls of my cave as I lay thinking of Sigurd and wishing him back by my side. I knew, but I was numb with sorrow, and for a long time I did nothing. Then, more recently, I came across a tribe of Thuets, Alans, who were traveling to the Western Empire. They spent one night in my cave, and the one who had a harp sang the song of the war sword as he had learned it from the Burgundian brothers.

"I set them right of course, and they promised they would sing the true version thereafter. And when they were gone, I made my plan. I found my way to Burgundian lands, and, at night, when I felt certain that all within were sleeping, I entered the hall of the brothers and found the sword—no difficult task. You saw yourself how the thing catches light in a way which only an enchanted thing may do. The proud brothers had not even thought to hide it. It was there on the wall above the high seat. I took it down noiselessly, and as soon as it was in my hands, I felt how it was thirsty for blood, how it was made to be sated. You know this too! I saw your face when you touched the thing! It was all I could do to hold myself back from taking it up against the brothers and the woman as well. But I understood also that this sword, Wodan's war sword, was meant to cut down armies, not a few insignificant Thuets who would suffer anyway a greater loss than life when they learned the thing was gone. I stole a horse. I rode feverishly. You know the rest."

I sat back on my heels and drained the rest of the wine from my cup. I could feel Edeco's eyes on me, burning with wonder. I was burning, too, with pride and something more. I had imparted my tale with vigor. It differed from the one that I had rehearsed with my brothers before my departure, yes, but it was no less a marvel. I had not meant to mention the Burgundians by name, and I could not think why I had done so, but I did not see how it would matter one way or another. And most of all, in spite of all my fabrications, I had managed to be true, or nearly so, to Sigurd. His name and his glory were secure, even here, in the City of Attila.

I set down the wine cup and glanced at the doorway, graced now by the lower edge of the descending sun. The light pouring in was golden.

"Why Attila?" Edeco asked softly.

I was prepared for the question. "Have you heard nothing?" I exclaimed, falling forward and planting my palm on Edeco's knee. "I grew up in the forest alone, living on what I could steal! I stayed here and there, yes, but only for short periods of time, and none of those I stayed with ever loved me or considered me one of his own. And, in truth, I preferred my aloneness . . . until I met Sigurd. Only then did I come to learn what it means to walk in the shadow of a great man, to be called friend by someone whose powers are equal to my own!

"Sigurd is dead, and I will never love a man that way again. But I have come here to seek the company of another great man, to lend my powers to a man who is, perhaps, in his own way, even greater than Sigurd. And I have brought with me the thing which only a great man may possess, which would cause chaos in the hands of a lesser man."

I jumped to my feet and tossed aside the skins as carelessly as Edeco had earlier. I reached into the sack, and spilling straw everywhere, pulled forth the war sword and held it up by the hilt. When I turned with it, the hot red orb of the sun was lower yet, filling the space now between the top of the doorway and the high palisade beyond it. And thus the sword became a torch in my hand, a wild, flashing thing which put the sun's light to shame. Edeco, who had bounded to his feet as well, abandoned his pretense of indifference now and let his mouth drop open. He drew back and shielded his eyes from the sword's fierce glare. Was it an accident, I wondered in my boldness, that the sun had chosen this moment to set? I had seen that it was setting, but I had made nothing of it; I had not planned to retrieve the sword. Again the warm honey scent permeated the little hut, and I fancied that it was Sigurd who had compelled me to take up the sword at just that time.

My triumph made me giddy. I heard myself laughing wickedly, as the valkyria, Brunhild, might have done. In response, Edeco's expression became even more bewildered, his bright blue eyes darting feverishly from me to the sword to the sun and around again. I felt his fear, his awe. I watched, amused, as he struggled to strike an attitude. His eyes still dancing, he brought his hand up from his side and growled, "Give it to me."

I drew back. "I will give it only to Attila."

"I will give it to him for you. You have my word," he said more gently. "Give it to me. I do not want to have to hurt you."

I laughed in his face, for as I had the sword, the notion was absurd. But the guard, who had halted his horse to learn the cause of the commotion, had seen the thing now, too. I lowered the sword and handed it to Edeco. He took it up as if it were a fragile thing. The guard saw the exchange and began, reluctantly it seemed, to pace again.

"Attila returns tomorrow," Edeco said, his gaze sweeping along the length of the sword. "I will keep the sword until then. I will tell him all that you have told me. I have no doubt that he will send for you." He gestured for the sack.

Gudrun's Tapestry

As soon as he was gone, I spread out the skin I had slept on earlier. I was anxious to see Sigurd again, to discuss with him what I had said and done, if only in a dream. His scent was still heavy in the hut; I had no doubt that his phantom would still be available to me. I lay down and closed my eyes, but my mind was racing, and I could not fall asleep. In spite of my efforts to empty my mind, it bustled with my image, with the way I had spoken, the way I had planted my hand on the Thuet-Hun's knee, the way I had pulled forth the sword and held it up as if to silence the setting sun.

I saw myself over and over again as I imagined I had looked to Edeco, a small, thin woman laughing sardonically and holding light itself in her grip. My only regret was that my audience had not been Attila. I marveled at how evil I had become; at how much I had enjoyed my wicked charade.

But the evening progressed, and, gradually, my conceit was shaded by another perspective. I had drunk from the same cup as my enemy. I had laid my hand on him as if he were a brother. I had despised the Huns all my life, and yet I had spent a time conversing with one—for he was a Hun in mind if not in blood—and it had never once entered my thoughts that this Hun, this Thuet who was a Hun, might well have been in Worms when the blood of my people flowed like a river. When I had held the sword up to the sun, I had felt an impulse to strike Edeco with it, but not because he was my enemy. The truth was more that in holding the thing, I had felt myself an extension of it— and thus had been overcome with an urge to experience its power.

The night was slipping by. I could sense the sun yearning to rise again, but still sleep evaded me. The honey scent was gone now, and I wondered whether I had only imagined it earlier. What force had caused me to mention the Burgundians like that? Would it really make no difference? I had taken some pleasure in marking my brothers as villains. How was that possible? I had even taken pleasure in tainting myself.

Perhaps it was not madness after all that had made me feel so emboldened, so oblivious, so giddy—all feelings which eluded me now as cunningly as sleep. Perhaps, I thought, the curse had found a way to reach me. Since the time I had first received the sword from Gunner's hand, I had amused myself by thinking that I was too good, too much a true Burgundian, to be contaminated. Now I wondered. Now I was ashamed.

I crawled into the corner and trembled with humiliation. I felt alone, afraid, as if I were a marmot without a tunnel on hand, separated from its colony by time and space and allegiance. I was sick with longing for Sigurd, and I tried with all my being to conjure up his presence again, to detect once more his honey scent. But I smelled nothing but my own fear. And soon I came to suspect that the illusion of Sigurd's presence, like the illusion of my valor, which had been building for days and days, had been yet another trick of the sword's. I was sick with fear and self-loathing. I gagged but could not vomit. And when I had spent myself and finally fell asleep, I dreamed of nothing.

Chapter 2

Humbled now by the knowledge that the source of my former powers had been outside myself, I did not much care when Edeco failed to come for me the next day, nor on the one after that. I was determined to use the time to summon up a new force, this time from within. To encourage myself, I invented various scenarios in which I met with Attila, and I wondered which one would most resemble the real event. But another day passed, and then another, and still I was not summoned. How many days passed in all I could not tell because after nine or so, I lost count—or rather I gave up counting in an effort to deny my despair.

I need not have bothered; with or without my consideration of the passing time, it had plenty enough to feed on. The meals that were brought twice daily became increasingly meager, until they consisted of no more than a crust of bread and a bowl of water. The various Hun women who brought them hurried in and out, taking no time to concern themselves with the steady progression of my emaciation. Nor was I given a taper, and thus, except for those brief moments when the curtain was pulled aside to admit my indifferent attendants, I had no light, no company, no distraction other than the endless pacing of the guard's horse outside my prison.

Now, to stave off madness—which no longer seemed desirable to me—I made a game of recalling all those events which had brought me to the region called Pannonia. This enabled me, for a time, to hold on to some vestige of my identity and purpose. I realized all too well, as the days crept by, how easy it would be to drift back into the less painful but infinitely more insidious prison—where time was suspended and events were devoid of meaning—in which I had spent two long years of my life. But the events I summoned up to stabilize myself, like the scenes I envisioned with Attila, began themselves to lose their meaning after a time, and I felt myself slipping in spite of my efforts. I could no longer stand to live alone within my own mind. I ached for work, for something to do with my hands. I pulled hairs from my head for days on end and braided them together until I had made a fine, thin chain the length of the hut. But the futility of this labor discouraged me, and eventually I gave it up. I ached to be able to hasten the time through slumber, but I could sleep only sporadically. And even here I was afforded no diversion, for my dreams were dreams of shadows and silence. I tried to pray, but I had no sense that the gods could hear me. I tried to imagine my brothers' faces, hopeful as they had been when I had last seen them, but I saw only my own face in my mind's eye, and how audaciously I had gone about making Gunner and Hagen colleagues in my quest. I tried to imagine my dear child's face, but its sweet features became increasing inaccessible. I began to suspect that I would never be sent for, that I would be forced to live out my days thus, in bleak isolation on foreign, godless lands. And so, with my regrets and the recollection of my folly alone unfaded in my mind, I came after all to desire what had previously seemed the less desirable of the two prisons—the dark abyss where thought and hope and emotion are strangers. I hovered near its entrance, but even here I failed to gain admittance.

One day I heard the curtain being drawn, but not the quick footsteps that usually followed, and I knew that Edeco had finally come. I was curled up in the corner with my face to the wall, covered with more skins than the cooling weather warranted. Several moments passed before I could bring myself to look in his direction. He had left the curtain open behind him so that the daylight poured in and scorched my eyes. "You failed to keep your word," I croaked. My voice was the voice of an old woman, unused since his last visit.

"Attila is a busy man," Edeco mumbled.

My eyes had still not adjusted to the light. I could see his shape, but not his face. "Too busy to see the woman who brought him the war sword?" I asked bitterly.

"You are bold to speak so," Edeco responded.

Yes, I was bold, but not because I suddenly felt enlivened with spirit and purpose. Rather, I felt so vague and shapeless, so weak in mind and body, so close to death, even eager for it, that I no longer cared what I said or how I said it. It was a wonder that I'd had the wits to recall the war sword at all. Certainly it had been some time since I had thought of it. I had referred to it as one refers to a thing in a dream, pointlessly. I turned back to the wall and pulled the skins closer around my head.

"Get up," Edeco said. "I will take you to Attila now."

His voice was gentle, and it stirred an emotion in me. What right had he to speak to me so kindly when he had left me alone to wallow in darkness, to grope for sensibility amid my own stinking thoughts? I turned to look at him once more. I could see him now. He loomed over me. In his bright eyes I saw his pity, and also his disgust. I was disgusting. I was an animal. His neglect had made one of me. My hair was matted. My body was wet and stinking beneath my cover of stinking skins. "You must get up," Edeco declared. "If you feel you cannot manage it, I will have the guard come in and help you."

"Go away," I muttered, but Edeco remained, looking down patiently. After some moments I threw off the skins and slowly uncurled my stiff limbs. As I turned over onto my stomach, I saw the last meal that had been brought in. Except for the flies, it had not been touched. I could not remember the last time I had taken the trouble to eat. Shakily, I got to my knees. Edeco's bejeweled arm shot out to aid me, but I withdrew from it, preferring to fall. His arm followed the course of my descent, and I noticed that his palm was red and badly blistered. I gathered what saliva I could in my parched mouth and spat into it. His fingers stiffened and then curled slowly over my spittle. As if we both were curious to see what the clenched fist would do, neither of us moved for a moment. At length it withdrew.

"Get up, Ildico," he said again.

His resolution infuriated me. I got to my feet and stood a moment, considering my dizziness and staring at his burned hand as it came up to take my shoulder and steer me toward the doorway. Outside, I closed my eyes against the blazing sun. I reeled, but this time I did not balk when Edeco caught me. When I regained balance, I nodded, and, leading his horse, Edeco steered me around the back of the hut. I was startled to see, in the distance, the village life taking place. I had forgotten about the village and the villagers. I had forgotten the look of the place, the endless sky, the restless grasses stained with huts, the high wooden palisades. Edeco held on to my elbow and we approached the scene slowly. It seemed imaginary, insubstantial. Still, as we grew nearer, I lowered my head, ashamed, even among my enemies, to be seen as I was.

We moved past Attila's palisade toward the one that surrounded it, through which I had come on my first day. It seemed to take forever to reach it, and I fancied that I heard snickers and mocking exclamations from the people we passed on the way. When we arrived at the gate, Edeco turned his horse over to a guard. Then the gate was opened and we entered the tunnel-like chamber that led to the world beyond. I wondered whether I would be set free now—or rather, turned lose, without horse or weapon or food or water, to fend for myself for as long as I was able. After my long imprisonment, I would have welcomed the opportunity to walk in freedom until I collapsed. But midway through the tunnel, Edeco turned me into one of its several tributaries and led me to the wooden door at its end. He rapped once and the door was quickly lifted, revealing, beyond it, a large stone bath house beneath a wooden roof. The woman who had lifted the door stepped back to permit us passage. There were four others within, two at each side of the pool, all of whom bowed low to Edeco.

Edeco snapped his fingers and one of the women rushed over. She turned me toward her and began to pull at the broaches that held my robe together. The others rushed up behind her, as if they would all take part in the effort. I pushed the first woman's hand aside and turned to Edeco, crying, "Do you intend to watch me bathe?"

"You are not to be left unguarded," he said flatly.

"You can wait out there!" I pointed to the door.

My manner caused a stir among the women, a few of whom began to laugh behind cupped hands. I had forgotten the sound of laughter; I turned to stare at them.

Edeco whispered harshly into my ear, "You are not to speak to me that way."

It cheered me to see Edeco on the verge of abandoning his feigned patience. In the hope of pushing him further, I cried, "Where do you imagine I will get to?"

His eyes flashed. "Attila would not have you speak to anyone."

I spread my arm to take in the women. "Is there anyone here who would understand me?"

"There are many ways to make oneself understood," Edeco replied crossly. He took hold of my arm and jerked me toward the waiting attendants. I waved them away and quickly undid the broaches myself.

In a moment I was naked. My haggard body caused more snickers among the women, and I turned to see whether Edeco was likewise amused. Though the set of his lips revealed his persisting anger, he was looking aside, seemingly concerned with some small flaw in his riding whip. I accepted the soap which one of the women offered and lowered myself into the pool, which was warm and large enough to swim in. I ignored Edeco's presence after I saw that he would continue to ignore mine and took my time about my bath. My pleasure in the bath was enormous. And I was glad to be among other human beings—even if they were Huns—people to know, if not to care, whether I lived or died.

When I'd had my fill, I climbed out and allowed the women to dry and dress me. My new garment was coarse, somewhat too short, and far too wide, but it was clean. Two of the women affixed my broaches and other trinkets to it while another stood behind me and set about untangling my hair. The woman with the comb was not gentle, but even her roughness brought me pleasure. I bent my head back and let my attendant jerk it about as she liked.

When they were done with me, the women filed out, the last one taking my badly soiled garments along with her. Only then did Edeco look up. He seemed surprised to see that I was smiling. I had not realized it myself until I saw his expression. Had my hatred, I wondered, dissolved along with my stench? I examined my feelings and found that it had, though it confused me to think such a thing possible.

Now we set off for Attila's palisade, still at the slow pace made necessary by my weakness. When the gates were opened, I saw beyond them colorful tents fashioned from skins and some beautiful fabric I had never seen before. It looked as soft as baby's skin, as fluid as water. I knew that it must be silk, which I had heard about, from my brothers and others.

At the entrances to these tents, women sat on colorful rugs, chatting and drinking from gold goblets not unlike the ones that Sigurd had brought back from the dragon's cave. The women were also draped in the wondrous fabric, the silk, and they were far more comely than any of the other women I had seen. They had to be Attila's wives. I had heard he had many. As we passed them, they ceased their conversations and bowed their heads to Edeco.

Beyond the tents was Attila's hall, a long wooden structure still at some distance in the great courtyard. Several groups of guards sat on their horses near its entrance. At our approach, one of them slid to the ground and lifted Attila's door to shout some Hunnish exclamation inside.

Edeco pushed me in so roughly that the guards outside laughed. Startled by his sudden change in attitude, I turned to look at him before facing Attila, but he was already standing at attention, his back straight and his eyes staring straight ahead. And thus I was surprised when I turned back and saw no one.

I took the opportunity to let my eyes wander over the fine furnishings, the beautiful planked floor, the tapestries that hung along the walls, and the gold—gold goblets, gold serving trays, gold swords hanging beside gold shields between the tapestries. I had never seen so much gold before. I glanced at Edeco. Although his eyes were still staring ahead, his lips were curled into a self-satisfied smile. I studied the pieces again. The war sword, which would have made the others seem common by comparison, was not among them. I studied the tapestries, thick colorful things depicting life-sized men hunting, warring, marching, thieving. Not all of the figures were Hunnish. Most were clearly Roman, probably stolen from the palaces Attila had ravished each time he marched on the Eastern Empire. The furnishings consisted of tables, a very long one along the south wall and several smaller ones grouped close together along the west wall, and chairs. All of the chairs were made of wood except one, and this one was a long couch covered entirely with red fabric, silk, and positioned at the center of the hall facing the doorway. The north wall was curtained in a pale-colored silk, and I supposed there was a bower beyond it. If Attila was within, he would have to be there. And sure enough, there was some movement in the curtain, and, a moment later, one corner was drawn aside.

The first thing I saw was the war sword. And as if I were seeing it for the first time, I gasped. Then I gasped again when I managed to tear my eyes from it and look at the man who carried it, for Attila's face was somehow familiar to me.

With his broad chest, thick neck, large shapeless head and scanty beard, in most ways Attila looked no different from any of the other Huns. He was, perhaps, even shorter than many. What distinguished him were his eyes. They were more deeply set, and darker, the pupil and the color around it being so nearly the same shade that it was hard to say for certain what he looked at as he approached. They were ominous eyes, as motionless and irresistible as the eyes of the dead.

He moved forward slowly, then stopped and spread his arms. Stiffly, Edeco stepped into his embrace. His face still expressionless, Attila clapped his hands on Edeco's back once and then dropped them. Edeco stepped back immediately and said some words in the Hunnish tongue. Attila's eyes swept over me and away. Then he turned and moved toward the red silk couch, where he made quite a ceremony about settling himself, lifting his legs and stretching them out along its expanse, and then, after laying the war sword across his lap, stretching his arms out along the couch's arms. When he had positioned his head just as he wanted it against the back of the couch, Edeco began to speak again. Attila responded without looking at either of us. His voice was deep, and his words, it seemed, carefully chosen. I noticed that he wore no jewelry, and his garments, though not made of marmot skins, were very plain.

"Lower yourself now," Edeco said.

I bowed, but apparently not low enough, for all at once Edeco's arm shot out and struck the small of my back, sending me to my knees. I peeked up to see Attila's reaction, but there was none. His head was turned slightly aside, and he seemed to be staring at nothing, his posture so relaxed that he might have been asleep with his eyes opened. He looked older in profile, forty, perhaps. A moment passed. Then he said something more to Edeco in his low voice. Edeco said, "Go closer now so that he can see you."

I went on my knees across the floor to the foot of the couch. I felt weak and very much in need of nourishment. In my mind's eye, I could see again the scrap of bread covered over with flies. It seemed nearly desirable now. I began to sit back on my heels so as to not to lose my balance, but Edeco shouted, "Stay on your knees," and I forced myself to stay as I was, tottering from side to side.

The two men spoke at length while I bent my head and concentrated on staying upright. Finally, Edeco said to me, "Attila wishes you to know that your gift is most welcome. He heard my account of how you acquired it some thirty days ago when you first arrived, and he would have you know that he thinks you a woman of great courage. Now, if you wish, you may speak to Attila."

Thirty days ago? Not sixty? Not one hundred? For all that I'd had time to practice my speech, I could think of nothing now but the impossibility of a mere thirty days having passed. "I am grateful to Attila for permitting me this audience," I stammered. I bent my head lower and tried to remember why I was there. "It is indeed an honor to find myself in the company of so renowned a man. I would be further honored, now that I am no longer a prisoner, to be permitted an audience with him on occasion, so that I might hear for myself what feats my gift enables him to accomplish. And I pray they will be many."

I was satisfied with my little speech, but not with the quaking voice that had delivered it. Attila had listened without looking at me, without the slightest indication that he was at all interested. Nor did he look at Edeco while he translated. Afterward, Attila remained silent for so long that I began to think our meeting would conclude without any response from him at all. Then his black eyes darted toward Edeco. He said some words, hesitated, and added some more. He moved his head farther aside so that now

I found myself looking at his ear and the scar that began its descent just near it. Edeco said, "Attila regrets to inform you that you are to remain a prisoner, but—"

"You cannot mean it! I will not go back!" I shouted mindlessly.

"But," Edeco continued, "as a token of his appreciation for your gift, you will be given all that you want or need from our people in the way of food and clothing."

I shot him a look. "Our people?"

Edeco took a quick breath and continued. "Furthermore, you will be permitted to bathe regularly. You will be given wine as you desire it. I myself will come to you at intervals to make sure you are not wanting for any convenience. And, on occasion, Attila will send for you. This is how it will be until Attila decides what to do with you."

I got to my feet. Edeco's hand came down on my shoulder, but now I refused to succumb to its pressure. "What to do with me?" I cried, looking at Attila, desperate to catch his eye. "Is this how I am to be treated? Like an animal?"

Attila remained motionless. Edeco laughed. "You professed to have grown up in caves. You should be used to living like an animal."

It took a moment for me to make sense of the reference. "I slept in caves," I cried bitterly. "I did not spend my days in them. I was free to come and go. We Thuets love our freedom."

The amused smile fell from Edeco's face. "There is no such thing as freedom, woman," he sneered. "We are free only to choose our limitations."

"Then let me choose mine. Let me leave the City of Attila."

"You will never leave."

I glanced at Attila, who had still not moved a muscle. "Then let Attila take my life. Tell him it would please me if he would let his fine gift sate itself first with the blood of the woman who bequeathed it."

Edeco laughed, then translated. With his face still turned aside, Attila grunted. Their amusement inflamed me. My hand struck out toward the hilt of the war sword, prepared, in that instant, to do the job itself, but Attila found it first. His fingers fell over it idly, as if he had only meant to alter its position. At the same moment, Edeco grabbed my shoulders and dragged me back a pace. Attila yawned. He said something to Edeco and Edeco said to me, "Attila appreciates your dilemma, but he is loathe to let any harm come to the woman who brought him the gift of the gods. He will call for you again at some later date. Your conduct today makes it necessary for us to conclude this interview." As Edeco turned me toward the door, I stole one last glance at the great Attila. He had crossed his feet and closed his eyes. A slight smile was at play on his lips.

Outside, Edeco took my elbow, but I twisted away from him and we walked along in silence. When we reached the isolated hut, I stepped in saying, "Perhaps I could be moved into the village. I would speak to no one. I give you my word. Ask the women who come each day to feed me whether I have tired to speak to them. They will tell you I have not. Not a word have I said to anyone."

To my relief, Edeco came in behind me. Beyond him, the guard began to ride. "That is impossible," Edeco said.

His tone was gentle again, as his hand had been when he had tried to take my elbow. In an unanticipated burst of supplication, I took hold of his hand and clung to it, though I could feel his reluctance to have it held. "What have I done?" I cried. "What crime have I committed? You must not leave me here alone." My eyes swept over the floor. A meal had been laid out for me in my absence, a real meal, with plenty of meat and bread and cheese and fruit and a jug of wine. Now I was torn between my desire to detain Edeco—for all that I hated him I did not think I could suffer another day or night alone with nothing but my own company—and my hunger. I loosened my hold on his hand and it slipped away quickly. "I cannot live this way," I murmured, looking still on the meal. Once again I wondered whether Edeco had been at Worms when the kingdom of the Burgundians was destroyed. He had to be at least thirty; he would have been just old enough to have participated. I sank to my knees saying, "I must eat." But when I looked up again, I saw that he had gone.

CHAPTER 3

"One day a herdsman living outside the city came to the gates begging to speak to Attila. Attila granted the herdsman an audience, and the herdsman told him how, earlier that same day, he had noticed that one of his heifers was lame."

I was sitting cross-legged in the center of the dark hut the night that

Edeco pulled aside the curtain and said these words. At first I thought them to be some new excursion of my imagination, but Edeco was carrying a taper, and for all that his words made no sense to me, I recognized the light at least as being genuine. He set the taper down and seated himself.

"Upon closer examination," he continued, "the herdsman saw that the beast had cut its forepaw, and that there was a long trail of blood leading off into the higher plains. The herdsman followed this trail half a day, and it brought him to a stretch of deep grasses not far from the city gates. Therein he found a sword, protruding from the earth so that only its hilt and a part of its blade were visible. He marveled that such a thing could go undetected so near the gates, and he marveled again when he went to pull it forth and burned his hand on the fire that shot out from it at that very instant. And then he knew that it was an enchanted thing and meant for the man whose palace the gates enclosed.

"Attila rode at once, taking the herdsman and one of his officers along with him. When the three reached the place where the sword grew out of the earth, Attila commanded his officer to retrieve it for him. But as with the herdsman, just as the officer reached for it, a fire shot out and scorched his palm. Then Attila got off his horse and went to retrieve the thing himself while the herdsman and the officer looked on anxiously lest the master should scorch his own precious palm. But though the thing began to blaze anew when Attila went to touch it, the flames eased as his fingers grew nearer, and at the moment of impact, they abated altogether. And then Attila knew that the gods loved him well and had sent him the thing to urge him on toward the destiny he had heretofore only imagined."

Edeco folded his arms and smiled. Although my mind was weak, sometime during his tale I had come to comprehend it. I was deeply pained, but I knew better than to let it show. I reached for Edeco's hand, and he was happy enough to give it to me. I held it near the taper flame and turned it palm up so that I could see the scars. "And the guard who peered in the night I arrived and you learned the true story of the sword's origin?" I asked.

"The unfortunate man met with an accident," Edeco said smugly.

I gave him back his hand.

"I would have burned my entire body if Attila had so required it," he whispered. His eyes searched mine, as if for some reaction to his declaration. When I failed to provide one, he took it upon himself to imagine one for me. "You are appalled," he said loudly. "It is clear that the Frank meant everything to you. But consider this, Ildico. The important details are true. The sword was fashioned by the gods. You said so yourself. And it did find its way to Attila for precisely the reason I stated."

"True enough," I managed. "But the god who fashioned it was a Thuet, not a Hun."

Edeco's features relaxed now that he had gotten something of a challenge out of me. "Thuet god, Hun god, Roman god, what difference does it make?"

"Have the Huns gods? I would not have thought so."

Edeco leaned forward. "The Huns had no gods before the war sword. Now they have one, and his earthly manifestation is Attila."

"Earthly manifestation? Do you mean to say that Attila claims to be a god in man-shape?"

"Yes, in a manner." Edeco considered. "Or perhaps it is more like the Roman god, the Christian one who is said to have sent his son to Earth to preach his word."

"What god is that?" I asked.

Edeco laughed and glanced at the doorway as if to see whether anyone was listening there. "I know little about him myself other than that his son was weak while he walked the Earth and did not resist when the masses set about ending his life." He laughed again. "I see now that I erred when I compared Attila to him. In any case, it is fortunate for you that Attila believes that the war sword was fashioned by the gods and sent to him."

"How so?"

"Why, Attila would have had you killed by now if he did not believe that. He believes the gods chose you to deliver the sword for a reason. And until he decides what that reason is, your safety is assured. You may not realize it, but you are a favored prisoner here. The others, and there are many, share lodgings to the east of the City of Attila. They are starved and beaten regularly by the guards who attend them. In fact, Ildico, had you not made the blunder that you did in telling me the story of the war sword, you should be living now in one of the silk tents that grace Attila's courtyard, another of his wives."

"What blunder did I make?" I asked.

Edeco laughed heartily. "Did you think for a moment that Attila would repeat your story to his armies when they asked how he came by the sword? It is a thing to marvel at, for certain. And all those who have seen it have marveled well enough. But do you think Attila tells them that he got it from a tribeless Thuet who stole it from a Burgundian who stole it from a

Frank who stole it from a dragon who stole it from the gods? He might as well say it was a gift from the Romans, woman."

"But the Romans give him gifts regularly. You told me that."

"Not gifts with the power to defeat them."

"I see," I said, though I was still perplexed.

"You see, Ildico," Edeco continued, "when you told me your story, you made it all too clear that you would never stand to see the Frank's glory diminished. We cannot have two versions of the sword's origins going around, now can we?"

I shook my head. "Then tell Attila that I am prepared to deal with him on this matter. He can say what he likes about the war sword, if only he will set me free."

"Attila cannot take that risk. He has great plans for the sword that the gods gave—"

"I gave it to him."

Edeco laughed and pointed a finger. "You see, you still persist."

"I only meant to say—"

Edeco's face became stern suddenly. "I know what you meant to say."

"But you must tell him—" I began to plead.

Edeco stood up. "I will tell him nothing on your behalf."

To my horror, I found that I was more distressed to see that he was leaving than I had been to learn that Attila had invented a new story to explain how he had come by the war sword. Edeco's coming into my hut with Attila's fabrication on his lips was the first unexpected thing that had occurred in many days. Prior to it, there had only been the meals and the pacing of the guard, and in between, brief intervals of slumber, so that I did not know where one day left off and the next began. "Please stay," I said weakly.

Edeco looked down on me. A smile appeared on his face and he lowered himself again.

I looked away, ashamed now to have petitioned my enemy. Then I recalled that part of my purpose in coming to Pannonia was to deceive my enemies just so. I had lived for so long alone in the dark that this recollection came as a surprise. I brightened a little and taxed my mind to think of something to say to him now that I could justify such conference. "This story," I said at last, "will it be sung now in Attila's hall along with the others?"

"Sung? How so? What others?" Edeco asked. He looked annoyed.

I was amazed. "Do the Huns not sing of their ancestors? Of the wars they fought? Of their conflicts and struggles since the beginning?"

Edeco shrugged. "We have one song only. It is a song of praise for Attila."

"I thought all peoples—" I began.

"The Huns were nomads until they came to Pannonia," Edeco interrupted. "Why should anyone want to hear a song about that?"

"Oh, but Edeco," I cried. "The Huns deprive themselves there. Why, to hear the songs of your ancestors played out for you . . . . My brother Gunner—" I stopped myself short and stared at him.

He nodded, almost imperceptibly. Then he smiled.

"Of course," I went on hastily, "this Gunner was not my real brother. My real brothers are dead, as I told you. I hardly remember them. This Gunner I am thinking of, the one who sang so beautifully of the Thuets coming down from the cold countries, was the son of the leader of a tribe with which I once stayed for a time. Now let me see. Were they Vandals? Alans? Aye, gods, I cannot remember."

Edeco's damaged palm came up between us to silence me. Beyond it, I saw that his pert smile was still set on his face. "You cannot remember what tribe, Ildico? It surprises me that you would remember the man but not the tribe he hailed from. And yet you must have been very close to this Gunner to have called him brother."

I lurched forward and, forcing myself to smile, I grabbed Edeco's hand as it was descending. "Ah, Edeco, it was a long time ago. The mind plays tricks with distant memories, making some clear while others fade entirely. And as for my calling the man my brother, let me assure you; on Thuet lands it is no uncommon thing to speak of a good friend that way, even when he is not one's brother in blood." It occurred to me suddenly that my gesture seemed more an appeal than the playful rebuke I had meant it to seem. I dropped his hand at once.

Edeco smiled. Then, taking up the taper, he got to his feet again.

At first I dwelled on my blunder so intently that I drove myself as near to despair as I had ever been. But gradually I came to see that I would give myself away, and thus my brothers, entirely if I did not find the means to improve my state. Attila had the sword, and the sword was cursed; I had only to keep myself alert and wait. In the meantime, I added more skins to those that already lined the walls of my hut—for the nights were becoming colder—

and I reviewed the words that had passed between Edeco and me during our meeting. I came to believe that it would not matter, in the end, that I had disclosed my brother's name. And I came, too, to understand my desire for my enemy's company—and to forgive myself for it. Our meeting had gone badly, but at least my mind was alive now, with reflections, speculations, and notions concerning the future. What did it matter that I was not free to come and go? I was free, at least, to contemplate how I would one day reveal the true story of the war sword. And, as it had been confirmed that Attila truly valued the thing and intended to put it to use, how far off could that day be? It would make him bold and greedy, as it had made Sigurd bold and greedy, and thereby, likewise, ensure his destruction.

Perhaps some part of the reason that I was able to view the future in a different light was that I now had light. Though Edeco had taken his taper away with him when he departed, he must have seen my eye stray after it, for the following morning, when the Hun woman came with my meal, she brought a taper with her, and then another when she returned again in the evening. Furthermore, my meals, as Attila had promised, continued to be adequate, and the Roman wine, which I had grown to like for its sleep-inducing properties, was brought regularly. And, too, Edeco began to come occasionally to escort me to the bath house.

A pattern was taciturnly established. Out in the village, on the way to the bath house, Edeco rode and I walked before him with my head bent, like the humble prisoner he would have me appear. Then, in the bath house, perhaps in gratitude for my resignation, Edeco kept his head turned and feigned to be concerned with some other matter. And he appeared again at the door of my hut sometimes in the evenings, saying that he had come to be certain that I was not wanting for anything.

Not for a moment did I imagine that his kindnesses were connected to anything other than his ambition to extract some further information from me. But I also saw, as the days passed, that Edeco took some pleasure in our meetings, and I resolved to use his tolerance of me to my advantage.

At first, our discussions were competitions: Edeco probed for details concerning my motives in coming to Pannonia. I attempted to shift the conversation back to Attila and the war sword, for I longed to have some confirmation that its power was beginning to work. But when I eventually came to see that Edeco would tell me nothing of Attila's present disposition, I began to ask Edeco questions about Attila's past. By then, Edeco, who had likewise grown bored with his line of questioning, was happy enough to describe

Attila's feats, which I feigned to admire (though no more than I thought would appear credible under the circumstances), hoping that one day he would slip, as I had, and say more than he intended. He did not mention Gunner again, and my fear that he might yet do so eventually passed when I saw how easy it was to get him to speak about himself.

Edeco was one of Attila's three personal guards, the others being Berichus, a Hun, and Orestes, a Roman. How cunning on Attila's part, I mused when I learned this, that he should choose a Hun, a Thuet, and a Roman to attend him. Clearly, he feared insubordination, and thus, by having one guard to represent each of the factions from which it might come, he hoped to avert it. I learned, too, that Edeco was born to Skirians, who, like the more numerous Ostrogoths, had come under Hun dominion early on, when the Huns had first come to Pannonia. As Hun subjects, they quickly adopted Hun customs, such as deforming the faces of their sons so that they would learn to endure pain. Like other Thuet peoples, the Skirians had always been skilled farmers. Since the Huns themselves had no knowledge of farming, and no desire to learn it, the Skirians and Ostrogoths took on the task of providing the Huns with food and wool. And of course, they also provided men for the Hun armies.

Most of the Skirians took Hun wives to prove their loyalty. But Edeco, who boasted that his loyalty had never been a concern, chanced to be attracted to a woman from his ancestral tribe. This was when he was still very young, and though a member of the Hun army, not yet a personal guard. He and his young Thuet wife produced two sons, Humulf and Odoacer. Just after Odoacer's birth, there was an uprising among the Skirians, and though Edeco's wife had no part in it, she was killed inadvertently when the Huns put it down. It was to appease Edeco for this grave error that Rua (who was the Hun leader at the time) took him into personal service. And Edeco was appeased. When Rua died, his nephews, Bleda and Attila, kept Edeco on, but it was Attila who loved Edeco most, and when Bleda died (Edeco could not be led to say that Attila killed him, though that was the way I had heard it back on Burgundian lands), Edeco served Attila alone. He then had much to do with convincing Attila that unlike the previous Hun leaders, his name would become immortal. And in return for his loyalty and his love, Attila granted Edeco every kindness, including much gold and the second highest rank among his men. Only Onegesius, a Hun and the owner of the great palisade wherein the bath house was located, ranked higher.

I learned something, too, about Attila's wives and children—or rather, sons, for though other Huns might father daughters, Attila had his own killed as soon as they were born. Those of his wives who produced girl babies in succession were likewise killed, or, if Attila favored them, sent to live in exile beyond the city gates. It was one of Edeco's tasks to go among the silk tents of Attila's wives and choose for the master, when he could not make up his mind himself, the one with whom he would sleep on a given night. Since Attila's wives had no other task than to keep themselves comely for their common husband, they were all anxious to be chosen, and there was much jealously among them.

So, too, was there jealously among Attila's sons, so much so that a guard had to be assigned to them to keep them from killing one another. But there was only one among them, a youngster called Ernac, whose demise would have actually distressed Attila. According to Attila's best-loved soothsayer, there would come a time, after Attila's death, when the Huns would grow weak, but this Ernac would know the way to make them strong again. And thus Ernac had his own personal guard to protect him from his brothers.

I had occasion to make very good use of this information one day when Edeco was escorting me to the bath house. As we were going through the village, we passed a group of boys—some Hun, some Thuet, some part and part—who were making a game of tormenting a poor marmot who had apparently wandered too far from its tunnel. The boys, many of whom had sticks, had formed a circle around the thing, and each time it tried to escape, one of the boys drove it back again. Just beyond the circle of boys, a guard sat watching from his horse. Edeco touched my shoulder with his riding whip and commanded me to halt in a loud voice such as one uses to speak to a subordinate. Then he bent over his horse and whispered in my ear, "Can you guess which boy is Attila's beloved Ernac?"

"That is easy enough," I replied. "It is the one from whom the guard's eyes never stray." We both looked at Ernac. He had left the fringe of the circle for its center and was, it seemed, attempting to skewer the marmot on his stick.

"Perhaps I tell you more than you should know," Edeco mused.

I dared to glance at him and found him smiling. Then he went to bring up his horse so that we could continue on our way. But a sudden notion caused me to cry out, "Perhaps you will not mind then if I tell you more than you should know. There is one among these boys who is destined for greatness, but it is not Attila's Ernac." Before he could react to my sedition, I pointed a finger. "See that one there? The tall boy who stands somewhat apart looking as if he would like to join the others but looking, too, as if he is loathe to hurt the thing unnecessarily?"

Edeco's eyes hardened. I went on quickly. "I saw a face such as his, but older, one night in the flame of my candle. He was marching, leading a band of men. But the men he led were not Huns. They were Thuets. I sensed that they were marching on the Roman Empire, but my vision withered before I could be certain."

Edeco squinted his eyes and lifted one hand from his horse's reins. But his hand stayed motionless in the air and his gaze, which drifted from me to something beyond me, became unfocused. Finally, he touched my back with his riding whip and cried, "Get along, woman."

Of course I knew the boy was Edeco's own Odoacer. A few days earlier, some of the same boys had been playing near the western palisade, which is to say not far from my hut. I heard them laughing and calling to one another. Since no one ever ventured so far from the heart of the village, I drew the curtain and peeked out. My guard had ridden off to admonish the mischiefmakers, and thus I was free, for a moment, to observe. When the boys saw the guard approaching, most of them scattered immediately. But one of them, a Hun, stayed put and called out, "Odoacer," as if in warning. Then a head popped up over one of the small knolls between my hut and the palisade, and I knew it must belong to Edeco's son. The Hun boy, meanwhile, ran toward the guard, calling out some vapid explanation as he went. When he saw that Odoacer had cleared the knoll, he ended his explanation abruptly and ran after him.

At the time I made little of my discovery, except to think that I might mention the incident to Edeco so as to flatter him by telling him that I found his boy comely. It was not until we stopped to spy on Ernac that I realized that I might put my knowledge to a greater use. And even then, I had no idea what I would say about Odoacer until I found myself saying it. It was almost as if my prophecy were a true one after all and had come to me entirely unbidden, as prophecies do to those who have the Sight. Now I was quite pleased with myself. After my first meeting with Edeco, I had never again spoken of myself as a valkyria. Such a contention coming from so enfeebled a woman, I had thought, would only make Edeco laugh. But I was not so enfeebled anymore. The ease that Edeco took in my presence of late assured me that he might yet tell me something that would serve my purpose. And, too, Edeco's constant need to prove his allegiance to Attila to me had something of the opposite effect. There was a chink there, and through it I thought I discerned some deep-rooted, perhaps unconscious Thuet loyalty in the man. Was it not possible that just as I had chosen to feign love for Edeco so that, somehow, someday, my people might prosper by it, that Edeco had chosen to feign love for Attila so that he and his sons might likewise prosper? We are free only to choose our limitations, he had said. But his reaction to my invented prophesy, his looking off into the distance with his brow furrowed and his eyes as hard as stones, seemed to indicate that he was not beyond envisioning something more. My words had been nothing less than treasonous, and yet Edeco had not spurned me for saying them—an act of treason in itself.

One evening Edeco came to my hut in a particularly good mood, and I dared to say to him that I should like to know something of the Hun language, some simple words that would enable me to thank the Hun serving women who brought my meals. Edeco looked at me suspiciously at first, but I laughed and exclaimed, "Oh, Edeco, what harm can it do for me to speak a word or two of kindness to other women? Even in the bath house, where my face is now familiar, there are times when I should like to exchange a word or two with my attendants. I have no desire to become fluent. Indeed, I do not have the capacity for it."

"Only a few then," Edeco relented. And thus he taught me the Hunnish words for please and thank you and some others to say by way of greeting. But in our conversations thereafter, when I asked him in a casual manner for the word for this or that object or idea, Edeco continued to oblige. I would repeat the word once, and then quickly turn our conversation back to where it had been. But after Edeco's departure, I would repeat the new word over and over again, until it was committed to memory and stored away with all the others I had learned from him, available for some use in the future—though what I could not guess.

I also learned from Edeco that the Romans had a written language, which was not used, as were runes, to cast spells or alter events, but only to make record of them. It was bitter cold the night that Edeco brought this information. We had divided the skins up between us and were taking turns holding our hands over the taper to keep them warm as we conversed. We had been talking about the Roman wine and its warming properties, and Edeco had added, "The truth, Ildico, is that the Romans have many such skills which we Huns would like to lay our hands on."

I cut him off, saying, "Aye, building skills and law and—"

"And writing, yes." And when he saw by my look that I had no idea what he was talking about, he laughed and explained.

I was not much moved at first, especially when Edeco admitted that the lines the Romans made, characters or letters, had no magical significance. But Edeco seemed determined to convince me otherwise. "Think of it, Ildico," he cried. "You spoke once of tribal songs, sung to commemorate one's ancestors. But should a tribe be wiped out, by famine or war, those songs, too, would cease to exist. The written song, on the other hand, would remain long after, unless the tribe were wiped out by fire, for others to find and sing."

I laughed. "Who would bother to seek out such a thing among the remains of the dead?"

"No one, perhaps. I used the songs only as an example. There are many other ways in which writing has been useful to the Romans."

"Name them."

Edeco's eyes twinkled. "I shall, my ignorant friend." He studied his hands in the candlelight. "Here's one—laws. The Romans set all their laws down in writing."

"And how is that better than setting down one's laws in spoken words?"

"Have you never heard of a situation where a man professes not to have heard the law on this or that matter? If laws are written, no man who can read can claim such ignorance."

"Name more."

Edeco's eyes wandered and returned again. "Their wealth, the number of gold coins they have accumulated. The leaders have every man in every village say what they have, and then it is recorded. Then, when the time comes to collect taxes, the leaders know exactly what to expect. And messages! Written messages are sent as a matter of course."

I laughed again. "Where I come from, messages are sent easily enough. A good rider on a fast horse is all that is necessary, Edeco."

Edeco shook his finger at me. "Aye, but you miss the point. Suppose I had some message for Attila alone—"

"Why, then you would go to him yourself."

"Suppose I could not. Suppose some matter obliged me to stay where I was. If I knew how to write, which I do not, I would write my message on a scroll and seal it. If the seal was unbroken when Attila received it, then he would know no eyes had seen it but his own."

Gudrun's Tapestry

Now I was interested. "Name more," I demanded.

Edeco raised one brow. "Have you ever known a man whose thoughts were superior to those of other men? One who could influence others with his knowledge?"

I thought of Sigurd's uncle, Gripner. "Yes," I said cautiously.

"When that man dies, his thoughts, his wisdom, must also die—"

"Unless they are written. I see."

"And more, Ildico. The Romans prepare their speeches first in writing. That way, they are sure to leave nothing out or to be anything less than eloquent when they deliver their appeals to the masses. They even declare their love in writing, or at least the diffident among them do, those whose faces would otherwise redden and blunt their tongues." Edeco shook his head. "And more, if I could name them. Births, deaths, marriages, all these things the Romans make record of."

"How did you come to know all this? You must tell me."

Edeco laughed. "It is not as uncommon as you think. There are many people on the Earth who share this skill with the Romans, Thuets among them."

"None that I ever knew. Does Attila know how to write?"

"It is a tedious thing to learn. Attila has neither the time nor the need to do so himself. There are plenty of men living within the walls of the City of Attila to do it for him. For instance, there is the Roman bishop who—"

"Bishop?"

"Aye, a man who professes to be acquainted with the gods."

"Go on."

"This bishop came to Pannonia once to rob the Hun graves of their treasures. Attila caught him at his task and would have killed him on the spot, but then he thought better about it. One's enemies, Ildico, are often more useful than one's friends. Attila made a deal with him. He would let the bishop go if the bishop would promise to open the gates to his own city some nights later. Now Attila not only had the excuse he had been looking for to cross Roman lines, but his success there was also assured. He marched on the bishop's city, took much gold and many men, and brought the bishop back as a token of his gratitude, for of course the bishop's people would have torn him apart when they learned he had been the one to open the gates. Now he is one of Attila's most trusted scribes. And there are others, some of whom have come from far away lands begging to be allowed to record for Attila."

"Has Attila so much to record?"

"Of course! A great man like Attila must make a record of all sorts of things. He sends his demands to the Eastern Empire in this way. He sends the names of the men he has captured and lets the Romans decide how much gold each man's return is worth to them. Even his dreams are recorded, for naturally they have much influence on the decisions he makes." He waved his hand in the air. "And all things in between."

"I see," I said. And when Edeco had gone that night, I sat trembling against the cold and seeing more and more clearly how such a skill might be useful to me. And during the next several days I had fantasies wherein I learned to write and used my skill to tell the truth about the war sword. In these fantasies I composed Sigurd's story over and over, choosing only the most agreeable words to convey Sigurd's valor and Sigurd's fall. The notion so excited me that it was all I could do to keep from sharing it with Edeco. Nevertheless, in subsequent visits, he could not help but see how interested I had become in writing generally, and one evening he brought me a sample of it, characters drawn on a sheepskin parchment.

He entered, as he often did, without any greeting. With his expression full of significance, he held the thing out to me. I locked my eyes on his and stood up to receive it. Then I unrolled it quickly, and there, on its smoother surface, were the pretty, rounded characters that Edeco had described, drawn in a purplish ink. I studied them long and carefully, so long, in fact, that I forgot Edeco's presence. And when I remembered and glanced up at him, I found, to my astonishment, that he was scrutinizing my face with the same intensity with which I had been pursuing the parchment. I was horrified of the affection I thought I saw in his eyes.

"What does it mean?" I asked.

"A dream," he murmured.

"Attila's dream? How did you come by it?"

He straightened then, but his eyes remained heavy. "Attila sorts them out after a time and keeps only the ones he deems important to his political future. The others are burned. I took this one from the burn pile. You may keep it."

He was standing very close to me, so close that I could hear him breathing, and had not the parchment been between us, I feared, he would have moved closer yet. "Does Attila know you have taken it?"

"Why should he care? It was discarded."

I bit my lip. I could imagine myself in the middle of the night when no one was likely to come, endlessly copying the letters with a stick onto the earthen floor. My fingers, which had been idle for so long, burned with the desire to have such a purpose. "But if one of the serving women should see it here.... It troubles me, Edeco. What can be more personal than a dream? I am so grateful to you for bringing it to me, for giving me the opportunity to see this wondrous thing you have told me so much about, but if someone were to find it in my hut... perhaps when we are gone to the bath house... might it not look as if we were...?"

Edeco's eyes hardened suddenly. "Conspiring?" he finished for me.

He ripped the parchment from my hand and quickly rolled it up. He turned, but before he could leave, I reached out and clutched his shoulder. "I was only thinking of you," I pleaded.

"Do you think Attila takes my loyalty so lightly that he would believe me capable of such a thing? Of conspiring against him with you, a Thuet?"

"I did not think that far along. I only saw that it would seem—"

"No more!" he shouted.

His exclamation hung in the air between us. I let my hand slide from his shoulder and stared at his back, at the light curls that covered his neck, so similar in color to my own. A moment passed. Now I could hear the guard riding back and forth beyond the curtain. I wondered whether I should ask Edeco to forgive me, to allow me to accept the parchment after all, for indeed I did covet it. Before I could decide, he turned back to me, and in the next instant, I found myself in his arms, and, to my astonishment, my eyes filled with tears. He held me tightly, his lips brushing my neck as some emotion I had long forgotten surged in me.

All at once I saw their faces—the faces of my loved ones, my family—in my mind's eye, as clearly as if they were standing before me.

I was amazed and alarmed to see the range of passion my enemy's embrace evoked in me. It was as if I had been waiting for this, waiting for some gesture of love that would link me again to all that I had lost. Nor did it matter to me that the gesture might well be feigned for reasons I could not imagine. The faces of my loved ones were bright and smiling, looking at me as if it were only across some river and not some great godless void too terrifying to name.

Edeco spoke, but in the jumble of my wild musings, I failed to hear him. I bade the vanishing faces of my loved ones farewell and asked Edeco to repeat himself. He held me back from him, saying, "Only this, Ildico. If I could write, there are things that I would say to you which my tongue has no expression for." He released me before I could respond. On his face I saw the same wide-eyed, half-frightened look I had seen on his son's when it had shot up over the knoll. He touched my neck with his knuckles, letting his fingers linger a moment under my chin. Then he dropped his hand abruptly, his fingers already clenching as if they had betrayed him, and went out into the night.

Sapaudia

Chapter 4

We had been in Sapaudia a full year when the Franks arrived. They were our first visitors there. In Worms, before the siege, we'd had many visitors; many kings were made welcome in my uncle's great hall. But after the siege, when my uncle's hall had fallen to ashes and the dead among us so greatly outnumbered the living that we had neither heart nor hands enough to give them proper burials, most of these visitors, these kings and noblemen, took their tales and their laughter and their gifts elsewhere.

Truly, we did not fault them. To have done otherwise at that time would have been a conscious act of self-destruction. The Romans had used us to teach all the Thuet world a lesson. Our vanquishment, they hoped, would keep other Thuet tribes in a state of submission. Thus, only by avoiding us could our Thuet brothers prove to the Romans that their vile lesson would be heeded. And had it been the Romans themselves who came on horseback to obliterate us, our brothers would have come in droves with their spears and their battle-axes and their war cries. But the cunning Romans knew this all too well. They paid the Huns to do it for them.

Only the Franks—Sigmund, Sigurd's father, and Gripner, Sigurd's uncle, whose disdain of the Romans exceeded their fear of the Huns—continued to visit us at Worms in the years between the siege and our resettlement at Sapaudia. When Sigmund died, Gripner came just as regularly, and always Sigurd was at his side. In this way, Sigurd and I came to be friends when we were very young.

Two years before the siege, my uncle, Gundahar, seeing that we needed more lands than the greedy Romans would part with, laid claim to a portion of the lands the Romans call Belgica. Aetius, the Roman general, crushed his effort right away, and many of our people died. And so, between our defeat at the hands of the Romans and our massacre at the hands of the Huns, there were very few of us left. One could say that the Burgundians were no more, there being hardly enough of us to constitute a tribe let alone a kingdom. In fact, we might have said this ourselves in the beginning had we voices with which to speak. But the sight of our dead all around us, floating in a sea of blood and Hunnish arrows, left us numb and speechless. For a long time a mere look was even too painful an exchange.

Mostly, my people slept back then, as people do when they cannot bear to remember. They awoke only long enough each day to do their most urgent chores, and, sometimes, when they had the heart for it, to eat. And even working and eating, their faces were the blank unflappable faces of dreamers. I, however, being a child, did not sleep. I mourned bitterly for my people, especially for my uncle, but then my need to mourn passed from me and I could not understand why the sorrows of my people persisted. People battled, people died. The world was like that. But our world had come to a standstill. Father, who became king after my uncle was slain, was, perhaps, the greatest sleeper of all. Having no chores to do himself, for he was old even then, he awoke only to eat. And sometimes he could not even manage that. Sometimes his eyes would blink and his head would bob in the middle of a meal, and Mother or I, whoever was nearest, would quickly sweep away his bowl so that his face would not drop into it.

My brothers slept less than the others. Though older than I (Guthorm had not been born yet), they were still young, and likewise bothered by the deep sleep the Burgundian survivors had fallen into. But they were obsessed with their bitterness, and their lengthy conversations, which I was permitted no part in, were always about the vengeance they would take against the Huns. This, as far as I could see, was as much a waste of time as sleeping. In their wild fantasies, they marched to Pannonia alone, the two of them, and cut the Huns down one by one until there were no more.

Mother was not much better, although, having lost her father and four brothers during the siege and then to learn just after it that she was pregnant, her conduct was no more than could be expected. When she awakened in the afternoons, she would put on a false face and try to pretend that nothing was wrong in her household or beyond it. "Look how the sun shines today!" she would call merrily from the barn door. "Listen to the birds. Oh, we are so fortunate to have sunshine and birds and enough good people to milk the cows and goats and tend the fields!" And then she would collapse in a heap on the earthen floor, blubbering until she slept again.

The good folk she referred to were not so much our people as our servants who, when the Huns first arrived on our lands, fled as fast as mice. But when they heard what destruction had befallen us, they came back again, pleading to be allowed to help us put our lives back together. Most of them had been with us so long that they no longer remembered the tribes of which they had once been a part. In heart, if not in blood and courage, they were Burgundians too. Their pain was no less than our own. And though they forced themselves to stay awake so as to make up for their desertion by working at the tasks that would keep us alive, they moaned and sobbed and wailed and had no drive to stir our spirits.

And so it is understandable that something happened in my heart when Sigurd came riding into this world of death and decay and folly and madness. Even before the siege, when my people were still themselves, I had never known any one of them to be as spirited, as hungry for adventure, or as quick to take on a challenge as Sigurd. And afterward, when these were precisely the qualities that my people lacked, Sigurd seemed a god to me, full of the tales of his doings—some of which were clearly exaggerated for my benefit—and full of the quests he planned to pursue in the future. For me, he was the emblem of the future in a world that refused to be seduced by one. How he loved to speak of the elves and the frost-giants! Leaping about beside his much-loved horse Grani, he would show me how the frost-giants moved when they were angry and how the elves curled up between the boulders when they were afraid. He would beg me to run off with him into the forest where I might see one of these creatures for myself, and though I never did see a single one, what a wondrous thing it was to sit with my hand in Sigurd's, panting from having run so far so fast, looking up at the sky through the tree tops. His visits were never long enough for me. And when he left, I always felt that he took the best part of me away with him. It was as if he were my soul's repository.

One day, when Father was using the palm of his hand to support his head as he finished his dinner, one of our freemen came into the barn where we were living (the halls having all been burnt during the siege) and addressed my father as "king." That was the day Father finally awakened. "Bah!" he shouted. "What king? Can a man who has only a few hundred subjects be called a king? There are no kings here. This is a barn, not a palace. See, the walls are chinked, and the wind blows in at night."

We never learned what the poor fellow had come to say, for some time during Father's harangue, he ran off. Father went back to his seat, and, still grumbling over the man's audacity, he finished his meal. But when he was done, he did not go back to sleep. Mother, who was due to deliver her child any day, slept. And eventually my brothers became bored with their latest conspiracy and went to sleep too. But Father did not sleep. He paced. He went along the walls fingering the chinks as if he had never noticed them before. He came over to the corner where I was sitting wrapped in skins against the cold and patted my head. And the next day, when I awakened, amazed so see him pacing yet, he told me to run out and gather together all of our people to hear the king speak.

This was no easy task. Even with the help of my brothers, who came out later to assist me, it took most of the day to assemble the surviving Burgundians and their servants. Some awakened readily and promised to come to our barn momentarily, but when we went back to see what detained them, we found them asleep again. Some had to be poked and prodded into wakefulness and then escorted to the barn. Some said, "What king? Gundahar is dead, is he not?" But eventually we managed to gather together every last one of them. And then, amid the shuffling and the yawning, the bent heads and the sprawled legs, the dried tears and the fresh sniffles, my father the king stepped forward and made the most eloquent speech I have ever heard.

He declared that we had lived without hope too long, and that the time had come to turn our hopelessness inside out. He commanded that all men take up their drinking horns again and be merry. He called for children. He said that we were all as good as dead ourselves if we failed to set our minds to replenishing our kingdom. He reminded us of the struggles our ancestors had endured when they came south from the cold countries to establish themselves on lands where things grew without coaxing. He said he expected every married woman among us who was not beyond the child-bearing age to bear a child within the year. And he swore that in his own house the example would be set. There would be mead and music and song and new life.

We were not to rub out the past, to forget it, he warned. That would be a serious error. We were to sing about it and still be merry; we were to remember the dead and still to yearn for life.

The task was formidable, and at first our people paid little attention to his decree. They slept less perhaps, but they continued to go about their business ploddingly and with their heads hung low. But as Father had promised, he set the example for them. He forbade my brothers to speak of the Huns until the time came when there would be Burgundians enough to make such discourse sensible. He insisted that Gunner take up his harp again and play until his fingers bled. Mother he made to sing, not about the sun and the birds, but about our ancestors, their hardships and accomplishments, while Hagen and I danced around the hearth. And gradually, our people came to follow the king's example. Our women began to walk over the graves of the dead, as women do when they long for children. Our men offered sacrifices to the gods so that they might assist in the effort to replenish the kingdom. In the evenings, we gathered together, men and women and children alike, beneath Wodan's sacred trees, and we sang so loud and so long that I sometimes feared we would set the stars to tumbling. And the gods heard our voices and children were born, their cries obliterating the ghostly cries of the dead. Our pretense was a pretense no longer. The life-spirit had come back into us.

Mother had given birth to a child sometime before the siege, but the child, a girl, was blue and sickly, and Father refused to accept it. He had it laid out under one of Wodan's sacred trees in a cold bed of new snow. But Mother had longed for that child, and when Guthorm was born in the midst of Father's enforced celebration, another blue and sickly child, and this one marked with the sign of the vacant as well, Mother cried out when she saw Father's scowl appear on his face. He paced the floor and eyed the child who had been placed upon it for his inspection. And in her long shrill cry there was something that made Father cease his pacing. Perhaps he was thinking of the gods and of how he had prayed to them that the Burgundians should be blessed with many children. Or perhaps he was thinking of the example he had promised to set for our people. In either case, to the amazement of us all, Father took Guthorm up and sprinkled him with the water of life and smeared his lips with sweet honey and gave him for his birth-gift the sword which he had intended for a healthier son.

Within the span of every evil there lies a core of solid goodness. Guthorm was that core. Guthorm, whose existence was merely the consequence of the death and destruction that had preceded him, brought great joy to all of us, despite his flaws—or, perhaps, because of them. For in his face we saw the simple innocence our sufferings had caused us to cast off in ourselves.

In the sixth year after the siege, Father struck a bargain with Aetius, and we were granted new lands farther south. And thus we came to settle in Sapaudia. But my father the king, who had breathed new life into the Burgundians, lived only long enough to see his new hall erected. He became ill on the way to Sapaudia and died some weeks after our arrival.

Father had been dead nearly a year when Sigurd came to our new lands, a day I recall as well as if it were yesterday.

Chapter 5

I climbed up onto the roof of our hall to chase the goats down, but then I stayed to sit for a time among the dandelions that had come to life in the turf there overnight. From my post, I could see beyond the steep, reed roofs of our servants' dwellings all the way down to the forest that marked the southern boundary of our pasture, and just before the forest, the mound of turf that marked Father's grave. Someone was playing there, running up one side of the mound and rolling down the other. "Guthorm," I said warningly.

Of course he did not hear me—or at least not in the way that other people hear; he was much too far away for that. But he heard me in another way, a way which was particular to him, his gift. He froze at the top of the mound and studied all that fell within his scan until he discovered me. Then he jumped to his feet and came running, his short legs sprawling crazily and his arms making great circles in the air. The cows and sheep and goats took no note of him as he went flying through their pastures. The servants, some of whom were afraid of him, went about their plowing more earnestly as he passed them by. He tripped once and tumbled. Then he picked himself up and stood for a time staring at his feet. Perhaps he was wondering why they worked so often against him. Whatever his distraction, it was clear that he had forgotten me.

"Guthorm," I whispered again.

And soon he was just below me, jumping about at the edge of the roof and making a noise from deep within his throat. I pointed to the flat-topped rock that the goats used to step up onto the roof, and when he mounted it, I grabbed his arms to hoist him up. But he had depended too much on my strength, and instead of him being pulled up, I was pulled down.

I hit my knee on the side of the rock as I tumbled. Guthorm fell on top of me. The pain in my leg and his weight across my body caused me to throw off the tenderness I had felt for him only a moment before. "Monster!" I cried. "You know you are not supposed to play on Father's grave. I cannot count the times I have told you."

He rolled off me and sat up. I sat, too, and observed the place where my robe had been torn. I could see my bloodied knee through the tear.

Gudrun's Tapestry

"What if Gunner had seen you? What do you suppose would have happened then?"

Guthorm began to cry. Although he was seven, he still cried often. Since he did not talk, his cries and grumblings were all we heard of him. "Do not cry," I said. "It cannot do any good. Come. We will go to Father's grave together and ask him to forgive you—or surely something terrible will befall us all." He gave me his hand.

"Go down now," I said to him when we had reached the grave, and I prostrated myself to show him what was needed. He had stopped crying by then, and he took my prostration to be a game of sorts. He had it in his mind that if he poked at me long enough, I would be happy to roll down the mound as he had done earlier. It was some time before I could calm him and rid him of his mirth. But then, when I had put together in my mind the words I would use to beg Father's indulgence on Guthorm's behalf, I heard the trample of horses and the laughter of men coming through the forest, not from the path to the west that led to the halls of our freemen, but from the south, where my brothers hunted.

I sat up quickly, thinking, Huns! Like the servants, I had come to believe that once the Huns learned that enough of us had survived to warrant a new settlement, they would come again to finish us off for good. Before leaving Worms, we had heard that the leaders, Bleda and Attila, of the great tribe which had attacked us were calling for all Hun tribes to unite under their dominion, and that then they would come down hard on all their enemies. I had never seen these fierce brothers. Along with Mother, I had been hidden away when the siege began. But it was said that the Huns were as strong and as powerful as horses, and that they loved war better than they loved life. Of the two leaders, I was told, Attila was the more hideous to look upon. And indeed, many times in my dreams I had seen him as he had been described to me, a small, broad-shouldered man with a flat nose and a scanty beard and something in his eye so evil that it made men shudder and women swoon. I never considered myself to have the Sight, but these dreams were so real that they convinced me that the day would come when I would look into Attila's evil eyes and see my own reflection staring back at me. And thus, despite my brothers' insistence that the Huns were too preoccupied making war on whole countries to care that some few hundred from the kingdom which had once numbered eighty thousand had survived, I continued to live in fear of them.

"Oh, Father," I prayed hastily, "rid me of my fears and give me the courage that befits a Burgundian." But the men came closer and I grew more afraid.

There was no time to run up through the pastures, so Guthorm and I crawled around to the far side of the mound. As the men came out of the forest and entered the clearing to the east of us, we slipped from the back of the mound into the forest. There we clung to the trees and waited to hear the war cries of the Huns. Once I opened my eyes to glance at Guthorm, and seeing how ridiculous he looked with his eyes squeezed tight and his cheek so hard against the bark of the tree that he seemed to be merging with it, I was ashamed, for his stance was merely an imitation of my own. Still, it was some time before I could bring myself to relinquish my hiding place and stand where I could see what was happening in the pastures.

I can only suppose that it was the drumming of my heart, a drumming which the thought of Attila had initiated, that had kept me from realizing sooner that our visitors were too small a company and riding too casually to be the despicable enemies I had imagined. I flushed at the thought of my own foolishness as I watched Gunner come down the hill from our hall with his arms spread to greet the men. Two of them had slipped off their horses and were moving toward Gunner, also with their arms outstretched in greeting. One was old. The other was young and wore his hair longer than that of his companions, a distinction in Frankish lands which marks a nobleman. Gunner embraced the older one first, then Sigurd.

I knew that Gunner would be angry if I came up directly, and yet I did not see how I could stay away. I ran along the edge of the forest, careful to keep myself hidden, and then up along the east end of the pastures where the servants were plowing in the fields with their oxen. When I reached the servants' huts, which were all in a row, it was easy enough to go from one to the other without being noticed. The Franks had gathered to accept my brother's greeting just to the west of the last of these dwellings. It was behind this one that I hid. Guthorm, of course, was at my side.

I dared to peek out once, and when I saw Sigurd falter and blush in the midst of what he was saying, I knew that he had seen me out of the corner of his eye. My own face grew hot, too, and I sank down aside my hiding place to bask in my pleasure. Guthorm, however, was still peeking out and would give us away if he continued. I grabbed at him, but he had recognized Sigurd, too, and he would not be contained. I could imagine how we would appear to the onlooker, a vacant-faced child lunging forth from behind the hut and being pulled back by the arm of someone otherwise concealed. And when I heard a sudden burst of laughter, I knew that we had been discovered. I waited to hear whether Gunner would scold me, but as his reprimand did not follow, I came out slowly from my hiding place, holding my robe so as to conceal the tear in it.

"Lift your eyes, sister," Gunner called. "A friend of yours honors us today with his visit." I lifted my eyes to meet Sigurd's, but then Gunner put his arm around Sigurd's shoulders, and, laughing, turned him toward our hall.

All the Franks had dismounted by then, and some of the servants had left their tasks to take charge of their horses. With the Franks going one way and the servants and horses another, it was a moment before I could look the men over to see who had ridden to our lands at Sigurd's side. Of course the old man was Gripner, Sigurd's uncle, and now that I was subdued enough to think about it, I was astonished to see him. The last time I had seen him, more than a full year earlier at Worms, he had complained that he was already too old to be riding, and that his eyesight was quickly deteriorating. And now we were so much farther away. In fact, it was a curiosity that the Franks had come to us at all so early in the growing season.

The last of the group to enter our hall was also familiar to me. Regan, the dwarf, had been an advisor to Sigmund, Sigurd's father, before he died. As Gripner and Regan had never gotten on well, Regan had ceased to join Gripner in his travels after Sigmund was gone. I had not seen him in some years, and I was not pleased to see him now. Dwarfs, of course, are as old as time, and to see one is bad luck—unless he loves you well. Regan loved me not at all. He had no love for anyone whom he suspected to have as much power over Sigurd as he did. His presence, along with Gripner's, portended some matter of importance.

I took Guthorm's hand and we ran to Marta's hut. Old Marta was not within—she had probably been summoned up to our hall to help Mother when the Franks first approached—but I knew she would not mind if I went in and used her threads to mend my robe. When I was done, Guthorm and I went down to the river which winds its way to the east of our fields, and there we bathed in one of her quiet pools. Clean and respectable again, we made our way back to Father's grave to finish the business we had begun earlier.

Guthorm, who liked to sleep when the sun was high in the early afternoon, was drowsy by then, and he listened quietly by my side as I begged Father to forgive him his mischief-making. When I felt certain that Father had been satisfied by my words, I begged him to forgive me as well, for having desires that were contrary to his. For although I had no reason to believe that Sigurd's visit had anything to do with me, I hoped with all my heart that he had come to ask my brothers for permission to marry me. Sigurd and I were both eighteen years, the right age to think of such matters. But I knew, even as I begged Father to give me some sign that he had come to change his mind, that my wish was a foolish one. On our way to Sapaudia, Father, who had known he would be leaving us soon, made it clear to my brothers that his only daughter was to make a marriage which would serve the needs of the Burgundians. We were already on the best of terms with the Franks; there was nothing to be gained by my marrying one of them. His declaration was no surprise. Even at Worms, when the subject of my marriage came up, Sigurd's name was never mentioned. Since Father's death, Gunner had taken it upon himself to remind me of Father's wishes. A harsher man than Father had ever been, he insisted that I was not to spend time with Sigurd alone when he came.

I led Guthorm to the cluster of sacred oaks nearest our hall and let him lay his head on my lap while I sang him Balder's song. I knew it by rote, and I knew, too, that I could sing it through and linger on my self-pity simultaneously. Balder had a dream one night, and in his dream he had been killed by violent means. In the morning he awoke and told Frig, his Mother, of the terrible dream he had had. Balder was not one to have such dreams; Frig knew immediately that the dream was a warning. And thus she went around to every living thing—Moon and Sun and Earth and Night and Day and Wind and Fire and Sea and Tree and Rock and River and Mountain and Flower and Bird and Beast—and made them all give her their word that they would bring no harm to Balder, the sweet god of innocence and light. And every living thing was agreeable. Only from the mistletoe had Frig failed to extract a promise. And when she realized her oversight later, she shrugged, for the mistletoe was quite harmless anyway.

Oh, what a time the gods had then. They spent their days throwing rocks and tree limbs and fiery torches and other such things at Balder, and all the things they threw ceased in flight just short of hitting him and dropped to the earth at his feet. And no one enjoyed these games as much as Balder. But one day, destructive Loke, who knew about the mistletoe, who had caused Frig to overlook its presence in the first place, made a sling shot for Hoth, the blind god. And putting the mistletoe into it, he showed Hoth where to aim. Because he was blind, Hoth had been outside the games previously; he was pleased now to be included. He laughed as the mistletoe flew through the air, as did all the others. But when the mistletoe struck and Balder fell down dead, all the laughter ceased—except for Hoth's and Loke's, which could be heard thundering over every hill and down through every valley in every land all the world over.

Guthorm had fallen asleep. It occurred to me, not for the first time, that he was very like the innocent Balder, and every bit as vulnerable. I looked up from his sweet face and saw Mother coming down from the hall with a bowl of milk in one hand and something bundled and held in her skirt with the other. She smiled when she saw how sweetly Guthorm slept, but as she handed me the milk and unwrapped the bread and cheese from her skirt, her smile slid away.

"What are they talking about?" I asked, trying to sound casual.

"Nothing that pertains to you."

My heart fell, but I took a hunk of cheese and tried to appear untroubled. Guthorm opened his eyes, and seeing the food, he sat up quickly and joined me. Mother ate a little too, but distractedly, and continually glancing over her shoulder toward the hall.

When we had finished, Mother dusted the crumbs from her lap and got to her feet. In the sunlight, her aging, white skin appeared fragile, and the lines at her mouth and brow, more deeply etched. "When the men come out," she said sternly, "I will expect you to come right in and help. We will be baking many loaves of bread tonight."

"When will they come out?"

"Soon enough, I wager," she replied. Then she turned back to the hall.

Guthorm had closed his eyes and was already at rest again with his head on my lap, and I leaned against the tree, thinking to follow his example. But knowing that Sigurd was just within the hall made repose impossible. I stared at the hall door and waited. In a while, it was lifted, and the dwarf came out to stretch his short arms toward the sun. Since I could not very well scramble out of sight with Guthorm's head on me, I held my breath and looked aside and hoped he would not notice me. But I heard him call out "Girl!" and I knew I had been seen. I roused Guthorm and stood up. "Tell your servants to fetch our horses," Regan demanded.

"You cannot be leaving already!" I blurted out before I had time to recall that Mother had indicated that the Franks would be staying. But the dwarf only laughed and re-entered the hall.

I did his bidding, and then I hurried back to stand amid the oaks while the men emerged from the hall to mount their horses. Sigurd was the last of the visitors to come out, but as both Gunner and Hagen were at his side, I dared not approach. Still, I stood boldly now beneath the trees until I caught Sigurd's eye. When he saw me, he gestured to the north with a thrust of his chin so subtle that anyone watching would have thought he had meant only to free his face from the golden curls that clung to it on so warm an afternoon. Then he mounted his horse and rode off with the others, down through the pastures and into the forest to the south.

"Listen carefully, little brother," I said, taking Guthorm's shoulders. "You must go up beyond the hall, over the hill, and into the forest and find our rock-horse. When you get there, you may hear Mother call. I may call too. But you are not to come back. You are to stay with the rock-horse until I come for you. Then we will mount him together and ride away to far off lands. Do you understand?"

The rock-horse was a large rock, the shape of which resembled the head and back and rump of a horse. I had taken Guthorm to play on it many an afternoon when my chores were completed. I had no doubt that he could find his way alone. Whether he had understood the latter part of my instructions, I could not say. But there was nothing to be done about it. I turned him in the right direction, and with his eyes dancing and his arms swinging at his sides, he skipped off. When I could no longer see him, I furrowed my brow and rushed in to Mother.

"Guthorm has run off again!" I exclaimed, panting to suggest that I had been running.

Mother was down on her knees beside the stone hearth at the center of the earthen floor. She had been using a small iron shovel to make a pit in the ashes for the breads that we would soon be baking. Now she looked up at me and blinked. "How is that possible? He was just with you."

"Aye, but then everything happened so quickly. The horses were brought up, and then men came out, and . . . . Or perhaps it was the dwarf. I suppose he saw the dwarf and was afraid."

She sighed to let me know that she was annoyed. Then she got to her feet slowly and moved toward the door. As I followed her, I saw her head turn, and I looked in the same direction instinctively and saw Gripner sitting on the long bench against the wall. He had his head turned aside, and he was holding a cupped hand over his mouth.

I ran over and bowed low. "Good sir, forgive me. I did not see you there or I would have—"

"Go, go," he interrupted, and when he made to wave me off, I saw the grin that his hand had been concealing.

Giddy with the knowledge that Gripner knew my secret—for Gripner had the Sight—I ran out and joined Mother. She was holding her hand over her eyes to shield them from the glare of the sun. "Shall I call out?" I asked.

"No. If he had a mind to returning, he would have heard us already," she said, turning slowly in a circle and scanning every direction. "Well, I suppose you will have to go look for him. Your brothers and the others have gone to hunt. What a pity that we have to send our guests to hunt for their own food. There was a time when we should have . . . ." She broke off and let her hand slide over her eyes. Then she dropped it and turned from me, crying, "Go before he gets too far. Then hurry back. I told you I need you."

After we had settled in on our new lands, my brothers sent three of our freemen to the Franks to inform them of the incredible event that marked my father's death and to give them the map that revealed the course to Sapaudia. One of the three, Havel, an older man, had always been particularly kind to me, and not knowing that my father had decreed that I was to quell my love for Sigurd, he had asked me whether I had some message for Sigurd before he left. Since my brothers were on hand, I merely said that I wished Sigurd to know that our new lands were lovely, and that Guthorm and I had found ourselves a secret place to the north of our hall amid the birches. In this way I hoped to let Sigurd know that our friendship was still discouraged, but that I had found a place where we might meet alone nevertheless.

Breathless, I burst into that same birch forest now and ran in the direction of the rock-horse. With the sunlight flickering on the leaves and bouncing off the slim white trunks, the forest was dazzling—a perfect place to meet with Sigurd. And sure enough, he was there. He and Guthorm were kneeling beside the rock-horse's head, offering him the grasses they held in their palms. Sigurd's own horse, Grani, was grazing nearby. Guthorm was so intent on his game that he did not even look up as I approached. Sigurd did, but only to smile. Then he went back to speaking to Guthorm in his low, soothing voice.

My heart leapt at the sight of him. *My dear one*, I thought, approaching, *my darling*, but to my dismay, when I opened my mouth, I found myself crying, "Sigurd, I am so afraid of the world!" And then, like a fool, I burst into tears.

Sigurd jumped up and wrapped me in his arms.

"I heard you this morning marching through the forest," I cried.

"I saw you and Guthorm hiding behind the burial mound."

"I thought you were Huns."

"Huns!" He held me back to study my face. I tired to press myself against him again to hide it, but he lifted my chin. "Huns?" he repeated softly, amused.

"I thought you were Attila. I was going to take Guthorm and flee and leave the others to suffer his wrath."

Sigurd laughed and held me close again. "You would not have done that," he whispered.

"I fear I would have. You do not know me anymore. I have become even more of a coward since we arrived here. I think of the Huns constantly, and in my mind I am always planning how I will escape when they arrive. I dream of Attila more often than I care to admit."

"You would not have left the others."

"How can you be certain?"

"I know you, perhaps better than you know yourself. You have a great reserve of strength. You will see that one day."

"Now that you have come, I will find the place where I am strong again right away."

Sigurd laughed. "You will not need it anytime soon. The Huns have their minds set on much bigger prey. We had news of them recently. They marched on Constantinople, taking many Roman cities along the way. Theodosius, the Eastern Empire Emperor, could not stand up to them. He begged for terms."

"Is it true, Sigurd? It has been so long since we have had any news. We are isolated here, so close to the Western Empire that we fear they hear us when we raise our voices in song. Thank the gods that the Huns and Aetius are allies. The Huns are not likely to march on the Western Empire as long as that is the case. Did you see any Romans on your way?"

"None."

By now Guthorm had wiggled himself in between us. He was standing on the rock-horse with one of his arms around each of us, leaning into us so that we had to lean toward him to keep him steady. When we saw that he was unlikely to withdraw, we sat down, pulling him down between us. He rocked from side to side, humming contentedly. I had not stopped smiling since I had made my admission concerning my fears. "You are taller than you were before," I declared.

"And you are more beautiful."

I blushed. I have Mother's dull eyes and drab yellow hair, but nothing of her height or smile. "How long will you be with us?" I asked, eager to change the subject before Sigurd could detect his error. "You must promise to stay for days and days. Our hall is not nearly so large as it was at Worms, but—"

Sigurd reached past Guthorm to set his fingertips on my lips. "Be still," he said gently. "I will tell you what you need to know. Tomorrow we ride northeast to the foot of the high mountains. Then the others will turn back and Regan and I will ride into the mountains alone."

I gasped. "The gold?"

"Aye, the gold," Sigurd said.

I had no need to hear more. I looked at my knees and brought to mind all that I knew about Regan and the gold. Regan had been on the Earth in the first days when the gods and the dwarves and the elves and the frost-giants were as common a sight as trees. That was a dangerous time, even more dangerous, some say, than now, for the dwarves and the elves had powers, and the frost-giants were evil through and through. Alas, the gods do not take up their man-shapes anymore, and though there are still plenty of elves and frost-giants, their numbers are greatly diminished by comparison. Like my people, those left seem afraid to show themselves. And as for the dwarves, they are practically non-existent. Since they cannot tolerate sunlight, Regan told us one evening when he had come to Worms at Sigmund's side, most of them died over the years and years since the beginning, by turning to stone when they failed to return to their caves in the hills before dawn. In this way, Regan and his brothers were an exception to their race. Their maternal grandmother had been only half-dwarf, and she had passed some of her non-dwarf blood onto her daughter who passed it onto her sons. To have dwarf powers and still the freedom to go about by day as well as night, Regan had professed, was a gift from the gods who had favored Regan's grandmother and arranged the union in which she was conceived. It was Regan's status as a dwarf who had not only known the gods but who had once been in their favor and could speak of their doings with authority that had endeared him to Sigmund.

The connection between Regan and the high mountains was this: the gods once had a great chest of gold, more gold than anyone had ever seen before. But they lost it to Regan's father in a game of dice. Knowing that the gods were more cunning than they were, and that they would not rest until they had their gold back again, Regan's father, Heathmar, took great pains to determine where and how to hide the gold. Finally he decided to put it into the pool of water beneath the great waterfall that fell from the other side of the hill wherein he lived with Regan and his other sons. He told Andari, Regan's youngest brother, to assume the shape of a pike so that he would be suited to watch over the gold. This was a boon for Andari. The dwarves loved to take on animal shapes so as to experience animal joy. There is no joy greater than that of the fish who swims all day and all night and thinks of nothing. But Andari had to take care. Just as the gods were vulnerable when they took on man-shapes, dwarves risked losing their longevity when they made themselves over in the images of animals. But the gold was safe for many years, and Andari, the pike-dwarf, came to love his watery home and his watery life even more than he had once loved his life in the hillside living among his brothers.

But one evening, when Regan's brother Ot had taken on an otter shape so as to visit Andari, the evil-minded Loke saw him leaving the hill and followed him around it to the pool of water. And when Loke heard Ot and Andari discussing the status of the gold, he quickly assumed his man-shape and threw a rock at Ot, hitting him dead between the eyes. Then he carried Ot's otter body away from the pool to where the other gods had assembled to discuss their godly matters. He told them that he had learned the whereabouts of the gold, and the gods conceived a plan.

That night some of the other gods took on man-shapes, too, and went with Loke to Heathmar's home in the hill. Heathmar and Regan and Fafner, Regan's third brother, were all within. The gods showed Heathmar Ot's flayed body and told him that they would restore Ot to life only if the gold was returned to them. Heathmar, however, was greedy. He surmised that the gods had followed Ot to the pool, and now he feared that Andari, in his own greediness, might be tempted to remove the gold to another hiding place. He had long missed the gold that Andari had taken to the pool. What good was gold, he had come to ask himself, if it could not be enjoyed? So he conceived his own plan. He could live without Ot, he told the gods, but not without the gold. Since the gods had killed Ot, they would have to pay a man-price. The retrieval of the gold and the promise never again to interfere with it would suffice. Under Heathmar's direction, Regan and Fafner bound the gods before they could cast off their man-shapes. Only Loke was left untied, and him they sent off to the waterfall to recover the treasure, the condition being that if Loke failed, the other gods would remain bound forever.

At the waterfall, Loke sat all night with a net casting for Andari the pike. When he finally caught him, he threatened to kill him and swallow him whole if Andari did not reveal the exact location of the gold. Andari, who no longer cared about gold or gods, was happy to show Loke where to dive. But after he had been set free, and for no other reason than to remind Loke that he was a fish who was more than a fish, Andari jolted out of the water, laughing, and put a curse on the gold. It would, he declared, bring untimely death to its keeper, whether he be a god or a man. Only dwarves, who Andari still had some love for, were exempt.

Loke returned to the hill-home of Heathmar, and while Heathmar and Regan and Fafner looked on, he removed the gold from the chest and placed it piece by piece on Ot's otter body. Then he told Heathmar and his sons about the curse that Andari had put on the gold. He assured them that he and the other gods could be counted on to keep the promise that would buy them back their freedom, for the gold was no use to them cursed. Heathmar unbound the other gods. And after they had gone away, grumbling because Loke had permitted such a thing to happen, Heathmar told his sons that he would hide the gold himself now, and that he alone would know where. Regan and Fafner argued with him. If the gods had agreed to let them have the gold forever more to make amends for Ot's death, then surely some portion of it was theirs, too, as they were Ot's brothers and entitled to some of his man-price. But Heathmar refused to listen to them, and when he had put all the gold back into the chest, he turned himself into a large black bear so that he would have the strength to drag the chest away. But before he could do so, Fafner drew his sword on him.

While Regan was spilling his tears over his father's bear-body, Fafner pulled the chest away. By the time Regan noticed, Fafner was already out of the cave and down the hill. Furthermore, he had turned himself into a huge dragon, a feat difficult even for a dwarf, and, with his great, earth-quaking stride, he was dragging the chest in the direction of the high mountains.

"I can hardly believe this, Sigurd," I said. "Are you going to tell me that after all these years you and Regan are going off to recover gold that is cursed to begin with?"

"A dwarf's curse is nothing like a god's curse. Regan says a dwarf's curse withers over time."

"Then what of the dragon? Fafner? Surely he has not withered any. I have heard folk say that they have seen smoke and flames of fire coming from those mountains."

Sigurd fingered the small iron hammer, a replica of Thunor's, which hung from a chain around his neck. There was mischief in his eyes, but, hoping to hide it from me, I suppose, he lowered his head. "Regan says that together he and I will be able to slay the dragon, Fafner. Regan is old and weak now, and not as powerful as he was when the world was new, but he is still more cunning than most."

I got up from the rock-horse. "'Regan says, Regan says.' You have always believed everything that Regan says. How do you know there is really any gold at all? Your only proof is that Regan says so. If there was gold, would not someone have gone up for it long before now? Certainly Regan has told the story to enough people."

"Why, Gudrun, you surprise me here. Listen to yourself. You know as well as I that there is no Thuet so dishonest.... Regan is the only one who has a claim to—"

"And the dragon? Can Regan be more cunning than a dragon-dwarf who has had nearly all the years since the beginning to brood over how he might subdue his assailants? Tell me no more of what Regan says. We have enough to think of here, in the shadow of the high mountains. There are the Romans to whom we must pay tributes so that we can live in peace. And the Huns, who know no peace."

Sigurd shook his head. "You astonish me, Gudrun. Perhaps you have changed after all. At Worms, there were plenty of times when my plans concerned you, but I never knew you to come up against me like this."

I fell on my knees before him. "None were as dangerous, Sigurd. When I was a child, I shuddered each time Regan spoke of the gold and the dragon. I think somehow I knew the day would come when he would involve you with them. I cannot bear it. If I should lose you—"

Sigurd slid off the rock, and taking my hands in his, he knelt before me. "I beg you to listen, Gudrun. Regan feels his end is at hand. He has had dreams and other warnings. Except for Fafner, who will soon be dead, he may very well be the last of his race. If he is to die in peace, with any chance at all to attain Valhalla, he must avenge his father's death. He is set on it, I tell you. He will go into the high mountains with or without me. But he is too feeble to slay the dragon in his man-shape, and too old to change himself into any other. I must go with him. Though he is a deedless man who never took up the sword in his life, it was through his instruction that I learned to use my sword, through his reminisces of the animal-shapes that he once took on that I learned to make myself as strong as a bear and as fast as a fox and as silent as a hawk. You say your courage comes from me. Mine comes from him. I owe him this much."

While I listened, I promised myself to say nothing more to antagonize Sigurd, for I thought that I would rather lose him than taint his love for me.

Yet, as soon as he was through, my mouth opened, and my contrary notions came tumbling out anew. "I do not believe that Regan is so weak," I declared. "I do not believe his death is at hand. He is a dwarf, one who can tolerate sunlight. He is using you, Sigurd. After you slay the dragon, he will slay you and take the gold away for himself."

Sigurd laughed. "The man who slays me will have to be a better man than I am. Regan will not be the one."

His laughter brought me back to Worms, to an afternoon that we had spent casting spears in the pastures. Sigurd had me hurl his spear at him, and then he caught it in mid-air with a backhand motion and swung his arm in such a way that the spear was brought up in one movement and ready to be cast back. We did this over and over, until Sigurd could do it with his eyes closed just by listening to the sound of his spear slicing the air. I had not wanted to cast spears at Sigurd, for naturally I was afraid that he would miss just once and be taken from me by my very own hand. But he had laughed when I argued with him, just as he was laughing now. And eventually I gathered my courage and trust in his spear-skill and cast the first spear. When I saw with what ease he caught it, I was ashamed that I had failed to match my confidence in him to his own from the onset.

"Why must you risk your life for gold?" I mumbled.

"All men want gold."

"Why?"

His eyes flashed. "Remember, Gudrun, that the Franks were also conquered by the Romans, and though they did not turn the Huns on us and wipe us out, many of our tribesmen were taken away to live as Romans and march in their armies. Gold buys power. It buys men. And here is something more for you to think about, Gudrun, my love. If I return with the gold, I will be able to buy you."

"Buy me?"

Sigurd fell back on his heels and pulled me down beside him. "When I come back with the gold, smeared with the dragon's blood, do you think your brothers will continue to find reasons to keep us apart? No, they will want us to marry then as quickly as possible. The Franks and the Burgundians will be as one in power and wealth."

This was something that had not occurred to me before. The notion of being able to marry Sigurd and the conviction that the gold was still cursed, no matter what Regan said, scrambled about in my mind together and left it a field of chaos. "What do my brothers say?" I asked.

Sigurd laughed. "They are pleased, of course. I have not talked to them about our marriage yet, but it is there, said or unsaid, as it has always been. Surely it has occurred to them that if I succeed in this venture, I will pay a handsome bride-price for you. But your brothers are not fools. Now that I have informed them of my plans, they want to ensure my loyalty to them whether I marry you or not. The cunning Gunner has requested that tonight I become one with him and Hagen, a brother in blood."

Now it was my turn to be astonished. "Cunning Gunner?" I asked.

Sigurd laughed again. "Do not be a fool, Gudrun. In all the years that I have known your brothers, they have never once spoken of their love for Sigurd, son of Sigmund and Frankish noble. But now that there exists the possibility that I may soon be Sigurd, slayer of the dragon and possessor of his hoard . . . ."

I moved away and answered harshly. "You do my brothers a great injustice. They have always loved you well. If they have offered to mingle their blood with yours, it is because they love you and for no other reason. They would not do such a thing for a few gold coins. And if you accept their blood only because you hope to secure me . . . ."

Sigurd dropped his eyes. "Of course," he whispered. "Forgive me. I only meant to show you—"

I put my hand up to keep him from repeating his offense. My brothers' motives were their concern. Our blood ties obliged me to defend them, as Sigurd well knew. "What does Gripner say about all this?" I asked to change the subject.

The question seemed to startle him, and he hesitated before answering. "My uncle is an old man."

"Aye, but he has the Sight. Surely he has had something to say."

"His visions are no longer reliable. And he is the first to admit it." Sigurd brushed his hands off on his tunic and got to his feet. "We should go before we are missed."

I got to my feet quickly and turned toward Guthorm. He had been standing beside Sigurd's horse, but now he was already approaching us. Sigurd put his arms around me, but I could not bring myself to return his embrace. He released me promptly and moved toward his horse. As Guthorm was passing him, however, he swept him up in his arms, much to Guthorm's delight, and kissed his forehead loudly. Then, after setting him down again, and without looking back at me, he mounted Grani and rode off through the glimmering birches. I regretted my anger immediately, but I had no courage to call him back.

Gudrun's Tapestry

Mother was at work on the loaves when Guthorm and I entered the hall, laying out the dough on the stone slabs surrounding the hearth. She did not look up. Gripner was no longer about. I got to my knees and began to work at her side. "You saw him, did you not?" she asked moodily.

"You said his mission had nothing to do with me." Guthorm was poking at the dough. Mother slapped his hand and gave him a battered wooden bowl to play with. "But you see, if Sigurd returns with the gold, Gunner would be a fool not to let us marry."

"If he returns, it is very likely Gunner will agree to let you marry."

"Then why did you say—"

She looked at me significantly. "You are your father's daughter, Gudrun, not Gunner's."

On the way to Sapaudia, before he died, Father had taken to saying that he had grown too old to be useful. This was, in some sense, true. Unable to endure the trek on horseback, he had ridden up in the oxcart among our possessions like a child, watching and speaking little. Sometimes his head drooped down on his chest and he slept. Many times he was in pain, though I knew this not because he complained but because his features twisted suddenly for no apparent reason. His hair had grown white by then, and his face so deeply etched that when his smile came, a thousand creases wavered and changed direction. Sometimes his memory failed him, and other times he simply could not seem to find the words he needed to express himself. When this happened, he would demand to have Guthorm put up in the oxcart beside him, and with his arm around his youngest son, he would smile and scan the sky as if his destination were other than ours.

There is no dignity among our people in the straw-death, the death that is the consequence of old age. Valhalla is a place for brave men who die in battle. Those who succumb to the straw-death are carried instead to live in Hel among the women and children and cowards and all the others who in life failed to wield the sword, to be ruled over by the dark goddess whose name is the same as the place she governs. But there is an alternative, and Mother took us aside and prepared us for it. And indeed, one evening after we had eaten, Father called for his skins—the bear skins which men wear to give themselves courage in battle—so that he might sacrifice himself to Wodan and thereby buy his way into Valhalla by his own hand. It took both Gunner and Hagen together to dress him in them. They did so silently, each eyeing the other meaningfully. When Father was dressed, Gunner and Hagen came to sit with Mother and me on the long bench against the side wall of our hall. Guthorm was there, too, playing at my feet with the hem of my robe. But even he seemed to know that something was different, for after a time he stopped playing and watched Father along with the rest of us.

In the distance we heard the first rumblings of thunder. Thunor was welcoming us to our new lands, letting us know that he would shortly provide the rain that we needed for our early crops. We listened to his greeting and watched Father in the firelight. He was breathing deeply, through his nose, staring straight ahead with his eyes wide open. He seemed to be oblivious to us. He seemed to be listening to a voice that we could not hear. As the moments passed, his breathing became deeper yet, and his eyes wider, until they looked like they would burst forth from their sockets. His mouth hardened, the skin around it quivered, and he seemed to grow taller in his seat. And meanwhile the thunder grew louder. Then all at once Father let out a scream and rose from his chair. I felt my own body lift, my impulse being to run to him. But Hagen, who had taken my hand, tightened his grip on it. And Father did not fall. Shrieking, he went running out through the open door, his sword flashing overhead. As if we were separate limbs of the same body, we all got up at once and went after him, pressing ourselves together at the threshold to see what he would do. In his bear skins, he looked much larger, and his vigorous howls seemed those of a younger man—indeed, a warrior. And Thunor saw and heard him too, it seems, for all at once a great, jagged bolt of fire lit the dimming sky and brought Father down where he stood with his sword held up to Valhalla. There is no greater honor for an old man than to be brought down by lightning. Thunor had singled out Father for Valhalla after all.

Had I a right, I wondered as I worked at Mother's side, to desire to go against the wishes of a man so well loved by the gods? Would it set the gods against me? And surely I tainted my brothers as well as myself, for it was doubtful that a few gold coins were what my father had in mind when he said that my marriage should serve all of the Burgundian people. If my brothers were seeing now that my marriage to Sigurd might benefit them directly, it was because I had, by making my desires clear to them over the years, made accomplices of them.

Gudrun's Tapestry

We had our feast with the Franks, and then we took torches and went down to the edge of the forest, very near to the place where Father was buried. The men had all drunk great quantities of mead by then, and there was much shouting and singing among them. Our servants heard the uproar and came out from their huts to join us in the cool night air. And thus we stood, voices and light in a half-circle, the Franks and the Burgundians and the servants of the Burgundians, as Gunner and Hagen and Sigurd went down on their knees and dug a hole in the earth with their hands. Hagen was about to draw his short sword when he was stopped by Gunner's grip on his wrist. "Guthorm should not be outside our blood-bond," Gunner declared.

"I should be honored," Sigurd said as he scanned the half-circle for Guthorm. Finding him, he beckoned, and Guthorm went forward hesitantly. Then Hagen drew his sword, and holding it in one hand, he drove the tip into the palm of the other while the Franks and the Burgundians cheered behind him. Guthorm, who seemed mesmerized by the sight of the blood gushing from Hagen's palm, began to make a grumbling noise which, when the shouting had subsided, threw all the Franks who were within earshot into fits of laughter. Sigurd stopped them with a gesture. Guthorm tried to flee then, but Gunner grabbed his arm. Mother, who was standing beside me, bit her lip. "He is frightened," I called out.

"Be still and take your turn," Gunner insisted, ignoring my plea. And he prepared to prick Guthorm's palm with the bloodied sword. But all at once Guthorm broke loose and charged to my side. Again there was laughter among the Franks. Gunner was about to come after Guthorm, but Hagen shouted, "He is not sensible of our rites. Leave him stand among the women." Gunner relented and turned back to Hagen. He took the sword from him and quickly slashed his palm. Then he passed the sword to Sigurd, who did likewise. Then Sigurd and Gunner gripped each other's hands, palm to bloody palm, and the blood ran down their arms and along the sides of their tunics and into the receptacle they had fashioned out of the earth. "Brother," Gunner cried. "Brother," Sigurd responded. Then Sigurd and Hagen joined their hands and did the same. In the firelight one could see a glistening in Hagen's eye as the rite was completed. There was a great shouting from the crowd as Gunner and Hagen and Sigurd covered the earthen vessel that held their blended blood with more earth and marked the spot with a rock.

Back in the hall our party took up their drinking horns again and there was much merriment. A brother to my brothers now, Sigurd soon grew bold and abandoned his place next to Gripner in the seat reserved for honored guests and came to sit by my side on the long bench. I pressed my hand into his to show him that I was no longer angry with him.

Gripner asked for Gunner's harp. When he had it, he began to sing in his aged voice about the Visigoths, the brave and cunning Thuets who broke into the empire a long time ago and who, under the leadership of Alaric the Bold, waged a great war upon their hosts so that the Romans might come to know that they were not invincible.

A young Frank whom I had never met before took up the harp next. He sang a sad song about how the first Thuet tribe to be conquered by the Huns, the Ostrogoths, was made to give up its customs and put itself in the Huns' service.

Then Gripner asked for the harp once more. This time he sang of the lament of the Franks when they had been defeated by the Romans, and of the brave men among them who had drawn their swords against the mighty Aetius.

His song was so beautiful that Gunner, who had tears in his eyes, removed one of his gold arm-rings and offered it to Gripner to thank him for his words, for there was nothing Gunner appreciated more than beautiful words strung together to recover the past. While the rest of us lived with some hope of the future, Gunner had given up his hope sometime between our preparations to leave Worms and our resettlement at Sapaudia. His hopelessness had made him bitter, and his bitterness had made him mean. Music and poetry were the only things that stirred him anymore. Inspired by Gripner's song, he took his harp back and sang the Franks the song which they had all been waiting to hear, the lyrics of which described Father's passing. Although they already knew the story, they were anxious to hear the details, and there was great joy among them when they heard the elegance that Gunner lent them.

While the Franks were still lifting their drinking horns and toasting to Father's good fortune and Gunner's gift, Sigurd whispered to me, "One day men will sing of me that way."

I looked at him. He was smiling, and his eyes, shiny with constrained tears, were set on the men who were still exclaiming over Gunner's song. "Is that so important to you?" I asked.

"Yes," he answered bluntly. "There is nothing I want more than to be remembered at night in the halls of good Thuets when their hearts are light and their minds are at peace."

Although my love for Sigurd was as vast as the sky that holds the world bound from end to end, I had all afternoon been fighting off the thought that Sigurd was either a fool, for allowing himself to come so easily under Regan's influence, or worse, that he was greedy and cared more for gold than for men. But now, in Sigurd's rapturous face, the counterpart of his pleasure, I saw the truth clearly. Sigurd wanted what all men want—to be remembered, and through remembrance, loved.

The fire was low by then, and some of the Franks had fallen asleep over their drinking horns. Although Gunner could not be coaxed to sing anymore, he still played his harp, repeating the melodies that we had heard earlier and reminding us of the stories that had accompanied them. And so sweetly did his fingers work at their task that those who were sleeping smiled, and those who were awake rolled their cloaks into bundles and used them to rest their heads. Hagen brought in his straw-stuffed mattress, still rolled and bound, and offered it to Sigurd, but Sigurd refused it. Then Hagen brought me the sheepskin rug that I used to cover myself at night. He and Sigurd draped it around me. Then Sigurd took my cheek into the palm that was still covered with my brothers' blood and pressed my head toward him until it came to rest against his shoulder. And thus we slept together, seated on the hard bench against the hall wall, surrounded by our peoples, and without the need to describe to each other the immensity of our happiness.

CHAPTER 6

They came all at once, the geese, hundreds and hundreds of them, filling the sky above the moor like a storm. Having become used to Guthorm and me the Summer before, they went about their business directly, and, for the most part, paid us little attention—except on the days when we could spare them some crumbs. Then they were all over us, fighting amongst themselves and pleading to be recognized. A few times, when we had no crumbs, one of them would waddle over idly and speak to me in her goose tongue, telling me that she understood my concerns, or so I liked to think.

Their young came into the world covered over with downy feathers and with their eyes already open. In no time they were ready to leave their nests to swim and eat beside their elders in the shallow, murky lake. When they abandoned their nests for good, having grown too large for them by midsummer, Guthorm and I gathered the down feathers which their mothers had plucked from their own soft under-bodies to make the bedding for their young. The feathers would be given to the Romans, a portion of the tribute they expected each year. But I had it in mind to hold some aside for myself, for it was my wish that Sigurd and I would sleep on a feather mattress when we married. Yes, I had decided that I would rather marry Sigurd and spend the rest of my days begging Father's forgiveness than refuse to marry him and spend the rest of my days in despair. Of course this decision, which cost me little time and less thought, was based not only on the assumption that Sigurd would return from the high mountains, but that he would have the dwarf-dragon's gold in hand as well when he did. As Sigurd had observed, it was the gold—and not the man who had gone after it—that would have the power to prompt my brothers to go against my father's wishes. I had no way to know then how grave would be the consequences of my resolution.

While my days on the moor were quiet, my evenings were noisy events filled with many people. As we expected the Roman tax collectors shortly, our freemen came up to our hall regularly to meet with my brothers and to take stock of our possessions and decide what portion of them could be spared to appease the Romans. Hagen felt that we might be conservative in our offerings that year. Since the Huns had marched on the Eastern Empire, he argued, the Western Empire would have come to realize that it was to their advantage to be indulgent with their "barbarian neighbors," as they called us. The greater part of the Western Empire's army had for many years been made up of Hun mercenaries. But the Huns were fickle now, as we had learned from the Franks, and the Romans would be looking to fill the void. And who knew better how little we had to begin with than the Romans? Gunner, however, disagreed. He insisted that Bleda and Attila's pact with Aetius was as strong as ever, and thus it would be a dangerous thing to provoke the Romans by giving them less than they expected. Our freemen were divided on the issue, and it took the space of several evenings before it was decided. In the end, there was a compromise. We would hide what little gold we had, but we would offer the Romans salt and skins and soap and turnips and beets and down and half our season's honey crop. The Romans had a great love for honey, though they did not ferment it and make it into mead as we did. They used it instead to make cakes, and their women, it was said, mixed it with milk and made a lotion that turned their skin soft. Furthermore, we would give up half of our servants to march in the Roman armies. This was not an easy decision for our people to come by, but since there were more servants among us than there were Burgundians, there was no alternative for it if we were truly to rebuild our kingdom as Father had decreed. And the Romans would not know the difference. A barbarian was a barbarian to them,

Gudrun's Tapestry

a Thuet a Thuet. Our freemen drew lots to see whose servants would go. Our own personal servants were not to be affected.

When these matters were behind us, we occupied our evenings with hive-hunting, for the nests were full of honey by then. Everyone took part in this activity. The servants repaired the ladders which had been weakened the Summer before or fashioned saplings into new ones. Guthorm and I were given the task of carrying the vessels which would be filled with the honeycombs that Hagen collected. Gunner assigned some of the servants to work with him. Our freemen, along with their families and servants, did likewise.

We were at this task the evening the Romans came. Hagen carried Guthorm up on his shoulders as we made our way into the depths of the forest that night. He liked to sing while we hunted the hives. Since he never sang when Gunner was about—for Gunner always mocked his loud, tuneless voice—Hagen saved it up for the times when he was not. Like Gunner, Hagen composed his own songs. But unlike Gunner, whose songs were always the melancholy laments of days gone by, Hagen's generally reflected his mood, which was jolly more often than not. On this night he invented a song to appease the bees whose hive we planned to plunder. In it, he equated the upheaval of their hive with our own upheaval at Worms. But he assured the bees that they would build a new hive, and that now, knowing of the dangers of the world, their new hive would be stronger and higher up. I followed behind Hagen, and when he started his song for the second time, I sang along with him. One of our servants, a man called Clumar, followed behind me, carrying the ladder and the torch. Clumar did not sing, and I could tell by his look that it did not please him to hear us either.

When we arrived below the nest that Hagen had singled out earlier in the day, Clumar made a bundle of the twigs, and touching his torch to it, passed it on to Hagen. Then he held the ladder steady while Hagen climbed. The bees stirred immediately, and in their great rush to flee from the smoke, many flew into the fire. We did not like to see them die. Though we had all suffered our share of their stings, their sweet gift was more than adequate compensation. They were the middlemen whose life-purpose was to bring Wodan's honey to his people, just as we were the middlemen whose life-purpose was to generate a new kingdom of Burgundians. There was no one among us who failed to thank Wodan for sharing his honey-magic with the bees, for what is more wonderful than honey? But on this night, Hagen had no opportunity to offer his thanks. In fact, he was not even able to finish cutting into the nest. He was still up in the tree in the process when he saw the torches in the distance, far too many and too close together to be those of our fellow hive-hunters. He let out a call, like that of an owl, to alert whomever might be within earshot, and then he scrambled down the ladder, the pleasure of his task drained from his face. Unlike Gunner, who insisted that we could learn much from our alliance with the Romans, particularly their tool-skills and building-skills, Hagen despised the Romans. He argued that there was nothing to be learned from men who were content to live within walled cities. "Clumar," he cried, "take my sister and Guthorm to your hut and keep them there until the Romans are gone."

    Clumar stood for a moment with his mouth open, undoubtedly trying to find the words that would alert Hagen to the fact that he did not like to have Guthorm under his roof. He was a superstitious man, and I had many times seen him make the sign to ward off evil when Guthorm passed too close to him. But as there was nothing he could say that would not stir Hagen's wrath, he sighed and turned to lead us away while Hagen took the torch and set off in the other direction to meet the Romans.

    As soon as Clumar had ushered us into his hut, he went out again into the night to tell the servants who had not gone into the forest that the Romans had arrived. The buzzing that ensued rivaled the one that the bees had made at the sight of the smoking twigs. As I expected, Clumar did not return, but as I did not like Clumar, I was glad to be left to fend for myself. I could forgive him for regarding Guthorm as an emblem of evil—he knew no better—but he seemed to regard all others likewise, though to a lesser degree. He held back from laughter and conversation, his small gray eyes always darting about so that no one could ever guess what he was thinking. I do not think I ever saw him smile. If a battle broke out, Guthorm and I would be better off without him.

    But it was unlikely that there would be a battle. After all, this was the Roman tax-collecting contingency, not the army. If Hagen had hidden me away, it was likely because of the rumors we had all heard about the Romans' fondness for "barbarian" women. Before long I could see the Romans going by through a gap between the logs that made up Clumar's wall. They were half-hidden behind the metal helmets and the metal vests—body walls, Hagen called them—which they wore over their tunics. There were perhaps fifty of them, and they rode in tight rows of five abreast, a pretty sight to see. At the rear of their assemblage was the horse-pulled wagon that would carry away our offerings, and behind the wagon Hagen appeared walking beside their leader, conversing with him in our language. When the Roman assemblage came to a halt, Hagen whistled for the servants. They came out from their huts hesitantly while the Romans dismounted. After tending to the Romans' horses, they went off to the place where the honey and the other offerings had been stored.

Gunner came into my field of vision, still carrying his honey vessel and dragging his ladder behind him. But he dropped these things at once so as to be able to greet the Roman leader with opened arms, as if he were a brother. I had wondered how Hagen had greeted the leader, but when I saw his eyes narrow as he watched Gunner, I knew that his own greeting had not been so affectionate. When Gunner and the Roman released each other, the Roman cried out an order to his men, and two of them struggled to lift a large wooden vessel out of the wagon. The Roman said something to Gunner which I could not hear but which made Gunner laugh abruptly. Then Gunner and the Roman began to walk in the direction of our hall while Hagen and the other Romans followed behind.

I had assumed that the wooden vessel contained Roman wine, and I knew I was right when I heard the sound of laughter and shouting wafting down to me from the hall. In Worms, the Romans had never been so amiable, and we had never been so hospitable. Since it seemed the chances were good that the Romans would be spending the night, I began to look about for bedding for the drowsy Guthorm. I found only a cloak, a coarse, foul-smelling thing, and I spread it out on the earthen floor and made Guthorm lie down on it. Then I sang him Hagen's hive-hunting song until he fell asleep.

It was late and growing cold. Clumar's fire needed replenishing. Since there was no wood stacked beside his hearth, I went outdoors. But there was no wood by the door either, and I did not like to rob the other servants of their night's supply. I stood for a time in the darkness, until I had gathered enough courage to go up to where our own wood was stacked close to the hall door. I was so intent on not being seen through the lifted door that at first I did not notice the figure seated on a rock to the left of me. I gasped and dropped the logs I had already gathered, and they went rolling toward the black silhouette. "Sister?" it asked.

I ran to Hagen's side. He looked about, and seeing that no one was watching us, slid over and made room for me on the rock. Then he handed me his drinking horn. I took a sip, and realizing what it was, I spit it out immediately. Hagen laughed at me. "Do you not like the Roman wine?"

"I like nothing about the Romans."

"Nor do I."

"They why must you drink their wine?"

Hagen ran his fingers over my cheek. The wine made him smell bad. I could hear Gunner's laughter distinctly above the din coming from the hall. "I like nothing about the Romans except their wine," he said. "Their wine is good. Very, very good." And he drained the rest from his horn.

"And our brother?" I asked. "It seems to me that there is much he likes about the Romans."

Hagen looked at me. In the moonlight I could see the scar that divided his face in two, running down his forehead at an angle, across his nose, and down one cheek. He had received it long ago at Gunner's hand, an accident which occurred when they were jousting. It made him look fierce, and it kept the women away from him. I did not usually notice it myself, for his face was otherwise handsome. He had a straight, strong nose and a prominent jaw. His lips were generous, and his eyes were very blue and large. On this night, however, the moonlight seemed to crawl into the hollows of his scar and settle there. "Do not underestimate Gunner," he warned me. "He remembers all too well what the Romans did to us in the past. You can find uses for the skin and the teeth of the wolf and still hate the wolf, Gudrun."

"Aye, but to embrace the wolf?"

Hagen glanced at the hall door. "Hush. You will be heard. Go away now. You should not even be here."

"I do not care if I am heard," I said, but softly, for in part I did. And I would have said more had not Hagen clapped his hand over my mouth just then. Together we watched a young Roman come stumbling out of the hall with his drinking horn in his hand. He looked up at the stars for a moment and then made a sign with his free hand which I had never seen before. Then he staggered over to the oaks. We could hear him urinating behind one of them.

"What sign was that that he made?" I asked when the Roman had gone back into the hall.

"He was praying to one of his gods, I suppose." Hagen began to laugh. "The Romans cannot hold their wine, you know. I hear they put their hands down their throats to make themselves vomit when they have drunk too much. Then they sleep, and when they awaken, they begin drinking all over again."

He went on laughing, so that I knew he'd had a bit too much of the Roman wine himself. When he was quiet again, I asked, "What do you mean, his gods?"

"Did you think only Thuet peoples had gods?" he asked.

"Do you mean to say the Romans pray to Wodan and Thunor and—"

"Foolish girl, no. They have gods of their own."

"But how is that possible when our gods created the world and man to live in it?"

Hagen slapped his knee and howled with laughter. "I had no idea my sister was so ignorant," he cried merrily. "Go back to Clumar's hut now and pray to Wodan for wisdom."

I got up briskly. "I will pray to Balder that my brothers will one day learn kindness," I retorted, and I went off scowling, but full of love for Hagen. But the thought of the Roman gods looking down from Valhalla, mingling with our own gods, or perhaps warring with them, began to frighten me. When I could no longer hear Hagen's laughter behind me, and I began to run.

I lay for a long time shivering. I had left the logs behind, and now I could not muster the courage to go back for them. To keep from thinking of the Roman gods, I thought of Gunner and wondered whether he would seek to advance his alliance with the Romans. It seemed to me that this was his objective, and I realized all at once that he would think nothing of marrying me off to one of them if he thought a more fruitful alliance could thus be attained. This notion frightened me even more than that of Roman gods in Valhalla, and I snuggled up as close to Guthorm as I could on Clumar's stinking cloak. In spite of my efforts to fall asleep, I found myself trying to imagine what it would be like to be married to a Roman. I knew little more about them than that they were ruthless and greedy and their women loved honey. I saw myself, in my mind's eye, rubbing honey on my skin and praying to gods whose names and deeds were unfamiliar to me. In the background of my musings, I heard horses galloping through the pastures; the servants of our freemen were riding up on their masters' horses to be taken back to the Western Empire along with our other offerings. I pitied the servants who would be leaving, and I prayed to Wodan that they would be well treated.

I awoke before dawn, still upset and too cold to move a muscle. I realized that I had spent the entire night shivering. I could not remember my dreams, but I was certain that Gunner had been present in them and had married me off to a Roman after all. Again I heard horses, and I assumed that this was the Romans preparing for their departure. Since I was reluctant to leave Clumar's hut until I was certain that the Romans had gone, I tried to go back to sleep. I closed my eyes and thought of Mother and wondered whether she, too, had been made to spend the night in one of the servants' huts. I imagined that she was with Marta, safe and warm by the old woman's hearth-fire. Thinking of the fire, I fell asleep again, but immediately I found myself lying in snow, surrounded by Romans, whom, though I did not dare to look up at them, I recognized by their well-made boots. They were standing over me, talking about me in their language. I narrowed my eyes to slits so that they would not realize I was awake. And I prayed that they would soon tire of inspecting me and go away. And then, all at once, I was elsewhere, still lying on the cold ground, but this time in the high grasses at the moor. The Romans were gone, and instead I was surrounded by geese. Like the Romans, the geese were talking about me, but their language I could make some sense of. They were commenting on the fact that I was shivering and trying to determine what could be done about it. Then the leader among them suggested that they gather together and press themselves against me. This they did, and all at once I was warm and at peace. But then one of the geese bent his head over mine and kissed me gently on my cheek. Even in my dream state I recognized the kiss as a genuine one, and I floated up out of my dream. "Mother?" I mumbled, my eyes still closed because the dream seemed yet within my reach. I heard Guthorm's deep-sleep breathing, but nothing else. I could feel the weight of the covering which had been placed over me, which I had mistaken for the gathering of geese. "Hagen?"

Still there was no answer. Surely none of the Romans would have covered me and kissed me so gently. It was as quiet without as it was within, and I could feel daylight pouring in through the gap in Clumar's wall. I felt certain that the Romans had gone. I opened my eyes and studied the back of Guthorm's head. His pale hair was matted; already he needed another bath. "Gunner?" I asked more loudly. But I knew it was not Gunner; Gunner seldom kissed me. Then it occurred to me that it must be Clumar, for who else would enter Clumar's hut unannounced but Clumar himself? Outraged, I sat up at once and turned to confront him. And there, looking amused, was Sigurd.

Now I believed myself still dreaming. But as I would not put the sight of such a phantom to waste, I threw myself into Sigurd's arms, and there I learned that I was indeed awake. How we clung to each other, laughing like two children while we watched Guthorm come awake. To our further amusement, Guthorm at first merely stared at Sigurd, his eyes wide and his tongue making circles around the edges of the dark gap that was his mouth. Then he crawled out from under Sigurd's cloak and into our embrace. I would have been happy to stay thus entangled forever, but after a moment Sigurd got to his feet, dragging Guthorm and me up with him. "Let us go quickly," he said.

"For all that I am worthy of you now, I would not want your brothers to find me here with you. I spent a part of the night watching from the edge of the forest. The Romans left shortly before dawn. Then I saw Clumar coming out from a hut which I did not recall to be his. I went to him, and he told me that you and Guthorm spent the night here."

I looked into his eyes and marveled that I could have ever imagined that he would fail at anything he attempted to do.

We walked together, hand in hand, Sigurd and Guthorm and me, rounding the row of huts and heading up the hill to the hall. The sky was overcast now, and the air was cool and full of moisture. Hagen and Gunner and Mother were sitting outside the hall door, beneath the oaks, probably discussing the meeting with the Romans. Gunner was the first to look up. When he saw Sigurd, his mouth dropped open. Hagen, looking to see what had startled our brother, jumped to his feet and came running. Mother sat motionlessly, her mouth still set to form whatever word she had been about to say. I covered my own mouth with my free hand to conceal my pleasure.

"Brother," Hagen shouted. "You are back! You are alive!"

"I have the dragon's gold," Sigurd declared.

By this time Gunner, too, had found his feet. He reached Sigurd and embraced him heartily. "Let us go at once and offer a sacrifice of thanksgiving for your return before we hear another word," he cried.

"That would please me," Sigurd said. He stepped forward and bowed before Mother.

She lifted her chin and smiled, but I saw in her eyes that she had not counted on Sigurd's return. "This is good news," she said flatly. "I will see to the sacrifice." She got up at once and started down the hill, calling for the servants as she went.

Soon after, Mother and the servants emerged from the pastures with a good fat lamb, and we started down the hill to meet them. Then we all went together to the sacred grove not far from Father's grave at the edge of the forest. Sigurd and Mother and my brothers and I entered the grove while the servants stood at its entrance, stretching their necks and pushing against one another. Since there had been no time to fashion a proper garland for the lamb, Mother called to one of the servants to pick her some flowers from outside the grove. She twined them together deftly and stuck them beneath the rope that had been knotted around the lamb's neck. Then Gunner took the end of the rope and led the lamb to the stone altar at the far end of the grove. There he bowed before turning back to lead the lamb to the grove entrance.

Three times he led the lamb to the altar and three times he led him away. The forth time, he lifted the lamb and held him up for all to see. The servants began to sing. Guthorm hummed and swayed happily at my side. Gunner placed the bleating, kicking lamb on the altar, and Hagen drew his sword, saying, as he looked from one sacred tree to the next, "We thank you, Wodan, for the return of our brother and for the good deeds which he has done in your name. Accept this fat lamb as a gesture of our gratitude." As he drove his blade into the lamb's heart, the voices of our servants swelled. We lifted our own voices then, and together we sang Wodan's praises while the lamb's life-spirit rose, almost visibly, and his life-blood ran bright and red over the sides of the altar and onto the earth. Hagen withdrew his bloodied sword and held it up, and our hearts were glad together.

When the last of its life-spirit had been absorbed by the spirits that inhabited the grove, the lamb stilled. Hagen cut into it and pulled out its heart and liver and lungs and entrails, the parts that Wodan loves best, and placed them in a heap on the altar. Then he smeared the blood from his hands onto each of the sacred trees while Gunner drew his sword and severed the head of the lamb, and, forcing the blade through the lamb's skull, pinned it to the largest oak.

Gunner called for fire, and one of the servants pushed through the mouth of the grove with an armful of twigs and logs. Another came forward with a torch, and the fire was ignited before the altar. And all the while we sang, lifting our voices to Valhalla. When the fire was hot enough, the lamb, which Hagen had flayed by then, was placed on the logs and roasted. We sang while it cooked and we sang while it cooled. Hagen ripped it into portions and passed one to each of us within the grove and then without to the servants. Our voices, harsh now from so much singing, quieted, and when every man and woman and child had received his share, they ceased altogether. Then, silent but much elated by the connection that we had made with the gods, we ate the flesh of the lamb in the cool dark womb of the grove.

The rain came all at once, falling hard and cold through the tops of the trees. Hagen dismissed the servants immediately. Sigurd wrapped his cloak around my shoulders and Guthorm's and pushed us out of the grove.

In the hall we gathered around the hearth. I was deeply chilled and my teeth chattered despite the nearness of the fire. I sneezed once, and then again. There was a dull aching at work in my head. When I felt the next sneeze coming, I set my lips hard against it so that I would not desecrate the day of Sigurd's return with my disturbances, but the sneeze came anyway.

Gudrun's Tapestry

When the others had warmed themselves sufficiently, they left the hearth to Guthorm and me and took their rightful places in the hall—Gunner and Hagen on the high seat that had once been Father's, and Sigurd on the seat opposite at the other end of the hall. My place was on the long bench beside Mother, but I could not bring myself to retreat from the fire.

"Well," Gunner began, addressing himself to Sigurd, "the time has come for you to tell us of your venture. Leave out no detail, brother. We have waited long enough to hear your words, and we will want to remember them."

Sigurd smiled proudly. "I will tell you all," he said in a loud voice, for although our hall was not nearly so large as the one at Worms, there was still much space between Sigurd's voice and my brothers' hearing of it. My own hearing, meanwhile, seemed to have gone bad with the sickness that was rapidly overtaking me. I had to concentrate hard just to distinguish Sigurd's words from the din that filled my head and from the sound of my own sneezes and sniffles.

"Why not go into your bower," Gunner snapped suddenly.

"She shivers," Hagen said. "Let her stay where she is. She will want to hear this too."

"She can hear well enough from the bower," Gunner said, but Hagen only stared at him, and finally Gunner sighed and turned his attention back to Sigurd.

"Regan, you will note," Sigurd began, "has not returned with me." He dropped his eyes from those of my brothers suddenly and looked down at his feet. This was what Sigurd always did when he wanted others to know that he was troubled, for his face was otherwise incapable of expressing sorrow. Sigurd's upper lip was long and narrow, and at each end of it there was a dimple. When he was a child, his father would fly into a fit of rage to see his son's naturally bemused expression yet on his face after he had been scolded. And thus Sigurd had learned that by lowering his head he could keep his father from becoming inflamed. The habit served him well, and he had hung onto it.

"We noted this," Gunner said impatiently.

"But let me begin at the beginning," Sigurd said, lifting his gaze.

"Bring us some mead, Mother," Hagen interrupted.

"At this early hour?" she cried.

But Hagen, whose eyes were fastened on Sigurd, made no response, and thus Mother got up and brought out drinking horns for Sigurd and my brothers. When they had been filled, Sigurd began again.

"Regan and the Franks and I rode to the foot of the high mountains and camped there the first night as planned. We offered a sacrifice, a good-sized buck that we had come across during the course of our ride, and as with today's sacrifice, there was evidence that it was accepted. Then, in the morning, the others turned back for Frankish lands, and Regan and I rode on alone.

"Travel was slow. The mountains are steep. We made our way cautiously, for many times we thought we heard the movements of frost-giants beyond the trees surrounding us. Had we come across any frost-giants earlier, we could have gotten away from them easily enough. As you know, they are slow-moving. But on the steep mountainside, they would have posed a threat. But we climbed and climbed, and we saw nothing.

"In all, it took us ten days to reach the top of the highest mountain. And when we did, we found that the air there is not as well-distributed as it is at lesser elevations. Breathing it made us light-headed at first, and slow to go about our business. Nor were there many beasts to be found up there. We were lucky to come by a rabbit each night to share for our dinner. And we were cold, brothers, for it seems that when Winter retreats from tribal lands, she stops just short of a complete withdrawal and sits poised on the mountain tops gathering strength for her next assault."

"The dragon," Gunner urged. "Get to the dragon."

Perplexed, Sigurd stared at Gunner for a moment. Then he continued. "Regan had brought along a forked limb from an apple tree, and with this limb, on which he had cast a spell, he was able to direct us, after three days more, to the dwarf-dragon's cave. We came to it at night. And as we stood at its entrance holding our torches low, we heard the dwarf-dragon's breathing, so loud that it set the shrubs at the mouth of the cave to trembling. I confess, brothers, I was afraid that Fafner would catch wind of us, but Regan assured me that dragons are dull creatures, and that as long as we took care not to let ourselves be seen, Fafner would suspect nothing. So we hid our horses at some distance from the cave, and then we hid ourselves in the brambles above the cave entrance and waited for dawn.

"Fafner arose late in the morning, making a grumbling so great that it loosened some rocks from the mountain and sent them tumbling down its face as though they were mere pebbles. Then he came forth from the mouth of the cave, and plodding along on his monstrous feet, he made his way to a small lake to the west. The path he took, we noted, was well-worn, and we were assured that he traveled it regularly. We knew then that we had only to hide ourselves along this path to be able to slay him and rob him of his wealth."

Gudrun's Tapestry

Gunner got up and retrieved the mead pitcher from its place at Mother's feet. He refilled Sigurd's drinking horn and then Hagen's and his own. "So tell us, brother, what did this dragon, this Fafner, look like?" he asked as he sat down again.

Sigurd's brow rose. "Look like?" he asked laughing. "Well, that is not easy to say."

Gunner sat forward and cocked his head questioningly. Sigurd stared back at him, the color rising in his face. Then all at once he laughed and shouted, "You see, he was enshrouded by fog and flame."

"Fog and flame?" Hagen asked, his eyes as round as moons.

"But you saw his feet," Gunner prompted. "You said he had monstrous feet."

"And so he did. There were times when we were able to glimpse this or that part of him through pockets in the fog and the flame, and thus did we see his feet. But never did we see the whole of him at one time. His feet were monstrous things, and there were two of them, as far as I could tell. And his head was a great, ash-gray thing covered with scales like those of the snake. His eyes were two round dark pools, each as large as the head of a man. And . . . ." Sigurd closed his own eyes so as to better recall the dragon. "And with every breath he drew fire from his lungs and spewed it forth. He was large, as large as three men together. No, four. He was as tall as four men together, and far thicker." Sigurd's eyes popped open. "Wodan alone knows what he found up on that barren mountain top to sate such a body."

"But you said he went regularly to the lake," Gunner retorted. "I would have guessed that he went there to fish."

"Aye, and so I thought myself at first. But a great many fish it would have taken to sate him, brother, and this was not a large lake."

"But there must have been enough—"

"It does not matter what he ate. Go on," Hagen urged.

Sigurd lifted his drinking horn to his lips and stared for a time at my brothers, his bemused expression a contradiction, surely, to his thoughts. "After a time, the dragon returned to his cave and did not leave it again that day. That night, while the dragon slept, Regan and I made our plan and went to work. The flame and the fog which kept us from seeing Fafner, we reasoned, would likewise keep him from seeing us—if we were hidden well enough. And so we dug a great hollow in the earth at the place where Fafner's path rubbed the edge of the lake. The earth there was soft, and the digging went easily in spite of the thinness of the air. And into this great hollow I lowered myself, for such was the nature of our plan. Then Regan covered the hollow with branches and set off for the other side of the lake.

"Once again, in the morning, the rumblings came. And at the sound of them, I drew my sword and made myself ready. The rumblings were soon followed by footsteps—clump, clump, clump, clump. The earth shook around me. I feared it would fall in and trap me forever. Clump, clump. He came closer. My heart beat so loud in my chest that I imagined he would hear it. And perhaps he did, or perhaps he had more wits about him than Regan gave him credit for, for all at once he stopped along the path and held fast his fiery breath as though to listen. But the cunning Regan had foreseen such an event. He had stationed himself at the far side of the lake, at the point that was directly opposite Fafner's path. And when he saw Fafner's hesitation, he jumped up suddenly from his hiding place and called out Fafner's name."

Sigurd stopped to catch his breath and drink again. My heart beat wildly to think of him in so much danger. Gunner and Hagen, I noted through my sore, blurred eyes, were sitting on the edge of their seat, watching anxiously for Sigurd to drain his horn. Even Mother looked attentive. The rain was falling harder now, louder. I drew closer to the fire, and Guthorm, noticing the gap between us, slid over beside me to eliminate it, bringing along with him the dead ant that he had been rolling in his fingers.

"Having seen Regan, or having heard him as the case was, Fafner started coming again, faster than before, and with great determination. Clump clump, clump clump, he came. Regan egged him on. 'I have come for the gold,' he cried out from across the lake. 'Did you think you could keep it from me forever?'

"Fafner came faster yet, breathing hard, clump, clump, clump, clump, as fast as a horse when its rider has stirred it to a gallop. And indeed, the earth around me did begin to cave in. I lifted my sword and prayed to Wodan that I would not be buried alive . . . ." Sigurd looked aside, toward Mother, but he did not actually focus on her. He jerked his head back all at once. "Or worse, that the dragon would catch one of his monstrous feet in my hollow and crush me—a possibility which I had not thought of before. And then, all at once, his great body was within my view. And just as he was about to take the step that would bring him into contact with my hollow, I leaped up and plunged my sword into his heart. Then I fell back into the hollow, and his blood gushed forth and filled it with its dragon stench." Sigurd paused.

I sneezed and saw his eyes dart over to me.

"And then?" Hagen cried.

"And then," Sigurd said slowly, "the life-spirit went out of the dwarf-dragon forever. He groaned only once, and then he rolled over my hollow and into the lake. Immediately his great dragon body was sucked into it. By the time I emerged from my hollow, blood-soaked and covered with earth, only my sword could be seen protruding from the icy blue waters. I jumped in and mounted Fafner even as the lake was swallowing him. I withdrew my sword—no small feat, for his thick dragon flesh seemed to have closed in around it. Then from the far bank I heard Regan calling to me, 'His heart! Cut out his heart! What man will believe us if we return without the heart?'

"I had thought myself to bring back his head, or one of his great gray feet, or his long snapping tail. But he was sinking too quickly into his watery grave, and his head and his feet and his tail were no longer visible to me. So I reached into the wound that I had made in his flesh and fished out his heart. It came out freely, as if there had been no sinew to hold it in place. It is here, in my pouch."

Sigurd reached into the sheepskin pouch that hung from his side near his sword. Gunner and Hagen rose from their seat immediately and crossed the floor together. I forced myself to get up, too, and peered over my brothers' shoulders. The thing in Sigurd's palm was black and covered with maggots. I quickly returned to the fire.

"But this heart is too small to have belonged to such a creature!" Gunner exclaimed. "Why, it is as small as a child's!"

Sigurd looked up at him innocently. "That is just what I said to Regan when I saw what I held in my hand."

"And what did Regan say?"

"Regan bade me to recall that Fafner was a dwarf who had created for himself the body of a dragon for his own vile purposes. His heart remained the heart of a dwarf. Look carefully. You can see the rift that was made by my sword. And you will see, too, where I bit into it so as to acquire something of the dragon's strength. Is that not proof enough?"

Gunner laughed nervously. "Brother, I do not doubt you. I am only surprised to see a thing so small after all that you have told us about the creature." He exchanged a look with Hagen and returned to his seat. Hagen nodded to Mother, and she got up with the mead pitcher.

"And the gold, brother?" Gunner asked in a whisper which was evidently meant to conceal his anxiety about it.

"Ah, yes. The gold. The dragon's hoard. It was there, as we had known it would be, in the dragon's cave. The great chest that the gold had once been kept in was empty, and the gold, finger-rings and arm-rings and drinking cups and broaches and swords, the likes of which no man has ever seen before, were scattered about, as if the dragon derived his pleasure merely from looking on these things—as well one might! These weapons and adornments illuminated the otherwise dark cave. What a sight! And there was one sword . . . a thing so beautiful . . . " Sigurd shook his head as if he were at a loss to describe it properly. "Its hilt," he said, lifting his hand, "is carved in such a way . . . . Regan said it was fashioned by Wodan himself. But I digress. More of that later.

"Regan and I wasted no time in searching the rest of the cave. When we were certain that there was nothing else of interest to be found in it, we collected the gold and filled up the chest. Then we slept. We awoke later in the day and prepared to leave. But even together we could not lift the chest. So we brought our horses around to the cave entrance and retrieved Grani's side-sacks. We removed the gold from the chest and placed it in the sacks and managed to drag them out to Grani, Regan's horse being too old to take on any of the weight.

"It was slow going down the mountain. In fact, it was far more difficult than the ascent had been. Grani seemed to buckle under the weight of the gold. And Regan, who had accomplished the goal that he had carried in his heart for so long, seemed to grow weaker by the moment, very much as your father grew weak once he had made your people to love their lives again. And when the sun began to bother him as it had never before, Regan declared that his time was at hand. I urged him on by reminding him of the esteem that would be his when we returned and those who loved him learned that he had done the thing he had set out to do.

"We were cold, as I have said, and we found little to eat. And there were other dangers. We heard the howling of wolves both day and night. We heard the footsteps of the frost-giants, who were surely watching us from behind the boulders that cover the mountain. And we seemed to stumble over our very feet." Sigurd broke off and looked at Guthorm. Guthorm sensed his gaze and looked up. Then Sigurd lowered his head almost to his knees, speaking louder to compensate. "And alas, brothers, it was in this way that Regan was lost. I saw him stumble in one particularly dangerous spot where our path along the face of the mountain was perilously narrow. I made to grab hold of him, but Grani and his great load were between us . . . and thus I failed. He went tumbling down, bouncing off the rocks like a cloth doll. But he never cried out. I tell you, he was ready, and he went peacefully. Still, my descent was a sad affair after that." Sigurd lifted his head and searched my brothers' faces. "When I reached the bottom of the mountain, several days later, I looked for his body in earnest. But it was nowhere to be found."

My brothers looked at each other. Then Gunner said, "Surely some beast had devoured him by then."

"And so I thought, too. But I should have been happy to have found his bones, or a fragment of his cloak. I had only his horse, and he I slayed and buried in Regan's name in the meadow which seemed most likely to be directly beneath the place from which Regan had fallen. And I prayed that he might accompany Regan, whither I know not."

For a time there was silence. Again my brothers exchanged a look, perhaps each hoping that the other would be bold enough to bring the story back to the matter of the gold. Sigurd, meanwhile, sat on the edge of his seat with his hands dangling between his knees and his head lowered as if his discourse had tired him out. Finally, he looked up. "There is more."

My brothers became alert.

"Something else of interest occurred before I set off for your lands. I came across a valkyria."

"A valkyria," Gunner repeated, rising to his feet.

"Then you know of such creatures?"

"Know of them? Why, of course. They are women of great power who bring fortunes to those whom they choose to serve. I have heard men say that they have the power to choose whom among the dead is worthy of Valhalla. They escort the chosen dead there themselves." He looked at Mother. "When our mother was a young woman at Worms, she knew a valkyria. In fact, this valkyria was present at my birth. It was a difficult birth. I was turned 'round in her womb, and it was thought that both she and I would perish before I could be gotten out. But the valkyria, called Ildico, was sent for. And on the wall of the bower in which Mother lay, Ildico carved a powerful rune. And thus was I born and Mother's life spared so that she might bring forth more children into the world."

Gunner lowered himself to his seat again. Mother nodded and opened her mouth, but before she could speak, Sigurd said, "She was called Brunhild."

"And where did you find this valkyria called Brunhild?" Gunner asked.

"After burying Regan's horse, I slept one night in the meadow. When I awoke, I saw in the distance to the north black smoke rising out of the trees and into the sky. I hid Grani and went on foot to find its source. And there I found wagons in a ring, as if the travelers who had owned them had been expecting an attack. It was these wagons which were burning. Scattered about on the earth were bodies, men and women and children. They were unknown to me, but their dress and wagons assured me that they were Thuet peoples. I walked among them, trying to determine who their attackers had been, but I found no weapon or other evidence of their foes. I was about to dig a grave for them when I heard from within the circle of burning wagons a voice calling weakly for help. I leaped through the flames and into the center. And there, at my feet, was what I first took to be a Roman soldier, for Brunhild was wearing a helmet and vest not unlike those that I have seen on the heads and breasts of Romans. Blood trickled out from a wound in her thigh, spilling onto the ground at my feet. Crying out curses against the Romans, I drew my sword and was about to slay her. But before I could do so, she managed to remove her helmet, and I saw that she was a woman. Still, I held my sword ready, for woman or not, I believed that she was responsible for the deaths of the poor folk that I had seen outside the fiery circle. But then she raised herself on one elbow and spoke to me in our language."

"What did she say?" Gunner asked.

"'I am no Roman. Do not kill me.'"

"And what did you answer?"

"'Who are you then? And how did you come to be dressed like a Roman?'"

"She told me then that she was a valkyria, and that she had come among the poor folk of the wagons to choose the dead for Valhalla. But the Romans who had attacked them were there in the forest when she first sensed the mishap and was donning her helmet, stolen from the Romans some time back. Upon seeing her, they followed her back to the site of the attack, and a struggled ensued between Brunhild and the Roman leader. She fought him hard, but when she saw that he would overcome her, she feigned submission and let him drag her into the circle of wagons. There he forced her to the ground. But as he began to have his way with her, with the other Romans standing about between the wagons, laughing and shouting and hoping their turns would follow, she engraved in the earth a rune of great power, a fire rune."

"I did not know such a rune existed!" Gunner exclaimed.

"Nor did I. But her story was convincing. I had no reason to doubt her. And there was the fire—"

"Go on. What then?"

"Then the flames leaped out of the wagons. And the Romans who had gathered to watch her violation ran away in fear. The Roman leader, seeing the flames rise about him, jumped to his feet and drew his sword. But his attention was divided between trying to slay Brunhild and trying to pull up his britches, and when a flame from the wagon nearest took hold of him, he bounded out of the circle of fire and went running after his fellows. It was in the course of his flight that he inadvertently wounded her thigh. The wound was deep nevertheless, and Brunhild had lost some blood. She found she was unable to escape from the flames which she had called forth to save herself. But as she lay there, anticipating death, she carved into the earth yet another rune, this one for help. And that, she told me, was shortly before my arrival.

"I lifted her in my arms and leaped once more through the circle of flames. I placed her down on a grassy spot away from the sight of the dead. There was a stream nearby, and with its waters I washed her wound clean. Then I ripped a strip from the bottom of the tunic she wore and tied it above her wound. Then, when the bleeding ceased, I thought to distract her from her discomforts by telling her something of my own adventures. To my surprise, she showed no sign of astonishment. I asked her how it was that my words failed to amaze her, and she reminded me that valkyrias have the Sight. She had foreseen, she said, many years ago, that she would come upon a dragon-slayer who would bear the gold of the gods.

"If I had had any doubts about her, I doubted no more, brothers, for although I had told her all that I have told you about Regan and Fafner, I had been careful not to mention the gold. Of my motives, I had told her only that I went to the dragon's cave at Regan's side to help an old friend avenge the death of his father. Then she said that in order to thank me properly for saving her life, she would grant me one request, and if that one request fell within her rune-wisdom, I should have it.

"Brothers, I was speechless! All at once I could not think what I wanted most in this world. I asked her to name the runes she had knowledge of. And thus she named them—runes to bring victory in battle, to keep one's drinking horn safe from poison, to ensure good health, to sharpen one's mind, to soothe the wind . . . and how many more I cannot begin to tell you." Sigurd laughed. Then he took a hasty swallow from his horn. "Brothers," he cried, "I am a greedy man. I wanted all these things. And when I told Brunhild this, she said that she would give herself to me in marriage, and thus would she be at my side all the days of my life to provide for me always the very rune each day demanded."

Sigurd got up from his seat and approached the hearth. He sat down beside Guthorm and reached over him to touch my hair with his fingertips.

His eyes were still on my brothers, and thus he did not notice the tears that were gathering rapidly in mine. "I told her, brothers," he continued, "that my heart was elsewhere, that I would have Gudrun for my wife or no wife at all. She was quiet after that. She looked off at the smoldering wagons and pouted, as women do when they wish to have things go their way. Now I feared that she would hesitate to grant me even the one request that she had previously offered. But all at once I saw that the solution was simple enough. And I told her then that I knew of a king who would be pleased to have a valkyria for his bride, that this king was the nephew of a great king who had once ruled over more people than there are stars in the midnight sky, but that his people had been cut down, and that now his nephew longed to rebuild his kingdom. With this poor but noble king, she could put her rune-wisdom to good use. I told her, too, that this king was my brother in blood and would soon share with me the dragon's riches, the gold of the gods. And I asked her, brothers, if I arranged her marriage to this king who was my brother, and thus made her my sister, whether she would still see fit to share with me the profits of her rune-wisdom."

I turned to look at Gunner. His lips were spread into something akin to a smile. "And what did the valkyria say?" he asked tentatively.

"The valkyria said she would meet this king, and if he pleased her . . . ."

Gunner threw his head back and roared with laughter. Hagen laughed, too, and slapped Gunner's back with his broad hand. I looked at Mother and found her looking at me. I turned back to the fire.

Gunner jumped to his feet. "Why do we hesitate?" he cried. "Let us go to her at once. Where does she wait? How many days' ride should we prepare ourselves for?"

Sigurd lowered his head. "The valkyria insisted I come back for her alone."

"Speak up, brother!"

Sigurd peeked up but kept his head bent. "I say, she insisted I come back for her alone. I do not know why. She would not say. She waits yet near the circle of wagons—a day's ride from here, no more."

Gunner sat down hard.

"Why did you not bring her back with you today?" Hagen asked.

"She had yet to go among the dead of the wagons and choose for Valhalla those who are worthy. It is a sacred rite, of course, and one that she must perform alone. I dug a grave before I left, and she promised to bury the bodies herself. Furthermore, she had no horse. The horses of the wagons had been cut loose by the Romans when they attacked. And Grani was loaded down as it was."

My brothers fell into silence and looked off in different directions, the story of the valkyria having robbed their minds of the recollection of the gold. Then it returned to them. "And the gold is safely hidden?" Gunner asked.

"It is. I buried it during the night at the river's edge. It will please me to show you the spot. Then, if some danger should befall me when I ride off for the valkyria, you, at least, shall profit from my labors."

"And what," Gunner began thoughtfully, rubbing his fingers on his fleshly chin, "if I do not like this valkyria? Perhaps I will find her homely. I would not have a homely woman for my wife even if she be acquainted with all the runes in the world."

Sigurd laughed heartily. "Brother, her rune-wisdom is no mere acquaintance. I tell you, it muddles one's mind to think how useful she may be to the Franks and the Burgundians. And as for her aspect, think on it no further. She is a thing to behold. You will not be disappointed."

Gunner threw his head back once again, and his laughter filled the hall. "Let us go then," he shouted. "Hagen and I will choose a good horse for the valkyria and ride out with you as far as the river. You will show us where the gold is buried, and then you will do as the valkyria bade and go alone to fetch her. Women have their reasons, and a valkyria must be obeyed. We will expect you to return within two days. We will save the story of your feat for the feast that we will then have in your honor."

"Gunner?" I said quickly when I saw that Sigurd had risen to feet. He looked over at me, his expression astonished, as if he had forgotten I was there. "Would it not be better if Sigurd rested one night and went for the valkyria in the morning? After all, he has only just returned to us, and what part of the night he did not spend burying the dragon's hoard, he spent watching for the departure of the Romans at the edge of the forest." I dared not add that it was raining and cold, for men such as Sigurd and my brothers scorn such matters. When Gunner made no response, I looked to Sigurd for help. He seemed to be weighing my words.

"It is better to go now," Sigurd said at last. "The Romans may yet have it in mind to come back and search for the valkyria."

"How likely is that?" I whispered, thinking of the flames leaping from the wagons at her command. But Gunner heard me and stepped forward.

"Sister," he shouted, "do not hold the man back. His quest will bring fortunes on us all."

Mother, who had been silent throughout, jumped up from the bench. "Wait," she cried. "If Sigurd and Gudrun are to be married, then it is only right that we should have the betrothal rites now. It will take but a moment. Grant us that at least."

In amazement, we all turned to look at her. "This is no time for such matters, woman," Gunner said finally.

"I say it is."

Mother and Gunner continued to stare at each other. Gunner was holding his lips tight, breathing through his nose. His eyes were narrowed and his face was red. Mother's face was stern and motionless.

"All right," Gunner said at last. "Let us have them then, but let us have them quickly. Leave out the trifles and do only what is necessary. There are more important matters—"

"There are few matters as important as making a promise to one's life-mate," Mother interrupted.

But Gunner had turned and was already stomping back to his seat. He threw himself down on it and sat pouting, with his wide chin resting on his fist and his head turned away from us.

The rite of betrothal demands that a woman shed tears for the family she will leave behind when she sets out to make her life with her mate. But as most betrothals are joyous occasions, these tears are usually forced. I did not have to force mine. Rather, I had to force myself to keep them in check so as not to appear to overdo. I got to my feet and slowly unknotted my hair. Then I unclasped one of the two broaches that held my robe together at my shoulders and removed from the chain that hung between the broaches my key and scissors and comb. While holding my robe together with one hand, I fastened the loose end of the chain to the broach again with the other. Then I fastened the key to the chain at my waist, where it would remain until the end of my days or Sigurd's. I used the comb to pull my loose hair across one shoulder and over my breast. Then I used the scissors to cut one long strand. I replaced the scissors and the comb on the chain. Beyond the sound of the rain beating down hard against the walls and the crackling of the hearth fire, I could hear Gunner's impatient sighs. Sigurd had gone down on one knee and was waiting for me to hand him the strand of my hair. I looked into his eyes directly for the first time since we had all come into the hall, and I thought I saw some impatience there. But he kissed my hand gently as he accepted the strand. Gunner, thinking that the ceremony was over, got to his feet.

"Wait," Mother said softly. "Her hair has yet to be bound. And Sigurd has yet to walk three times before her with his sword unsheathed."

"Her hair, his sword . . . . Time passes, woman!" Gunner shouted. Then he sighed and sat down again.

Mother came forward to bind my hair, not in the knot from which it had previously hung loosely, like the tail of a horse, but in a tight clump at the back of my head so that my neck was exposed.

When she was finished, Sigurd got to his feet and bowed low to me. Then he drew his sword and walked past me three times.

"How lovely she looks," Mother whispered.

From the other end of the hall I heard Hagen mumble an affirmation, but I did not look over for fear of seeing Gunner's expression.

"I will return to you in no time," Sigurd whispered. "We will plan our wedding then."

"Are we done now?" Gunner shouted.

Mother nodded. I bent my head low and listened to the footsteps rushing for the door. When the three had gone, Mother stepped in front of me and took me by the shoulders. "I have a plan," she whispered. "I know what we can do to secure Sigurd's love for you."

I looked up at her, horrified. How strange it seemed that Sigurd's love for me should be an issue. I could not remember a time when I did not love Sigurd or he me. We had grown together—playmates, secret-sharing friends, sweethearts. And though I had been speculating on the matter of Sigurd's love since he first mentioned the valkyria, I did not like to hear another voice my fears. "What plan is that?" I asked dully.

"Ha!" she cried. "Valkyrias are not the only ones with powers. I know of a brew which we can make easily enough. You need only to have Sigurd drink it down when he returns to insure that his thoughts will not wander from you again. Do you feel well enough to come with me to collect some roots from the forest floor?"

I did not feel well at all. My eyes were burning in my head, and I ached all over. Though I had long been at the side of the fire, I shivered still. And the rain seemed to fall harder even as I considered it. But in my mind's eye I could see nothing but the image of Sigurd riding off swiftly in the direction of the high mountains to fetch the valkyria, the lock of my hair perhaps in his pouch with the decaying dwarf-dragon's heart, near his person but far from his thoughts. I went into the bower to fetch my cloak.

Chapter 7

Gunner, who had never been so animated, took charge of the preparations for the feast himself. He would have invited all our freemen if that had been possible, but half of them, having lost their servants to the Romans, were too busy with their additional chores now that it was time to harvest, and as he did not like to hurt their feelings by inviting all of the other half, he decided to ask only the ten or so who were in some way related to ourselves or to Gundahar—in other words, the noblemen. These noblemen he rode out to solicit himself, and he asked each of them to bring along some small gift so that Sigurd would not doubt that he was welcome among us. Hagen he ordered to pursue the grandest beast he could, while Mother and our servants baked breads and cakes and gathered berries from the forest beneath the persistent rain cloud that hung over our lands.

I myself had no part in these preparations, for I was by then debilitated with fever. I never left my bower, and what I know of the ordeal I learned from that distance. Nor was I able, on the second day, to take part in the feast—if one could call it that. From my bower I heard my brothers welcoming in our noblemen, but their voices, which were robust at first, became somber as the evening wore on. I expected to hear Gunner singing the story of Fafner and the gold to his guests while he waited for Sigurd and the valkyria to appear, but I heard nothing of it. And when it grew late and our honored guests had still not come, Gunner declared, "We will begin without them. I know of no god or man who would stand by to see this much food wasted." And then I heard no sound at all, except that of spoons beating on bowls, until it was time for the guests to mumble their thanks and go.

I was glad then to be so ill, for my wild thoughts seemed far off, as if they were the thoughts of another and were merely being advanced to me. And so close to death did I imagine myself that by contrast Sigurd's tardiness seemed of small account. I fell in and out of sleep so many times that night that after a time I could make no distinction between the two. At one point I heard Mother say, "I have some rune-wisdom and so does Gudrun. Is that not enough?" to which Gunner replied, "If Sigurd is to be believed, the rune-wisdom of the valkyria exceeds yours and Gudrun's by far. It must be the valkyria." And later, I heard Mother say, "They can be dangerous, these valkyrias. She will not give him up so easily. And did you see the look in his eye when he spoke of her? She put a spell on him with her runes. I feel sure of it. Do you think you can change that? She will bring nothing but disaster to this hall." But again, I do not know whether these words actually passed between them or whether they were only the product of some dream I devised in my feverish state.

Later yet, I dreamed a dream which I knew for certain to be a dream, and though it was Attila's face I saw therein, I was relieved to know my state for what it was. Attila was in our hall, seated on the high seat on which only Gunner and Hagen may sit, on which Father sat until he heard the voices of the gods calling to him. Across the hall, in the seat reserved for the honored guest, my brothers sat squirming under Attila's hateful gaze. Meekly, Gunner asked, "To what do we owe this honor, master?" And Attila answered, "I have come to unite the Huns and the Burgundians together. I will marry your sister."

As I awoke in the morning feeling somewhat better physically, my concern over Sigurd's tardiness increased proportionally. I lay for a moment between Mother and Guthorm listening to the wind, and then I felt that I must get up and see whether Sigurd might have come after all, late in the night while we slept. I got to my knees and waited for my dizziness to pass. Then I got to my feet and tiptoed out of the bower. My brothers were both asleep in the hall, where men sometimes end up when they have been up late and drunk too much mead to get themselves to bed. Hagen was near the hearth. His empty drinking horn was on his stomach, and there it rose and fell as he snored. Gunner was stretched out on the long bench, his head turned to the wall and his long, heavy arms dangling on either side of him. To my surprise, I saw that he had reddened his already reddish locks with ashes and goat fat. I hurried across the hall and peeked into my brothers' bower. It was empty.

I went back into my bower to take my place again between Mother and Guthorm, neither of whom so much as stirred. As I wiggled into place, I took note of the two small wooden vessels that had been prepared for me. They were in the corner of the room, and so close to Mother's outstretched arm that I feared she would upset one or the other when she awakened. One I had made much use of, for it contained the brew that Mother had made to rid me of my sickness. The other was the potion which we had made together for Sigurd. If she disturbed one, I hoped it would not be the latter.

It had rained steadily for three days, and I imagined that, in concern for her health, Sigurd had found a shelter for the valkyria, and thus the reason for their delay. But my jealous mind provoked me, asking, What of my health? Has Sigurd no concern for that? Still, the rains had ceased now. I could see beyond the small bower window, which was covered with the opaque membrane which encases the unborn calf, that the sun was shining. It seemed a good omen, and my hope rose up again and, strange to say, claimed the seat in the forefront of my mind in which my suspicions were already firmly seated. And thus they perched together, simultaneous and side by side, the one inventing images of the valkyria lying in Sigurd's arms, sheltered from the rain in some grove or beneath some rocky ledge, while the other directed my eyes to take note of the sun and the chance that Sigurd might yet return and that I would have no need, after all, to give him the brew which Mother's unwitting fingers might at any moment disturb. In truth, I did not like to think that I was capable of giving it to him, for I could not imagine how I could get him to drink it without lying to him. He had accepted the lock of my hair, I reminded myself. He had passed three times before me with his sword unsheathed. What is, is.

Gunner awoke in the hall and called out Hagen's name. Hagen must have sat up hastily, for I heard the drinking horn that had been on his stomach collide with the stones surrounding the hearth. Then I heard his voice, still gruff with sleep, saying, "We have slept too long. Let us hurry out and see about more game for surely Sigurd returns tonight."

"Let him return or not," Gunner grumbled. "I do not care one way or the other. Let him have the valkyria and the charmed life she offered him. We will have the gold—if he did not dig it up already."

There was a moment of silence. I could imagine Hagen gesturing toward my bower almost as well as if I had seen him myself. And I knew I was correct when I heard Gunner say, "Brother, she will have to know sooner or later."

"Then let it be later," Hagen whispered. "We do not know ourselves yet. Any number of things could have happened. For all we know the man is dead, cut down by Romans. In any case, dead or alive, he is our brother. There is no taking that back. He said he would return. And when he does, he will explain his delay, I wager, to your satisfaction and Gudrun's, too. Trust him a bit."

"I trust no one," Gunner said grumpily.

Hagen laughed. "I pity you then, brother. There is nothing in life more valuable than friendship, and from what seed does it bloom if not trust?"

"Bah. I will tell you what is more valuable than friendship. Life itself.

Was that not the message that our father bade us to hold in our hearts? And I will tell you something else as well. My life will be longer than yours for having the sense to know it."

The last of Gunner's words had come from farther off. Apparently he had gotten off the long bench and was moving toward the door.

"You know you do not mean that," Hagen cried after him. "You are impatient, that is all. And you slept poorly. Where are you going?"

I heard the door being lifted. "To make sure that the gold was not dug up during the night."

"Fine," Hagen began. "Go. In the meantime, I will—" but the door was lowered again before he could finish. "—hunt," he mumbled to himself.

Mother and Guthorm were still sleeping deeply. Once more I wiggled out from between them and went into the hall. Hagen, who was sitting cross-legged, brooding, did not hear me enter until I said his name. He straightened quickly. "Gudrun! Are you better then?"

"Somewhat."

He smiled, and the pattern of his great scar altered. Then he took up the poker and began to stir the embers in the hearth. "I heard," I said.

He went on stirring. "He is just disappointed. He did not mean what he said."

I knelt down beside him and put my hand over his so that he was forced to put the poker aside. "You believe that Sigurd will return today, do you not?"

Hagen nodded, but he kept his eyes on the fire, which was slowly coming to life. I squirmed beside him. "Hagen," I whispered, "when Sigurd told us of his quest, there were looks which passed between you and Gunner which I could not account for."

He shrugged and said nothing. I increased the pressure of my hand on his, but still he continued to stare into the fire. Some moments passed before he finally lifted his gaze, and then he studied my face for just as long. "Go back to bed, Gudrun," he said at last. "I will not be the one to point out that which you fail to see yourself."

I laughed nervously and released his hand. "I have no idea what you mean to say."

"Only this: Sigurd may have paid too high a price for the gold."

"How so?"

"Go back to bed, I say. This does not concern you anymore than it should me. Go back to bed at once."

I got up abruptly and went back to bed.

Because of the chill in the air, the door was down that evening when Sigurd returned, but we heard the approach of the horses anyway. We heard the valkyria's laughter even before Sigurd called out. As if we had not been expecting anyone, we all ceased our activities at once and stared at one another. Then Gunner put down his harp, which he had been playing softly by the hearth-fire, and, patting his unnaturally reddened hair, he rushed to the high seat. Hagen put aside his drinking horn and went to lift the door. Mother and I were sitting on the long bench, embroidering. Guthorm was at our feet.

When Sigurd entered, I made to rise and greet him, but when I saw that his gaze did not fall on me, I sat down again. "Brother," he cried, addressing himself to Gunner and smiling triumphantly, "I present Brunhild." And he took the valkyria's arm and led her to stand before Gunner's seat. Gunner rose uncertainly while Brunhild, who was giggling, bowed before him.

Even in her coarse men's weeds, muddied from travel, Brunhild was, as Sigurd had promised, a thing to behold. She was tall—nearly as tall as Sigurd. And though she was thin, her hands and forearms suggested good bones and strength. Her skin was the bronzed skin of one who spends her days outdoors. By contrast, her light, watery blue eyes stood out like jewels. She did not wear her hair knotted and hanging down her back as other Thuet women do. Rather, it fell loosely over her shoulders and breasts, light locks streaked white in places and as shiny as silver. Her feet were bare and dirty, but long and finely formed. Over her arm, I noted, she carried Sigurd's cloak.

It is difficult to say how I felt to see her standing there beside Sigurd, holding his cloak. Or perhaps I shrink from describing my emotion because I knew immediately—though I had never experienced such a feeling before—that it was a sordid, shameful, dangerous thing. Of course, I had been jealous since Sigurd had first mentioned her, but now my disposition was beyond jealousy. This was jealousy at its depth. This was the root of jealousy from which one looks up and sees only blackness. I felt defeated by her presence, and I moaned.

The valkyria could not have heard me, for I barely heard myself. But her watery eyes slid away from Gunner at just that moment, not to me, but toward me, and then quickly back to my brother again. "I have heard many fine things about you," she said, smiling her enchanting smile.

Gunner, who had previously been speechless, now moved his lips comically in an effort to reply, but before he could do so, Brunhild began to laugh. At first, Gunner seemed to be alarmed, but then his look changed, and he began to laugh as well. In a moment he was roaring with laughter, as was Sigurd. But then Brunhild stopped laughing abruptly and turned in my direction, a trace of her mirth still on her lips—but gone completely from her eyes.

I rose from my seat. "I am called Gudrun," I croaked in a voice still harsh from my illness.

She bowed her head to me, and when she lifted it again, her smile had vanished entirely and her eyes had hardened. My own eyes seemed not to have the power to break her hold, and I was afraid.

Luckily, Mother rose just then and bowed, saying, "I am Grimhild."

Brunhild hesitated a moment longer and then slowly inclined her head toward Mother and nodded. Then she turned to look at Hagen, who had not yet moved from the door.

He managed to mumble his name—but in a way which revealed that he was as dumbstruck by her beauty as the rest of us.

Guthorm, who had been playing quietly with his wooden bowl, sensed her gaze when it fell on him next. He looked up at once, and then he threw his weight against my leg and grabbed hold of my ankle. I waited for someone to introduce him, but no one did. It was as if, under her scrutiny, he had all at once become an embarrassment to us. We watched her watch him with her eyes wide and amused. The silence became awkward. Then all at once Brunhild turned away and cried, "I have met you all. Now let us eat!" We were not used to such boldness; Hagen and Mother exchanged a surprised look. But Gunner threw his head back and laughed heartily.

As we had not been certain that Sigurd and Brunhild would return that evening, Mother had not called in any of the servants, and no one thought to do so now. Thus we went about the business of readying the meal ourselves, and as quickly as if it had been Wodan himself who had demanded it. While Hagen and Gunner assembled the table, Mother rushed to fetch the food and the mead pitcher. I struggled to free myself from Guthorm's grip, and with him crawling behind me on all fours, I went to fetch the washing bowl and drying cloth.

When the table was assembled, Gunner turned to Sigurd and said,

"We must apologize to you, brother. Thinking that you were going to arrive last night, we gathered together with our freemen and set out a great store of food. When you failed to arrive, we ate the food ourselves, as we did not want to send the Burgundians away hungry. Hagen and I had no luck hunting today, and thus we have only some cold meat, day-old bread, and our own meager company to offer you." I could see by the glint in Gunner's eye that his professed apology was really a cunning attempt to get Sigurd to reveal the cause for his delay.

Whether Sigurd saw this, too, I could not tell. He was silent for a moment, and then he clapped his hand on Gunner's back and said, "It is enough, brother."

I had been moving toward Hagen, and he toward me, when Gunner had spoken. And like Hagen, I had halted to listen for Sigurd's response. Now I went back about my task, and when Hagen had finished with the bowl, I turned to Brunhild. I barely lifted my eyes to her for fear of finding myself again at her mercy. But to my surprise, when I did peek up, I saw that a perplexed look had come over her beautiful face. Her eyes swept from the bowl to my face and back again, as if she had never come across a washing bowl before. Sigurd, who was still at her side, saw her confusion and stepped forward to plunge his own hands into the bowl. When they were cleansed, he wiped them on the drying cloth and hung it back on my arm. Then he took his cloak from Brunhild, gently, so that their eyes met. They smiled at each other. When she had washed and dried her hands, she turned toward the table, and without asking Gunner where he would have her sit, she climbed over the bench to perch on the spot she had chosen for herself.

Once she was seated, with her back to us, Sigurd finally looked at me. He touched my cheek. "My love," he whispered. But the valkyria seemed to have heard, for just then she turned her head as far back as it would go, and one watery eye strained to detect us. Horrified, I continued to stare at her even after she had turned away again. And when I turned back to accept the remains of Sigurd's greeting, I found that he had already moved away.

Many men have lifted their drinking horns in our hall, but few have done so as often and with as much gusto as the valkyria did that night. Even more amazing was her appetite. While we all looked on, she devoured all that was before her and then scanned the table for more. And all the while she laughed, finding the most common remarks to be amusing. It was not very long before my brothers were attempting to outdo each other in the number and quality of their anecdotes. Gunner, for instance, told her how he had tricked the Roman tax-collectors into leaving behind their barrel of wine. But then Hagen confessed that he had tricked Gunner into thinking the barrel was empty so that he might have what was left for himself. Next, Gunner professed that he had poured out most of the wine into another vessel before Hagen ever got to it. Nor was Sigurd outside this competition. He insisted that the Romans had brought up two barrels of wine but had only offered one to the Burgundians. The other, which was for their own use, he had stolen and hidden during the night while the Romans were up at our hall drinking up most of the first barrel. How they laughed—Brunhild and Hagen and Gunner and Sigurd—at their nonsense.

"What tribe do you hail from?" Mother asked, her voice breaking into their laughter like something dangerous.

Brunhild glanced at Sigurd, who smiled encouragingly. "No tribe," she said gayly. "I was separated from my parents when I was very young."

"But where were you raised?" Mother demanded.

"Here and there," she said, and she laughed her high-pitched laugh again. And as if "here and there" was the cleverest thing they had ever heard, my brothers and Sigurd laughed along with her.

"But where did you learn your rune-wisdom?" Mother went on.

Brunhild's eyes opened wider. "I was born with it."

Mother, whose lips were parted and ready to expel the next inquiry, waited patiently for the latest round of laughter to subside. Then she said smugly, "Gudrun has some rune-wisdom too. She learned it from the sister of my father when she was very young. It is because of her that we have never had lightning strike this hall. And on her account, too, that the fire you see burning here has never leapt beyond the rocks that contain it."

Brunhild, who had taken Mother's boasting as an opportunity to lift her drinking horn to her lips, laughed abruptly now, spraying the table with mead. She covered her mouth and waved her thin arm in the air. "Forgive me," she said when she had gained some control. "I do not mean to . . . ." But her laughter returned and kept her from completing her apology.

Mother stared at her coldly, waiting for an explanation. When Gunner was able to control his own laughter, he provided one. "Woman," he cried. "Can you fail to see? Brunhild can make fires, not merely keep them in check!"

Mother thought about that, and then, unbelievably, her lips began to stretch into a smile. I felt my cheeks growing hot. I longed to say something in my own defense, but I had been rendered witless. Nor would I have been heard over the laughter of the others anyway. Yet I wished to laugh myself, for in truth, the comparison was comical. And moreover, I knew that it would please Sigurd to see me cheerful. But I could not speak and I could not laugh. I thought all at once of Clumar, the servant who lacked the wits to laugh and converse with others, and I guessed I knew his secret now. He, too, had a black heart, whatever the reason, and his witlessness was merely its reflection.

"The moon is full tonight," Gunner said to Brunhild when she had finally completed her meal. "I would be pleased to show you the site of my father's grave and tell you something of his passing."

"I have no objection to that," Brunhild replied, and she shot up from her seat. But her expression was staid now, and I supposed she hated to leave her larger audience for an audience of one. I watched Sigurd's eyes follow her to the door. Just as she reached it, she turned sharply and their eyes met. Gunner did not fail to note this exchange.

When they were gone, our hall was so still that one seemed to hear the echo of the valkyria's laughter rebounding from the walls. Hagen made one attempt to speak to Sigurd on the matter of his journey, but Sigurd answered evasively, saying only that there had been no dangers. The moments that followed were awkward until Mother got up and began to clean the crumbs from the table. We were all happy enough to follow her example, and in no time the bowls and the drinking horns were cleared away and the table disassembled. I went to Sigurd then and said that I, too, had an urge to walk beneath the moon. Sigurd nodded and moved toward the door. And Mother, seeing that Guthorm had heard and would follow us out, wisely snatched him back and held him squirming to her breast.

"I can see you are unhappy," Sigurd said as soon as the door was down behind us.

"Not at all," I lied, and I began to walk.

But Sigurd persisted. "You do not like her, do you?"

I stopped to look at him, and though I knew better than to answer honestly, I could not manage to do otherwise. "I do not. She is a fool," I said crisply.

Although his lips remained curled at the corners, Sigurd's eyes became rigid, and I could see that he was angry. "You are jealous. You must be, or how could you say such a thing?"

My tears came all at once. "Do you love her?" I cried.

I searched Sigurd's eyes for the answer, but before I could discover it, he grabbed me and pulled me to him. "Do you truly believe that I could stop loving you within the span of a few days, Gudrun, and fill the void with the love of a stranger?"

My thought was that Sigurd had spent more time alone with her in the past few days than he had with me in the past several years. I longed to lash out at him and ask him what events had caused him to be with her so long. But that would have been unthinkably discourteous, and my responses already lacked courtesy enough. "Gunner loves her already, and he has known her only one night," I whined.

"Silly Gudrun," Sigurd whispered. He took my arm and we began walking up toward the forest to the north of the hall. "Gunner does not love her. He loves her face and the sound of her laughter. And why should he not? Her face is flawless, and her laughter is music more sweet than that which issues from Gunner's harp. But a woman is more than her face and her laughter, and one does not discover the expanse of a woman within so short a time. We, on the other hand, have known each other long and well. When I say that I love you, I am referring not merely to your face and your laughter—" He stopped suddenly and took hold of my shoulders. "Let me hear no more from you on this subject, Gudrun. You give me no credit when you suppose me to be so shallow." And he began to walk again.

"I am truly sorry," I croaked as I hurried to keep pace with him. "You will not hear me speak that way again."

Up at the rock-horse, among the birches that glittered in the moonlight, I decided to prove to Sigurd that I had put the matter of Brunhild out of my mind. "Let us speak of our wedding," I said in a voice which I hoped sounded cheerful.

Sigurd had been staring out at nothing. Now he turned to look at me, his expression strange. It was a moment before he responded. "If you like," he said. "Here is my plan. Tomorrow I leave for Frankish lands. I have put that off long enough now. I must get back and let my people know what happened to Regan, and naturally, they will want to know the rest, as well. When I return, we will have the weddings—yours and mine and Brunhild and Gunner's. I suppose your mother will have to sleep in the hall with Hagen and Guthorm for a time. Then, when the growing season comes around again, we will leave the others and make our way to the hall I share with my uncle. I have given some thought to Guthorm, too. If you like, he can live with us until we come again to your lands. He can go back and forth, whatever you want. We will visit often enough, I wager."

His response had been blunt, matter-of-fact. "That suits me," I said, and I could think of nothing more to say on the subject. We sat like strangers, until Sigurd began to rub his stomach and yawn. "Are you tired?" I asked.

"Very. Would you mind?"

"Not at all." I was already up on my feet.

I tiptoed into the bower and took my place between Mother and Guthorm. It was narrower than it had been before because an additional mattress, which was empty at the moment, had been laid out for Brunhild. I pulled my sheepskin rug up over my shoulders and settled myself. My black thoughts had tired me out, and I was ready for sleep. I kissed the back of Guthorm's head and was about to close my eyes when all at once Mother whispered my name, startling me. "You failed to give him the drink," she whispered harshly.

"I had no opportunity." Out of curiosity, I had tasted the brew myself earlier in the day, and it tasted badly—far worse than the medicinal brew. I could not think of a way to get Sigurd to drink such a thing without telling him the reason for its preparation. And now that he had proven to me how repulsive my jealousy was to him . . . . Still, there had to be a way. Sigurd's little speech, meant to reassure me of his love, had the opposite effect. It seemed to me that it was forced, perhaps even rehearsed. When I lifted my head to look at the vessel that contained the brew, I saw only the smaller of the two vessels, the one that held the medicinal brew. "Where have you moved it to?" I snapped.

"In the corner, near Guthorm," Mother whispered. "I moved it so that the valkyria would not notice it and become curious. Will you give it to him tomorrow?"

"He rides back to the Franks, first thing."

"Then you must rise early and give it to him before he leaves. Tell him it is something you made to ensure his safe travel."

"But there are few dangers between here and there."

"There are always dangers. Tell him you had a dream and foresaw some horror. Use your imagination, daughter. Now go to sleep so you can rise early."

"I will," I said, but I did not go to sleep for some time. I did use my imagination however, though not in the manner Mother intended. I used it to imagine that Gunner and Brunhild had argued, and that when they returned, she would awaken Sigurd and bid him to take her away at once. I used it to imagine that Sigurd and Brunhild had only returned to dig up the gold, that their participation in our paltry feast had been a sham, and that when the rest of us were asleep, they would rise and go to the riverbank together. And when Brunhild and Gunner came in that night, and Brunhild found her way into the bower and took her place on the other side of Mother and almost immediately began to snore, I used it to imagine that her snoring was a pretense, that she could hear my thoughts and feel my hate—for how could the black, fiendish presence of my hatred, which had coiled itself about me like a snake, which was consuming me, suffocating me—be anything less than apparent to the object of its inclination? Yes, I used my imagination—far into the night. And when I slept, I slept the deep, dreamless sleep of exhaustion. And thus I failed to hear when Sigurd awakened in the morning. When I awoke, he was, of course, long gone.

Chapter 8

What did Brunhild do during the day? No one knew. But one thing was certain—she slept a good deal when she was not doing it. The birds and the sunlight and the voices of Mother and Hagen and Gunner in the hall, which were plenty enough to rouse Guthorm and me, had no effect on her. When we quit the bower each morning, she was still sleeping soundly on her stomach, with her head turned toward the wall and her arms pinned to her sides like flightless wings. It was usually mid-day, when my brothers were returning from their hunting or from meetings with our freemen, when Mother and I were just finishing with the cows and the goats, that Brunhild made her first appearance, her long silver hair flowing behind her like a shaft of sunlight. And then she did not speak of her dreams, as other people do when they have just awakened. She merely offered Gunner and Hagen her enchanting smile and Mother and me her less-than-enchanting nod (Guthorm she never greeted at all) and went off about her business taking the northeast path into the forest. That was the last we saw of her until evening.

One day, when Brunhild was just going off, Mother questioned Gunner. "That girl is no help," she said. "Where does she go? What does she do? You must have asked her?"

Gunner, still mesmerized by the sight of Brunhild's hair visible yet among the trees in the distance, mumbled, "She is not a woman like yourself. She does what she does. It is not for us to question."

As if to obstruct his view of the silver butterfly flitting away into the forest, Mother shoved me in front of him. "Nonetheless," she insisted, "there are ways she could make herself useful. She could be instructing Gudrun here in the ways of the runes. Can you not ask her to take your sister along sometimes?"

Gunner laughed. "Anyone can write a rune. It is merely a matter of connecting one line to another. What makes Brunhild's runes work is her power, and that, you will recall, she was born with—a gift from the gods like the bees' gift of honey."

While he spoke, he kept his gaze set over my head, and when his eyes began to shift, I knew that he had lost sight of Brunhild. He sighed once, then turned, and mumbling something about sharpening his sword blade, he left us, Mother and me with our milk pails and Hagen with two dead rabbits lashed together and hanging from his shoulder.

Mother shook her head. "We hear about her powers often enough. But I have seen no sign of them myself. Have you?"

Hagen lifted the rabbits from his shoulder and inspected them. "I have seen how her glance sets Guthorm running if Gudrun is not near to grab hold of his wrist. And look at the effect she has had on him."

We all turned to look at Gunner. He was sitting beneath the oaks with his arms folded and his sword across his lap.

I saw very little of Brunhild in the days between Sigurd's departure and return. We ate at the same table each evening, but saying no more than "pass this, pass that" to each other. And as she slept late and I retired to the bower early, ostensibly to work on my feather mattress but in fact to nurse my black thoughts and let fly my increasingly reckless imagination, we were rarely ever in the same place at the same time. Gunner did not see much more of her than I did (or at least he did not see her alone), though of course this was not his doing. From my bower I heard him ask her on several occasions, "Will you come and walk with me tonight?" But her response, though always kind, was firmly negative—she had tired herself out during the course of her day, or she had eaten so much that she could not lift herself now, or, more often, she would rather stay put and hear him play his harp.

And Gunner was content then to take up his harp for her, and when he had done with one strain, to take it up again. He sang to her about our father and how he had bargained with Aetius. About our uncle, Gundahar. About the Burgundians we had once been at Worms and the sorrowful vulnerable lot we had since become—and much more. In this way, Brunhild came to know all there was to know about us while we still knew next to nothing about her. Once, when Gunner had put down his harp, I heard him say, "We need you, Brunhild. You can change the fate of the Burgundians with your runes. What rune will you write for us?"

Brunhild replied, "I will know what rune to write when the time comes to write it."

"Write one now," Gunner persisted. "Be our entertainment tonight. Make the fire soar, though not so high that it brings the hall down. Make day of night. Make my harp to play itself; the gods know my fingers burn with all the strains that I have played for you."

Brunhild's response came quickly and harshly. "Do you think I would write a rune for some trifling matter? To see you laughing or amazed? The force that drives my runes is not some wide river ever flowing. It is more a stream which is apt to dry up if the gods do not see fit to fill it. When the times comes, I will know, and only then will I write my runes."

I was so intent on listening for Gunner's response that I did not hear Brunhild's footsteps coming until she had already reached the bower. She caught me sitting over my sack of feathers with my hands still and my ear straining toward the hall. "What ails you?" she snapped, and then she pulled her mattress closer to the wall and lay down on it with her back to me.

As far as I know, this was the only time that Gunner and Brunhild ever crossed each other during Sigurd's absence. And the next day, Gunner went out of his way to make amends. He rushed to her side when she made her appearance beneath the noon day sun, pulling from his tunic some flowers he had managed to hide from the rest of us. And that evening (and, indeed, on all the evenings that followed), he made no attempt to get her to walk with him. He went right to his harp when our meal was done, and he played her the strains that she professed to love best—and, moreover, one new one telling of the enchanting valkyria who had come to our hall to enrich our lives with her beauty and her grace; her runes he wisely did not mention.

My life was not enriched. The days that passed were the longest I had ever known. As I quickly learned, when one's heart is black, when one's spirit has perished and one's body is forced to endure without it, a day is an obstacle, a mountain to be surmounted. I continued to believe that Sigurd would marry me—for Sigurd was a man of his word—but I had already invested much time imagining how he would look off at nothing, as he had when we sat on the rock-horse the night of Brunhild's arrival, when we lay on our feather mattress as man and wife.

Nor was Mother's life enriched. Though she no longer questioned Brunhild, her face was rigid when Brunhild was about—and much of the time when she was not. Guthorm's life certainly was not enriched. He had thrived always on my kindnesses and Mother's, and we had no mind for such matters now. Hagen was Hagen, a practical man and a man of good humor, and if Brunhild changed his life at all after his initial astonishment at her beauty, I could not say how. Only one life was enriched, and that was Gunner's. Gunner had become a new man. Though one could see in his eye that he continued to take note of Guthorm's mishaps, he refrained from scolding him for them now. Nor did he speak sternly to Mother and me when we disagreed with him on some account. Rather, he was indifferent to us. Whatever we said or did was fine with him, as long as he could keep his eye on Brunhild (which he did unceasingly), fill Brunhild's drinking horn, carry Brunhild's bowl, strain his voice and bloody his fingers on his harp to please her ear.

And who could blame him? Her beauty remained startling, her laughter music. Her voice was as sweet and low as a Summer breeze. Her movements were quick and purposeful, and yet she carried herself like a queen, with her chin lifted high and her watery gaze at once candid and imposing. And for all that she wore a tunic not unlike my brothers', no one could ever mistake her for a man. Her confidence in herself and her powers endowed her with a strength which the rest of us had forgotten. And yet, there was about her a vulnerability as well. Sometimes, for instance, she would shudder, as if she knew some secret too terrible to share. And the way she slept at night, with her arms tight against her sides . . . . It made one want to bend over her and pull her rug up to cover her shoulders. No, I did not blame Gunner for loving her, and had I not believed that she loved Sigurd and he her, I might have cherished her myself. But as it was, she served only to remind me of all the things that I was not. My dwarfish stature, my gritty voice, my laughter (which I had forgotten the sound of but which I was certain was a sordid thing compared to Brunhild's), all these deficiencies which I had hardly given a thought to before were foremost in my mind when she was in my sight.

Fortunately, much of the time I was too busy to dwell on Brunhild, for there was much work to be done, and with the exception of our 'honored' guest, we labored each day side by side with our servants at those chores which mark the end of the growing season. Our chief task was the hay. It had to be cut and gathered and formed into rain-shedding cones to be stored as fodder for Winter. The amount of hay had to be reckoned carefully so that we would know what number of livestock could be kept alive over the Winter and what number should be slaughtered at the beginning of the new season. And there was the wheat to be harvested, along with the other late crops. For my brothers, there were many consultations to be had with our freemen, who were performing the same tasks on their own pastures, but some without the aid of their servants.

When our preparations for Winter had been completed, when the wheat was cut and stored and the hay cones were drying in the fields, Gunner called for a day of rest before our servants went off to aid those of our freemen who had lost theirs. Gunner, who had never before given a thought to the servants (who had always needed Hagen to remind him that they were something more than oxen), assembled them all together very early on the morning of that day and made a great speech about all the good work they had done. He promised them that they would be his guests in our hall when we had our end-of-the-season feast. The servants all cried out their praises for Gunner, and then, uncertain what to do with a day to themselves, they retreated into their huts.

As I watched them disperse from my place on the edge of the roof, I wondered myself how I would get through a day without work. Now my mind was already filling with the future, and all the shadowy, sorrowful images that I usually conjured up at night were beginning to take on a more authentic form. We were expecting Sigurd back any time now, and I had no doubt that my worst fears would soon be confirmed for me.

The sun had not yet risen above the trees when I heard a rider approaching from the opposite direction, and when I turned, I saw Hagen. He had ridden off just before supper the day before to play at tables, or so he had said, with Vascar, one of our freemen, and he was only now returning. Of course, we all knew his real purpose. Vascar had an unmarried sister, and Hagen had taken some interest in her of late. I crouched down to hide from him, but he spotted me anyway and brought his horse up beneath me. When he saw that I would ignore him, he dismounted and climbed up to sit by my side. His face, when I finally bothered to look at it, was tranquil—Gunner, Hagen, Brunhild, their faces were all the same. I did not need to ask to know that Vascar's sister had begun to return his affection. He cupped my chin in his hand as I was turning away from him and said, "Sister, I do not know you anymore."

I pushed his hand away. "I do not know myself."

He slid down the roof some so that he was more or less in front of me. "Perhaps Sigurd will not know you either when he returns."

"What of it? It is too late to matter one way or the other."

He laughed. "You sound like Gunner," he mumbled. He considered. Then he laughed again. "I should say, you sound as Gunner used to. It is as if you exchanged your humor for his."

This hurt me deeply, though I tried to show no trace of it. All at once he pulled me toward him and kissed my cheek, my eye, my brow, in his rough manner. I pushed him away and set my gaze on the sun, which had just cleared the treetops. "What do you call this force that governs you now, Gudrun?" he asked. "Hatred? Envy? Hopelessness?"

"All that and more," I said flatly.

"Well, girl, the time has come for you to cast it off. I had hoped you would reach this conclusion on your own, but Sigurd will be back with us soon enough, and time is running short. Do not let him return to a bitter, joyless woman. Look around you." He threw out his arm. "Now is a time for rejoicing. The hay is drying. The wheat is cut. And how many other fortunes have befallen us . . . . Sigurd and the gold, Gunner a changed man, full of the hope now that Father's words failed to inspire in him, eight children born to the Burgundians this season, five of them boys and all of them strong and healthy . . . ."

"It is easy enough for you to count our fortunes, Hagen," I said bitterly before he could think of more. I was staring hard at the sun, hoping a focus would help me to hold back my tears. In all the days since Sigurd's departure, I had not cried once. To do so now would be to topple a dam confining high waters.

Hagen took me by the shoulders and shook me. "You are not listening to me. I know your thoughts, though you keep them to yourself. But has it ever occurred to you that you might be mistaken? I wager you are. I wager Sigurd loves you as he always has. Aye, I saw the way he looked at Brunhild that night, but then I looked at her that way myself. The woman I love has none of Brunhild's charms, but plenty of her own. Surely Sigurd feels the same. But do you think he will continue to do so when he sees you like this? You are no longer lovable, sister. You must do something—"

"I cannot," I cried. "This force, this blackness, has taken me over. Go away. Leave me alone. The woman you love . . . . You speak to me from the spire of your own satisfaction. Come back when Vascar's sister has tired of you. Speak to me then of hay and wheat and hope. Then I will listen."

Hagen tightened his grip on my shoulders and spoke to me more harshly than he had ever. "You will listen now. Are you so weak that you have allowed this blackness, as you call it, to bury you? Go down to the pool at the side of the river and search for the image of your face, woman. Look past the scowl and the dull gaze and perhaps you will see what you fail to see now. You are a Burgundian. Does that mean nothing to you? You belong to a race of people who, despite all adversity, refused to perish. We were born to survive, cannot you see that? We are the ones who banded together and vowed to cherish life, to make a new life—perhaps not for our children, but for our children's children and theirs. Does that not obligate each of us to conduct our lives in a vigorous manner? To grapple with these trifling matters? Have you forgotten, Gudrun, who fathered you? Whose blood beats in your veins? I see that you have. And why? Because the Burgundian history is but a story to you, an entertainment to be sung by free men—well, nearly free—in the safety of their halls. But our safety was paid for in blood. Do you think our ancestors thought of envy and love when they fought their way down from the cold countries? Did we think of envy and love when the Huns and the Romans came down on us? Rejoice, if for no other reason, that you have the leisure to contemplate such matters."

"Do go away, Hagen. You are truly tiresome today."

He let up his grip. I ripped a blade from the turf and stuck it in my mouth and looked toward the horizon indifferently. Hagen watched me for a moment. Then he slid off the roof and went for his horse.

I regretted his departure immediately—though I could not will myself to call him back. As I watched him ride away, down through the lower fields and into the forest, I found myself thinking of Sigurd, and then of Brunhild, and of the aura of innocence that I had detected emanating from her when I had last crawled past her sleeping body to quit the bower. All at once it occurred to me that perhaps she was an innocent, as Guthorm was. It was not her fault that she was as lovely as she was. I decided to go down to the river and contemplate these matters further.

I slid down the roof and dropped to the ground, and as if to confirm the accuracy of my thoughts, I found myself face to face with Brunhild. We both let out shrieks of astonishment. Had she been moving any faster, I would have knocked her down. Some exchange was called for, and as "What are you doing up so early?" seemed inappropriate under the circumstances, I said, "It is warm today, even at this early hour."

She looked away. "Yes. It has not been this warm in some days. You would never know the cold season was already upon us."

We had had our exchange, and yet she lingered. It puzzled me. "I thought to go down to the river," I dared to say. "There is a spring up behind the hall. Surely you have seen it. We burn peat there to heat the rocks so that we can bathe in the Winter. But it is not as pleasurable as bathing in the river. That is why I thought that today, being so warm . . . ."

I ceased my rambling all at once. Brunhild had turned back to me, and with her head cocked to one side, she eyed me suspiciously. I noticed, for the first time, that her watery eyes were streaked with green. I studied her long fair lashes and her finely tapered chin. "It is warm," she mumbled.

Inspired by her indulgence, I cried, "Come with me! We can bathe together." I held my breath to await her response.

Her smile came slowly. "I am for it," she said at last. Then she laughed her high-pitched laughter. "Let us go to the river . . . like sisters. I am for it."

My heart soared. I was speechless. I held up one finger to show her that I would be right back and ran into the hall to fetch the soap. Mother, who was helping Guthorm into a fresh tunic, jerked her head up and eyed me questioningly. I ignored her, and having found the soap, ran back out again.

Brunhild was standing just where I had left her, the morning sun ablaze in her hair. Her smile was still in place, and I was grateful for it, although now it seemed to me that it was more a smile of amusement than of camaraderie. She had called me sister, and I could not contain myself. Though she had not one line on her face, she looked older standing there grinning at me, wiser. I asked myself, Why should Sigurd not love her? She is a beautiful, wise, charming woman, a valkyria, my sister now, and when we have had our weddings, Sigurd's sister as well. Why should Sigurd not love her in the same way that Gunner and Hagen love me? "Let us run," I cried.

Brunhild laughed. "Run? Why, I have only just awakened." She cocked her head again and her eyes swam over the expanse of cloudless sky. "I will run," she said. "It may do me good. It may wake me up, for I think I may be dreaming."

I laughed at her remark, and I felt as if I had never laughed before. I laughed and laughed until the dam burst and the flood waters broke free from my eyes. Brunhild saw them streaming and laughed too. We began to run. And while we ran I thought, *We have been so unfair to you, Mother and I. No wonder you sleep late into each day. My sister. How terrible to find yourself in the hands of strangers who have lost their capacity for kindness. No wonder you think you are dreaming now.* And since I could not very well say these words to her while we were running so hard and laughing still, I rearranged them in my head so that I might say them properly when we reached our destination.

At the bank of the bathing pool, which was quiet and safe in the crook of the river's arm, we collapsed, gasping for breath, our eyes still wild with laughter. I was anxious to make my confession. I had embellished it by now. Now I thought to be completely honest, to tell her how her beauty and her charm and Sigurd's high regard for her had initiated my black thoughts and hence my unforgivable behavior. I imagined that she would laugh at me, and that then she would take me in her arms and console me. It was this consolation I craved. But when I finally caught my breath and was about to spit out my exclamations of love and sorrow and misery and regret, she turned to me and said, "Must he always follow?"

I looked back toward the moor across which we had come and spotted Guthorm flying through it, his arms flapping in the air like broken wings. "He knows where I am all the time. I cannot get away from him," I stammered. "He will not bother us. He just likes to be where I am. He will not bathe unless I force him to. He does not care to be wet. He—"

Guthorm arrived and threw his arms around my neck, not so much a hug as an effort to drag me away. I laughed at first as I tried to free myself, but when I saw the appalled look on Brunhild's face, I ceased laughing. "Stop," I shouted. Guthorm's lower lip came out, but as his eyes slid away, they fell on a toad that was making its way along the bank, and he got down on his knees immediately to watch its progress. "He will not bother us now," I said. But Brunhild's expression remained repulsed.

She sat back, so as to have a better look at Guthorm as he crawled along the bank. "He does not like me," she mumbled.

"He is afraid of you."

She laughed abruptly. "He is not the first. Men are always afraid that they will anger me and that then I will use my powers against them. Women are afraid I will use my powers to take their men from them." She shrugged. "I do not much care. I would sooner have people afraid of me than not." She picked a flower and began to twirl it in her fingers.

Now I guessed that she knew my thoughts and was providing me with an occasion to utter them. All at once I felt manipulated. "I have not seen your powers," I said softly.

She stopped twirling her flower and smiled tauntingly. "Have you not?" she asked, her eyebrows rising.

She got up slowly from the bank and began to undress. In a moment she had shed her masculine garments and was wearing nothing but the chain that hung from her neck, her only piece of jewelry. I had noticed this chain a thousand times, but the pendant which hung from it had always been concealed beneath her tunic. Now I saw that it was a small hammer, fashioned from stone and not unlike the one that had hung from Sigurd's neck for as long as I had known him. I felt myself trembling. It was shinier than Sigurd's but otherwise just the same. She saw me staring at it, and her hand came up to cover it. Her eyes flashed with amusement. "Is it his?" I croaked.

She laughed and dove into the pool. She swam prettily, hardly disturbing the waters with her long, strong strokes. All at once she arched her back like some huge fish and went under in the place where the pool was deepest. I stood up to look for her. Moments passed. I struggled out of my robe and slid down the bank. The water was icy cold. Treading water to stay afloat, I felt all around for her with my feet. Whether I wanted to save her (for by now it seemed she had been under far too long) or merely to have another look at the pendant, I could not say. Then I heard the water break and Brunhild soared up behind me. I turned at once, and with my eye focused on her throat, I swam toward her. I could hear her laughter even above the splashing that I made with my wild, awkward strokes. Just as I reached her, she went under again. For a moment there was silence. Then she emerged close to the bank. She hoisted herself up and sat panting, her fingers around the pendant, her face aglow with sport.

Trembling with cold and confusion, I swam back to the bank and climbed out. "You mock me. Is it his or not?"

"It is not," she snapped.

I looked away. "Then why did you let me make a fool of myself?"

"Why should I not? Since I came here, you have made your distrust plain enough."

"Then I have been mistaken?" I ventured hopefully. "Is that what you mean to say?"

"Mistaken to let it be so obvious." Her eyes were hard and cold now beneath their familiar mist. "Look, Gudrun, why not just say what is on your mind. What you want to know is, do I love him."

She was wrong. That I did not want to know. But as I stared back at her with my teeth rattling from the cold, she told me anyway. "I do. And moreover, he loves me."

"You put a spell on him," I mumbled after a long silence in which I seemed to retreat from my very existence.

She laughed. "I can see you would like to think so. But you are wrong. I had no need to. He will marry you. He feels he has no choice. And he fears your brothers' wrath. But he does not love you. And thus I must marry your brother, for all that he is ugly and vain and weak in his will, so that I can remain close to Sigurd."

Now it was my turn to laugh. "You lie," I cried. "If Sigurd loved you he would want you by his side. As it is, we plan to leave come next growing season. You will be here with Gunner, and we will be gone to live on Frankish lands."

To my horror, her expression did not alter. "Sigurd and I will work that out. There is plenty of time between now and then."

Her composure enraged me. Slowly, she got up and began to slip her tunic over her head. While her arms were still entangled in the sleeves, I stood up and slapped her shoulder. It was a weak gesture, the sort I might have used with Guthorm, but for an instant it rendered her motionless. Then, as if she had agreed that it was weak and could not be bothered to respond to it, she resumed straightening her tunic. I felt something on my leg. I looked down and saw Guthorm. I had forgotten him. I shook myself free and shouted into her imperturbable face, "Sigurd loved me from the time—"

"Aye, loved!" she shouted back. "And I have no doubt he loved you well. But that time is over now. Go to him if you do not believe me. Ask him yourself. Do you think it took us three days to journey here because I could not bear to travel in the rain? The rain does not bother me, and neither does the cold. You forget that I spent my life living in the forest with no roof over my head. Look at yourself. Your urchin body is blue with cold. You tremble. Your teeth rattle. When I met you, you seemed more dead than alive."

"I was sick."

"You are weak. You do not deserve a man like Sigurd. You had no appreciation for his quest. He told me so. You hardly lifted your head to hear his words when he told you and your brothers how he came to slay the dragon and acquire his gold."

"He said that to you?"

"He said a good many things to me. We spoke of you at length during the course of our journey. A fearful little thing, he called you. But when we were quite near to your hall, we came to a cave, and after that we did not mention your name again."

"No more," I cried.

"We knew by then that Sigurd's precious honor would make it necessary for us to part soon enough, and thus we used what time we had left well, so well that we could not bring ourselves to leave in time for your feast, so well that all through the night we did not give a thought to the consequences of our delay."

"Sigurd would not have done such a thing. He is a brother to my brothers. He would not have—"

"Betrayed Gunner? Yes, yes, I know all about it. Sigurd went on and on about it even as he was laying down his cloak for us. Let me take you there now. Let me show you the place where Sigurd built the fire just at the mouth of the cave—not for warmth, we knew we would be plenty warm in each other's arms—but so as to be able to see each other's faces while—"

I could hear no more. I pushed her toward the edge of the bank, but as she was falling, she grabbed hold of my arm, and we fell in together. I swallowed water, but I got my footing on the steep, sandy bottom and propelled myself upward. For an instant I saw her face, and I heard Guthorm moaning loudly from the bank. Then she was gone and Guthorm was gone, and I was being held under. I found her legs and toppled her. We emerged together, scratching, pulling, pushing, gasping for breath. Guthorm was howling now. She pushed me under again. I grabbed hold of her foot, but it slid out of my hands. When I emerged again, I saw her climbing up onto the bank, her tunic clinging to her, her muscular limbs straining against it like rocks. I made to grab her foot and pull her back in, but she was up and out before I could do so. I slid back into the water and watched while she wrung out her hair. Then she picked up my robe and threw it in. "Scat!" she shouted, and Guthorm, who had been perched on the edge of the bank with his arm stretched toward me, jumped up and ran away. "There," she said. "I am refreshed. I believe I will return to the hall and have your mother prepare me something to eat." She turned and started for the path.

The City of Attila

Chapter 9

While the others remained indifferent to my words of greeting and gratitude, there was one among my various attendants who bothered to acknowledge them with a nod and a half-smile. And thus, one morning when the girl appeared with my milk bowl and basket of bread, I gathered my courage and said to her as she was leaving, "Tell Edeco that I should like to bathe." The young Hun stopped near the doorway and glanced at me over one shoulder so that I could see the glint of fear in her eye. "I must be allowed to bathe," I repeated.

When the curtain was drawn later that day, I prepared myself for the sight of Edeco's face—though I had not seen him, or anyone, other than my attendants, since the night that Edeco had brought me the sheepskin parchment which I had refused to accept. That was when the weather was still cold. Now it was warmer, and I had spent the best part of the new season isolated, full of fears, and sustained only by the hope that Edeco's last words to me had been truly said, and that they anticipated an allegiance that we would one day share. But it was only the girl again, hauling in a large bucket of water. Gravely disappointed, I got to my feet to help her set it down. It was less than half full, and when the girl backed away from it, I saw where the rest had gone. "Forgive me," the girl mumbled when she saw me eyeing her wet robe. I took a step closer to her, but her face took on the fearful look that it had when I had spoken to her earlier, and she backed toward the door. I spread my fingers out pleadingly and struggled to tell her that I was grateful for the water, that it was no matter that most of it had been spilt, but that I wondered why it had been necessary when it would have been so much easier for Edeco to come as he used to.

The girl blinked her eyes, and I saw that she had failed to understand me. I tried again, speaking slower and rearranging my fragmentary sentences as best I could. Finally the girl nodded. "Edeco is gone," she said.

"Where did Edeco go?" I asked, trying to conceal my emotion.

"Away."

The word was unfamiliar to me, but the Hun girl waved her hand in the air as if to designate something far beyond the doorway. "Away, away," she repeated. And then she retreated herself.

Although I sorely needed the water after all this time, I was too distracted to make use of it now. I paced and bit my fingernails and wondered whether it were possible that Attila had somehow learned that Edeco had shown me the parchment, and to punish him, sent him into exile. I waited impatiently for the girl's return, but more days passed, and then I began to worry that the girl had mentioned our conversation to one of the others and had thus been relieved of those of her duties concerning me. Desperate now, I began to observe the other women who came and went, hoping one of them might give me some signal, some gesture of kindness that would indicate that she, too, might be approached. But none did, and I felt on the verge of yielding to madness once more, when one afternoon the Hun girl came again with a bucket of water.

This time when she had set the bucket down, she giggled and held out her robe so that I could see that she had not spilled anything. I praised her as best I could, and while the girl was still smiling, I asked casually, "Attila? Is he gone too?"

"Away, too. Like Edeco and the others," she whispered furtively before leaving.

Now I felt a great sense of relief. If Edeco and Attila were gone off together, with others, then certainly they were about some campaign. I washed my body thoroughly, and then I lowered my head into the bucket and washed my matted hair. Clean again after days of having had to endure my own filth, I felt I could be patient, that whether I should have to wait a day or a year, the time would come when I would hear that the sword had worked its havoc on Attila. I resolved to keep myself in good spirits and to avoid having any more risky conversations with my new friend.

One day I heard a roar go up, and as the weather was hot and dry again, I thought at first of fire and rushed to peek out from behind my curtain. The guard, who had stopped pacing to look off toward the village, noticed me and raised his riding whip threateningly. I hurried away from the doorway and to the back of the hut, where I pressed my ear against the wall. Now I thought the roar was more the sort that horses make when many men are riding swiftly together. Beyond it were cries and shouts, but I could not determine whether these expressed joy or horror. It occurred to me that the Romans might have learned of Attila's absence and were marching to lay siege on the City of Attila. But when I heard my guard's horse resume its pacing, I decided it must be the Huns returning. "I am free," I cried aloud, and I let my tears run down my face. And when they ceased, I set about praying words of thanksgiving—though it seemed an impiety to pray now when I had given so little thought to Wodan and the others for so long.

That evening, when the Hun woman came with my meal, I searched her face for some confirmation that Attila was dead, but I saw nothing beyond the usual indifference. And the expression on the face of the woman who came in the morning told me nothing more. I noted, in my taper's light, that a rash had formed all along my arms. And it seemed to me that my heart was beating all too rapidly. I feared I would die before the good news ever reached my ears. Another woman came in the evening and replaced my untouched breakfast tray with my supper one. I opened my mouth to speak to her, but before I could form an inquiry, she was gone again. A while later, as I was spreading out my skins for sleep, the curtain opened once more. I turned, ready now to interrogate whomever it might be. But my mouth snapped closed when I saw that it was Edeco.

"Ildico, how do you fare?" he asked, his expression officious.

For a moment I could only stare at him. Then I answered, "Well enough, considering. And you?"

His smile came slowly, but the tenderness that I had seen in his eye each time I had envisioned him was not present. "We were victorious. I am very well and much richer than before."

My heart plunged. "Then you marched again on the Eastern Empire?" I managed to ask.

"Yes."

I turned from him. "Did you know when I saw you last that you would be marching?"

"We left the very next morning. Did I fail to mention it? Attila had word last Winter that the earth beneath the Eastern Empire had begun to turn in on itself. Entire villages were swallowed up. The wall of Constantinople crumbled. He took this as a sign that we should march. I wonder that you do not bother to ask about him."

I shrugged. "I assume he is well. You would not have counted yourself victorious otherwise."

Edeco beamed. "He fought like a god. The war sword brings him luck."

I turned back to him slowly, and to hide my anguish, I asked, "Did you take many villages?"

"Whole provinces—Illyrium, Trace, Dacia, Moesia, Scythia—"

"The names mean nothing to me," I snapped. Then, more gently, I added, "I know little about the Eastern Empire."

Edeco's smile broadened into something akin to a sneer. "Then let me choose words that are compatible with your ignorance, Ildico. Much blood was spilt. Many Romans died. We tore down their churches. The booty was great. I do not think they will cross us again."

"And how did they cross you?" I asked, repulsed by his arrogance.

"They failed to live up to the terms of our treaty."

"What terms were those?"

His boastful smile vanished. He straightened. "None that concern you." Then he added, "You are changed, Ildico."

I studied him a moment. "I might say the same of you."

He looked surprised. "I would have thought that our victory would have had some meaning for you."

"Indeed it does."

He went on as if he had failed to discern the sarcasm that had crept unbidden into my tone, saying, "I have something to say to you on Attila's behalf. This, at least, should stir you some." He hesitated, but seeing that I had no response, he continued. "In his deep gratitude for your gift, Attila has come to agree with me that you might now be initiated into the village life. You are to join the women who serve him his evening meal, a position of much esteem, I assure you. A guard will come for you each evening to escort you to Attila's gate. A girl will meet you there and bring you into the palace. She will show you what to do. You must watch carefully and keep your mouth shut. And you must be careful never to lift your eyes to Attila or any of his guests, myself included, while you are serving. So you see, Ildico, as long as you do not make some blunder, your solitary life is behind you. Attila is kindhearted, is he not?"

I bowed. "Tell him I am most grateful."

"I shall. He is still outside the city gates, but he returns tomorrow. You will begin your first night of service then. Do you have any questions?"

I had many, but none that I could ask of Edeco. I shook my head.

The prospect of my new position brought some new hope to counter my disappointment, but whether it was connected to my purpose or the desire for distraction, I could not be certain. I no longer knew the difference between the two. Edeco was right; I had changed. But then Edeco had changed, too. Before his departure, it had seemed that he was very close to becoming, if not my ally, then at least my confidant. Now he seemed as much Attila's man as when I had first come to Pannonia.

As Edeco had promised, a guard came late the next afternoon, and for the second time since my arrival, I found myself enroute to Attila's hall. But this time, when the gates were opened to admit us, it was not the silken tents of Attila's numerous wives that my eyes beheld. They were there, of course, not far off in the distance, but the great swarm of men who sat on their horses in Attila's courtyard kept me from seeing all but flashes of their bright colors. My guard, a stern-looking Hun on a squat Hunnish horse, indicated that I was to wait by his side just inside the gates until further instruction. He kept his riding whip on my shoulder, and when the Hun who would take me to the hall approached through the crowd, he informed me by bringing it down hard. I flinched against the pain and turned to see the familiar face of the young Hun girl who had obliged me by answering my questions. After all my time alone, the boisterous horsemen frightened me, and I was glad that I should not have to go among them with a stranger. The Hun girl bowed expressionlessly, but as soon as the guard turned, she smiled and touched my hand.

Most of the crowd was made up of Huns, though there were Thuets scattered among them, and all were drinking from gold or silver goblets while they laughed and shouted and toasted one another. They were, I discovered as I followed my companion, divided into two groups, those who sat between the gates and the silk tents, and those who sat between the tents and the hall. Hun women carrying wine jugs wove their way among them, stopping to pour for whomever required it. Attila's wives, who were sitting outside their tents, looked very much as if they would like to be going among the jovial men themselves.

When we got past the tents and through the second swarm of horsemen, I saw a sight which nearly brought me to my knees. On either side of Attila's door, a great many poles had been erected, and atop of each was the black, bloated, bloodied head of one of Attila's victims, men and women and children alike. I gasped, not realizing that I had stopped walking until I noted that the Hun girl had stopped to wait for me. Her expression indicated that she was amused to find me so startled by the sight. It had been a long time since I had seen so many severed heads, and then it had been at Worms and the heads had been those of my own folk. Except for the few Hunnish faces among them—deserters, I supposed—these faces were Roman. But the terror

I felt moving through me was just the same as if it were the Burgundians all over again.

The girl was still watching me, but now she looked impatient. I commanded my legs to move, but they had gone slack, and my eyes still lingered on the wild eyes and black, protruding tongues of Attila's victims. The sound of my bogus name in my ear made me jump. I turned to see Edeco, his face ruddy and full of laughter. "Had we been able to procure more poles," he said leaning over his horse, "the dead among us would far exceed the confines of Attila's courtyard." I could think of no response. His slurred words indicated that he had already had more to drink than he had ever had in my company. "And of course," he went on, "we took them alive when we could. The Romans will pay a handsome price to buy back their citizens."

Edeco brought his horse up and rode away laughing. The Hun girl grabbed my wrist and got me moving again. In a moment we were in Attila's hall, which was empty except for the women who had come in to fetch wine jugs from the long table against the south wall. The Hun girl placed a jug in my hands and indicated that I should go outside with it.

I wandered through the crowds dazed, remembering that I was carrying a wine jug only when I felt a riding whip or a hand come down on my shoulder. I did not even realize when the jug was empty until the Hun for whom I thought I was pouring exclaimed. I ran back into the hall for more wine, and then out again, praying all the time that I would not encounter Edeco again, for it seemed to me that he had a purpose in saying what he had to me, and that it was linked to something vile.

I had gone out for a fourth time when a sudden hush fell over the crowd. Beyond it I could hear the voices of singers. The horsemen began to separate, leaving a path from Attila's gate through the tents and to the hall. I found myself close to the gate and at the edge of this path, and thus, when the gates were opened, I had a clear view. In the distance I could see Attila riding on his Hunnish horse—or rather, I saw a rider holding a shaft of fire over his head, for Attila was too far off to be otherwise recognized. Behind him rode rows of men for as far as the eye could see. On either side of Attila, young Hunnish girls walked, scattering flower petals and singing what could only have been their song of praise for their master. Their voices made my heart swell with sorrow and longing. Walking behind the girls and holding white cloth canopies over their heads were women, who were also singing. The villagers who were not part of the ceremony were lying prostrate on either side of the procession. When Attila came closer, the men within his courtyard dismounted and prostrated themselves, too. I quickly joined them on the ground. The girls and the women who were walking with Attila stopped just outside the gates, and as soon as Attila had entered, the gates were closed behind him so that the greater number of his troops likewise remained without.

    I glanced up as Attila was going by and saw that he looked somber, almost bored, his eye falling on nothing and no one. The girls and the women continued to sing, louder now, as if to make up for the fact that the gates were between their song and their master's indifferent hearing of it. When Attila had dismounted and gone into his hall, everyone got to their feet again. Through the crowd, I saw the Hun girl hurrying toward me. Waving for me to follow, she turned quickly and began running toward the hall. I ran behind her, looking straight ahead so as to avoid the anguished faces of Attila's victims. As we reached the door, I glimpsed Attila, already settled on his red silk couch, and, to my horror, staring right at me. The Hun girl entered and prostrated herself before him. As soon as she got up, I followed her example. Then I hurried behind her to the long table. The jugs of wine had been moved back, and now the table was laid out with great quantities of food—breads and fruits and cakes and meats such as I had never seen before. Some of the other serving women were taking these foods and dividing them up into bowls. Others were carrying the bowls to the several small nearby tables. I took up two bowls and set to following their example. A group of boys of various ages came in together, each prostrating himself in turn before Attila. As Ernac was among them, I surmised that these were Attila's sons. Unlike his brothers, Ernac went down on the floor beside his father rather than at his feet, and Attila, who was looking at the next group coming in, reached out his hand and patted Ernac's head. The second group contained Edeco and several other bejeweled men. They, too, took turns prostrating themselves. The third group to enter was Attila's wives. We went among the three groups carrying over the small food-laden tables. As we set them down, Attila's guests found chairs for themselves. Then Attila got up, taking the war sword with him, and lowered the door.

    Now the hall went dead quiet. As Attila was settling himself again, the young Hun girl came forward and handed me a wooden cup filled with wine. Since all of the tables had already been provided with gold and silver goblets—and perhaps because of my distracted state—I assumed that this ordinary wooden cup was meant for me and made to lift it to my lips. The girl's gasp stopped me short. And as if to conceal my blunder from the others, she went up on her toes before me. Then she whispered, "For Attila, fool!" and nudged me into motion.

I began what seemed the longest journey of my life. Though I kept my eyes on the wine, I had the sense that everyone else in the hall was watching me. Indeed, the only sound was that of my feet dragging across the floor. I felt myself bent over, hunched, but I had no power to straighten. My legs seemed to be buckling beneath me. I was delirious with fear and confusion.

When I finally reached Attila's couch, I saw that his hand was already extended. I pressed the wooden cup into it and stood to watch my own hand, which was quaking violently, retreat. Now I seemed to hear an enormous sigh, as if all the onlookers had been as anxious as I that I should hand the cup over without incident. I turned at once and hurried back to the other serving women, some of whom were eyeing me sternly. Then I stood like them with my back to the long table and watched as Attila raised the cup to his lips. When he had had his sip, he passed the cup to one of his sons, and this boy took a sip and passed it along to the one beside him. When the cup had gone all around, from table to table and guest to guest, the last to drink from it, one of Attila's wives, got up and carried it back to Attila. Like me, she moved slowly and kept her eye on whatever was left of the wine.

Next Attila made a long speech, hesitating often so as to choose his words carefully. He looked at no one while he spoke, and his voice was so low that he seemed to be talking to himself. I understood enough of his words to know that his subject was his recent victory, though his demeanor reflected none of the jubilation one would have expected after such an event. I was horrified, when he finished, to see the Hun girl coming at me with a wooden tray. I tried to push it back on her, but the girl shook her head and stepped away.

Unlike the small tables which I had helped to carry and which contained every sort of exotic food, Attila's tray held nothing but a single bowl of meat. I could see with the corner of my eye that he was already straightening himself on his couch to accept it. Again it seemed as if my every step took me no closer to him until I was actually there. As I bent to lower the tray, my eye fell on the war sword at his side. It glared like the sun in the torch-lit hall, and I fancied it was mocking me, daring me to lift it and drive it into his heart. Since Attila made no move to take the tray from my hands, I had no choice but to lower it onto his lap. I was just about to release it when all at once he seized my wrist. Repulsed by his touch, I forgot myself and glanced up at him. I saw his indignation and quickly looked away. He released me and I hurried back to the other servants.

As soon as he began to eat, conversations at the various tables rushed in to fill what had been a prolonged silence. The Hun girl handed me a wine jug and pointed to Attila's door, which one of his sons was in the process of lifting. Gladly, I went out with the other serving women to go again among the troops. They were less rowdy now, and some of them sat staring solemnly at the doorway as if in envy of the few who had been admitted. Conversely, when I went back into the hall later for more wine, I found that the guests inside had become clamorous. As I was turning to go out again with a full jug, my eye fell on the source of their merriment, a dwarf who was dancing among the tables. I was startled to see such a creature in Attila's hall, and for a moment I could only stare. The dwarf was twisted in such a way that his head seemed to protrude from one shoulder. His complexion was dark, darker even than that of the Huns, but otherwise he had none of their features. In fact, he looked like no one I had ever seen before. As he fluttered from table to table, he stammered in the Hunnish tongue, rolling his eyes and contorting his face in every possible manner. I glanced at Attila and saw that while he was watching the dwarf just as intently as the others, he seemed to take no pleasure in his antics. Then I remembered the wine jug in my hand and hurried out.

I was just coming in for another jug when a loud clap brought me to an abrupt halt. The laughter in the hall ceased instantly. A silence followed, and then Attila gave an order concerning the dwarf, and one of his officers jumped to his feet and escorted him roughly from the hall. Then the entire assembly stood up. The other serving women, I noted, were rushing to carry the tables away, though the remains on some suggested that not all the guests had finished eating. I hurried to join them. As I passed Attila, I saw that his tray was still on his lap, and I wondered whether it was my place to remove it. Fortunately, before I could decide, Attila lifted it himself and set in down on one of the tables that two servants were passing by with. Meanwhile, the guests formed a line, each of them prostrating him or herself before exiting.

Edeco, who had gone to open the bower curtain to admit one of Attila's wives, was the last to join the leave-takers. While he was waiting for his turn to prostrate himself before his master, he caught my eye and gave me a look which could have only meant that I had somehow disappointed him.

I looked away and began to remove the food bowls from the tables, thinking that they should now have to be wiped clean. But when all the bowls had been stacked on the long table, the Hun girl touched my wrist and jerked her head to indicate that it was time for us to leave as well. Except for the two old women who stayed behind to take charge of the final clean-up, the servants went forward together to prostrate themselves.

I was no sooner out the door than Edeco grabbed my arm and pulled me away from the others. Most of the courtyard crowd was gone now, and those who had not gone were in the process of retreating. Edeco dragged me toward the gates, his face full of anger. When we reached them, he let go of me and shouted, "You did not obey me!"

"You failed to tell me that I should be the one—"

He struck me across the face; the slap was more a show of authority than an actual attempt to hurt me. Nevertheless, I would have cried out from the shock of it if he did not then quickly cover my mouth with his hand. He looked about himself, as if to see whether he were being watched, but there was something in his eye which made me think that he was disappointed to find that he was not. This interested me no end. "You dared to look into Attila's eyes while you were serving him," he cried.

"He startled me," I cried when he dropped his hand from my mouth. "Forgive me," I added, fearing that he would slap me again.

He took my arm and we went around Attila's palisade. He walked briskly, dragging me along. It was dark now, but out in the village a good many men still lingered in groups on horseback. There were also several couples sitting on the grassy knolls, whispering in the moonlight. The couples dwindled as we went farther. By the time we reached the area wherein my hut was located, we saw no one at all.

Edeco seemed as surprised as I was to find that there was no guard posted at my doorway. He pushed me into the hut but stayed outside himself cursing under his breath. A tray of food and wine had been set down for me. In all the excitement, I had forgotten that I'd had nothing to eat since morning. I sat down to it eagerly. After a time, Edeco came in. "The guard has still not come," he complained. He began to pace, stopping every so often to look outside.

A woman came for my tray, but when she saw that Edeco was within, she bowed and hurried away without it. "I do not understand why my behavior in the hall is so important to you," I began. "Why should you care? If Attila should use his sword to slice off my head, what would it be to you? You would have one less prisoner to concern yourself with."

Edeco continued to pace and did not respond. But I was eager to get him talking, for I thought perhaps his behavior indicated that he had something to hide from me and I was determined to find out what it was. "Who was the dwarf?" I asked more casually.

"Zerco," Edeco answered, still pacing. "He belonged to Bleda once. Now he is Attila's."

His response was bitter, but as he had responded, I went on. "It surprises me that such an old man is not treated with more respect."

He stopped to look at me. "He is no older than Attila. It surprises me that you would think otherwise." He resumed his pacing. "Zerco's mind is as crippled as his body. His only function here is to entertain."

"Attila did not seem much entertained by him."

Edeco stopped again. "And your function is to serve, not to make observations."

"One cannot help but observe. Even animals must pause to take in their surroundings. It is a condition of life."

Edeco stopped pacing for good and stood with his arms folded, looking down at me. "Is it now? Then tell me what other observations you have made here in the City of Attila."

"I have observed that your manner varies, depending on whether you are alone with me or in the presence of others."

Before he could respond we heard the guard approaching. Edeco stepped out and spoke to him harshly. The guard's reply was low and penitent, and I could not make it out. Edeco came back in and closed the curtain behind him. "Then you observe well," he said.

"May I ask you then why you are sometimes so unkind?"

"You may not," Edeco snapped. But a moment later he hung his head and mumbled, "You know the answer as well as I."

I jumped to my feet and thrust myself before him. Though he did not move away, his eyes darted in every direction so that he reminded me of the marmot we had once seen cornered. "Edeco," I whispered, taking hold of his scarred hand. "We are both Thuets, are we not? And I know—"

"Tell me nothing of what you think you know," Edeco warned.

I took a step back from him and went on quickly. "Why, Edeco? Is your loyalty to Attila so great that you would feel compelled to betray me? You said nothing to Attila when I told you of the vision I foresaw for your son. Look at me. Look into my eyes and tell me you do not see your own Thuet reflection staring back at you. We are just the same, Edeco! We must play at being Attila's slaves while we are here in the City of Attila, but we both know that no Thuet can be at peace with himself while he lives within the confines of another man's walls."

Edeco grabbed my shoulders, and with his lips pressed together in anger, he shoved me back until I hit the wall. Then he glanced over his shoulder to see if the guard had heard the thump. "Do you hear yourself?" he whispered harshly. "You are sick—sick to imagine that I have any other ambition than to serve Attila. I may be a slave, but I am a rich one. Can you truly imagine that I would give that up for the privilege of calling myself a Thuet again?" He released me roughly. "Your implications disgust me. I never gave you any reason to believe we had such vulgar thoughts in common." I opened my mouth to protest, but he shouted, "Never!" Then he glanced at the doorway again. "What I could not say to you before," he went on rapidly, "I find I can say now, in my anger. I cared for you once, Ildico. I hammered Attila to get him to take you on. And now you have—"

"Your mother was a Thuet," I cried. "And your father. They came down like mine from the cold countries to—"

"I will hear no more from you!"

"And your sons, Edeco."

"My sons will do well to inherit my riches when I am gone."

"Your sons are capable of coming by their own riches. That is what I foresaw. If you continue your sham, that is the thing they will inherit, your status as Attila's fool. You are no more a man than Zerco."

Edeco leaned into me. "I should kill you now," he whispered, "but angry as I am, I would likely make it quick. Attila will want to plan something more . . . ." He broke off and shook his head with disgust. Then, turning, he kicked my tray and sent it flying as he marched out.

Chapter 10

All that night and the next day I waited, even during the brief moments when I managed to doze, for the guards to come and drag me away. But no guard came for me until evening, and then it was only the same one who had come the night before to escort me to Attila's gate. As I walked beside the Hun girl through the courtyard—which was empty now except for a few guards and the faces of Attila's victims still set out like vulgar sentinels before his door—I searched the girl's face for some sign that she knew that my death was imminent. But if she knew anything, her movements failed to betray it.

Attila was not about yet. We joined the other servants, who were chattering quietly at the long table. When one of the older women handed me Attila's wooden tray, I breathed a sigh of relief, for it seemed to me that if I were meant to place Attila's bowl of meat on it, then Edeco could not have said anything to Attila after all. But a moment later it occurred to me that this could be a sham; from everything I knew about Attila, it would be just like him to wait until I had delivered his tray to strike me down.

Attila entered from the bower. I put the tray aside, and as I was prostrating myself with the others, I glanced at him, looking for some indication that he knew he was in the company of an agitator. He gaze swept over me, sure enough, but it did not linger.

His guests began to file in. Tonight only his sons and some eight or nine of his officers joined him, Edeco among them. I brought Attila his wine cup and relaxed somewhat when I saw him drink from it. He passed it around, and when it came back to him, he said a few words too low for me to hear. The others nodded solemnly in response, and though Edeco nodded too, he kept his eyes on the table, as if he could not bring himself to look up at his master. I brought Attila his dinner tray. It contained the bowl of meat, and a second bowl, of dates, which one of the older women had added at the last minute. When Attila seized my wrist, as he had the previous evening, I was no less startled and I let out a cry. There was a collective gasp, but when he let go of me the next moment and chuckled, and his guests chuckled too. The evening went well enough after that, and I decided that I was safe, for Edeco would be considered as much an insurgent as I was if it were known that he had withheld the facts of my sedition for so long.

All that Summer and Winter, except for the few occasions when Attila went off on some business outside the city, I served him. And by listening to his speeches—which were a prelude to every meal—and to the women with whom I worked, I came to have a fairly good understanding of the Hun language. Furthermore, the women came to accept me as a fellow servant, a boon now that I no longer had Edeco to speak to. Once I asked the Hun girl, who had begun to escort me to the bath house in Edeco's place, to mention to Edeco that I should like to speak to him. But when I saw her next, the girl informed me that he'd said he had nothing to say to me and that I should not send word to him again. On the few occasions when our eyes met inadvertently in Attila's hall, Edeco quickly looked away. Attila, who seemed to notice nothing but who, in fact, noticed everything, said once to Edeco as he was turning sharply from my glance, "So, friend, I see you have not yet made it up with your Thuet." Edeco nodded and blushed while the other officers laughed, and I came to understand that in order to be relieved of his duties concerning me, Edeco had made his master to believe that we had been intimate and had a lovers' quarrel. And my affection for him grew then, for I guessed what turmoil his divided loyalties must be causing him.

As for Attila, after my first few evenings in his service, he seemed to take no more notice of me than he did the other servants. Except for the fact that I was still guarded when I was in my hut, I began to see that my life was no different from theirs. We were all Attila's slaves, and we lived in fear of stirring his wrath, which, I learned, could be done quite easily.

Most of Attila's anger was directed at his sons, Ernac being the only exception. Ellac, who was the eldest, practically a man, was the one with whom Attila was roughest, for Ellac most often seemed to forget that Attila's chief desire was for uncontested obedience. On one occasion, for instance, noting that Ellac had not eaten one of his cakes, Attila told him to pass it on to Ernac. Ellac replied, "I was about to eat it myself, Father." And Attila, who had seemed so calm only a moment before, leaped up from his couch, knocking his tray to the floor, and punched Ellac so hard that he flipped over the back of his chair, his feet upsetting the entire table. Attila hollered for him to get up, but Ellac, who was groaning and holding his face, did not stir. With his own face as red as his couch, Attila walked over to where Ellac lay and kicked him several times—his face, his chest, his back, his genitals—so that I thought surely the young Hun would die. When Attila had released all his anger, he went back to his couch. "Ellac," he said softly, "now give your cake to your brother." Ellac's bruised fingers found the cake, which was lying with the overturned bowls in a puddle of blood, and he crawled to Ernac's feet with it and held it up. Ernac took it, studied it for a moment, and with his smile turning to a sneer (an expression which made him look much like his father), he rubbed the cake into Ellac's face. Attila, who seldom laughed, burst out laughing then, and his guests, who had been holding their breath throughout the ordeal, quickly joined him. Later, when I went with the others to clean up the mess, I found several of Ellac's teeth in it.

Attila slapped his other sons often—though never as violently as Ellac—for everything from dallying over their meals to speaking out of turn. But what was most disturbing was that one could never say when Attila would strike. He was generally quiet during meals, and after he had made his little speech, content to eat his meat and dates (which were the only foods that he would touch) and listen to the others, though he showed no real interest in what they were saying. As one could never tell when he was getting angry, the boys often overstepped their bounds. Sometimes Attila seemed not to notice, or, in any case, not to care. But other times his reactions came swiftly and seemingly out of nowhere. Young Ernac, with his fatuous grin, always gained from these displays, for after Attila had his revenge on whomever had annoyed him, he generally called Ernac to his side and stroked his cheek as if he were some small, furry animal.

Once, in the middle of a meal to which Attila's wives had been invited, Onegesius, Attila's first officer, came into the hall holding two Huns by the scruff of their necks. When Attila saw them he jumped up, again without any regard for his tray, and began to admonish them in a fierce voice. The men had been among Attila's troops when he had last marched, but they had run off and had only just been captured. At first there was much commotion. While Attila was shrieking at them, they were crying out vapid explanations for their desertion. Hereca, meanwhile, who was one of Attila's wives and the mother of Ellac, rushed to stand in front of the two deserters with her arms spread, for one was her uncle and the other her brother. Attila, who always had the war sword at his side, pushed Hereca out of the way, and with one blow, beheaded both men. For a moment there was no sound or motion in the entire hall save the thump of the bodies and the rolling of the heads on the floor. Then Attila turned to Hereca, the bloodied sword still steaming in his hand and his lips pulled so far back that one could see his molars. Hereca saw what was coming and went down on her knees immediately. There she covered Attila's feet with her kisses. I could hear her lips smacking all the way from the long table where I was standing with my fist in my mouth for fear of crying out. With the exception of Ellac, who was hiding his face in his hands, every eye was on the war sword, which was throbbing now and dripping blood over Hereca's head. Then Attila, who looked disgusted by the sight of the woman at his feet, made a decision, nonetheless, in her favor. The sword dropped to his side, and he contented himself instead with kicking Hereca several times while, between her shrieks and groans, she cried out praises and words of thanksgiving. When Attila had enough, he settled himself on his couch and called for more food. This was the cue for his guests to resume their meal and conversations. And thus, with no one daring to acknowledge the heads, the bodies, the spilt food, the river of blood, or Hereca, who lingered on the floor amid it all, the meal commenced.

On another occasion a Hun was brought in who had been accused of fondling one of Attila's wives. This time Attila took his time about getting up from his couch. He even took the time to place his tray on the floor. In a low voice, he asked the man to hold out the hand he had used to touch his wife. Attila's look, as he studied the hand, was merely amused. I waited for him to laugh, as he had on other occasions when I had expected worse. But he took a step back from the outstretched hand suddenly and raised his sword. The next thing I saw was the Hun's hand flying in the air. It landed on one of the tables, in the bowl that Scotta, another of Attila's officers, had been eating from. While Attila climbed back onto his couch, the man went running out the door screaming and holding his bloody limb. Scotta stared at the hand with his eyes wide, as if he had never seen such a horrible sight. Attila smiled at Scotta, and Scotta quickly adjusted his expression likewise, and, snapping his fingers in the air, called for a new bowl. But then just as everyone began to converse again, Attila leaped up with his sword and threatened to cut off Scotta's hand if he did not take the Hun's hand out of his sight.

By early Spring, my knowledge of the Hun language was adequate enough to enable me to decipher Attila's objectives when he made plans to march again. There was a tribe of Huns who were still living independently of Attila near the Black Sea. The chieftains among these Huns had been receiving gifts for some time from the rulers of the Eastern Empire, who wanted to buy their allegiance. But one of these chieftains, a man called Curidachus, was at odds with others. Curidachus had sent a messenger to Attila to say that he would vow his allegiance to him if Attila would cut down the other chieftains. Attila, after consulting with his soothsayers, agreed. And when the guard failed to come for me a few evenings thereafter, I knew that Attila was already marching.

He was gone only twenty days. But during that time I lived like a prisoner again, and I was happy enough when the ordeal was over. Unlike the occasion of Attila's return after the Roman siege, there was no celebration this time. And thus I hoped to learn that the battle had gone badly for Attila. But this was not the case. Though no one spoke of the attack on the evening of Attila's return, on the one following, a messenger from Curidachus was ushered into the hall by Onegesius. He announced that he had come to thank Attila for cutting down the other chieftains and bringing peace again to their tribe. He said, too, that Curidachus would not fail to implement the terms of their agreement.

Attila put his tray aside and got to his feet. He looked the messenger over for a long time before he spoke. Then he said, "If Curidachus is so grateful, then how is it that he did not come to thank Attila himself?" Though his query had been put forth mildly, I saw that his fingers were clenching the hilt of his sword, and I held my breath as I went among Attila's guests with the wine jug.

The messenger bowed his head low and responded, "It is difficult for a man to gaze upon a god, for if it be impossible to look upon the orb of the sun, how could one behold the greatest of gods without injury?" Whether this had been a part of Curidachus's message or invented by the messenger on the spot to save his own skin, I could not guess.

But Attila appeared to be well satisfied, for he smiled and nodded thoughtfully. Then his black eyes darted to Ellac. He put his sword aside and went to stand behind his eldest son, placing both hands on his shoulders. "Tell your master," he said to the messenger, "that in my great love for him, I have decided to grant him an even greater boon. This fine young man, Ellac, my first born, will return with you. Onegesius will ride to install him beside Curidachus to help govern over your people. With Ellac ruling at his side, I have no doubt that your peace will be long lasting."

Ellac's terrified expression and the snide look that Attila exchanged with Ernac assured me that this was no more a tribute for Ellac than it was for Curidachus. And when I saw that Ellac and Onegesius were not present the following evening, I knew that Attila had wasted no time in sending him off.

The seasons changed again, and other than the fact that Aetius had sent Attila a new scribe, I learned no news—though Attila dined, more often than not now, with only his closest officers, and they conducted much of their conversations in whispers. Nor did the strangeness of seeing Edeco day after day and never having the opportunity to speak a word to him dissipate. He seemed not to notice me at all now, and I came to think that he had forgotten me altogether, along with the thoughts which I had once stirred in him. In fact, even Attila grew lax in his concern for me, for although I continued to be guarded over when I was in my hut, I was told by one of the other women that I might begin to make my way to the palace in the evenings by myself. And thus I went through the village alone each evening, happy enough to be free for a time, and always hoping that I would run into Edeco on my way, always planning what few words I would say to him before he rushed away—for though I continued to long for my own people, my darling daughter particularly, it was now a hopeless longing that I did not expect ever to be gratified. My life was in Pannonia now. And if I had ever truly believed that the time would come when I would find a way to cut Attila down and leave his wretched city, I did not believe it any longer. In fact, when I thought of it now, I laughed at myself, as people will laugh at the antics they devised as children.

One evening Edeco was not present at dinner. As there were occasions when Attila's chief officers did not appear, I made little of it. But I realized the following evening that Orestes, Attila's Roman, was not about either. And when a few evenings more passed without either of them, I began to suspect that Attila had sent them off on some mission, perhaps to the Eastern Empire. I had once heard Attila tell his men that although the Eastern Empire had been prompt in paying its tributes, they had failed to return all of the Hun fugitives he had demanded, and they had not yet evacuated some lands south of the Danube which they had promised to him as a part of their treaty agreement. I decided that these were the matters that Edeco and Orestes had gone to negotiate. I missed Edeco's presence sorely. I had no idea how far away Constantinople was, but I imagined it was a good distance, and I did not expect to see him again for some time.

One afternoon during the Summer, one of the Hun women came to tell me that I would not be needed in the palace for some days. When the woman saw my look of concern, she laughed and explained that Attila was only marching to a Hun village to the east of the City of Attila where he would take yet another wife, a woman called Eskam whom the soothsayers promised would bear him many sons. And thus, when I heard a horse galloping toward my hut some five evenings later, I assumed that Attila and his bride were back, and that with the other women rushing to prepare to serve (for it was already dark by then), this rider was a guard coming to tell me to get myself to the palace immediately. And I was pleased, for my five days alone in the hut had been as objectionable as any of the longer periods. I got to my feet, and running my comb hastily through my hair, I pulled back the curtain. Edeco was just dismounting. I dropped the comb and stepped back from the doorway.

As if he had been riding hard for some time, Edeco was breathless, but he was smiling too, and looking at me with some pleasure in his eye. He stooped down to retrieve the comb and held it out to me. "I am back," he announced.

"Aye, I can see that for myself," I mumbled.

"Would you like to know where I have been and what I have been about?"

I hesitated to answer. But as Edeco's smile seemed genuine, I answered honestly, saying, "I suspect you went to Constantinople to negotiate on Attila's behalf."

He pointed a finger at me. "You are a clever woman. That is it exactly. And while I was there, something out of the ordinary occurred. Would you like me to tell you about it?"

"Do," I urged, trying to conceal my delight in his presence.

His eye fell on my wine jug. I sat down quickly and patted the spot across from me. Edeco sat, too, and took a deep swallow from the jug.

"Well," he said, wiping his mouth on his sleeve, "let me think where to begin. I went to Constantinople with a message for the Emperor, Theodosius. Orestes, who speaks the Roman tongue, went with me. And after we had passed Attila's message on to Theodosius, a certain Roman noble called Bigilas, a man who speaks my language as well as others, called me aside. And so, leaving Orestes to fend for himself in the Emperor's palace, I went with this Bigilas to the palace of Chrysaphius, another Roman noble, a eunuch much favored by Theodosius. The palace of this eunuch was splendid, immense and full of riches. And as I had not expected one of Theodosius's men to have a palace comparable to his own, I suppose I exclaimed. And the look that I saw pass between Bigilas and Chrysaphius assured me that my exclamation was precisely the sign they had been hoping for."

"What sign?" I asked, confused.

"Why, that I could be bribed."

"They bribed you?"

"Aye. Let me get to the heart of it. They promised me that if I would kill Attila, I could return to Constantinople with my sons and live in a palace just like Chrysaphius's, and that my sons would be nobles. So you see, Ildico, the vision you foresaw so long ago was not a portent of my son's future. It was merely a portent of the bribery I was to encounter. You must have misinterpreted."

"Ah," I said, "I wondered myself whether I had misconstrued the meaning of that vision. What did you say to these Romans, Bigilas and Chrysaphius?"

"I told them I would need fifty pounds of gold to pay the men I would need to help me carry out the deed."

I leaned toward him and looked deep into his bright Thuet eyes. "What happened next?" I asked.

"Chrysaphius got up from his chair as if he would go and fetch the gold right then and there. But I told him that Orestes was certainly already suspicious, and that if I returned with a sack of gold, he would only be made more so. Orestes, I assured them, was not to be trusted and would have to remain outside our conspiracy. Then we set about making our plans. I decided that Bigilas must be permitted to return with me to the City of Attila, ostensibly to translate Attila's response to the letter Theodosius was preparing for him, but in fact, so that after I had a chance to talk to the men I would include in the conspiracy, that I could send Bigilas back with instructions on how best to deliver the gold at some later date.

"Chrysaphius was well pleased, though it was clear that Bigilas had no desire to travel to the City of Attila. Still, he agreed to do so, and when we met the next day, Chrysaphius told me that he had spoken to Theodosius and that Theodosius thought we should also bring Maximus back with us—Maximus being a noble who is known to Attila—to carry Theodosius's letter. This Maximus, and his advisor, who was also to come, would know nothing of our plot.

"During the course of our travels I conspired further with Bigilas. One night I had him sneak to Maximus's side while Maximus was asleep and steal Theodosius's letter. It was unsealed, and Bigilas was able to read me its contents. He replaced it before morning with no one the wiser.

"When we reached Pannonia, Orestes and I left the Romans pitching their tents on the plain and rode here. We learned that Attila had ridden to take a new bride. We rode to find him right away, to inform him of the arrival of the Romans. He was very angry at first. In his letter to Theodosius, he had been adamant that no one but the highest ranking ambassadors should come to Pannonia, and Maximus is not one of them. But when we told him that the Roman delegation included Bigilas, and that Bigilas had conspired against him on behalf of Theodosius, he was amused, and very pleased." Edeco hesitated.

I took a deep breath. "Why should this please Attila?" I asked. "I should have thought he would only be made more angry."

"Why, Ildico, he was pleased on several counts. I wonder that you fail to realize. First of all, this knowledge gives him yet more leverage with Theodosius. Surely, you see that now he can insist that his tributes be increased. And Bigilas and Chrysaphius will be made to pay Attila for their lives—indeed, if they are spared—from their own personal riches. And keep in mind, too, that Attila is a suspicious man. There is always the risk that one of his officers may be tempted to conspire against him. Certainly plenty of his lesser men have attempted it. This event gave Orestes and me the opportunity to prove our loyalty to Attila, for a thing as precarious as the pledge of loyalty must always be renewed. And that, Ildico, pleased him very much."

No, Edeco, I thought to myself, *This event gave you the opportunity to prove your loyalty to Attila to me, and perhaps to yourself as well.* "And in turn," I said, "I suppose you will gain yourself from all this?"

Edeco beamed. "I already have. While we were enroute, we stopped at a village called Sardica where Maximus knew some people. They put us up for the night and prepared a banquet in our honor. There was plenty of good wine, and there was much toasting among us. Orestes toasted to Attila. Then the Romans toasted Theodosius. But Bigilas, who was drunk, shouted out that a god, meaning Theodosius, should not be toasted in the same breath as a mere man, meaning Attila. Then Orestes drew his sword, and I did too, as Bigilas must have known we would. And the other Romans, afraid that we would cut down Bigilas on the spot, offered us pearls and silks to spare his life. Look here."

Edeco fumbled in the goatskin pouch that hung from his neck. Then he held his hand out beside the taper. The stones that glimmered in his palm, four white and one black, were made even more lustrous by the sight of the scarred skin beneath them. "Do you know where these come from, Ildico?"

I shook my head.

"From the bottom of the sea. They are very precious."

I picked up the black pearl and studied it while Edeco slipped the others back into his pouch. "I will have these set in gold and made into an arm ring. The black one is more rare than the others. You may keep it."

I looked up at Edeco then, wondering why he should want to give me a gift now, when the last time I had spoken to him, he had threatened to have me killed. He returned my look with a tenacious stare, and all at once I realized that this was no gift at all. I was to pay for the pearl with my unspoken pledge never again to speak to Edeco from my heart on matters concerning Attila. I bowed my head and thanked him for his gift with the Hunnish words that he had taught me.

He smiled and relaxed. "After we told Attila about the plot, we told him how I had gotten Bigilas to read Theodosius's letter and what it said." He laughed. "You should have seen how pleased Attila was to see how cunningly I had played poor Bigilas. He told us to ride back to the Romans and tell them that he had no need to meet with them since he already knew the contents of Theodosius's letter. We could hardly keep from laughing when we saw the expression that came over Bigilas's face then. He could not decide whether we had betrayed him or not. And Maximus's face! Ho! That was something, for he knew of course that there was a traitor in the group. And while they were all exchanging looks, we told them that they might spend the night on the plain, but that in the morning they were to leave. Then we left them to quarrel amongst themselves and to consider what new offering they might make to gain Attila's ear. In the morning, we sent Scotta out to them to tell them to be gone. And as we had hoped, they promised more gold, more silks, more pearls, if only Attila would hear them. Scotta, who already had his orders, rode out of their sight, waited a time, and then returned to say that he had pleaded with Attila on their behalf and that Attila had agreed to grant them an audience as soon as he had married Eskam and returned to the City of Attila. He marries her tomorrow. I have got to ride back tonight so as to be in attendance at the wedding. Then we will all return together, Attila and Eskam and the Romans."

"What will Attila do to Bigilas?" I asked.

Edeco shrugged. "Only Attila knows that. But keep your eyes and ears open when you come to the palace to serve, and you will see how a great man makes the most of a perverse situation."

"I have already seen that," I said looking up into Edeco's eyes.

He acknowledged my compliment with a modest smile. "I must be off now," he mumbled, but he continued to stare at me motionlessly. Then he took my hand, wherein the pearl was yet enclosed and said, "I thought about you often while I was away, and I came to understand that when a woman is left alone, with no companions and no freedom to wander, her imagination is bound to turn on her. I hold myself responsible for the treasonous thoughts you once held. I should have pressed Attila to take you into service sooner, for once I saw you in his hall, working diligently and getting on so well with the other women, it was clear to me that you were yourself again, no more than a poor, lonely woman who came to the City of Attila to bring a god a gift, and perhaps to find a little adventure. My trust in you is restored."

"You are a wise man," I whispered.

And thus, on this deceit, our friendship was renewed.

Chapter 11

Attila's return with Eskam seemed as much a celebration as had his return from the Eastern Empire. Girls sang and tossed flowers. Women carried canopies over the heads of the girls and sang too. All the men who were not marching were prostrate. This time I was well to the back of the crowd in the courtyard and able to lift my head high as Attila and his entourage went by. Eskam, I noted, was a mere child, not even as old as my young Hunnish friend. She rode behind Attila with her head lowered and most of her face covered by her long, black locks. I saw Onegesius among the officers who rode behind her, and I concluded that he had just returned from installing Ellac to rule beside Curidachus.

As the servants were supposed to come in just after Attila—if they were not in already—I scrambled to my feet and fought my way through the crowd when I saw that he had entered. But Attila had invited a great many guests that evening, and there was already a throng at the entrance when I got there. "What do you think of Attila's new wife?" a voice behind me asked while I waited my turn to enter.

Startled to think that Edeco would speak to me so casually in public and with his fellow officers all about, I answered in a whisper, barely turning my head, "She is too young to appreciate her new status."

"Perhaps you are jealous," Edeco said.

I turned my astonished face toward him then. "That she should marry Attila?"

"No, of the girl's youth."

I turned away again, saying, "Aye, you may be right. My own is behind me. As near as I can figure, I have just turned twenty-three."

Edeco came up so close behind me that I could feel his breath on my ear. "Why did you fail to tell me? I would have brought you a gift."

"You did," I whispered.

He grumbled. "A loose pearl? That is no gift. I will take it back tonight and have it set on a gold chain that you can wear around your neck."

"No more," I cautioned, for we were almost to the door now, and I could see Attila's feet crossed at the end of his couch between the few heads still before us.

But Edeco only laughed and whispered, "Do not worry. My bond with him is stronger than ever."

I smiled. I had thought of myself as a servant for so long now that I had forgotten that in truth I was the daughter of a king. I was about to step into the hall when someone cut into the line in front of me, almost knocking me down. To my surprise, it was Ellac. "He fell from his horse and broke his wrist," Edeco whispered as Ellac went in. "Onegesius had to bring him back." And he began to laugh anew.

Edeco's boldness lifted my spirits, and I found myself humming as I carried over the tables with the other servants. The Romans entered, and as each one prostrated himself, Attila saluted him by name. I heard the name Maximus, and several others which were unfamiliar to me, but not Bigilas. I imagined that Bigilas was chained somewhere, perhaps outside the city gates, and I was pleased, in spite of my curiosity, to think that there would be no heads for me to have to step around that night. After a brief speech acknowledging the Romans and introducing Eskam, Attila gave the nod which was meant to inform the guards that Zerco should be brought in. Later, when the guests had had enough of him, Attila nodded again, and Zerco was rushed out. Then Attila nodded once more, and three of his sons stood up and began to sing the familiar song praising their father. But unlike the girls and the women, who had only sung the usual verses comparing Attila to the sun and the moon and the stars, his sons sang, too, of his battles and his victories.

At first I thought it odd that these people who sang so seldom should bother to add verses to their only song, but when the boys began to sing of the Roman siege and all the Romans who had died in it, I understood well enough. Nor was the effort lost on Attila's Roman guests, some of whom broke down and wept openly while Attila sat with his black eyes set on nothing and his lips quivering ever so slightly at the corners. Looking at him, I felt a rush of hatred, and it put an end to my good humor.

"This I never thought to see," I exclaimed later when Edeco came into my hut carrying my dinner tray. I leapt up promptly to take it from him.

"Think of me as your personal slave," Edeco mumbled.

I set the tray down beside my taper and glanced at him over my shoulder. I was astonished to find that he looked entirely serious. I forced a laugh. "Then I command you to sit and share my wine with me," I said. Edeco sat, but he continued to stare at me, his expression somber and intense. I could make no sense of the man. I thought of the pearl that he had given me, and of the pledge that I had made, albeit to myself, when I accepted it. "Where was Bigilas?" I asked.

Edeco sighed and took a chunk of bread from the tray. He turned it over in his hand and replaced it. "Last night after I left you and rode back to Attila's camp, Attila ordered me to ride to the Roman camp and bring the Romans to him. I had to wake them up. Then I stood outside Attila's tent while he admonished them on matters concerning Theodosius's letter. He never mentioned the conspiracy. When the Romans came out, I did as Attila had bade me and pulled Bigilas aside and ordered him to ride back to Constantinople for the fifty pounds of gold. So, to answer your question, Bigilas is somewhere between here and the Eastern Empire."

Edeco had been watching my hand travel from my bowl to my mouth and back again, and thinking that perhaps he was hungry, I lifted the bowl and held it out to him, but he only shook his head. "Who were all the Romans?" I asked. "There seemed to be far more than your account last night suggested."

As if his enthusiasm over the Roman intrigue had dissipated, Edeco sighed once more. Then he got up slowly and went behind me. When he reappeared, he had one of the skins in his hand. He rolled it up, and stretching himself out along the ground, he propped it up under one arm so that now I thought he must be tired or ill. "Some of them were from the Western Empire. They came to negotiate with Attila on some matter of their own. Apparently they did not expect to find their fellows here, for there was much exclaiming among them when they encountered one another. We put them up at one of the houses within Onegesius's palisade. We have men surrounding their quarters. We are sure to learn some useful information."

Again I scrutinized Edeco's face, for it seemed to me that he had related much more than he ought have. In a wavering voice, I asked, "What business have the Western Romans with Attila?"

Edeco looked up at me. "I do not know. Attila has yet to give them a private audience." Then he bit his lip and looked down at his hand, which he had turned palm up so that his scar was in evidence. "There is something more, Ildico. There are Thuets here as well. They arrived while Attila was out of the city."

I slowly replaced the piece of meat that I had been about to bite into. "Thuets?"

"Franks, like your Sigurd."

"But why—?"

"Again, I do not know. I doubt Attila will see them while the Romans are still here."

I could only stare. As if he read my thoughts, Edeco reached out and took my hand. It lay limp in his, and after a moment, he dropped it and sat up. "I almost forgot," he said stiffly. "I came for the pearl."

I had forgotten the pearl myself. I got up now to retrieve it from the battered wooden bowl which I had brought from home so long ago to remind me of Guthorm. When I turned with it, Edeco was already on his feet.

Edeco's candidness continued to such a degree in the days that followed that I often had to remind myself that I'd had proof of his cunning. Hidden somewhere beneath his new attitude, there was, perhaps, a design not unlike the one that had stirred him to manipulate Bigilas. But I was cautious only because logic informed me that I should be. In my heart, I continued to believe that Edeco would let no harm come to me. Even if I had not believed that, I would have been grateful for his company now that I was entirely resigned to living out my life in the City of Attila and could ask for little more than to have a friend who would look after me and bring me news of the world to fill my mind during its restless hours.

I learned from Edeco that the Romans from the Western Empire had come to Attila on behalf of their Emperor, Valentinian, to ensure the peace between them. This led me to wonder whether they had some reason to suspect that it was at risk. But when I mentioned this to Edeco, he said merely that all leaders must now see that it behooved them to pay tribute to the man who would soon rule the world. When the Romans were gone, the Franks became Attila's dinner guests for three consecutive evenings, but, as I had hoped, there was none among them whom I recognized or who seemed to recognize me. And as for the war sword, I concluded that even if one of them had recognized it as Sigurd's, he would have realized that it would profit him not at all to query Attila about his most precious possession. Edeco informed me that the Frank leader, who had been ousted by his brother for claiming his legal right to the throne, had come to appeal to Attila to take his side against his brother. I recalled that Sigurd had told me once that a cousin of his was inclined toward Attila. This concerned me at first. If the Franks were dividing for war, then surely my own brothers would come out on the side of the Frank's brother—and thus against Attila. But Edeco, who gave no hint that he knew the cause of my concern, assured me that although Attila had promised to come to the aid of the ousted brother in the future, he had no intention of actually doing so. The Franks who had come to Pannonia represented too small a tribe for him to bother about. But to placate them, Attila had given them quarters beyond the city gates, and the guarantee of further discussions in the future.

One evening during dinner, several guards came in dragging two Romans—a man and a boy. When Attila saw them, he stood up and called Edeco to his side. I put aside the wine jug I had just taken up and turned to watch. Attila clapped Edeco on the back and said, "Friend, look who has come to visit us. Why, it is your accomplice, Bigilas. And he has brought his boy along with him."

"The Thuet lies," Bigilas shouted. "I made no bargain with him. I came to bring you gold, Attila, on behalf of Theodosius."

Attila moved away from Edeco and began to pace before Bigilas and his son with a sneer on his face, his dark eyes twinkling roguishly. "Let us have the truth, Bigilas," he said in a voice that was almost gentle.

Bigilas sank to his knees, so that the guards on either side of him had to bend over to keep their hold on him. He answered just as gently. "You have the truth. I swear it."

Attila moved toward the boy. When he was in front of him, he extended his arms and placed his hands on the boy's shoulders. The smile he offered the boy was much the same as the smile that came to his face when Ernac was about. But the child saw through it and began to pant and to look about himself as if for some means of escape. Attila's smile widened. His hands slid from the boy's shoulders to his neck. He caressed his neck gently for a moment, and then, sliding one finger under the boy's chin, he said to the guards who held him, "Take this child outside and dip your blade into this vein here."

Bigilas was on his feet immediately, and struggling against his guards, he cried, "No, not him! If you want blood, take mine."

Attila cocked his head. "Then let us have the truth, Bigilas," he whispered.

Bigilas slipped to the floor again and hung his head. When he lifted it, he fastened his hateful gaze on Edeco, who had been standing with his hands at his sides and his expression officious ever since Attila had summoned him.

Slowly, Bigilas began his account of the conspiracy. And except for the fact that he included a good many more details, it was just the same as the one Edeco had related to me. When Bigilas finished, Attila put his hands behind his back and began to pace. "Do you mean to say that you thought Edeco could be bought?"

"Yes," Bigilas whispered. "I thought that."

"Then Edeco must have given you cause," Attila shouted.

I gasped. Edeco stiffened. Bigilas smiled slightly, as if he saw in Attila's query his chance for revenge. Attila, meanwhile, went to stand before Edeco and shouted up into his face, "If he did not give you cause, then why is it that you did not choose to bribe Orestes or one of the others?"

Bigilas glanced at his son. Gradually his smile dissolved. He lowered his head and stammered, "Orestes, being a Roman, chose his allegiance to you. Edeco, being a Thuet, was forced to succumb."

Attila, whose eyes never left Edeco's face, said softly, "Edeco, is your loyalty to me forced?"

"No, master," Edeco said in a voice equally low.

"Louder!" Attila shouted, and then, more softly and with his sneer quivering on his face, "so that our friend Bigilas can hear you."

Edeco lowered his eyes to look into Attila's. "No, master," he repeated. "My loyalty cannot be bought for it is naught but the emblem of my love." The two men stared at each other, Attila with an eagerness about his face, Edeco with no expression at all. All at once, Attila's gaze swung over to the war sword, which was lying on his couch. As if he had heard it speak some tender word to him, he smiled at it with an affection in his eye which even Ernac's presence did not elicit. Then he turned to look again at Bigilas. "Does your boy understand our language?" he asked. Bigilas shook his head. "Then tell him for me that I wish him to inform Theodosius that the loyalty of my men cannot be bought. This knowledge will save your Emperor much gold in the future."

Bigilas scrambled to his feet. "I will tell Theodosius myself, Attila," he cried while the guards tightened their grip on his arms.

"Your boy will tell him," Attila shouted. Then he said to the guards, "Take this snake out of my sight and put him in chains."

Bigilas began to cry out pleas and was so intent in his reluctance to leave that the guards had to carry him bodily. Nor did his pleading abate when he was outside the door. "You and you," Attila said pointing. Orestes and another, Elsa, stood up. "Deliver the boy to Theodosius. Tell him that the boy and the eunuch are to return with another fifty pounds of gold. Then, if I see fit, I will release Bigilas."

Thinking that perhaps Attila meant for them to finish their meals and ride in the morning, Orestes and Elsa hesitated. But Attila shouted, "Now!" and they stumbled over each other to reach the boy and the door.

Then Attila turned back to Edeco, who was still standing at attention. The hall was so quiet that Bigilas could still be heard crying off in the distance. With something sinister at play in the darkness of his eyes, Attila whispered, "Get out of here, all of you." Then his eyes swept from Edeco to those who had gathered at the long table, and leaving the tables just as they were, the servants ran out with the others.

That night I said to Edeco, "What if Bigilas had lied? I could see in his face that he considered it. He might have said anything in his anger. Had his son not been there, he might have told Attila that you gave him some clear indication that you were ripe to be bribed. That it was only later that you changed your mind and decided to disclose the conspiracy."

Edeco's mouth dropped open and his eyes grew large. Then his look changed to one of indignation. "He would not have been believed," Edeco declared. But his mood had been sullen since he had come to my hut, and it was apparent that he was as shaken as I was. He turned his head aside and stared at the north wall of the hut for a long time. I watched him carefully, wishing I knew what he was thinking. I was tempted to persist, to insist that he allow that he had been afraid, for if he admitted that, he would have to concede, too, that his bond with Attila was not as strong as he had once thought. But all at once a half-smile rose to Edeco's face, and, reaching into his pouch, he turned back to me. His hand emerged with the black pearl, set in a gold ring now and dangling from a gold chain. I took it from him and studied it. Then I slipped it over my head. Rubbing the smooth stone against my chin, once again I vowed, silently, to keep myself worthy of Edeco's friendship, the only pleasure left to me.

In the Spring, Orestes and Elsa returned with Bigilas's son. I did not see the boy because Attila marched out with an army of men—Edeco among them—to meet him on the plain. Still, Edeco informed me of all that had transpired. To appease Attila for his serious offense, Theodosius had sent the boy back with two high-ranking officers whom Attila had met with in the past. They presented Attila with the additional fifty pounds of gold, and in return, Attila gave them Bigilas. The eunuch had not come, but to make up for this, Theodosius's officers gave Attila other gifts.

I found Attila's leniency here amazing. I would have thought that he would have been furious to learn that the eunuch was not within the delegation. And I had been certain all along that Attila would kill Bigilas—perhaps before his son's eyes—before he let the Romans return to Constantinople. But when I said all this to Edeco, he shrugged and told me more about the Roman officers. They had pleaded with Attila, once the other matter had been resolved, to give up his claim on the lands south of the Danube. And here, too, Attila had consented.

"There will be peace then," I stated, bewildered.

"Aye, peace," Edeco mumbled. "We have given Theodosius everything he wants, and in return he has promised to keep up with his tributes and stay out of our affairs."

"Yet it seems to me," I ventured, "that Attila has given up more, since he has given up the lands I have heard him speak of as his own."

"Seems, Ildico," Edeco said, his eyes brightening. "And so it will seem to Theodosius, too. While the Emperor is speculating on the true meaning of Attila's complacency, Attila is free to turn his mind to other matters."

I straightened. "What matters are those, Edeco?" I asked, though I was afraid to hear the answer. While I watched Edeco chew his lips, as if he could not decide whether or not he should respond, I reached for the pearl and rubbed its smooth surface against my lips. It was my habit now to play with the thing.

Finally, Edeco smiled—cunningly, I thought. "Time is a stream ever flowing, Ildico," he said. "If one waits long enough, one finds the headwaters at one's feet."

I did not have to wait very long at all to find myself submerged in Edeco's headwaters, for only a few days later, two guards ushered two

Romans into Attila's hall during the evening meal. The one who spoke in the Hunnish tongue declared that they had come from the Western Empire and that he was a translator for his companion, who was a noble. The translator's Hunnish was not very good, and I was too far away to hear much anyway, but I heard the name 'Honoria' repeated several times in the course of his speech. After the last time it was spoken, the Roman noble bowed low and put some small object into Attila's open hand. Attila's fingers closed around it quickly while the fingers of his other hand went prowling through his scanty beard—a gesture indicating that he was considering something. He kept his eyes fastened on the noble. After a moment, he began to nod very slowly and deliberately. Then he turned to Onegesius and said, "Take these men to one of your houses. Make sure they are fed and made comfortable."

As it was unlike Attila not to invite gift-bearing guests who arrived during the meal to sit and share it, I surmised that this Honoria was a matter of such import that Attila was reluctant to discuss it even in front of his best men—who were the only ones in attendance that night. I kept my eye on Attila as I went about pouring wine for the assemblage. For a long time he sat with his fingers tight around his gift and stared off toward his bower. Then all at once he cocked his head and looked at his men with surprise, as if he had only just realized that he was sitting among them with his tray on his lap. "You may go now," he whispered. And his men, who had also been watching him expectantly, pushed their bowls aside noiselessly and filed out. Not long after, Attila dismissed his servants as well.

I paced and waited for Edeco to come. Although he came to my hut perhaps only one evening out of every ten, I could count on him to be there when something of interest had occurred. When I heard a horse approaching, I sat down so as not to appear anxious. Still, when Edeco entered, I found myself blurting out, "Who is this Honoria and what gift did she give Attila?"

Edeco's smile waned. "Honoria is the sister of Valentinian, the Emperor in the West," he declared coldly.

One of the Hun women came in with the dinner tray. Edeco and I stared at each other until she was gone. "And her gift?" I asked. "What does it portend?"

"Her gift was her ring. As to what it portends, you must have noticed, I had no chance to discover." Edeco shook his head, as if to dispel some dark thought that had invaded it. Then he sat down. "She's been out of favor in Ravenna for some time. My guess is that she sent her messenger to ask Attila to take her side against her brother."

"War with the Western Empire?" I cried, unable to conceal my alarm. Edeco eyed me irritably. But as my brothers were allies of the Western Romans, in dictate if not in spirit, I did not care that Edeco seemed in no mind to answer my questions tonight. "But there cannot be a war," I exclaimed. "Why, Attila and Aetius are friends . . . have always been friends. It was not so long ago that Aetius sent a scribe—"

"I cannot think why you bother to ask me questions when it seems you are capable of answering them yourself," Edeco cried, turning his head aside.

My own head was spinning so that I hardly heard him. "Does Attila even know this Honoria?"

Edeco shook his head. "He has never met her."

"Why is she out of favor in Ravenna?"

Edeco sighed. His look was the exasperated one that a mother bestows on a child who will not quiet. "Honoria had a palace in Ravenna," he began, spitting out his words. "It was managed by a steward called Eugenius. As her brother, the Emperor, has no children—his wife, it is said, is a virgin—there are many nobles in Ravenna who have sought to marry Honoria and produce royal offspring. But Honoria fornicated with her steward, Eugenius. And when Valentinian learned that she was pregnant, he had Eugenius killed. These events are recent. Whether or not she has delivered the child yet, I do not know. In any case, Honoria was banished to the Eastern Empire. But we learned from the Romans who came with Bigilas's son that her mother asked Theodosius to allow her to return. Her brother will most likely want to find her a suitable husband before she gets herself into any more trouble. But as she has sent her ring to Attila, I would say it is already too late. There. Now you have it, Ildico. Now you know as much as I do." And with that, Edeco got to his feet.

"So soon, friend?" I cried. "Stay and share my wine . . . and my meal as well. I observed that you had no chance to finish your own tonight."

"You use me, Ildico," he whispered, squinting down at me. "I am nothing to you but a source of information, whether to satisfy your curiosity or something worse, I do not care to guess."

I sprang to my feet. "It is true that without you I should be living in the dark without any knowledge of the world. But you mean much more to me than that."

"Do I, Ildico? I wonder. Your concern is never for me, for the affairs that complicate my life. You would rather know what Theodosius is about or who is Honoria."

"You led me to think that you were happy enough to share such knowledge with me. What am I to think? Your moods are more numerous than the trophies than hang from Attila's walls."

Edeco continued as if he had not heard me. "And there was a time when you shared your knowledge with me as well, but—" He broke off and turned away from me.

Amazed, I asked softly, "Can you mean my vision for your son?"

"No more," Edeco whispered, and he bolted out the door.

It was the young Hun girl who came to my hut the following day to tell me that I need not come to serve that evening. "What? Have they marched already?" I exclaimed unthinkingly.

"They have gone off," the girl responded, her dark eyes darting toward the guard pacing beyond the open curtain.

I did not sleep at all that night, nor the one after, for I was thinking of the danger my brothers might soon find themselves in. I told myself over and over that Attila could not have prepared for war so quickly, but still I paced and bit my nails and imagined that he had. On the third night, when I was so tired that I could no longer hold a thought together, I drank a good deal of wine in the hopes of finally getting some sleep. Finally I felt myself drifting . . . and soon I found myself caught in a dream in which there was a man watching me from the doorway.

He was silhouetted by the moonlight that streamed in through the gap in the curtain where his hand clutched it. I had blown out my taper; I could not see his face. "There will be war," he said.

Ah, it is only Edeco, I thought, and I took a deep breath while his declaration lapped at the edge of my consciousness. Then it entered. As I was getting up on one elbow, straining to break out of my slumber, he let go of the curtain and put an end to the stream of light behind him. "Theodosius is dead," he stated. "Marcian, the new Emperor, has sent an embassy to say that we can no longer expect tributes from the Eastern Empire."

Relieved, I sighed and let my head fall back onto the pile of skins. "Then you will march on the Eastern Empire," I heard myself mumble.

"And so I thought, too, at first. But Attila has decided to take Honoria's ring as a pledge of their betrothal. For her dowry, he wants half the Western Empire."

I made a noise in the dark, a cry such as an animal makes when it is cornered. Edeco went on. "Two of our embassies leave the City of Attila tomorrow. One will go to Constantinople to inform Marcian that war will result if he does not reconsider on this matter of tributes. The other will go to Ravenna to warn Valentinian that he had best not let any harm befall Honoria as Attila claims her as his wife."

I made no answer for a long time. I had begun to dream of my brothers, to see their dear faces floating before me in the dark. Edeco's words seemed a dream within a dream, and when at last they reached me, I asked, "In which direction will you ride?"

"Neither," he said stiffly, "though it pleases me to see that you bother to ask. I am to stay here to help Attila prepare for war." I went so far back into the dream of my brothers that I was startled when he spoke again. "There is more," he said. His tone was urgent, and it sent my brothers' images spiraling away. Now I could imagine Edeco's officious expression in the dark. It struck me all at once how strange it was to be dreaming of a voice in the dark, and I wondered whether I had ever had such a dream before. Edeco said, "I will not be coming to visit you here again, Ildico. Last night, while we were riding back from the plain where we had gone to meet with Marcian's embassy, I asked Attila to grant me permission to marry you. He was very kind. He took me aside, and we made a fire up on a knoll while the others rode for home. He explained that he has come to believe that all his good fortune in recent times—his successful march on the Eastern Empire, his uniting of the Huns, and now Honoria and her ring—are a result of the powers of the war sword. For a long time, he said, he thought it was enough to keep you alive to ensure that the sword would continue to bring him fortunes. But he saw that as he permitted you more freedoms, his fortunes increased proportionately. Ildico, Honoria is not the only woman Attila intends to marry. You will be his wife as well . . . though I doubt it will be soon. He is inclined to wait until these new events have taken their shape."

There was a silence for a long time, so that I wondered whether my dream of Edeco had passed from me. But then Edeco's voice came again out of the darkness, closer now than it had been before. "I must go, Ildico. I had Attila's permission to come to you tonight, for I made him see that I should be the one to tell you this news. In the future, I would be risking my life to come to you. No man would dare to be caught with any woman to whom Attila has laid claim. As of now, you are betrothed to him."

I heard myself laughing, and then Edeco's voice saying, "Is there humor in all this?"

"Attila seldom looks at me, Edeco," I whispered.

"A woman is a woman to Attila. You brought him the war sword of the gods, and thus he will marry you. It is that simple."

His voice was so close now that I thought he must be leaning just over me. I reached out my hand to touch him, but it sliced though the air and hit on nothing. "And you, Edeco? What is a woman to you?"

He hesitated. "Until I met you, nothing more."

"And how am I so different?"

"You have courage. Your heart is the heart of a man."

I had courage, I mused. It seemed strange that Edeco should think I had it still, and stranger yet that he should mention it when it had brought him only agitation in the past. My sudden recollection that all my courage was gone from me, that the thing that I had once admired so in myself had been as fleeting as it was precious, frightened me, and I cried out, "Hold me, Edeco. I am all alone."

"Do not tempt me woman," Edeco replied harshly.

Again a silence fell between us, and now I thought I could see the silence and the darkness merging and revolving around the place where I lay and where I imagined Edeco stood. Then Edeco's voice came again. "I must have the pearl back."

My fingers, which had been around it the whole time, tightened. "It has meaning for me, Edeco. I cannot give it up."

"Do not make me linger, Ildico. I betray Attila more by the moment."

"Betray? You use the word lightly tonight."

"Do I?"

I wished that I could see his face. I tried to make it materialize, but I had no power to do so. "What are you saying to me, Edeco? All this talk of courage and betrayal . . . . What does it mean?"

"Give me the pearl, Ildico."

I slipped the necklace over my head obediently. Then I reached out and found his outstretched hand. Our fingertips grasped and fumbled. "When you first gave it to me," I whispered breathlessly, "I promised myself that I would never again speak to you from my heart on matters where we have disagreed in the past. But now that you have taken it back—"

"Aye. I have set you free," he interrupted.

I could not imagine why I had said such a thing to Edeco. Nor could I imagine why he had answered as he had. And moreover, I had long since given up my ambitions. They had gone the way of my courage. To name them now seemed a travesty, a distortion of the truth. "I am sorry I caused you so much pain, so much confusion," I said, thinking to end it there. But then I said to myself, *This is only a dream, a senseless fantasy in which all things are possible and no one need account for them.* "I came to the City of Attila with no purpose other than to cut Attila down," I whispered, and I braced myself to be struck or kicked by Edeco's phantom.

"Then I will do what I can to advise you," Edeco whispered back, "though I cannot imagine that it will do any good. And as for myself, I will never play an active part in any plans that you may conjure. My heart is the heart of a coward—of a slave, as you were once kind enough to point out."

My heart is the heart of a coward's, too, I mused, and my mind stretched to take in all the nights and nights that I had bent over Attila to place his tray on his lap. On any one of them, I might have reached for the war sword. I might have tried. "I understand," I said. "You have your sons to think about."

"Were I thinking of my sons, I should pledge myself over to you completely. I think of myself, Ildico."

"No. You think of more than yourself, or these words would not be passing between us."

Again he sighed. "I do not know what I think of anymore. I think of my position with Attila, tainted now somehow by the very thing I sought to strengthen it. I loved him well enough until . . . . And I think of the vision you foresaw—a vision which lived in my own heart beside my love for Attila, though it was more a fantasy . . . until you saw it too. And I think of you, Ildico . . . . I would like to think that I came to all this from some place other than my feeling for you, but I cannot be sure. I am greedy for many things, and they are all in conflict."

In my dream state, Edeco's talk of visions only served to confuse me. But I had not failed to grasp his declaration of love. And that awakened my own emotion. "When Attila is dead," I whispered, "I will be honored to be your wife."

He was silent for a moment. "I told Attila that I would come directly to the palace and let him know how it went with you."

"Tell him I detained you with my joy. Tell him I fell to my knees crying, 'At last I know why the war sword led me here.'"

"I shall, Ildico."

The darkness swirled, sucking the silence into it. "But you must tell him, too, that I have no friend other than Edeco. You must be allowed to continue to come to me."

But to this Edeco made no answer, for he had already gone.

When I awoke the next morning, I was amused to think that I had dreamed so vividly, and I regretted that I could never share my dream with my friend, for how could I relate to Edeco a dream wherein he denounced his master? Smiling, I reached up to fondle my pearl, and I gasped when I realized that it was gone. I rummaged through the skins on which I had slept, but I could not find the thing. And then all at once I knew that my brothers were in grave danger, and, too, that I could no longer shun my obligation to find the means to cut Attila down.

I was beside myself in the days that followed, and I would have given anything to speak to Edeco of my concerns, but of course he did not come to me. I saw him in the courtyard on several occasions, but he only bowed his head and looked aside. The other officers, who had never taken note of me before, bowed too, now when they saw me approaching, so that I knew that they knew that I was betrothed to their master. And when I went into the hall one evening and heard one of my fellow servants saying to another, "I cannot think why he should want to marry a Thuet," I knew that Attila's mind was set and the abominable event would come to pass.

Now I set my own mind on feigning a new attitude, for if I were to find the means to cut down Attila, I had better not let my expression reveal my disdain. And thus I went into the hall each evening smiling and with my head held high, as if I were proud to think that I should become Attila's wife. Each time I bent over him with his cup or his tray, I bade myself, *Now! Now, take up the sword and do the thing that you were born to do, for tomorrow he may march again.* But my hand never heeded the order, and the conceit I wore on my face soon became a contradiction to the self-loathing I bore in my heart.

One night toward the end of Winter, Attila had a great many unfamiliar Huns to dinner—so many that there was a shortage of space. Six or seven men had to squeeze around tables meant only for four. I could not guess what their business was, for they did not speak of it. They were jolly one and all, and there was much laughter and toasting among them. Zerco was brought in to be mocked, and these unfamiliar Huns mocked him with far more gusto than had any of Attila's previous guests, striking out at him as he danced by, and then laughing so hard at his horror that their drink rolled down their faces. Even Attila seemed to find Zerco amusing on this occasion.

With all the shouting and laughter, it was a wonder that I was able to hear Edeco clear his throat when I bent over his table to pour for Elsa, who was sitting beside him. Though Edeco's eyes were fastened on Zerco, he nodded once when I turned to look at him. After that, I was in a panic, for I imagined that Edeco meant to inform me that Attila would be marching on the Western Empire in the morning, that these strange Huns were some of the men who would march at his side. And if it were so, then my chance to take hold of the war sword, to exchange my own meager life for the lives of countless others, Burgundians, surely, among them, was coming to a quick end. But I had already brought Attila his wine and his tray by then, and, furthermore, because of the crowd, several other women from the village had been brought in to serve, all of whom were so eager to please that one or another of them beat me to Attila's side each time he lifted his wine cup into the air to be refilled.

The banquet went on until very late in the night. After a time, I gave up my ambition, for now it seemed unlikely that these men would be fit to ride anywhere in the morning, much less off to battle. At length Attila began to yawn, and then he held his hand up in the air. Still chuckling over something one of the others had said to him, he declared, "Attila must sleep." The unfamiliar Huns went on talking and laughing even as the familiar ones began to file out. But Attila was in such a good humor that he only raised his hand higher and repeated his declaration. When the servants came to clear the tables from the floor, Attila's additional guests finally roused themselves. But Attila remained seated. And later, when the servants were finished and on their way out, the Attila they prostrated themselves before was already fast asleep on his couch with his lips stretched, as if he were dreaming already of victory.

Thinking that Edeco might be waiting for me outside, I kept myself to the rear of the other servants. But except for a few men still straggling toward the gates, the courtyard was empty. When we had passed through the gates, I broke off from the other women to make my way to my hut. It was then that I saw Edeco sitting on his horse, talking to Orestes and some others. As I passed them, they nodded and then went quickly back to their conversation. I was rounding the palisade. In a moment I would be out of their sight. I had an idea, but there was no time to think whether it made sense to execute it. I turned my ankle, and crying out, fell to the ground. I could hear the men chuckling behind me, and then a horse approaching slowly. I did not dare to lift my face from the dirt until I heard Edeco's voice. "Fool," he cried. "Perhaps we should have you take Zerco's place at the next banquet." The others laughed harder.

"Do not mock me," I cried in a pained voice, and I attempted to get up but then stumbled again.

Sighing as if he were much annoyed, Edeco slipped off his horse and, taking my arm, yanked me to my feet.

"In the morning," Orestes called behind him.

"Aye, in the morning," Edeco hollered back.

With Edeco leading his horse and me dragging the foot I had feigned to injure, we began to move across the field toward my hut. We could hear the others dispersing behind us, but neither of us dared to turn and look. Nor did we speak a word until we were close enough to the hut to see the shadow of the guard who paced before it in the moonlight. Then Edeco said, "We do not have much time. Listen closely. We have had our two embassies back from Constantinople and Ravenna. Marcian continues to refuse to pay tributes. Attila feels certain, therefore, that he is expecting an attack, and thus preparing for it. So naturally we will not be marching on the Eastern Empire at this time. Valentinian, meanwhile, has refused to give Honoria over to Attila. He says she is already betrothed to another man. We leave to march on them within the space of three days. But as Attila would not have them prepare for our attack, he is sending a letter to Ravenna to say that he deeply regrets the loss of Honoria but, due to his great love for Aetius, he will not stand in the way of the marriage Valentinian has arranged for her. The letter also says that he is planning a campaign against the Visigoths, who, as you know, abide within the boundaries of the Western Empire. Attila asks that Valentinian, in consideration of Attila's compliance concerning Honoria, not interfere in this campaign. Likewise, he is sending a letter to Theodoric, the Visigoth King, to say that he is marching on Ravenna, and that he had best not interfere. In truth, there is little reason to think he will. Aetius and Theodoric have been at odds for some time. But as Attila cannot take the chance that the two forces will unite . . . . Oh, yes, and I should tell you about the Franks, though how you will use any of this information for anything other than to stir your mind up—"

"To the point," I cried, my eye set on the guard whom we were fast approaching.

"After we have laid waste to the Western Empire, we will march to Frankish lands to install—"

"The letters must be switched!" I interrupted. Edeco looked at me bewilderedly. "The letters!" I cried again, impatiently. "The one to the Visigoths and the one to Ravenna. Theodoric and Valentinian will both realize that they have received the letter meant for the other and—"

"And join forces . . . ."

"Aye. Can you see to it?"

"I?"

"You must."

"But the letters have already been given out to their respective messengers."

"Were both in attendance tonight?"

"Yes, but—"

"Then both are surely fast asleep."

"The one sleeps alone, but the other has a wife."

"Then you must plan the speech that you will make in the event that you awaken her."

"And later, if she should say to Attila—"

"Would the messenger's wife seek out the ear of a corpse?"

"Ildico—"

"Do your sons ride with you?" We were close enough now for me to hear the guard saying something to his horse.

"No. They are not yet fully trained for such a march. But our army will be great. Few will be left behind. If ever there was a chance for you to escape . . . ."

"I will stay until I hear how the campaign goes . . . and whether or not you survive it—and I pray to Wodan you do, for I have grown to care for you much more than I thought possible."

"Ildico," Edeco whispered, and he tightened his grip on my arm.

I fought off the urge to exchange more endearments. "If you do not survive, I will find your sons and acquaint them with all that has passed between us . . . ."

"The elder one knows of your vision. He is for it."

"If Attila is brought down, perhaps they will see fit to leave with me before one of Attila's sons declares himself ruler."

"If we are cut down, you will have that chance, for the brothers will be at one another's throats for a good long time. There is none among them to take Attila's place. Our empire will cease to exist." Having said this, Edeco stopped suddenly and stared at me with wide eyes.

"Leave me now," I ordered.

"But Ildico, what if—"

"My name is not Ildico. It is Gudrun," I said hastily. "And I am more than a valkyria, much more. I am a Burgundian." And I hurried away from him.

The following evening, as I was limping toward the hall, I heard Edeco's voice behind me. I glanced over my shoulder and saw him walking with Orestes and Ellac. In a moment the three caught up with me. And as they were overtaking me, Edeco brushed up against my shoulder and breathed, "Done."

SAPAUDIA

CHAPTER 12

Brunhild came in through the open door with a brisk step and her mouth set as if she had something on her mind. I made to get up and fetch her the washing bowl, but I sat down again when I saw that she was heading for it herself. She submerged her hands hastily and wiped them on her tunic. But as she passed Gunner to take her seat beside him at the table, she remembered to take the time to bend over him and brush her cheek against his. He responded by grabbing her fingers and sweeping them across his lips, though he kept his eyes on Sigurd—as did Mother and Hagen and I. And Sigurd kept his own eyes fastened on his bowl, as if this would stop Brunhild from repeating her performance each evening or the rest of us from probing for his reaction to it. We were all sentinels now, stirred to our outposts by Brunhild's actions.

As Brunhild's new esteem for my brother had begun on the second day after Sigurd's return from the Franks, I felt certain that something had occurred between Brunhild and Sigurd on the first. But I had kept my eye on them all that day, and at no time did I see Sigurd stealing away to look for Brunhild or she to look for him. Whatever new turn their relationship had taken, it had taken it discreetly, through looks exchanged in passing, perhaps, or a word or two that I had failed to overhear. Now each time she passed Gunner, Brunhild made it a point to touch his face or his hand, and each evening when our meal was done, she petitioned him to come sit by her side. And Gunner, who one would have thought would have been delighted to receive these new attentions from the valkyria, seemed, instead, as puzzled as the rest of us. Though he responded quickly enough to her touch, trembling visibly with desire, when she implored him to join her on the long bench, he would hesitate a moment. His gaze, which was narrow and pensive then, would fall briefly on Sigurd, so that I knew that he knew that Sigurd's return was somehow connected to

Brunhild's transformation. Perhaps he suspected, as I did, that they had decided that in order to avoid suspicion on the matter of their love, that Brunhild had better feign indifference to Sigurd and devotion to Gunner. Apparently they failed to note that their behavior had the opposite effect.

"Whatever is coming is coming tomorrow," Brunhild announced as she reached for her drinking horn. She was referring to her prediction that the warm weather, which was still upon us even though the growing season was well behind, portended some misfortune on the way. Its nature had been the focus of our conversations for the last few days. But Brunhild had not been able to define it for us. The Sight was like that, my one-time sister had explained. Sometimes one stared into the fire or at one's shadow and saw clearly what lay ahead; other times one could only see the shape of the thing, but none of its features.

Now Sigurd dared to look up at her. "Can you say what it is yet?" he asked.

"No, but I have written a rune on all four walls of the hall. We will be safe enough here."

Gunner looked up abruptly, his mouth ready to express his delight, but when he saw that Brunhild's eye still lingered on Sigurd, he looked away again.

Sigurd's face reddened. Then he looked away, too.

"What of the rest of us?" I asked. It was the first time I had spoken to Brunhild since the day we had gone down to the river together. "Did you write runes on our freemen's halls as well?"

Brunhild answered with her face averted. "I plan to do so in the morning." She pushed her drinking horn across the table so that Mother could refill it.

"I will ride with you," Gunner offered. "It will give me great pleasure to see you do the thing you were born to do."

"That would please me," she answered.

"Perhaps you should ride tonight," I persisted. "If it is the Huns or—"

Her glance was fierce. "Not the Huns. Nor the Romans."

"But you said you did not know—"

"I said I did not know what it is. I do know what it is not."

"Leave these matters to Brunhild," Gunner said firmly.

Hagen got up and went to the door to check the sky. He had been checking it periodically ever since he had come in from his chores. The clouds had been gathering all afternoon. There had been thunder in the distance.

Now the clouds were close and low and dark, and tinged with an eerie greenish color. They looked like thick, turbulent bubbles. Hagen came back to the table smiling. "The weather will break very soon," he declared. "Whatever we face tomorrow, we will face it in cool weather at least, praise the gods." Of all of us, Hagen had taken Brunhild's prediction the least seriously.

Just then Gunner pushed his bowl away viciously.

"You are not finishing?" Mother cried out. As if it would ease the tensions that had arisen with Sigurd's return, Mother now made meals and housekeeping her greatest concerns.

"It is only the heat," Gunner complained. He got up from the table and began to pace, his fleshy face curled into a scowl. His tunic was drenched with sweat. "The gods have singled us out for this . . . this thing that is coming," he added. "I feel it to be true."

"Why should they?" Mother cried shrilly. "We have done nothing to offend them."

"Perhaps we have. Or perhaps one of us has." Gunner shot a glance at the back of Sigurd's head.

Sigurd, who could not have seen him, stiffened all the same.

Brunhild's laughter broke through the silence that followed. "It is the heat that makes you say such things, my love," she said. "Come back to the table and eat with the rest of us."

Sighing, Gunner returned to the table, but he did not reach for his bowl.

"The gods despise only those who are weak," Brunhild added softly with a glance in my direction. "They love those who are brave and unafraid to take what they want in life."

Gunner looked into her eyes and smiled gratefully, thinking, perhaps, that she was referring to him. "I wonder," he said. "Sometimes it seems to me that the gods take no interest at all anymore in the ways of men. Certainly they have no concern for the Burgundians."

"Say no more!" Mother cried. "You will bring their wrath down on all of us!"

"It will come whether I say so or not," Gunner shouted.

Brunhild laughed. "You contradict yourself, my sweet, every time you open your mouth."

Gunner turned back to her and studied her face curiously. Then he inclined his head toward Guthorm. Guthorm, sensing his stare, looked up immediately from his bowl. In a low deliberate voice, Gunner said, "When the survivors of a crushed race seek to replenish their kingdom, they look to the firstborn for guidance. This is our firstborn since the siege. Look at him."

Mother's eyes flooded with tears. "I never thought to hear you say such a thing," she whispered. "Are you not content to cross the gods? Must you cross your father, too?"

"Guthorm, the firstborn after the siege?" Brunhild exclaimed delightedly. "Why, you never mentioned it before."

"I feared you would leave us if you knew we were doomed from the start," Gunner replied.

Mother got up from the table with a start. Shaking her head, she swept Guthorm out of his seat. Guthorm managed to grab the last of his bread and pack it into his mouth before Mother turned to whisk him away toward the bower.

But before she could reach it, a blast of cold air came in through the doorway so powerful that it blew over Hagen's drinking horn and carried Brunhild's bowl, the only one that was empty, across the table. Mother froze in her place. Then she lowered Guthorm to the floor, and, eyeing the mess on the table, went for the cleaning cloth. "Do you see what you have done!" she shouted at Gunner. He barked a laugh. The rain began all at once then, and with it the lightning. "Lower the door," Mother demanded.

Hagen got up and moved to the door, but he stood looking out for a moment before lowering it. Turning, he said, "This storm will be fierce. Perhaps this is the terror Brunhild foresaw."

"She said the thing would come tomorrow," Gunner declared angrily.

Brunhild shrugged and waited for the thunder to abate. "Today, tomorrow.... Terror knows no time. Hagen may be right. What of it? Our walls are safe in any case."

Gunner rubbed his forehead. "Forgive me," he mumbled. "My head is full of storms of late."

The rain fell harder, and the thunder, almost constant now and very close, kept us silent for some time. Mother, who had finished cleaning up Hagen's mead, poured him more and then began to clean up the crumbs at Guthorm's end of the table. She stopped when the pounding began and looked up, as we all did.

This was a noise such as I had never heard before, far too loud to be rain. It was a terrifying sound that made me think that the gods themselves were banging their fists on the roof, and, after the things that Gunner had said, the notion seemed entirely possible. Hagen ran back to the door and began to lift it again in spite of Mother's pleas to leave it be. He lifted it high at first, and for a moment I could see that the evening had turned to night and that the night was full of fire. The wind rushed in and drove Hagen back a pace. He went forward against it and lowered the door, but before bringing it down completely, he got on his knees and extended his arm. When he turned, his eyes were wild in their sockets. He came to the table slowly, and reaching between Gunner and Brunhild, opened his hand. Sitting on his palm was a chunk of ice, as big as an apple. "The roof will not hold against this," he shouted over the pounding and the thunder.

Mother's cloth slipped from her hands and she began to beat her breasts. "What is happening?" she screamed. "Is it the end? Surely the end is at hand when Thunor throws rocks down from Valhalla!" She ran to where she had left Guthorm, and grabbing him to her, she fell to her knees and began to wail.

The drumming went on. My heart kept pace with it. I was praying innately to Wodan and Thunor when Sigurd turned to me and said, "Do not be frightened."

Brunhild's laughter crackled from across the table. "Is Gudrun afraid?" she asked, her eyes flashing.

I marveled that she had heard, for Sigurd's words had seemed like a whisper to me. "Why should I be afraid?" I responded. "I have utter confidence in the power of your runes."

Her eyes narrowed to slits.

Hagen, who had been watching her, laughed nervously. "The weather has made us all bold tonight," he said.

A new roll of thunder began. We sat in silence waiting for it to peak. Strange to say, it did not. On and on it went, getting louder and coming closer. It was so loud that it drowned out the sound of the pounding on the roof, a low rumbling, growing louder still. Sigurd inclined his head toward mine and whispered, "I must speak to you alone." I glanced at Brunhild to see whether she had heard. She had cocked her head to listen to the rumbling. I turned to look at the wall on which I had been leaning. It had begun to quake, and there were vibrations underfoot too, as if the earth itself were heaving and turning in. My ears ached, and I could not seem to catch my breath. I could think of nothing but slipping under the table, and I would have, I think, had I not seen Brunhild's eye fall on me just then.

The impossible roaring went on, louder and closer than before. I prayed harder. Guthorm appeared at my side and climbed onto my lap. I looked at Mother. She was still on her knees, crying now with her head thrown back, rocking, her arms wrapped about herself as if she did not realize that Guthorm had escaped from her. In spite of my fright, I remembered Sigurd's petition and turned toward him, but now he was sitting stiffly with his eyes wide open. The combination of the terror in his eyes and his natural grin made him look comical, and for an instant, I felt a ridiculous urge to laugh. I looked at Gunner. His gaze swept from wall to wall, as if he were waiting to see which would be the first to collapse in on us. He was holding Brunhild's hand so tightly that his knuckles had gone white. Hagen was standing behind him with his head cocked, oblivious to the ice-rock melting in his red palm. His eyes were wide and sightless like Sigurd's. He moved his lips, and though I could not hear his words over the terrible clamor, I made them out: "We are doomed." Aye, I, too, was sure we were doomed, and I regretted, as I glanced at Brunhild, that I should have to go to my death with the sight of her evil smile fading in my mind's eye.

I covered Guthorm's ears with my hands and tried to concentrate on my prayers again, but the only words in my head were the ones that Hagen had said. I closed my eyes and waited to die. And then, all at once, when it seemed that the roaring could get no louder or closer, it began to abate, and behind it, the awful pounding let up, too. How strange it was to hear only the rain again. As if we were all waiting to see whether the roaring would start up again, no one moved for a time. Then Gunner laughed and let go of Brunhild's hand. He turned to Hagen. "The next time Brunhild tells us we will be safe, you will believe her," he said.

Hagen smiled sheepishly. Mother, still on her knees, looked at each of us in turn and then at each of the walls. Her face was as white as new snow. She got to her feet slowly and stood motionlessly with her arms at her sides. Gunner called to her, "Bring us more mead. We have cause to celebrate tonight."

As if she had failed to comprehend his order, she blinked at him. Then she mumbled, hoarsely, "Let us hope our freemen have fared as well."

We had cause, later, to think that they had not, for when the winds and the thunder had subsided sufficiently, we all took torches and went out into the rain to access the damage. It was startling. The three great oaks nearest our hall—the sacred oaks of Wodan near which we had built our hall so as to elicit his consideration—had been torn up at the roots. It was as if Wodan, in his anger, had ripped them out of the earth with his mighty hand and thrown them down again like sticks. When he saw the sight, Gunner let out a cry and went down on his knees and struck his breast. Brunhild, who was standing behind him, put her hand on his shoulder.

The trees represented the worst of the damage, though not its extent. One of our servants' huts, we discovered after we had given up mourning for the trees, had blown away completely while the others remained strangely intact. We found one dead heifer right away, and later, three dead lambs. Hagen ran down to check on the horses and our storage huts. When he returned, riding his own horse, he reported that the barn had held, but the door had blown away and was nowhere in sight. The horses were fine, though wild with fear. Two of the storage huts had caved in while another appeared untouched—though its contents, much of our grains, had been sucked out of it. He was going off to Vascar's hall, he declared, to be sure everyone there was safe, and on from there to all the others. Gunner told him it would do no good to go off now in the dark, but as Hagen could not be swayed, Gunner went for his horse and rode off at his side.

The next day, even Brunhild got up early to stand amid the uprooted trees and broken limbs and wait for Hagen and Gunner's return.

Mother, who was expecting to hear the worst, had been mumbling to herself all morning. When she saw my brothers emerge from the forest, she said, as much to herself as to anyone, "I cannot bear it. This time I will not go on." I was thinking the same, but when Gunner and Hagen came nearer, I did not see the despair on their faces that I had been anticipating.

Hagen was the first to dismount. "Not a single death," he said, his eyes wide with amazement. "The destruction took a narrow path from the north. They had winds and falling ice as we did, but nothing more. None of their livestock. Nothing."

Now Gunner slid off his horse. His eyes were trance-like. "We alone were singled out," he whispered. "It is as if they meant to give us some warning . . . some message." He blinked and set his gaze on Brunhild. His hand, which was trembling, came up to rest on her shoulder. "But for your runes," he began. But his eyes came unfocused again, and his hand slipped back to his side.

Since Gunner and Hagen neglected to invite Sigurd to ride with them in the mornings that followed, Sigurd put himself in charge of the clean-up. Gunner decided that Beckmar's hut, the one that had blown away, need not be rebuilt. There were many empty huts on the lands of our freemen, and one servant less would make little difference to us. This was, Gunner reasoned, what the gods had intended when they had ripped up Beckmar's hut. Why else should they have carried it away? Gunner spoke of the gods all the time now, and with deference much like that which he had for Brunhild. He was determined to make sense of their message. One thing he professed to know for certain; the gods were anxious that he should marry the valkyria as soon as possible. Otherwise they would not have stirred her to mark our walls and save our lives. Now we were only waiting for our freemen to complete their Winter preparations and for our servants to return. Then we would have the mass slaughtering that always takes place at the beginning of the cold season so that the animals that cannot be kept alive through Winter should not go to waste. The weddings would coincide with the feast that followed the slaughtering, as celebrations always do.

In the meantime, Sigurd built a new door for the barn and butchered the animals we had lost in the storm. He divided the meat into parcels which Gunner and Hagen distributed among our freemen in exchange for some of their grains. Then Sigurd set to work on the oaks, turning them into logs for burning. All day long one could hear him hacking away tirelessly with his ax.

It became obvious during this time that Hagen had fallen out of favor with Vascar's beautiful sister, for he stopped riding out in the evenings to play at tables with Vascar. I hoped he would turn to me for consolation, but he did not. He spent all of his time away from the hall with Gunner. And as we were all together in the evenings, I had no opportunity to speak to him alone. Nor did I speak to Sigurd alone. I might have brought him his noon-day meal and sat with him while he ate it, but I asked Mother to go for me. She obliged me without comment. I avoided Sigurd for a reason. Since the night of the storm, I had come to believe that he wished to be honest with me, to tell me all about himself and Brunhild. I had kept myself sound since the incident at the river by telling myself that Brunhild might have lied. I had no desire to hear otherwise.

What concerned me more now was my brothers' neglect of Sigurd. And one morning I awoke with it in my mind that I must speak to them about it. I had no thought to be outright, but only, through conversation, to see whether I could discover the motive for their change. Or perhaps I only wanted to hear Gunner say that he feared that the valkyria loved Sigurd so that I could, for Sigurd's sake, convince him otherwise.

It was easy enough for me to get away. Mother was feeling ill that morning and had decided to linger on in the bower until she felt better. Guthorm, who seldom had the opportunity to lie in her arms, was happy enough to stay behind. Whispering so as not to awaken Brunhild, I told Mother that I would set about my chores, and hers as well, later, but that for now I had an urge to go off alone for a time. She looked up at me sadly and nodded in agreement.

By this time, my brothers had already been out hunting for a good while. I imagined I would meet them on their return. Once deep in the woods, who knows what directions they rode in, but they always returned by the same path. I called out a greeting to Sigurd as I passed him, and he turned from his work to smile at me. His smile was a paltry thing these days, and I imagined that the notion of marrying me in the near future was responsible for it. If it had not been the case that Gunner desired more than anything else to marry Brunhild, I would have set Sigurd free to marry her himself.

The forest to the south was used only for hunting, and I had never taken the path before. But with Mother indoors and the servants away, the only one who might have called me back was Sigurd—and he did not. My brothers spoke often of quicksand there, but I felt I should be safe enough—from that at least—as long as I stayed on the path. As for the wolves and other dangers, I tried not to think of them. I told myself that I was only a fearful little thing, as Sigurd had said, and that there were really no dangers at all. This sustained me until the path ran out.

I sat on a rock and reminded myself that Brunhild wandered alone all the time. Surely her fearlessness was some part of the reason Sigurd loved her. Still, she had the Sight and her runes for protection. I strained my ears to hear the sound of my brothers' horses, but I heard only the wind rushing through the trees. Time passed, and I grew restless.

It seemed to me now that there was a second path—though it was not nearly so well-defined as the one that had brought me this far—leading away from the blueberry bushes that surrounded me. I considered it for a time, and then I broke off several branches of the aging berries and began to follow it, scattering berries as I went in case I should have to come back alone. When all the berries were used up, I sat down again. And as I waited to see whether I would get the courage to proceed without them, I heard the sound of voices that I had been hoping for.

Still, I was reluctant to call out and announce myself until I was certain that the voices belonged to my brothers. As it was, the wind denied me certainty. I left the path and made my way through the trees, praying that I would not find myself face to face with thieves or frost-giants. But then I espied my brothers' horses in the distance, and a moment later, Gunner and Hagen themselves, sitting side by side against a large rock. The trees were thick between us, but I could see that their faces were grave, and I hesitated for a moment thinking that perhaps this was not the time to approach them after all. It occurred to me now that they would never believe that I had come this far alone, without horse or weapon, merely to engage in casual conversation. The whole idea seemed senseless, but as I was trying to decide what to do about it, I heard Gunner say Sigurd's name. Fearing they would notice me and think that I had been spying on them, I sank to my knees—and immediately saw that spying on them was not a bad idea. I began to crawl though the trees. I stopped when I could hear their voices clearly and, terrified by my audacity, held my breath.

"I, too, have spent many nights dreaming of it," Hagen was saying. "The sword alone, if it be as grand as he described it, would save us several men the next time the Roman tax-collectors come around. But we have managed all this time to refrain from even as much as digging it up to see whether it truly exists." He laughed abruptly. "Knowing Sigurd, there is always the chance—"

"My point exactly," Gunner broke in. "The man is inclined toward exaggeration. Shall we dig it up and have ourselves a look? He might have offered us that much by now."

"What? Are we thieves? Hold on to yourself, man. You of all people. The Burgundians look to you for guidance. Should you be caught . . . . Anyway, you will see some part of it when Sigurd and Gudrun marry."

"Aye, some small part, I wager."

Hagen shrugged. "Do not be so sure. He may be a fool, but he has always been a generous one."

"I disagree . . . about his generosity. I doubt he will pay so great a bride-price for her now."

Hagen laughed. "Must we start on that again? It seems we go around in circles."

"Do not be evasive, brother. Though you play at being as innocent as Balder, your thoughts are the same as mine."

"Your desire for the valkyria has made you mad. It drives your imagination to dwell in dark places."

"Do not speak to me of madness and dark places. Have you seen the way he looks at her?"

"I look at her, too. What of it?"

There was a silence for some moments, as if Gunner were contemplating this. Then he said in a gruff voice which I had to strain my ears to hear, "We are not men anymore. If we had died the night of the storm, we would have found ourselves in Hel washing weeds along with the women. The gods love those who go after what they want, as she who has some knowledge of them has said. We must prepare ourselves for battle against our enemies as all men do. What good will it do to make the Burgundians to be a kingdom again, if folk will say that the Burgundians are a kingdom of women?"

Hagen laughed again. "And who do you intend to fight, Gunner? Huns? Romans? You will have to fight the Franks first, if you take the life of one of theirs. As it is, they are our only true allies."

"But if we can prove to them that we had cause . . . . The time is now, I tell you. The opportunity is here. Why turn our womanish backs on it? You have a small view of the world, brother. You are like the worm who crawls all day and never sees beyond the next blade of grass. What is one man's life compared to the future of a people?"

"The one man you speak of is our brother. You have no proof that he broke—"

"Do I not? Lift up your head and look at the treetops!"

"I lift up my head and I see only that you are a dreamer. You speak as you did when we were boys. The gold would change nothing. There is not enough of it. One horse was all that was needed to carry it back. No doubt it would save us some men or the rest of our servants next year, but then what happens the year after that or the next one? In the end, we wind up what we already are, a small tribe surrounded by empires. We have no choice but to proceed as we have been: planting and reaping, bringing children into the world, and relying on the future to make sense of the present."

"Worm! Does it not bother you that we are not fit to challenge anything greater than the boar? That we spend our evenings like women, content to talk of household matters? Can you be happy wasting your life so?"

"I am happy enough as I am, thinking that I am the seed which in the future—"

Gunner grabbed his shoulder and shook it hard. "The gods are on our side this time. There has never been such a storm before! A storm within a storm is what it was. The gods brought the storm right to our door, as if to tell us that the time is now, that if we act, they will guide us, that we have their protection. Can you deny there was a message?"

Hagen jerked his shoulder free. "I admit, it has me puzzled."

"Well, then."

"Still, you cannot break the blood-bond without good reason."

Gunner threw his arms out. "I have good reason. That is what I have been trying to tell you! Do you think I am capable of breaking such a bond without it?"

"You have not asked her yet."

Gunner folded his arms. "I will ask her."

"Aye, you have said that before. Once you have married her. And thus there is no sense in discussing this until then."

Gunner shook his head. "Do you not understand? It will be too late then. He will be married, too, by then, and his heir may already be growing in our sister's womb. It must be before."

"What of the Franks?"

"We can give them some and say it is all."

Hagen turned away. Gunner watched the back of his head eagerly. Then Hagen turned back again. "You must ask her now," he repeated.

"I cannot do that. The gods intend that she should be my wife. Her rune-wisdom is as valuable as Sigurd's gold. That is why the gods sent her to me. You have seen what happens when I cross her. I cannot risk her turning against me before we are married."

"You must ask her now. Otherwise, I will have nothing to do with this."

There was a long silence. Then Gunner said, "Fine. We will do it your way. I will ask her."

I was already crawling back to the path as Gunner said this. I heard Hagen make a response, but I could not make it out. As soon as I was certain that I was too far off to be seen, I shot up from the ground and began to run. I ran hard, holding one hand over my mouth to keep from crying out or vomiting and the other over my heart to keep it from splitting it two. Now I gave no thought at all to the quicksand and the wolves. My thoughts were all for Sigurd. I was running to Sigurd to warn him. Somehow I managed to find the first path, and then I ran harder yet. But when I came close enough to my destination to hear the steady sound of Sigurd's ax, I stopped myself short and, gasping for breath, tried to think clearly. As I watched Sigurd through the trees, it occurred to me that I had not been thinking clearly at all. Now I saw that to tell him what I had heard was to give him sufficient cause to slay his conspirators. I hid myself behind a cluster of trees and tried to calm myself.

Some action had to be taken, but its consequence could not be my brothers' deaths.

I could not think. I could not clear my head sufficiently or still my racing heart. I could not stop my tears. I threw myself on the ground and stared at the mound of mossy earth before me. My tears blurred my vision and I could not bring it into focus. But I forced myself to concentrate. After a time, my breathing became more regular. Gunner had spoken of a small view. How small, I wondered, was mine? Some demon within me advised that I do nothing, that I let events take their shape unfettered by my personal desires. Gunner was right—the blood-bond had been broken. The notion of taking Sigurd's life and Sigurd's gold was not an inappropriate response. Had I a right to interfere? Were Father alive, he would surely say not. I could not think. And what if Gunner was wrong?—though it did not seem likely. If it was the future of the Burgundians that was at stake, did it matter?

I could not think. My thoughts were shadows of thoughts, and I could not carry any one of them through to its conclusion. I got to my feet and began to make my way back along the path into the forest. I walked hunched over, like an old woman, keeping my eyes on my feet. I would tell my brothers that I had heard, and then I would fall on my knees and beg them not to do the thing that had taken hold of their minds. I would snatch Hagen's short sword from the strap that crossed his chest and threaten to do harm to myself if they did not relent.

I stopped walking. If I told them what I knew, might they not feel compelled to do the deed much sooner? They knew I could not be trusted in matters where Sigurd was concerned. I turned back toward the clearing, walking slowly now. When I reached its border, I hid myself behind the same trees which had witnessed my discord moments before. I ran my hand over my face. It was puffy and scratched from my failed attempt to inflict upon myself a physical suffering which would be equal to my mind's anguish. One look at me and Sigurd would know that something terrible had transpired. Nor could I go into the hall without arousing Mother's curiosity—or Brunhild's.

I sat back against a tree and stretched out my legs. The leaves were gone now. The storm had torn them all away. The sky overhead was an icy blue—like Brunhild's eyes. The calm I had desired came over me gradually, but then it seemed that I was too calm. My mind, for reasons I could not penetrate, chose to focus on the sky and the tangle of leafless limbs cutting through it. I felt weak and tired. I think I may even have fallen asleep, for the blue and the silver above me turned to gray, and then the gray to nothingness.

Then the nothingness became blue and silver again, and in the moment of the transformation, my thoughts became unclouded. They were like silvery fish now, swimming though clear waters, and I was able to watch their unhurried progress without distraction. I saw what must be done.

CHAPTER 13

Brunhild emerged from the hall. As if to be sure that no one was watching, she lingered a moment, looking about. Then she marched over to Sigurd, who was stacking the wood he had been at all morning. When he saw her coming, he straightened. They exchanged some words, perhaps no more than a greeting. Then Brunhild laughed, and while Sigurd looked on, she made for the path that she took each day into the forest. I waited for her to pass me, and then I emerged from my hiding place and began to follow. When she stopped to drink at a stream, I came up behind her. "I will not stand in the way of your love for Sigurd nor his for you," I said.

Her body stiffened, but she dipped her hand into the stream and drank again. When she had wiped her mouth off on the hem of her tunic, she turned to look at me, her eyes bright with mischief and her mocking smile already in place. "Why, you are a sight!" she exclaimed.

Calmly, I repeated the words that I had come to say to her. She listened with her mouth opened and poised for laughter, and when I had finished, she did laugh. "What are you trying to say to me?" she asked.

"Sigurd will marry me and Gunner will marry you," I began in a ridiculous sing-song tone that challenged the earnestness I was attempting to put forth. "There is no way to change any of that now. But I will not stand in the way of your feelings for each other. In fact, I will encourage him to go to you. I will find a way to make him think that it would please me for him to take you as his lover. I will feign indifference to his love-making, if there is any of it. I will tell him I am not inclined toward that sort of thing. He will run to you. You will have Gunner, and Sigurd, too. I believe this is everything you wanted."

Brunhild's eyes narrowed, then drifted off to fasten on something beyond me. "I demand to know what you are about," she said softly.

"I am prepared to tell you. I have reason to believe that my brothers, who are hungry for Sigurd's gold, are plotting against him. They need only know for certain that the thing they suspect—that Sigurd broke his blood-bond with them in your arms—is true. Hagen has urged Gunner to come right out and ask you. Though Gunner fears that such inquiry will drive you away, he has agreed. You need only be convincing in making Gunner believe that you and Sigurd were never together. And of course, too, you must be sweet about it and not let him see you angry—"

"You ramble," she cried. "I have given Gunner no reason to suspect—"

"But you have. Your affection for Gunner did not begin until Sigurd returned. It has made him suspicious. How can you fail to see? Although your words are all for Gunner and your fingers always find their way to his flesh, your eye lingers on Sigurd more than is natural when you speak to him. Gunner knows, I tell you."

"You're wrong," she shouted. She glanced over her shoulder and lowered her voice. "If anyone has made Gunner suspicious, it is you. Why, you go about with a long face and never say a word to anyone. That is the thing that puzzles Gunner. You need only have behaved as if your mind were untroubled . . . ."

I was taken aback. I had not considered this, but now that it was said, I could see some truth in it. "I will then," I agreed. "But I must have your word that you will do as I have asked when Gunner comes to you with his question."

"What makes you think I would do otherwise?"

"I have seen your temper. In a fit of anger at Gunner . . . or Sigurd . . . ."

She smiled again. "I will hold my tongue. You have my word. But I will want something in exchange."

"I said that I would encourage Sigurd to go to you. Is that not enough?"

"Fool. He would come to me with or without your encouragement if not for the risk."

"Then here is something more. You spoke at the river of finding a way to be with Sigurd after the growing season begins again. I have thought it out. When we go to the Franks, I will feign sickness. I will say that I must have you by my side to care for me. There you and Sigurd will be free to do as you like."

"And who would believe that you desire my company?"

"Everyone, if we are seen to converse, to laugh, to go off together in the time left between now and then. Although it will not be pleasant for either of us, we must appear to be friends—sisters, as you once said—when Hagen and Gunner are about. We have all of Winter ahead of us. When the new season comes, we will have convinced them. Not only will this assure you a place at Sigurd's uncle's hall, but it will make Gunner believe that he was wrong to think the things he is thinking now when he sees that I do not appear to think them any longer. That you have made me see. I am asking you to play at a charade that will benefit us both. I need your cooperation, not only now but throughout the Winter. You may grow tired of Sigurd. And then you may not care what happens to him. But I give you what you want most now to ensure that if that day comes later, you will stick by our bargain."

"How do I know that you will stick by it? Who is to say you will not forget all about it once you are free of your brothers and me and living with Sigurd on Frankish lands? And what happens if you grow tired of having a husband whose affection lies elsewhere even before your move to the Franks? What of that, little sister? For all we know, you may be the one to tell Gunner—"

"Do you think I came by this decision easily?"

"Then give me some proof. Sigurd and I have had no opportunity to be alone since his return. Fix it so we can be, as soon as tomorrow. I will rise early, and in front of all of them, offer to take you with me into the forest. Then go to Sigurd and tell him what we are about. When he comes to us, you can hide yourself. And when Sigurd and I have had our . . . talk, you and I can be seen to return from the forest together. There must be a place where a couple can hide themselves."

"North of the hall, beyond the pine forest, there are some birches. No one ever goes there, but—"

Brunhild's smile quivered on her lips. "Good. Now we have a bargain."

As it turned out, Brunhild and I had no opportunity to carry out our plan. That same evening, as we were sitting down to our meal, two of our freemen came to us and announced that all Winter preparations had been completed. Our servants were already on their way back, and the great feast could take place whenever my brothers desired it. When Gunner heard this news, he pushed his drinking horn aside and stared at Hagen questioningly. Hagen nodded slowly. Then Gunner announced that the feast would take place the very next day.

But a feast the next day was evidently much sooner than what the men had in mind, for they looked at each other with wide eyes, and then one of them cried, "But then the slaughtering must take place tonight! It is nearly dark now, and the livestock have still to be brought up—"

Hagen interrupted him and repeated Gunner's command while Gunner sat back, satisfied with himself. The two men only stared.

Then Mother attempted to come to their rescue. "This makes no sense at all," she said. "Why, we will need a full day just for the baking of breads and the cleaning of meats, and the servants are sure to be exhausted when they arrive."

Gunner banged his fist on the table so hard that the men jumped and Mother's hand flew to her heart. "The baking and the slaughtering must all take place tonight," he shouted. "We are Burgundians. We are up to the challenge." He smiled cunningly. "I will hear no more about it," he added. Then he turned his smile on Brunhild. She smiled back and took his hand.

The freemen bowed and promised to return shortly with their fellows and all of the livestock that had been singled out to be slaughtered.

Gunner and Hagen pushed their bowls aside and went out right after the men. Mother snapped at me to hurry on with my meal so that we could get started on the breads. She was already laying out the grain sack near the stone slab at the side of the hearth. I had myself another bite or two, and then I hurried to her side. To my surprise, Brunhild soon asked to join us. Mother looked from Brunhild to me with her eyebrows raised. Then she turned back to Brunhild and said rigidly, "But of course you may." It was clear soon enough that Brunhild had never worked at breads before, and I took it upon myself to explain the process. She followed my directions quietly, bestowing on me, now and again, secret looks which I took to mean that her heart was not in her task, but that she was content—nevertheless and in spite of the fact that we would have to give up the plan we had made for the following day—that our charade should begin.

All of this left Sigurd sitting at the far end of the table regarding Guthorm and looking confused. But Mother took stock of him eventually and asked him to clear off the table. When he was done, she asked him to go outdoors and bring in more wood for the fire, and while he was out there, to check to see that there were torches enough for the activities that would soon take place. Sigurd did all this without a word, but when he returned later and Mother began to run off a list of other tasks that he might see to, Sigurd interrupted to say that he had one of his own and that it could not wait. And thus he left us.

When the loaves were formed and set to baking, Mother and

Gudrun's Tapestry

Brunhild and Guthorm and I went outside. By then our servants had returned, and our freemen and their families were arriving with their livestock. My brothers had fashioned a stone altar near the grove that encircled our fixed sacrificial altar, and our people were gathering around it. The moon, although somewhat less than full, was high, and as there were no clouds to obscure it, even without the torches we would have been able to see adequately. But the torchlight set our shadows to dancing, and with the moonlight overhead, the entire assembly seemed to swell and blaze. It had been some time since we had gathered together with all our people, and there was much rejoicing among us, over the feast which would take place the next day and, too, over the fortunes that had come to us throughout the growing season. There was also much talk about the great storm and speculation as to its meaning. What a fine crowd we made—though of course we were a pittance compared to what we had once been at Worms. Still, there was an excitement in the air which rivaled our gatherings at Worms, and no one spoke of days gone by.

When the order was given, we formed a great circle, and as we tightened it, we drove the livestock into the center. Frightened by the closing in around them, the animals stomped and kicked and bellowed. The children among us squealed with delight to see them in such a frenzied state. Leafy garlands, fashioned by our servants, hung around the necks of the animals, and as the animals stirred, petals broke loose and fluttered through the air like snowflakes. When Gunner grabbed hold of the first of the animals to be slaughtered, we lifted our voices and began to sing. We sang to Wodan and asked him to grant us a mild Winter. We thanked him for the mead which is his gift and which frees the tongues and minds of men. We beseeched him to keep us from abusing it, and, too, to keep our memories keen and to grant us soundness for our decision-making and courage for our hearts. We sang to the spirits of Wind and Storm and Fire and Water and asked them all to take pity on us. We sang to Frig, the wife of Wodan, and to Frey, her brother, and implored them to bless the feast and the weddings that would accompany it. We sang to Thunor, to thank him for the Summer grains which, except for what had been blown away by the storm, were stored now and would be sufficient to sustain us through Winter. And all the while the moon looked down on us as sweetly as a mother looks down on her children when they are at play. Our voices flooded the forest. The blood of our livestock flowed down the sides of the altar—until every stone was a glistening crimson—and became a puddle which became a stream which gushed off into the forest to encircle the trees with its warmth and bring life and vitality to the beasts therein. And we honored the animals who were dying for us and who, by their deaths, enabled us to better cherish our lives.

The shimmering light and the sound of my own voice among the voices of my fellow Burgundians soon began to penetrate my skin and to reveal the source of pride deep within which Hagen had once bade me to acknowledge. Though I had been vacillating all afternoon, now I felt quite certain that I had done the right thing by putting aside any notion of personal happiness in order to ensure Sigurd's safety. And though my heart was broken in pieces, I felt a surge of strength stir among the fragments. I am a Burgundian, I said to myself. I am Gudrun, daughter of a great warrior king, niece of the greatest Burgundian king who ever lived, and soon, wife of the man who slayed the dragon and returned with his gold. (And it struck me that I had taken far too long to come to see how proud I should be on this last point.) I have all this to hold on to. It will sustain me over the years just as Thunor's stored grains will sustain our people over the Winter.

When the sacrifices had been completed and a great heap had been made of the beasts' entrails on the altar, our songs ceased. Many of the smaller children, in spite of the commotion, had fallen asleep in their mothers' arms. Some of the older ones were resting against rocks and trees, very close to sleep themselves, and had now to be stirred into motion by their fathers. Guthorm had managed to stay awake and upright, but he was holding on to my skirt, sucking his thumb, his eyes slits in his round, expressionless face.

The crowd began to disperse quickly, for it was very late and our tired freemen and their families would need their rest for the next day. Before long, only my brothers and a few of our servants remained at the site of the slaughtering, for the skinning of the animals had yet to be done. I took Guthorm up to the hall and sang him to sleep with the same songs which we had sung to the gods. Brunhild entered, and without a word, stretched out on her mattress. Soon enough I stretched out on mine. Mother and some of the servants were out in the hall, removing the breads from the hearth and wrapping them in cloths to keep them fresh. They were chatting in low voices, and I went to sleep comforted by their murmurs.

I awoke early and crept out from among the sleepers in my bower and went across the hall to peek into the one opposite. Gunner and Hagen, who had surely been up most of the night, were sleeping heavily therein. But Sigurd was not with them. This was a shock. I thought I knew where he had gone, but I had fully expected that he would have returned by daybreak. It occurred to me now that perhaps some danger had overtaken him—or worse, that his repulsion at the idea of marrying me was so great that he had decided to take his gold and flee. As quietly as I could, I lifted the door, but as it creaked anyway, I did not bother to lower it behind me. The sky was already a crisp, cloudless blue, and the limbs of the pines in the distance were swaying gently. As I was standing there, I saw Sigurd emerge from the path to the west. He sat high on his horse with his free hand resting on the sack that hung from Grani's side.

He saw me and smiled—not the paltry smile I had become accustomed to, but the smile I had known all throughout the years before we had become strangers. Moved by his expression, I left the door and went toward him. When he got close, he jumped off Grani's back and caught me in his arms. For a moment, he held me so close that it seemed impossible that I should have ever doubted his love. The last time he had held me in that manner was the morning I had awakened in Clumar's hut to find that he had returned from the high mountains. His presence had seemed as much a dream then as it did now. And as I had not yet awakened from this last one, all the reality that had passed between was momentarily unimaginable. But it had passed, and suddenly concerned that Brunhild might be watching from the door, witnessing our embrace and wondering whether I had already failed at my end of the bargain, I released myself abruptly, exclaiming, "You missed the slaughtering last night. All the Burgundians were there and many asked for you."

Sigurd laughed. "Had I stayed for the slaughtering, Gudrun, I would have missed the feast. As it is, I rode hard to be here this soon. I left in such haste last night that I forgot to take along a shovel. I forgot how deep I had buried the gold. I had to dig it up with my hands." He held them up to show me. "I am delirious. I must rest."

"Go into the hall at once then. The others are not about yet. We were all up very late."

"I do not know whether I will be able to sleep. I fear I am too excited." Sigurd's smile broadened.

I turned to glance at the door, then I placed my hand on his to encourage him to speak.

"It has been so long since my eyes feasted on the sight of the gold of the gods, Gudrun," he declared. "I had forgotten how wondrous a sight it is. In truth, I spent more time than I ought to have, merely admiring it. And then it took me forever to choose among the pieces which would please Gunner most. And as I sat there in the quiet of the night with only the moon for company, I relived my journey into the high mountains. I relived the joy, the sense of accomplishment. . . . I learned this, Gudrun: when a man goes off to battle, he feels every bit a man. He feels a sort of exhilaration—almost as if he were more than a man, a god, almost. That is how I felt when I set off for the high mountains, and due to my triumphs there, I remained in that exhilarated state for some time after. But somehow, so gradually that I hardly noticed it, that feeling of strength and achievement slipped away from me, as it does when the battle is over and the men who have fought it have returned to their halls. I had thought this . . . this . . . sense of power—yes, that is what it is—would last me forever. I had not known how fleeting bliss is. But now, Gudrun, now that I have laid my hands on the gold again, it has all come back to me—what I did and who I am. I dread to go to sleep for fear that it will be gone again when I awaken. Do you understand what I am saying? You must think me a vain idiot, but—"

"Of course I understand," I cried. I wanted to tell him of the exhilaration I had experienced the night before, if only to convince him that it enabled me to understand his. But I saw no way to convey my experience without coming to the point where I should have to reveal the deed which had inspired it. "You have every reason to be pleased with yourself," I went on. "Even the gods take pride in their accomplishments. But go now. Sleep. What you feel now will be there when you awaken because you will have this sack of gold to remind you. And I will remind you, too, as I should have done before."

Sigurd squeezed my hand, then dropped it. "You are kind to me, Gudrun."

"How could I be otherwise?"

"Will you grant me one thing more?"

"Anything," I answered hopefully.

"Rouse one of your lazy servants and have him remove the sack and tend to Grani. He needs to be watered and fed. I rode him hard. Then, have the same servant bring the sack up to the bower and place it at my side. Do not try to lift it yourself. And of course, you must stay at the servant's side the entire time. Do not let the sack out of your sight until it has been placed beside me."

"I will do as you ask. Go now." Sigurd handed me Grani's reins and turned away. I could see by the way he walked that he was nearly aswoon with fatigue. Already the dream-like quality of our encounter was paling. And the embrace which had invoked it, I thought now, was linked to his excitement over the gold, nothing more. As I turned to Grani and studied the sack, I remembered the curse and my heart began to pound. It seemed to me that I could feel the evil emanating from it. I thought to strike Grani and cry, "Be gone, be gone!" but of course he would only return again, longing for his master.

In the middle of the day, when the sun was high and bright in the sky, Homel, a dear old servant who had been with us since my father was a boy, came to our hall to say that the bath had been made ready for Brunhild and me. The idea of bathing again with Brunhild made me shudder, but I took up the soap courageously, and with Brunhild behind me, I followed Homel out to the bathing pit, which was full and steaming. Homel tested the water with his hand, and satisfied that it was heated sufficiently, he left us. As the air was cool, we undressed quickly and climbed in. We washed and said nothing. I unbound my hair and washed it, too. Now that my betrothal was over, I would wear my hair down again, but this time in a net, as married women do. Brunhild would be expected to do the same, though I doubted that she would.

The bathing pit was small and meant to accommodate only one bather at a time. We had no choice but to sit close together as we waited for the sun to dry our hair. Our silence was awkward. But I glanced at Brunhild's face once, and when I saw the agitated look there, I began to feel giddy. I had a sudden urge to laugh wildly, though I could not imagine what I should be laughing at beyond the absurdity of our situation. Though I could not see them through the thicket which surrounded the us, I could hear our freemen and their families arriving for the feast. I was anxious to join them. Without a word to Brunhild, I climbed out of the pit and dressed myself. Homel was waiting outside the thicket, with his back to it. I caught him with his nose in the leafy wreath that he was waiting to place on my head. At his feet was a second wreath, for Brunhild. When he had positioned my wreath, he smiled and kissed me. "May the gods be with you today," he whispered. I found myself with tears collecting in my eyes, overwhelmed with a happiness which seemed strangely out of proportion to the situation.

Our hall was not large enough to contain all of our freemen and their families, but as we had been granted a lovely day, there were many who were content to take their food bowls outside. And thus, inside and out, there was singing and dancing and laughter and a great deal of eating and drinking. When everyone was sated, Gunner took up his harp and began to play. How quickly then did those of us who were indoors quiet. And as his music wafted out through the hall door, those outside quieted too and pressed nearer to the door to hear him. When Gunner had finished, others who had songs to sing came forth to take their turns. Since the story of the Burgundians is a sad affair, most sang sad songs, and before long there were many wet eyes to be seen in our hall.

But after a time, Hagen came forward and asked to be the next singer. Everyone brightened then, for it was no secret that Hagen's voice was poor or that Gunner derived pleasure in mocking him on account of it. But it seemed now that Gunner would be content to hear him sing, for his hands were already in place on his harp strings as Hagen announced to the crowd that his song would be one that no one had ever heard before. All men love to hear a new song, and thus the crowd pressed closer yet.

Gunner began to play, and Hagen, who looked uneasy for once, cleared his throat. His voice, at first, elicited some muffled laughter, but when his preamble was over and he began to sing of the dwarves who had walked on the Earth when the Earth was new and the gods went about as men do now, the laughter subsided.

I realized immediately that Hagen's song was going to be about Sigurd, and though I was confused by my brothers' sudden change in attitude, I was simultaneously thrilled to think that at last our people should hear of Sigurd's quest—even if it was Hagen singing it. I squeezed my way through the crowd to stand at Sigurd's side.

Sigurd smiled at me and returned his gaze to Hagen. I could see by his expression, which was one of mere interest, that he had not yet come to realize where Hagen was venturing with his words. But when Hagen got to the part of his story where the Franks arrived at our hall, Sigurd's smile lengthened and quivered, and he reached down to find my hand.

Immediately I looked for Brunhild, and I found her standing on the other side of the hall—looking quite beautiful in the robe that had been made for her—but with far too many people between us for her to notice my hand in Sigurd's. As we followed Sigurd and Regan into the high mountains, breathing the increasingly thin air and keeping a look out for frost-giants, Sigurd's face reddened, and his eyes began to moisten. His smile was wide and fixed now, so that it looked as if it had been carved out of wood. And it occurred to me, as Hagen described the dragon in words too eloquent to have been composed by him alone, that perhaps Gunner had already found time to ask his question of Brunhild—and that her response had satisfied him.

Gudrun's Tapestry

Our freemen stood amazed as Hagen sang of Sigurd's slaying of the dragon. Many turned to look at Sigurd, and those who were nearest to him placed their hands on his shoulders. When the song was done, and a few jokes had been made about Hagen's voice, there was not an eye in the hall which failed to fall on Sigurd. The Burgundians were waiting for him to speak. I let go of his hand and stepped away from him. But Sigurd, who was never at a loss for words, seemed to be now. His face was still crimson, and as if to control his emotion, he was swallowing hard and continuously.

The silence grew awkward, and, at length, one of the freemen whispered, "You must speak to our people, son. They are waiting."

Sigurd turned to look at him with round, inquiring eyes. Then all at once he lifted his gaze to my brothers and cried, "Give me but a moment." And calling out, "Make way, make way," he disappeared into Gunner and Hagen's bower. A murmur went through the hall then as our guests speculated on what Sigurd might do next. It fell a moment later when he reappeared with his sack slung over his shoulder. The crowd parted so that he could make his way to Gunner's seat.

He placed the sack at Gunner's feet and bowed low to him. Then he bowed to Hagen, who was standing behind Gunner. "Brothers," he said loudly, "I bring you Gudrun's bridal-price. It is none other than the gold of which you sang so wondrously."

The rumor of what was happening spread outdoors, and the hall became fuller yet. There was no man or woman among us now who could have moved from his spot even if he had wanted to. A second crowd had formed at the doorway, its members craning their necks and pressing forward. Only the children remained at some distance, and this only because those at the door chided them when they tried to come too near.

Gunner rose and returned Sigurd's bow. Hagen did likewise. Then, sitting again, Gunner reached into the sack and pulled forth a beautiful gold goblet. He studied it for a moment, his smile widening in his fleshy face, and then he held it up over his head where all men could see it. A roar went up from the crowd. Beaming now, Gunner called for quiet. He reached into the sack again and pulled out a gold crown such as my uncle once wore in Worms, only this one was far more beautiful, being studded with gems the likes of which I had never seen before. Gunner was delighted. Laughing, he turned it round and round in his hands. His laughter set others laughing, anxious to see the thing that pleased him so. When his arm shot up with it, another roar went up, this one greater than the last. Those in the rear of the hall pushed even closer together, and there was a great deal of shouting from those at the door who could not get in.

And thus, one by one, the pieces in the sack were revealed. How we marveled at all of them! There were six goblets more, and finger-rings and arm-rings, all studded with gems like the crown. There was a gold helmet and a gold shield and even a gold serving tray, the handles of which were made up of finely-crafted leaping bears. And all these pieces were so beautifully engraved that no one could doubt that they had once belonged to the gods. But the last piece that Gunner pulled forth was so beautiful that it made the others seem unremarkable by comparison.

It was a long time before Gunner completed his inspection of this last one. And in the meanwhile, our guests pushed and shoved one another to see what was detaining him. Gunner's jaw had dropped low, and his eyes, which were wide with disbelief, swept back and forth between Sigurd and the sword which lay on his lap. Hagen, who was peering over his shoulder, was equally amazed. Gunner's hand hovered over the hilt for a time, as if he would like to touch it but feared that he would desecrate it somehow. His smile was long in coming, but on its heels was his roaring laughter. He lay his hands on the thing suddenly and with resolution. And then he stood and held it high over his head. There was a hush from the crowd, and then a murmur which swelled into a roar.

Gunner laughed and nodded at our people encouragingly. "This is the sword of Wodan himself," he shouted, his eyes brimming with tears. There was more pushing, and I found myself in a corner where I thought I should be crushed. Gunner turned the sword around in his hands and held it by the blade now so that all men could see the hilt. I was near enough to see that it was beautifully engraved with dragons and bears and boars and all other manner of beast. Although it was not yet dark, the light in the room was quickly escaping, and someone lighted a torch and set it into the bracket on the wall. The sword came alive then, shining so brilliantly that it seemed itself to be the source of illumination. Our dazzled guests grew quiet once more, as if in reverence. And then another roar began among them, and there were shouts of praise for Sigurd and shouts of well-wishes for Gunner. At length, Gunner lay the sword aside and left his seat to embrace Sigurd. Words passed between them which, with all the shouting, I could not hear. Then Gunner lifted his hand to quiet the crowd. But they called back that they must see him holding up the sword again. And thus he took up the sword and they quieted at once.

"Friends," he began, "Burgundians, you have heard my brother sing of Sigurd's quest, and now you have seen its result." More shouts followed and Gunner waited patiently for them to abate. "This sword, this sword of Wodan's, this finest piece of the dragon's hoard, my brother in blood would bestow on me that I might lead my people once again to do the deeds that make a people great. This sword is hungry for blood! I feel it!"

Our people cried out even louder than before. Gunner's eyes glistened, and his smile was so unnaturally wide that he looked like one of the beasts growling from the sword's hilt. He had to wait a long time before the crowd saw fit to let him continue. Then, in a voice that made me think of our father, he shouted, "This sword is hungry for the blood of the Romans who profess to be our allies even as they deprive us of our servants and our wealth. This sword is hungry for the blood of the Huns. This sword has found its way to me for a reason. I could never again call myself your king and leader if I did not promise here and now that this sword, which has lain so long in the dragon's cave, longing for blood and action, will be sated."

A great cry went up. Gunner, who was trembling so with exhilaration that one could see his veins pulse in his neck, sat down and began to pass the other gold pieces to the men nearest so that they might examine them and pass them on. When all these pieces had been passed out, he turned and placed the sword on the ledge above his chair. Then he went among our people—but with his eyes constantly straining toward his new possession—and called for all men and women to take up their drinking horns again and celebrate.

And thus we drank. As some of the crowd began to move outdoors, the hearth fire was renewed, and those of us who remained within sang and danced around it. And if there was anyone among us who thought Gunner's proclamation premature, there was no one whose demeanor betrayed it.

When darkness fell, the tables were reassembled and the meats and fruits and cakes and breads were all brought out again, and once more our guests had their fill. Then the tables were taken apart and put aside so that the ceremonies could begin. Our guests seemed surprised now, as if, in all the excitement over Sigurd's gifts, they had forgotten that there were to be ceremonies as well. Laughing at their folly, they backed away from the hearth and made a circle around it.

Gunner called to Brunhild and she came forward and joined me. Walking together, we went around the hearth three times, and three times our guests sang out their good wishes for our happiness. Then we each removed the arm-rings which Mother had given us earlier in the day and threw them into the fire so that it might be appeased and so that all our future fires might bring us warmth and never destruction. The mead pitchers were passed around again, and as Sigurd stood by my side and Gunner by Brunhild's, we drank our bridal ale before our witnesses. More songs were sung, the last of which was a song describing the happiness of Wodan and Frig on their wedding night. Then the crowd became two crowds, and while one escorted Gunner and Brunhild to one bower, the second escorted Sigurd and me to the other.

To my surprise, Guthorm was fast asleep therein. I had forgotten all about him, and now I could not remember having seen him since much earlier in the day. Our witnesses began to shout for him to awaken, but their voices failed to stir him. When Sigurd turned and raised his hand to them, they stopped shouting. Shrugging indifferently, they backed away from the doorway, enabling Sigurd to pull the curtain closed behind him.

"He will not awaken, will he?" Sigurd asked.

"No, you can be sure of it," I answered hastily.

Sigurd took my hand and together we sat down on the feather mattress. It was dark, and I could see almost nothing of his face. I thought of Brunhild, in the other bower with my brother, and of our bargain. And anxious that I might otherwise fail to keep up my part of it, I brought up the subject which had been baiting me all night. "You bestowed a great honor on the Burgundian people tonight," I began cautiously. "Had I been the one to ride up into the high mountains and slay the dragon and acquire his gold, I fear I would have kept the war sword for myself, to spur the courage of my own people. And yet you gave it away."

Sigurd laughed and dropped my hand. He leaned back on his elbows. "My reasons are twofold, Gudrun." He hesitated a moment. "No, actually, they are three. First, by giving the sword to the Burgundians, I have, I hope, ensured that when the time comes for battle, the Burgundians and the Franks will fight on the same side."

"But we have been allies since my people first settled in Worms, and even before that."

"True enough. But these times are strange like no other. When I returned to my uncle's, I learned that a cousin of mine has been threatening to go to Attila and Bleda to offer them Frankish alliance."

"That cannot be. Such a man among the Franks?"

"His intentions are good. He is a man of foresight, and, like Gunner, he believes the day will come when the Huns will make war on the Western Empire. He thinks the Franks should be on the side most likely to win."

"Tell me you do not agree with him."

"Of course not. And neither does his father, who is brother to Gripner, and to my father while he lived. As you know, the Franks were never united as your people are. We have many leaders, and my cousin's father is only one of them. But he is a man all men listen to, and when he is gone—and that will be soon—my cousin will be listened to as well, unless his brother challenges him for the leadership. Anyway, these are not things to think of now with the Huns busy negotiating for terms with the Eastern Empire. If they think of the Western Empire at all, it is only with an eye to the future. Still, I gave the sword to Gunner because I believe even my cousin will think twice about his design when he knows that Wodan's war sword has fallen into Burgundian hands. My desire is that Thuet people will be united when the time comes to choose sides, and that then they will make the right choice together."

"But so many Thuet tribes have already gone over to one side or the other."

"Aye, and all the more reason to preserve the unity among the ones who have not."

"Your motive makes me proud," I murmured. "But you said you had three."

Sigurd sighed. "You will likely not be so proud of me when you hear the second, but I feel that I must tell you anyway. I only hope you will not be angry with me for speaking my mind to you—"

"You are my husband now. Speak."

"Your brothers are displeased with me of late. I am certain you have noticed. I thought to buy their fellowship."

I sought out Sigurd's eyes in the darkness, but the light from the hall did not penetrate the heavy bower curtain, and what moonlight came in through the small, high window above our heads enabled me to discern only the shape of Sigurd, the large black orb that was his head. "Let us not speak of the second reason," he said hastily. "Ask me for the third."

I was happy enough to do so. "The third, then," I said.

"The third reason is you."

"Me? How so?"

Sigurd sat up and took my chin in his hand and brought my face close to his. "I have loved you long, Gudrun. I felt your bridal offering should be equal to that love."

Again I searched Sigurd's face for some hint of his expression, but now that our faces were so close together that I could feel his breath on my cheek, even the dark shape of his head was indiscernible against the darker darkness. The last time Sigurd had declared his love for me, his words had been without conviction, the response, surely, to my envy and my tears. Had I somehow forced his tongue again? Or was he only, as perhaps he had that morning, confusing his affection for me with his excitement over the gold? Whatever the reason, this was something I had not counted on. In fact, it only made a snarl of matters that were snarled to begin with. As Sigurd kissed me, I forced my mind to consider the consequences. Would Sigurd go to Brunhild if he had come again to love me? But I was a fearful little thing. It was not possible. And if he did not go to her, what then? I had made a bargain, after all. I backed away and ended our kiss abruptly. But Sigurd laughed and pursued me all the more. And so helpless did I feel myself in his embrace that I said to myself, *One more moment, one more kiss, and then I will tell him the lie I have already rehearsed.* And while the logical part of my mind was urging me to tell him now and be done with it, the other part, so joyful to feel his touch, to be alone with him (or nearly so) in the dark bower while the mirth of the Burgundians went on just beyond it, bade me wait and wait, that there was time enough ahead to countermand my selfishness. And how quickly then did I turn my ear from logic and give myself to my husband.

Chapter 14

I awoke enclosed in Sigurd's arms, with Sigurd's breath on my face and Sigurd's skin against my skin. I saw immediately that the past was a contradiction and an inconvenience to my bliss. And thus I changed it. I told myself, first of all, that I had over-reacted to the conversation I had overheard between my brothers. That their words had been merely the idle reflections of two weary men who had come to feel emasculated by their circumstances. How difficult it must be, I mused as I ran my finger along Sigurd's slumberous smile, for my brother the king to acknowledge that his people were too few and too poor to take up arms against their enemies. Like our father before him, Gunner was a king in name only. And as if to confirm this for those who would assert otherwise, he had grown fat and melancholy over the years. But who would assert otherwise? No ambassadors from foreign tribes came calling at our door, bearing gifts and offering allegiance. Even our own people treated Gunner as little more than an elder brother, someone to be looked to when it was necessary to interpret the laws or remember the past. It was only natural then that Gunner should see in Sigurd's gold the opportunity to change these sordid circumstances. And I pitied him now, with all my revived and thriving heart. I told myself that between words and action there lies a great abyss which he had never actually intended to leap across—for had he truly proposed to take action, he would have done so immediately, as was his way. But he went to Hagen instead, whom he knew would offer resistance. Gunner had only dreamed of action, and recognizing his dream as a fantasy of evil dimensions, he longed, simultaneously, to be persuaded against it. And now he had the war sword. The trouble was ended.

I found, too, a new way to regard those matters concerning Brunhild. The idea of her joining us when we went to the Franks I put from my mind as something to be thought of later. And as for my more immediate concession, I said to myself, if Brunhild and Sigurd want to be together, well then, so be it. The danger inherent in their association will keep them from being together often. She cannot know, as I do, that Gunner would continue to want her anyway. And when they are apart, Sigurd will be mine. And should the day come when he turns from me again (and I no longer believed such a day would come), then I will have the memory of bliss—second only to bliss itself—to content me.

And so my delusions went. In fact, so thoroughly did I convince myself that after my initial conjectures, I gave these matters little thought at all.

The aspect of the days that followed only confirmed my beliefs. On that first morning after the feast, when we met in the hall to share the foods that had been left over, Brunhild was there with the rest of us, and she looked content enough to me. Gunner was as utterly transformed as a man can be. His smile, a sheepish one, never left his face. And yet, like a boy whose happiness embarrasses him, he kept his eye on his bowl. His skin glowed, and his movements, when he broke the bread or cut the meat, were the awkward movements of a man whose thoughts are elsewhere. He ate with haste, stuffing his mouth with more food than is becoming, but so sincere was his smile, which clung to his face even as he chewed, that I could not help but laugh. And when Brunhild heard me laughing, she looked up and smiled at me, as if, I thought, to say, *Yes, I have found happiness with your brother after all.* When my brother finished eating and began to yawn and say that he needed yet a bit more rest, how quick she was to finish her own meal and follow him back to the bower. And when the curtain closed behind her, Gunner's laughter came wafting out to the rest of us so that Mother blushed and Hagen quipped, "I will never marry. I see now how it makes men dull and lazy."

Thus the days passed, seven in all. The weather, meanwhile, was growing colder, and we expected the first snowfall shortly. Now we were all slower to rise in the mornings, dreading to get out from under our rugs and go about our chores—or in Brunhild's case, to wander in the forest. In the evenings, when we had eaten, we sought out the warmth of the hearth fire and occupied ourselves there as people do in the Winter—Hagen repairing tools and sharpening blades, Sigurd fashioning a new pair of shoes for Guthorm, and Mother and I working the wool that the servants had cleaned into threads on our distaffs while Brunhild sat idly and listened to Gunner's strains.

On the eighth day, however, all this changed. Gunner emerged from the bower alone that morning, and without the boyish grin that we had already become accustomed to. Looking at no one, he snatched a hunk of bread from the table and hurried outdoors with it. Hagen put aside his bowl and hurried out after him. A while later, Brunhild got up. She must have thought it was later than it was, for when she saw Sigurd and Mother and Guthorm and me still sitting at the table, she looked surprised. And before we could ask her to join us, she turned and went back into the bower.

I was outdoors with Mother, tending to the sheep, when Brunhild finally came out of the hall. Without so much as looking in our direction, she bounded over to where Sigurd was at work on the oaks and said something to him, seemingly curt. As she was turning away, heading for her usual destination, Sigurd noticed me watching, and he smiled. But his smile, I thought, though I was seeing it at a distance, had an uncertainty about it, as if the thing that Brunhild had said to him had oppressed him.

Sometime later, at Mother's request, I had one of the servants prepare the bathing pit for Guthorm. The sight of the steaming rocks upset him terribly, and I had to force him to remove his clothing. And thus it was that I was struggling with him beside the steaming pit, trying to get his tunic up over his head while I gripped one arm and watched the other flap as if he intended to fly away from me, when I thought I heard someone just outside the thicket, on the forest side. I let go of Guthorm and pulled some branches apart and peeked out in time to see Sigurd passing. My first inclination was to call him in to help me with Guthorm. But I saw that his eye was set on something up ahead of him, and when I pulled down more branches, I saw Brunhild standing at some distance along the path that led through the pines and up to the birches. She was facing Sigurd, waiting for him to catch up with her, standing in the one ray of sunlight that had managed to find a course through the thick limbs overhead. She was hauntingly beautiful there in that light, her unnetted hair afire and swirling around her radiant face in the wind. I let go of the branches and turned back to the bathing pit. Guthorm, of course, had fled. He had left his cloak behind. I put my face into it to smother the sound of my sobs. It occurred to me that I could still run out of the thicket and call to Sigurd to help me with Guthorm. Brunhild would see us and step into the trees, I thought, for it seemed likely that she did not care for me to know about this meeting. Then, when Sigurd came into the thicket, happy enough to think that I had failed to note his destination, I would exclaim that Guthorm had escaped. Their chance to go off together would be eliminated neatly . . . for the moment at least. But I took too long to act, and by the time I got back to the branches, they were already rounding a bend on the path. And at that moment I knew that I had been mistaken to assume that the memory of bliss was nigh to the thing itself; it was, in fact, its opposite.

I left the thicket and made my way along the path, berating myself for having become so furtive and deceitful. I went slowly, for the leaves beneath my feet were dry, and as I expected with every step to be discovered, I held Guthorm's cloak high and moved my head from side to side so as to appear to be searching. A twig snapped beneath my foot and I froze. "Guthorm," I called softly. I heard nothing, but when my heart stopped pounding, I saw the uselessness in going on, and I collapsed to the ground in tears. When I got to my feet again, I went back along the path in the opposite direction, and I passed the rest of the afternoon staring into the bathing pit and imagining the event I had not the disposition to witness for myself.

Much later, I heard movement on the path, and I reached the branches of the thicket in time to see Sigurd running by. He looked distraught, and I fancied he was concerned that Gunner should learn what he had been about. In my self-absorption, I had forgotten Gunner myself until that moment. I looked about for Brunhild, eager, for Sigurd's sake, that she should be seen to return at my side, but she was nowhere in sight. I washed my swollen face in the pit and rushed out of the thicket, thinking now that I must catch up with Sigurd before he entered the hall. But he was already entering when I emerged at the end of the path. I hurried along and entered myself a moment later, and Gunner, who was within, came right up to me. "Where is Brunhild?" he asked, his eyes narrowed. Sigurd was standing just behind him, staring hard at me.

I hesitated, wondering whether I should say I had just left her, but then I thought better of it. "Where indeed," I said. "She is gone off wherever she goes. Why do you ask me?"

Gunner turned to sweep his eyes over Sigurd and then back to me again. "One of the servants said he glimpsed her walking along a different path than the one she usually takes, the one that goes up behind the bathing pit."

I looked up toward the roof, as if considering. "No, he must be mistaken," I said as calmly as I could. "I am quite sure I saw her go the way she always goes."

Gunner grabbed my arm. "I thought to settle the matter by asking Sigurd here whether he had seen her. But when I went to find him, he was not at the oaks where he always is. It seems he went off, too, today."

I calculated quickly and concluded that I had come in too soon after Sigurd for him to have said much more to Gunner than that he had not seen Brunhild. I shook my arm free and forced a laugh. "You speak as if it were an outrage for a man and his wife to go off together."

Mother, who had been setting the table, turned around suddenly. "I wondered where you were," she said, "when Guthorm returned without you. I thought you planned to bathe him."

I laughed again. "Aye, I took him to the bathing pit as you bade me. But he ran off, the little monster. And as I could not find him, I sought out my husband's company." I held up Guthorm's cloak, still damp from all the tears I had shed into it. "I will put this away," I said. And I went quickly to the bower so that I should not have to look into Gunner's eyes again.

Guthorm was sitting in the corner where the mattresses were rolled and stored. He had found a hole in my feather mattress and was pulling out the feathers. As I knelt down beside him and put my arms around him, I heard the swish of the curtain behind me. "I must speak to you, Gudrun," Sigurd said.

I held Guthorm closer. "Not now. Can you not see that Gunner is suspicious. He thinks you have been with his wife."

"But Gudrun, that is what—"

"Go," I whispered harshly, glancing over my shoulder. And since he remained where he was, staring at me in amazement, I got up and hurried out past him.

The table was set. "Good," I cried, eyeing it. "Sigurd and I are famished after our walk."

Gunner took his seat and looked at me curiously. I smiled at him, but his expression did not alter. The door lifted and Brunhild came in. One could see that she had been crying. She closed the door and stood with her back against it, glaring at me as if whatever had upset her had been my fault. Horrified to think that she might say something to oppose what I had already said, I turned to Gunner and exclaimed, "You see how you have upset your poor wife? Look at her face. What terrible things did you say to her this morning that she should return still looking as sad as she did when she left?"

"What has come over you?" Gunner cried. "How dare you take such a tone with me."

I lowered my head. "I am sorry," I whispered. "It is not my affair."

Mother, who was pouring the mead now, said to me, "Where is Sigurd? Did he not see that we were almost ready here? Get him, and Guthorm too."

Gunner and Brunhild were staring at each other. I got up from my seat, and moving to the bower, I said, "We walked quite far. No doubt he is resting."

"I thought you said he was famished," Mother snapped.

"Aye, that too," I answered wearily. I pulled the curtain back a bit and slid in behind it. Sigurd was holding Guthorm on his lap. He looked at me pleadingly, his lips struggling to form his petition. "Come," I said. "We are eating." And I hurried out again before he could speak.

For the first time since her coming, Brunhild did not ask Gunner to take up his harp that night. Nor did he have a mind to take it up himself. Instead, he occupied himself with a bone carving he had begun the Winter before and never completed. The carving was supposed to represent Wodan, but to me it looked nothing like the god. In fact, with its fleshly face and wild eyes and angry mouth, it looked more like Gunner than anyone else. Perhaps Gunner thought so too, for he worked at it grudgingly, putting it aside at intervals to stare into the fire.

When it grew late, Gunner put the carving down for good and announced that he was retiring to the bower. He went off with his head hung low, without another word to any of us. Brunhild was not long in following. I waited a time, and then I put aside my distaff and bid Hagen and Mother and Guthorm a good night. Mother, whose mouth had been tight all evening, did not respond.

I was pacing when Sigurd came in. He grabbed my arm as he closed the curtain and said, "I must speak to you." His voice was loud and full of urgency. I covered his mouth with my hand and pulled him into the corner where our mattress was spread out. Much as I had no desire to be near him, I made him lie down beside me, and then I pulled our rugs up over our heads so that our words would not be overheard.

"What I must tell you will be painful," he began.

"Then let me spare you the pain of telling me what I already know," I snapped. "I know about Brunhild and the night in the cave. She told me herself. And I know, too, that you were together today. I was in the thicket at the bathing pit when you went by."

Our faces were so close together that I could feel his sharp intake of breath. "Gudrun," he whispered.

"Let me go on. I will say to you what I once said to her—though I thought of late that I should not have to say it: I will not stand in the way of your love for each other. But the risk you took today was frivolous. And its consequence was that I was forced to lie—"

"Gudrun, I do not love her."

"Do not deceive me," I cried. I lowered my voice. "Do not deceive me. I have played the fool long enough."

"Gudrun, you must listen to me. You are right about the night in the cave. It happened. I do not know how. Or I do. And I will explain to you as best I can if you will only hear me. But as for today, I agreed to meet her only to tell her that that night in the cave had been a mistake. You must believe me."

This I could hardly believe, now that I'd had all afternoon to set my mind on the reverse. Still, the tears of joy came welling up, and I had to fight to keep them back—for, in truth, I was eager to hold on to my anger.

When Sigurd saw that I would make no response, he went on quickly, saying, "You saw her face. You must realize I am not lying. She flew into a rage when she heard the words I had to say to her. She said she married Gunner only to be near me, that I should have told her before the weddings . . . . And I said I would have but that she seemed happy enough, and that anyway, we had no opportunity to speak. She would not believe that I would choose you over her. She said I was weak and dishonorable and connected to you only by my guilt. Aye, I am weak and dishonorable. And my guilt, Gudrun, clings to me more strictly than my shadow. But my connection to you has little to do with it, and I told her so. Then she fell to her knees, and with her arms wrapped around my legs, she swore to me that you came to her the day before our weddings and told her that you had no liking for love-making, that you begged her to become my lover so that . . . . I did not believe her. But she insisted. She said my kisses and embraces disgusted you. She told me to go to you and ask for myself. I said she lied. She insisted. She said to go and find you and ask. She said she would meet me where we met today again tomorrow, and that if I failed to come, she would go back to live her life among the beasts, for she would rather that than continue on as Gunner's wife, listening to him each night reciting the list of runes he would have her engrave on the war sword which I, she said, so foolishly gave him. She went on and on to name his flaws. I hardly heard her. I was thinking of you, of how I must find you and tell you about the cave, tell you that the man you married is everything she said, weak and dishonest and more, and ask you, too, whether the thing she said is true, though if it is, it is no less than I deserve."

This was a great lot to consider, and I took a long time with it. When I touched Sigurd's face, to show him that my anger had passed from me, I found it wet with tears. "I made a bargain with her," I began. "I did not keep it. My offense is as ignoble as yours, though my motive was worthier. I feared for your safety, Sigurd. I had reason to believe my brothers . . . . I went to her, and I told her that I would feign indifference to your love-making so as to ensure that you would go to her, if, in turn, she would make Gunner think that the night in the cave never happened. I even told her that I would find a way for her to join us when we go to Gripner's. I did not think it would make any difference. I thought I had already lost you. But on our wedding night . . . and ever since . . . . That was something I did not count on. We have both failed her. We have both deceived her. You must go to her tomorrow as she asked and tell her she was right to think it was only your guilt that kept you from her today."

Sigurd rolled away from me, onto his back. "I have made a great mess of things," he whispered. "I am a disloyal, dishonorable man. I never thought I should have to acknowledge these things about myself." He rolled back to me suddenly. "You know I was not always this way. You must despise me. How could you do otherwise?"

"I must hear in your own words what happened that night."

"It will soothe me to tell you. I wanted to sooner, but—"

"I know you did. I was not ready then. I am now. I must know."

Sigurd began slowly, his voice quivering with sorrow. "I came down from the high mountains a changed man, feeling my feat would carry me high for the rest of my days. And there she was, dressed in the Roman war weeds, blood gushing from her thigh. She was beautiful, extraordinary, a valkyria. And she did not keep her attraction for me a secret either. Still, I believed myself able to resist her. But when I went back for her, and we began our journey here, it became more difficult. We took to speaking of ourselves as gods. She never tired of describing to me how her rune-wisdom had brought fortunes to others. I never tired of telling her about the gold and how I had come by it. We let our minds wander. We invented settings in which her rune-wisdom and my gold and valor enabled us to prosper, to fight against the Romans . . . even the Huns. And though our words were mostly in jest—most of our imaginings being quite far-fetched, things that no man or woman can ever hope to accomplish—I would be deceiving you if I did not admit that the prospect of such an alliance began to seem a very fine thing to me.

"To shake myself free from her spell, I spoke of you. I said you were a good woman, content to live in peace and obedience to your brothers. She laughed. She said you sounded to her to be unfit to be the wife of a dragon-slayer, and I began to see you through her eyes." Sigurd grabbed hold of me suddenly, crying, "I do not mean to cause you pain. I tell you these things only to help you understand . . . ."

"Go on," I said.

He rolled onto his back again. A moment passed. "Our horses were tired by the time we got to the cave. And the rain had begun to fall harder. The thought of a warm fire . . . . But no, that was not it. Oh, Gudrun, how can I say these things to you? My tongue would cut down the truth at every turning. I needed no fire. It was Brunhild I desired. I was mad with desire for her. Gudrun, Gudrun, how can you ever forget and forgive me?"

I said nothing. For so long I had feared to hear Sigurd speak these words, but now that he was saying them, I listened almost dispassionately, as if the tale he told involved strangers. If I felt anything, it was pity, for I had never known Sigurd to shed a tear before.

"When we arrived at your hall, I was sure I loved her. I saw your envy and your pain. They were as clear to me as the pebbles at the bottom of a shallow stream. I could think of nothing but how I might break off our betrothal. I wanted only to be free of you. I'd had it in mind to stay some three or four days before returning to my people, but your face, your sadness, was like a blade cutting though me, reminding me of all that I could not have—those acts of valor which I imagined at Brunhild's side."

Sigurd laughed, a single ironic grunt. "I have grown womanish with these tears," he said. "How you must detest me. How I detest myself. But let me go on now that I have begun. When I left your hall, I found I missed you sorely—your friendship, that is. The way you have always had of listening to my troubles as if they were your own. I was confused . . . and ashamed. I wished that you had never been more than a friend to me, a neutral third party, a sister. How quickly then would I have turned back and begged you to listen . . . . And little by little I came to see that this trust between us was precisely the thing that made you so important to me, in a way that Brunhild could never be. I rode and rode, and her charm wore off some, though not entirely. I asked myself whether I would have wanted her so much had she been merely a beautiful woman and no valkyria. The answer would not come. I could not seem to separate the two. I could not tell what she meant to me apart from her powers. I wanted her powers. I wanted the future we spoke of. But I could not say whether I wanted her. And then I realized what I had done, how I had broken my blood-bond with—"

"Do you mean to say you realized only then?"

"I had put it out of my mind, as a thing to dwell on later." He fell silent.

"Do not dwell on it now," I whispered to urge him on.

He took a deep breath. "At home, Gripner watched me. I felt certain that he knew what I had done and was waiting for me to come forward and speak about it. When I was a boy, it always brought me comfort to know that my uncle knew of my wrongdoings. He always found a way to understand them. For Gripner, there was never good or evil where I was concerned—only mistakes. But how could I speak to him of this? Or, perhaps I feared he would forgive me, and I was not ready for that, for I had not yet forgiven myself.

"To be out of his sight, I spent several days alone in the forest, contemplating my error and praying to Wodan for guidance. I fasted, and, at length, I grew calm. But still I was not able to forgive myself. I began to think of Brunhild as kin, for by now I was convinced we shared—" He broke off.

"Shared what?" I asked.

"An evil element. A lack of desire to do well by our fellow man. And thus I came to feel that I was unworthy of you, of your innocent love. When I returned, my mind was still divided. And then there were your brothers . . . . Gunner always with his eye on me as if . . . . And then Brunhild looking at me as if to convey some message, the meaning of which I could not discern. But the night of the storm, when I thought that I should lose you . . . that we should lose each other, I saw that you meant everything to me, and that your goodness alone would save me. That your forgiveness alone would ignite mine. But we could not speak then, and afterwards, I lost my courage."

I wrapped my arms around him. "She put a spell on you with her runes. None of this is your fault."

"No, it is too easy to believe that."

"But I believe that, Sigurd."

"It may be so, but again, it may not. I must know that you forgive me either way."

"Then know that I do, that my love for you is too great to be rubbed out by one such blunder."

We held each other in silence for some time. Then Sigurd's voice came again, low and weary, into the darkness. "I must gain Gunner's forgiveness too. It is the only way."

I sat up. "You are mad. He would never forgive you. I know this to be true. He would kill you on the spot."

"Nevertheless, I must tell him all that I have told you. And anyway, if I do not, Brunhild may. Better he should—"

"No. You must promise to say nothing. This is madness, Sigurd. She will tell him nothing, not if you go to her tomorrow as she asked."

"And go to her again when next she asks? No. I cannot do it."

"You must. You must do whatever she wants. You must become her lover again. I will endure it. Or perhaps we will find tomorrow that she plans to go away. You said—"

"And do you think your brother so witless that he will not guess why she is gone?"

"Let him guess. You can deny it."

"No, Gudrun. He must be told."

"Then think of this, Sigurd. If you tell him, you will be endangering her life as well as yours. He will kill her too."

Sigurd sat up beside me. "Do you think so? After all, it was I who broke the blood-bond. She had no bond with him then herself."

"He would," I lied. "I know he would. His pride is greater than his love for anyone. Even Brunhild. And who is there to demand a man-price for her death?"

Sigurd plopped back onto the mattress. "I do not know what to do."

"I am telling you. Become her lover again. It is the only way. Only now you must be careful—"

"The way you press me here, Gudrun . . . . It makes me wonder whether the words that Brunhild said—"

"I care only for your safety."

"I will not go to her," he said resolutely. "Do not speak to me of it again. I broke the blood-bond once. I would only dishonor myself further to repeat the act . . . . And think of your part in it, Gudrun. You have already deceived Gunner on my account. I would rather die than contaminate you further. And who would benefit by it anyway? You? Gunner? Brunhild? No. Today has been the first in many that my soul has known any peace. And now, having told you everything . . . ." He drifted off, as if he had just thought of something else.

"Is there more?" I asked.

"No more," he mumbled. "I only meant to say . . . . Oh, Gudrun, sleep comes over me even as I speak."

"Do not sleep yet. You have yet to promise me that you will say nothing to Gunner."

"I cannot think on it anymore tonight. All these emotions, these womanish tears. So much to sort through. It seems I have done nothing but think for days and days and days. How tiring it all is."

"Aye, I know your meaning too well myself. Just promise me, or I swear I will never sleep again."

"I promise then, but I hardly know what it is that I am promising. And I fear I am a dead man either way."

As if our dreams had been one dream, we awoke at the very same moment the next morning. And as if we knew already that this day would end our happiness, we clung to each other wordlessly and with a desperation greater than any I had ever know before, for in Sigurd's eyes I saw both his fear and the reflection of my own.

The hall was quiet, and I imagined that Gunner was already seated in his high seat, waiting for us to arise so that he could confront Sigurd with the disclosure which, for all I knew, Brunhild had made to him during the night. Thus I made no move to rise. And Sigurd, who was surely imagining likewise, made no move either.

At length, Mother called from beyond the curtain to say that it was late and that she would soon be removing the breakfast foods from the table. That we had better come in and get our share. Her words did little to put me at ease, for her tone was rash. I imagined that Gunner, growing impatient, had bade her to call out to us. We clung to each other a moment longer, and then, grudgingly, we released each other. But our desperation persisted, and still we held each other with our eyes as we crawled out from under our rugs and got to our feet.

Before we reached the curtain, I whispered to Sigurd, "It will all end well. You will see." And I forced a smile.

I was about to draw back the curtain when all at once he fell to his knees before me. "This new day may bring the terror for which last night was only the foretoken," he cried hastily. "There are things I must say to you before we face Gunner and Brunhild, if she still lives. What happened between Brunhild and me was not the only grave error I made in recent times. It was the only one concerning you and your brothers, to be sure, but there is more. I must tell you now, for I fear I may not have another chance."

I could bear to hear no more. "This is not time," I said. "Whatever it is, it must wait."

"It must be now. I must know that you love me in spite of all that I have done. I must believe, when I breathe my last breath, that you loved the man I am, not the one you imagine me to be."

I grabbed his arms and made him stand again. "I will not hear you speak of death," I whispered. "And as for these other things that you would tell me, I will not hear them either. There are times when a man must weigh and decide, and when his decisions turn out to be errors, he must grieve for them alone and then discount them. Gripner was right to teach you that there is no good or evil for a person like yourself. Have you forgotten his lesson? There is nothing you can tell me now that would make me love you less. I have loved you all my life. And all my life I believed I could not love you more. But last night, when we shared our pain together, our secrets and our broken vows, I came to love you even more. You sully this new love of mine when you suggest that there is something you could say to me which would bring it to an end. Let us go, lest Gunner and Hagen begin to wonder why we tarry. And let us be hopeful."

I drew back the curtain before he could respond. To my astonishment, there was no one in the hall but Mother. "Where have they all gone?" I asked.

"They left early to hunt." She was wiping crumbs from the table, and she did not bother to look up at us.

"And Brunhild? Is she still within?"

"No, she went out shortly after them."

"So early?" Mother shrugged and continued wiping the table. Sigurd and I exchanged a look. "And Guthorm?" I asked. "Where is he off to?"

"He went with Gunner and Hagen, on Hagen's horse."

"To hunt?"

"Of course not!"

"Then why—"

Mother turned from the table then and I saw that her face was hard and the rims of her eyes were red. "I do not know," she shouted. She dropped the crumbs in her hand back onto the table, and grabbing her cloak from the long bench, she lifted the door and ran out.

Though we worked together side by side all that morning and afternoon, milking the goats and later, at our distaffs, Mother said not a word to me, and I concluded that she was worried about Guthorm. I might have been worried myself—for my brothers did not usually stay out so late, and they never took Guthorm along with them—but my thoughts were all concerning Brunhild. Still, I said to Mother, "Do not worry so. They will take good care of him." She only looked up at me with one brow raised and went back about her labors.

When it was clear that Gunner and Hagen would not return in time to provide us with our meal, Mother set about gathering what leftovers there were from the previous evening. I excused myself then and went out to find Sigurd. He was, as always, at work at the oaks. Two he had already cut and split into burning logs, and he was nearly done with the third. When I approached, he was just putting his ax aside for the day. In spite of the cold, he was drenched with sweat. I was about to say to him that I had seen no sign of Brunhild all day when I saw her emerging from the forest. Before I could avert my eyes, she called out, "It will snow soon enough, tonight perhaps."

Too astonished to answer, I nodded my head in agreement and watched as she went past us and into the hall. Then I laughed and said to Sigurd, "Did you see how pleasant she seemed? She has reconciled herself to the situation. My brother will make her happy, you will see. Everything will end well after all." Sigurd, whose eye was still fastened on the hall, nodded, but his expression remained one of concern. I wrapped my arms around his waist. "You cannot go on the rest of your life worrying about this," I said cheerfully. "I say it is over. Let us go in now and find a way to make Brunhild our sister. We have been thinking so much of ourselves that we have forgotten what a heavy load she bears. She has lost your love. And I pity her for that—for all that I am joyous to have regained it. Let us go in and see whether we can ease her pain."

When we entered, Brunhild was sitting alone at the table, and Mother was filling the drinking horns. Brunhild turned to look at me, the arrogance I was accustomed to seeing in her beautiful eyes replaced by an aspect of tranquillity. "We are not waiting tonight for your brothers," she said. "The food is ready. Your mother feels we should begin without them."

I sat down beside her, in Gunner's place. "How strange that they should take Guthorm with them today," I said.

She shrugged. "Not so strange. Gunner said to me last night that he regrets how little time he spends with the child."

This was not something I could easily imagine Gunner saying, even if he and Brunhild had made things up between them. "I wonder what keeps them so long," I persisted.

"I would not know," she said, looking away.

I got up to fetch the washing bowl, but I took my time about it, for I hoped that Sigurd might say a word to her, too, in my absence. But I heard nothing, and when I turned again, he was seated at the table, staring at his folded hands.

We were in the middle of our meal when the door lifted. Guthorm was the first to enter. Mother stood up when she saw him, and she would have gone to him, but he ran past the table and into the bower which was now Sigurd's and mine. Hagen came in next, and seeing Mother's expression, he shouted, "He is tired. Let him sleep."

"But he cannot sleep in there. He knows that. And he has not eaten yet," Mother cried.

Gunner entered, and I saw right away that his eyes were glazed over, like those of a man who has had too much mead. "Let him sleep," he said firmly. He sat down next to Brunhild and held out his hands to remind me that he needed the washing bowl.

"I see the hunt went well today, "I said as I brought him the bowl and looked at his bloodied hands. But as he made no response, I brought the bowl to Hagen in silence and returned to my seat.

That night, Gunner took up his carving, but before he got started, Brunhild asked him to play his harp. He stared at her a moment—incredulously, it seemed to me. Then he got up and went for it. He was mid-way into a melody when all at once the rigid look he had worn all evening vanished and he began to laugh. His sudden outburst was such a contradiction to the rising tension that we all stopped what we were doing to stare at him. Still chuckling, he said to Hagen, "Brother, sing for us again the song you sang on the day of the feast."

"You sing it," Hagen replied. "Those events warrant a better voice than mine."

"Oblige me, brother," Gunner insisted. "Your voice was good enough for us on that day, and it is good enough for us on this one as well. After all, a voice is a voice. Look what pleasure you brought Sigurd the last time you sang it. Surely his pleasure will be as great now." Gunner laughed and glanced at Sigurd, who was sitting with his hands frozen over Guthorm's new shoes, looking bewildered. His lips were parted as if to smile, but his eyes darted from Gunner to Hagen, and the smile did not come.

Gunner got up and began to pace, his harp in one hand. "Do you recall, Sigurd?" he asked, his gaze drifting to the war sword which was blazing on its ledge along the wall. "Why, you were speechless. And so you should have been. Hagen and I spent a good lot of time choosing the words and the melody for that song. We wanted to honor you properly, our brother in blood. Nothing but the best would do. And now that your song has been sung before all the Burgundians, you can be certain that it will be sung in many a hall for all the years and years until the end."

"The end?" Sigurd whispered.

Gunner roared with laughter. "Why, the very thought of hearing your song again flusters you, I see. Surely the world will end one day and all the good things on it will pass away. What end did you think I meant? Your end? You shall have no end, thanks to Hagen and me. Your feats have immortalized you." He stopped pacing and stood behind Hagen and stared down at the crown of his head. "Will you or will you not sing once more the praises of our immortal brother?"

"To what end?" Hagen mumbled wearily.

Gunner howled. "Everyone is distracted by ends tonight. What a vapid lot we are. To what end, he asks. I have told you to what end. To let our brother know that—"

"Enough!" Hagen shouted. "Begin the melody. I will sing."

Gunner reached down and planted his palm on Hagen's shoulder. Hagen looked away from it, and in the process, our eyes met—but he looked away from me too. Gunner came back to the hearth and began to play. With his head lowered, Hagen joined in singing. His tuneless voice lent a kind of mockery to Sigurd's quest. The first time we had heard the song, we had all been in a jovial mood and eager to hear Hagen's words. But now, the mood of my brothers' audience had been shaped by the lack of congeniality in their dispositions. Gunner's grin—which was almost a sneer—expressed his true intentions clearly enough; Hagen's singing of the song had been meant to scorn Sigurd from the onset.

The song was longer than it had been at the feast, for now Hagen added verses describing the gifts which Sigurd had bestowed on Gunner. While he sang of them, he lifted his head and looked at Gunner significantly, as if, I thought, to remind Gunner of Sigurd's generosity. But Gunner only smiled more wildly and stared at Sigurd. Hagen's last verse described the war sword, and I could not help but turn my head to look at the thing. To my horror, it seemed to have become even more animated, flashing there upon the wall as if it had ears to hear its praises. As if, like the Burgundians who had heard Gunner's speech, it could be stirred to a state of excitement.

Hagen finished, and Gunner's harp fell silent. Gunner nodded encouragingly, waiting for Sigurd to speak, but Sigurd was struck dumb. Gunner laughed; then he stopped laughing abruptly and got to his feet. He went directly to the war sword and lifted it down from its ledge and held it across his palms.

Horrified, I glanced at Hagen, but his expression told me nothing. His face seemed to be locked up, devoid of sense, almost like Guthorm's. Gunner came back to the hearth. Sigurd's stunned gaze clung to him. The sword flashed wickedly as Gunner brought it nearer to the fire. It was all I could do to keep from shielding my eyes from its glare. Then, in one quick movement, Gunner grabbed the sword by its hilt and jerked himself into a warrior's stance. Sigurd gasped. Gunner laughed and eased his stance. Still laughing, he turned and replaced the sword on the ledge, laying it up there tenderly, as if he were handling a baby. "I burn with desire to take it up against my enemies," he said. His whispered declaration seemed to fly out in all directions, to fill the hall. "And now," he announced, yawning, "I shall retire. I will see you all in the morning, if the gods so will it." He grunted a laugh and put out his hand for Brunhild. She bounded up to his side, smiling, the mischief come back wholly into her eyes.

I got to my feet as soon as they were gone and stood before Sigurd with my hand extended, mumbling something inane about retiring as well. I could feel Mother and Hagen watching me closely, but I kept my gaze on Sigurd. By degrees, he lifted his head. His look was as helpless as a child's. When he took my hand, his grip was slack. I all but pulled him to the bower.

Before entering, I turned back to look at Hagen. He looked away quickly, but not before I noted that his vapid expression had become something other—sympathetic, I thought.

Guthorm was asleep on the feather mattress. While Sigurd stared down at him, stupefied, I began to unroll Guthorm's mattress for Sigurd and me. But Hagen charged in before I could finish and scooped Guthorm up in his arms.

"Let him stay," I cried.

"He must learn," Hagen shouted.

We stared at each other. Then Hagen hurried out with Guthorm, pulling the curtain closed behind him.

"They have made up their minds," Sigurd said in a voice so low that I could hardly hear it. "The song was my funeral dirge. Tomorrow they will add a final verse to it."

I grabbed his shoulders. "Then we must be gone tonight."

"A man does not run from his destiny. Particularly when he has fashioned it himself."

"Perhaps we misinterpret—"

"Unlikely," Sigurd said flatly.

He freed himself gently from my grip and sat down on our mattress. I found his arm in the dark and tried to pull him back up, but he would not be moved. I fell to my knees. "Let us go. I beg you."

He clapped his hand over my mouth and we listened together to the strange noise coming from the other bower. At first I could not make it out, but as it grew louder, I was able. It was Brunhild—Brunhild laughing. Sigurd dropped his hand from my mouth, and we listened on, even after her laughter had subsided.

"We can wait until we are sure the others are asleep," I whispered hastily. "Then we can flee to your uncle's."

"With Hagen sleeping out in the bower?"

"Then in the morning, first thing, before dawn, before the others awaken. We must stay up all night waiting."

"It will not work," he said almost indifferently.

"It must. I beg you. You will not go against this one wish of mine."

Sigurd made no reply. Although I could not make out his face in the dark, I could imagine it, empty of fear now, almost peaceful, as if the life-spirit had gone out of him already.

We sat for a long time, not touching, not speaking. There was another sound. I held my breath to listen. It was the horrible retching sound of someone being sick. "Guthorm," I cried, and I got to my feet and ran out of the bower.

The torches had been extinguished and the fire was low. In the dim light I could see Mother bending over Guthorm while he vomited. Hagen was asleep, or pretending to be, on the long bench.

"Help me," Mother whispered when she saw me.

I ran for the washing bowl and drying cloth and brought them to her.

"Some light," she said, and I ran to find a taper. I lit it at the hearth and hurried back to her.

Guthorm had stopped heaving and Mother was wiping his face. His eyes were bright and red and frightened. Together we got him out of his clothes and wrapped him up in rugs and lay him down on Mother's mattress. We watched him wordlessly until his breathing became regular again. Then Mother began to cry softly. I touched her hand to comfort her, but she pulled it away from me. "The mess," she whispered.

I took the taper over to it and began to clean it up with the cloth. The odor was awful, but the sight was worse. Though much of it was fluids, there were also several meaty chunks therein. I brought the taper closer. Now I could see that some of the chunks were covered with hair and some with skin. The hair resembled the hair of the wolf, but I could not be certain. The skin was clearly snake skin. Sick with horror, I threw the cloth away from me. I looked back at Mother. She was bent over Guthorm, her shoulders trembling with her silent sobs. I reached for the cloth and finished cleaning the mess.

"We must go tonight," I whispered as I lay myself down again at Sigurd's side. "They have made Guthorm eat of the wolf and the snake. I do not know what it portends, but I know it is not good."

Sigurd made no answer. The regularity of his breathing assured me that he was already fast asleep. I thought to awaken him, but then I changed my mind. Even if he could be made to flee, it could not happen yet, as Mother was still awake. She would hear us and ask what we were about. And then Hagen might awaken, and Gunner too—if they were not already awake and waiting for us to make such a move.

I stared up at the darkness, determined to stay awake until I was sure that everyone was asleep. Then I would rouse Sigurd and demand that he flee with me. We might not get by Hagen, but it was our only chance. I rehearsed the words I would use to convince him. Words and words and words came into my head, and, for a time, they kept me from thinking about the evil thing that Hagen and Gunner had done to Guthorm. But the mind is a wonder, and while I was still at work making new combinations for my petitions, I began to ponder Guthorm's eating of foul things in earnest. I had heard of men eating such things before, in connection with spells for cunning and swiftness, those traits the snake and the wolf share. But the men who ate such things were evil themselves. There was no evil in Guthorm. Surely that was why his innocent body had rejected them.

Time passed, and there was no sound other than Sigurd's breathing. My own breathing seemed to keep pace with it. My mind released its monsters, and, tired as I was, I began to think that our flight could wait until morning after all.

Then the light changed, or rather, a light as soft as fog came creeping into the bower to displace some of the darkness. I said to myself, *Ah, at last I dream,* and I marveled that I could dream when all around me there was chaos. I looked to the source of the light and saw Guthorm. This troubled me some, for although Guthorm's presence inhabited most of my waking hours, I seldom dreamed of him. Beyond him, closer to the source of the light, was a second form—a woman, Mother. She seemed to be rising from out of the light itself, gradually at first, but then more quickly. She seemed to be wearing a mask, but when she came closer, I saw that it was only terror: terror marked her face grotesquely. Her lips were pulled back and her teeth were bared. Her pupils seemed to float. Her arms were outstretched.

I got up on one elbow to have a better look, and I saw then that Guthorm was wielding a sword. He was about to cast it. At me? But he was not looking at me. His blank gaze was fixed on Sigurd.

Perhaps I shrieked, for all at once Sigurd sat up beside me. The sword came flying simultaneously. I heard it slice the air, and then I heard a sound like a twig snapping as it bit into Sigurd's flesh. Sigurd yanked it out, and using the motion I had seen him use so many times, he cast it back again. When he recognized his assailant, he groaned. Mother caught Guthorm in her arms just as the sword entered his neck. Sigurd groaned again and fell back. His tunic was covered with black, a spreading black reaching for the whole of him. I put my hand on his chest, to hold his life-blood in. I heard a sound which I at first mistook for a ringing in my ears, its pitch was so high. Then I realized that it was Mother screaming. I said to myself, *What a dream this is! If only I could awaken.* And then I remembered something of the events that had preceded my dream, so that I came to see that it was not so strange a dream to have under the circumstances.

My hands were wet with blood. *How warm it is,* I thought. Then, to drown out the sound of Mother's screams, which were unbearable, I began to scream myself. And I thought that if I screamed loud enough and long enough, I would finally awaken. But my screams kept coming, and I felt no less a dreamer. My screams saturated the bower and rolled into the hall to merge with Mother's. I could not decide which was spilling out faster, my screams or Sigurd's blood. Then there was another sound, competing with mine and Mother's. This one I had heard before, and I quieted so as to be able to better listen to it. *Ah, yes,* I said to myself, *that is only Brunhild; Brunhild is only laughing again.*

The City of Attila

Chapter 15

It took me a moment to figure out what was different in my little world. Then I realized that there was no guard riding outside my hut. Thinking that the guards must only be changing shifts—though they had always done so just outside my doorway in the past—I crawled across the floor and peeked out. Then I crawled back to wait for breakfast. But neither my breakfast nor my guard appeared, and when no one came at dinner time either, I concluded that a guard could not be spared for me now that Attila was marching and that I had better go in search of food in the morning.

Edeco had said that there would be few men left, and he was right. Other than the guards posted at Onegesius's and Attila's gates, and a few others scattered in between, the only men I saw were the aged ones. The City of Attila was a city of women and children now. And as I wandered through it—hungry and fearful but savoring each step of my freedom—I could not help but note that the faces I saw looked more serene that those I was used to. I had left the hut with my cloak on, in part because the air was brisk, and in part because I felt safer covered up, but the air warmed gallantly for so early in the season, and as the only reactions my presence evoked were indifference or curiosity, I soon removed it. After a time I grew brave enough to look beyond the eyes of the guards and the villagers to the bright, cloudless sky and the golden grasses swaying in the fields as if to the rhythm of my own careless thoughts.

I was startled out of my reverie by a voice calling, "Ho! Ildico!" When I turned, I saw Eara, one of my fellow servants, sitting out in front of her hut. She had been surrounded by children, but when they saw me stop, they must have decided that my presence relieved them of their obligation to sit with the old woman, for they all ran off at once.

"My grandchildren," Eara explained, turning her smiling face toward me. She was one of the two women who stayed on in Attila's hall to deal with the scraps and the dirty bowls after the rest of the servants had finished their tasks. Her special status—which implied that Attila trusted her—and her brusque manner had kept me from conversing with her in the past. I could not imagine why she had called to me now, or why she looked so pleased to see me. Tentatively, I stepped forward and confessed to Eara that I was hungry and did not know where to go to look for food. Eara got up from her mat and gave me directions to the food tent. And when I thanked her and made to move away, she drew in her features in such a way that I thought she was disappointed to find me in such a hurry.

I had to go north past a good many huts before I found the line of wagons that Eara had described and the food tent just beyond it. When I entered, I found, as I should have realized, that the people working it were all Thuets. I imagined that some of them were from Edeco's tribe, and it was all I could do to keep from saying more than 'thank you' to them as I went from one to another to be served. When my bowl was full, I went outside and found a place to sit away from the others who had come outside with their bowls. I had never been to this part of the village before, and though the sights were the same as elsewhere, I was enjoying the difference in perspective, when all at once I heard a sound behind me—a low wail. I put the bowl aside and looked around but saw no one. Then I chanced to look where the wagons were all lined up together and espied, wedged between two of them, a woman of my age. The woman was bent over, but her face was uplifted and contorted with pain or anguish. Her suffering passed even as I watched her, and her features relaxed. Taking a deep breath, she sat back against a wheel spoke. She was very beautiful, and, clearly, Roman.

I turned to look at the sky again, but now I was distracted. And when I heard the Roman cry out again a while later, I got up with my bowl and went toward her, between the wagons. My shadow arrived ahead of me, and she tensed as she looked on it. But when her gaze reached my face, she smiled at once. "I heard you cry out," I said in the Hunnish tongue, although I did not expect to be understood.

The Roman moved a dark strand of hair away from her face. "It was nothing," she said.

I stared down at her. I had never come across a Roman woman before. I was torn between curiosity and an instinctive contempt for the people who had set the Huns on the Burgundians. "How is it that you speak Hunnish?" I asked.

She glanced beyond me, as if to see whether anyone was watching. "I am married to a Hun. And you?"

As her expression remained pleasant, so that I thought she must not mind being married to a Hun, I resolved to be careful how I answered. "I serve Attila in the evenings," I said. "I live alone in a hut beyond his palisade. I am not married."

We stared at each other for so long that I concluded we had nothing more to say to each other and was about to take my leave. But then I noticed that she was fingering a large green stone that hung from a chain around her neck. Unconsciously, I reached up to fondle my own stone and dropped my hand abruptly when I remembered that I would not find it. "How did you come to marry a Hun?" I heard myself ask.

"I was taken prisoner during the siege of my village. The man who cut down my parents and my brothers claimed me as his wife."

I clapped my hand over my mouth, as startled that the Roman should relate this with a smile as I was by her words. She dropped her stone and brushed her fingertips against the hem of my robe. "Sit," she said. "Tell me how you came to serve Attila."

Now it was my turn to look beyond the wagons, for it occurred to me that the Roman might be a scout planted by Attila to learn from me all that Edeco had failed to learn. But I saw in the next instant how ridiculous the notion was, and I sank down beside her saying, "I wandered too far from home. Some Huns found me and brought me here. At first I stayed alone in my hut. But then one of Attila's men, a man who calls me his friend, pressed Attila to take me into service." I looked away, marveling at how easily deceit came to me now that I had become so practiced at it. When I looked back again, the Roman was clutching her leg. She groaned, then closed her eyes and breathed through her mouth until the pain passed. "What is it?" I asked.

She rolled her skirt up quickly and I saw the huge open gash across her thigh. It was swollen and red at the edges and black in the middle with puddles of pus. "You must get help," I exclaimed.

She pulled her skirt down over the wound. "It is not so bad. The pain comes and goes. It is worse today than usual. It will likely heal on its own."

"But it will not. I have seen men die of lesser wounds." I was already getting to my feet, but the Roman put her hand up to stop me. I stared at her palm, for I thought I felt some power—some energy emanating from it—almost like the energy emitted by the war sword. Frightened and intrigued, I sat down again and stared at her.

"I cannot go for help," she stated calmly. "The man who inflicted it, my husband, forbade it. If he learned I went for help, he would do worse to me, I am certain."

"But how could he do such a thing?"

She laughed. "I suspect he was jealous. He does not mind when I speak to Hun women because he could not bear it early on when I knew nothing of his language. But one day he caught me speaking to another Roman, the wife of a Hun like myself, in our own language, which he would have me forget. This wound was meant to remind me of my error. I have had it for some time and it has not killed me yet. So you see, you need not worry."

"But I must go," I cried. "Suppose he learns that you spoke to a Thuet and wounds you again on my account?"

"No," she cried, her dark, almond-shaped eyes flooding with petition. Then she smiled and said more gently, "It has been so long since I have had anyone to talk to like this. The Hun women do not trust me and never speak to me of personal matters. Besides, no one will notice us here. And even if someone did, who would tarnish such a glorious day with such an evil purpose?"

We both looked up at the sky instinctively, and I said to myself, *I am no better than the Huns. Because she is no Thuet, I did not trust her either.*

"You must have noticed," the Roman added, "everyone seems more at ease now that Attila is gone for a time."

Now I felt an impulse to overturn my distrust by telling her of the scheme that Edeco and I had devised, and that, consequently, Attila might never return. But I remembered that I had been played once before by a beautiful woman who appeared, briefly, wise and congenial. "Has your husband gone with him?" I asked.

"Yes."

I shook my head. "I cannot think how you can be so pleasant when you are married to such a monster. I thought my own miseries the worst until now."

The Roman looked at me with her head cocked and one of her long, finely-arched eyebrows ascending. "I have had to learn to forgive him. Otherwise I should have died of despair long before now."

I could not help but laugh. "Forgive him? How is that possible?"

The Roman smiled warmly. "Have you never had to forgive someone yourself?"

"Aye," I answered. "But that was my brother. And even that was a difficult task which I should never have accomplished without much help."

"All men are brothers," the Roman responded.

I stared at her quizzically.

"But you asked me about my husband," she went on. "Forgiving him was not easy at first, but time passed and gradually I managed it. I have come to realize that he does not see that his ways are wrong. Right and wrong have no meaning for him. He can distinguish only between the Hun way and the way of others. It is sometimes necessary for me to remind myself that had I been raised among the Huns and taught early on that glory comes from domination, it is likely I should be much the same." She hesitated, her milk-white finger at play on her lower lip. "Would you like me to tell you the story I keep in mind to drive off my anger when it comes?"

"Indeed, I am most curious."

"It is a story Jesus told."

"Jesus?"

"The son of God made man and sent to Earth."

"Then you are a Christian?"

"Yes. Now listen. There was once a king who decided that he had better bring his accounts up to date. And in the process, he came across the name of a man who owed him twenty pounds of gold. He sent for the man and demanded payment. But the man fell to his knees, and after telling the king of his woes, he begged the king to be patient until he could find the means to repay his debt. Now the king, who was as rich in empathy as he was in gold, said to the debtor, 'Go. Your debt is forgotten.' And the man left immediately. But as he was heading home, musing over his good fortune, he encountered a man who owed him four pounds of gold, and thinking that now that he was debt-free he might use the four pounds to get himself ahead, he insisted that his debtor pay him on the spot. The debtor fell to his knees and begged his creditor to give him more time. But the creditor, who had already forgotten the king's leniency, had his debtor sent to prison."

"I fail to understand," I said. "What has all this to do with forgiving the man who killed your family and wounded you?"

"If you think of the king as God, you will see. There is not a day that passes when God does not forgive me for my debts. And so who am I to refuse to forgive the debts of another, whether he asks or not?"

I shook my head. "I do not grasp it. One is obligated to forgive his own . . . . But one's enemies? It makes no sense to me."

"Have you an enemy, friend?"

"Aye, and his name is Attila. He and his brother cut my people down when I was very young. There were some eighty thousand of us before they came. Now we number—" I broke off, startled to see how easily I could forget myself. And when the Roman lay her fingertips on my arm, I began to cry and had to hide my face in my hands. "I have been here so long," I mumbled. "And I never before said those words—"

"Cry, my friend. I will comfort you. And you will be comforted again in Heaven," the Roman whispered.

I dropped my hands from my face and looked down to where the Roman's fingers were fondling my arm. Again I was struck by the warmth that seemed to emanate from them. "You do bring me comfort," I whispered back. "But tell me, what is Heaven?"

The Roman sat back, folded her hands on her lap, and lifted her gaze to the sky.

"We call the place Valhalla," I said. "I wonder is there any difference?"

The Roman opened her mouth as if to comment but then changed her mind.

"I lied before," I said. "I did not wander too far from home. My home is far away, across the plain and over the mountains to the west. I came to the City of Attila freely and with a purpose. I came to find the means to cut Attila down. And I may have succeeded. I will know when this campaign is done." I searched her face for some sign of alarm but saw none. "I detest him," I continued. "I shall never forgive him for what he did to my people—and yours either, for that matter, for I never knew a Roman before, but now I see that you Romans are not at all what I once thought."

She laughed. "I am not representative of all Romans, friend, though I promise you, I am no better than most. Still, there are some among my people who are worse. In the village where I grew up, for instance, there were a great number of unjust men. These men were councilors, and their task, once, was to see to our civic lives. But they were also the city tax-collectors, and when they found that through bribery and corruption that they could grow in wealth while the rest of us declined, they were quick to forget about our civic lives and concentrate on their own needs. We were lucky to have the church to turn to. It protected the poorest among us . . . until Attila came and tore it down."

"Then you must understand why it is right that Attila—and these tax-collectors too—be cut down before more people are harmed by their actions."

The Roman smiled. "I should like to tell you another of Jesus's stories, if you would not mind too much."

"I invite you to do so."

"Then here it is: There was a man who had two sons, and one day he asked each of them to go into the fields and work them. The first said no, but later he reconsidered and went to work. The second son said yes to his father, but he had no intention of going. And as soon as his father's back was turned, he went back about business of his own. Which would you say was the better son?"

"Why, neither. It seems to me that if this Jesus wanted to set an example, he would have invented a third son, one who said yes and then went right off to the fields."

"But you see, the point of the story would have been lost then, for the people he intended it for were either like the first or the second son."

"Then the point is lost on me as well. I can only make sense of it if a third son is included. If the listeners were more like the first and the second, then the compliance of a third would have given them something to strive for."

"Perhaps. But let me explain it the way my father once explained it to me. The corrupt among us are often like the first son, who said no but later changed his mind. Perhaps he changed his mind so late in the day that he could hardly be of use in the fields. The point is that he did change his mind. Time is God's gift, friend. He doles it out as He sees fit. Until night falls, who is to say that it is too late for a corrupt man to change?"

"But what of the second son who was more cunning and had no intention of doing as his father bade? I can think of at least one person as corrupt as he."

"He, too, may change his way of thinking."

"Now I understand," I said, but in truth I was still perplexed.

Perhaps the Roman saw through me, for she set her gaze on me sternly and said, "I hope to meet with you again, friend, and I do not mean just here in the City of Attila. Do not poison your thoughts with notions of harming Attila."

I grunted. "If Attila comes to rule the world, you will change your thinking fast enough."

The Roman clapped her hands together. "Then let us pray to Jesus that never comes to pass. Have you never heard it said that when people pray together—"

"Forgive me, but I cannot think what would happen if my gods learned that I had prayed to another."

We stared at each other in silence for a moment, and then I turned away. I was thinking, and not for the first time, how godless the world had come to seem since my coming to Pannonia. I could not understand the folly of the Roman's god, who would have folk turn their backs on their enemies even as they drew their swords on them. But her talk of this Jesus, as it put me in mind of Wodan and the others, was a boon for me. My mind drifted off on its own, far away, so that all at once I seemed to hear the voices of my fellow Burgundians rising up to stir the ears of the gods. I seemed once more to see the sacrifice, the blood-stained altar, the blood-smeared trees—and all the time our voices reaching up and up to Valhalla, becoming one voice, the voice of a people bound together by blood and custom and hearts that are full. That was an uplifting like no other. And it grieved me to think that my existence in Pannonia had put it at such a distance, for whether my people had come together to mourn or to rejoice, to plead or to praise, our connection to one another and to the gods was so pure and so profound then that it transcended the event that had assembled us. And when we went our separate ways, we took something of that holy connection away with us.

I turned to the Roman. "It would please me to tell you about my people and our gods," I said. And I proceeded to tell her all that I had been thinking and more. She smiled sweetly throughout, and afterwards we said nothing for a long time.

"No one is all bad," she finally whispered.

I came bounding down to Earth and turned to look at her.

"My husband, for example. For all the evil that he has done, he has grown fond of me. As long as I obey him, he treats me with kindness. And he allows me privileges which the other Huns would scorn him for if they knew."

"Such as?"

"Well, for one, he allows me to write as I please, as long as I do it in his language."

I sat forward excitedly. "I know of writing. My friend . . . he told me. What is it that you write?"

The Roman drew a circle in the sand with her finger. "Letters, mostly."

"And he permits you to send them forth with messengers?"

She laughed. "I do not write them to be sent. The people they are written to are all dead."

Now I looked at her with some concern, thinking that perhaps she was mad. All this talk of forgiving one's enemies . . . and the force which I had felt emanating from the her hands . . . . I had never met anyone like her before.

"When I first came to the City of Attila," she continued, "I found myself thinking the same thought over and over again: If only I could speak to my family. If only I could tell those who loved me about my ordeal with the Huns. I felt I was losing my mind by keeping my sorrows all to myself."

"Aye," I interrupted, "I know the feeling well enough."

"Then I began to write the words of discontent which I had carried around so long in my head. And as I described each of my miseries, the pressure they had exerted when I had only been able to think of them was relieved some. I suppose I was really only writing to myself. Even so, the writing of those matters made them less somehow. Now, when I look back on them . . ." She sat forward suddenly so that we were shoulder to shoulder. "Do you know how to read at all?"

"No. But I saw some writing once, on a parchment made of goatskin."

The Roman smiled. Then she sat back and sighed. "I was going to say that if you knew how to read a bit, you might take my letters should anything happen to me."

"But nothing must happen to you!" I exclaimed.

"I am not afraid to die."

"You must live for my sake. I will not do without you. Though our ways are different, I find that I love you already."

The Roman turned to look at me. "How are you called, friend?"

"Here in the City of Attila I am known as Ildico. On my own lands, I am called Gudrun."

"I am called Sagaria."

"Sagaria," I repeated, looking up and noting that the line for the food tent was now extended outside of it.

She had followed my gaze. "We should go," she whispered. "The whole village will be coming now. It is that time."

Her hand came up to fondle her green stone, and again I missed my own stone sorely. "It is lovely," I said, indicating it with a flick of a finger.

She smiled. "It is very special. See here." She slipped the chain over her head and held the gem with both hands. Then she twisted it, and as I watched in amazement, the stone divided and became two. It was hollow inside, and the bottom part seemed to be connected to the upper by an invisible hinge. "My father gave me the gem when I was still a babe. I kept it full of rose petal. After he was gone, I used to open it and think of him. But I made the mistake of telling my husband about it, and the next time I opened it, it was empty. He must have emptied it while I slept, for I never take it from my neck. Smell. The scent remains."

I bent my head and sniffed. But the lengthening line before the food tent caught my attention again and I looked up at Sagaria with apprehension.

"We must part," Sagaria said hastily. "As soon as these villagers have eaten, the Thuets will take their wagons and go."

"We must meet again tomorrow," I cried, and I grabbed hold of her wrist. To my astonishment, it was burning. And then I understood the nature of the force which I had felt issuing from her hand.

Sagaria saw my look. "I have had the fever for some days," she said. "It will pass."

I thought of Eara, of the disappointed look she had given me when I left her. "I have an idea," I whispered. "I think I can find someone who may be willing to give us something for your leg. No one need know about it."

But Sagaria's eyes were all for the crowd now, which was becoming noisy. "You go first," she said. "I will be a long time getting away myself, and we should not be seen to leave together."

"No, you go. I will not rest until I know you have returned safely."

Sagaria put her burning lips to my cheek and kissed me softly. Then she got up clumsily, and dragging her bad leg, she went out between the wagons in the direction opposite the throng. When she passed from my view, I lay down and searched for her from beneath the wagons. With her awkward limp, she was easy enough to pick out. When she disappeared again, I rolled under one wagon and came up on the side of the next in time to see her entering a hut not too far off in the distance.

That night my imagination was a wild, uncontrollable thing. I fancied that I would heal Sagaria, and—as I had forgotten all about Edeco in the excitement of having found a friend, and such an intriguing one—that Sagaria and I would find the means to escape. Then, remembering Edeco all at once, I imagined that Sagaria and I would wait together for his return and to learn that Attila was dead, and that then the three of us would steal off together to begin a new life, picking up my sweet daughter and her caretaker, on our way. Then I thought of Edeco's sons and included them in my fantasy—and then my young Hun friend, too. And I laughed aloud to think how my brothers' faces would pucker and fold when they saw me coming with my daughter and her nurse, three Thuets more, a Roman and a Hun.

I went to Eara's hut directly in the morning. Once again, she was sitting outside, but this time there were no children about. I was frightened, for other than a smile and a look of longing, I had no reason to think that I could trust Eara any more than I could trust anyone else in the City of Attila. But when Eara spotted me and called out, "Did you find the food tent all right?" I was encouraged.

I went closer and knelt down on the mat in front of the old woman so that my words would not be overhead. "Aye, I found it, thanks to you. But now I have another favor to ask, and I pray you will grant it to me without question."

Eara's smile vanished and she searched my eyes, one, then the other. "Come in," she whispered at length, and I had the feeling that she knew already what I had come for.

Her hut was no larger than mine, but so cramped with straw baskets and piles of skins that I wondered how she found room to lie down at night. "Speak," Eara said.

"I need a cure—" I began.

"Aye," Eara said, nodding.

"Were I familiar with the plants that grow here in the City of Attila, I would have made one myself, but—"

"This cure is not for you," Eara interrupted.

I stared at her. "No. A friend. She has the fever . . . from a gash that does not heal."

Eara searched my face again. Then she whispered, "Describe it to me."

I did as she bade, and all the time Eara stood with her face close, nodding. When I finished with my description, she turned slowly and looked over her several baskets. Then she went to one of them and rummaged through it. When she turned again, she was holding a swatch of sheepskin in her hand, rolled up and tucked in at the ends. She unrolled it carefully and showed me the black glob at the center. I bent to smell it. The scent was strong and unfamiliar.

Anxious to find Sagaria, I thanked the old woman hastily and turned, but before I could retreat, she grabbed my shoulder. Again, her eyes swept back and forth across my face. Then she turned and went to another of the baskets. She had to dig deeply to find what she wanted. She pressed a second swatch and into my hand. "Poison," she whispered, her dark eyes flashing. "It promotes a quick death. Painless. If her leg does not heal, and the pain is too much, give her this."

I dropped the second swatch into the neck of my robe and ran out in a state of confusion. I could not remember having told Eara that Sagaria's wound was on her leg. I took this to mean that she knew about Sagaria—or that she had the Sight. And for all that the old woman had given me what I wanted and more, I wondered whether I had made a grave error in going to one of Attila's two most trusted servants. But there was no time to think of it now.

We had not set a time for our meeting, but as I had assumed that Sagaria would be as anxious for it as I was, I was disappointed when I arrived and did not find her. Too excited to eat, I paced between the wagons for a long time, and when the sun was well past the place where it had been when we had met the day before, I decided to go to her hut. I knew she would be upset to find me there, and that my going might bring about dire results, but I did not know what else to do. I wandered among the huts near hers casually, as other women were wandering, and when I reached hers, I darted in without looking back.

She was lying on a bed of skins, and she looked even more radiant than she had the day before. I called out to her, but it seemed a long time passed before she became aware of my presence. And then she only looked at me. I took the salve from my robe. "I worried so when you did not come to the wagons," I said getting to my knees. "I have a cure. I will apply it now. And then I will get food and bring it to you, for it is clear you are not well enough to go yourself."

"You should not be here," she whispered. Her voice was very weak.

I pulled up her skirt and as gently as I could, began to apply the salve. The wound was raw and painful looking, and yet she did not as much as wince. My eyes filled with tears. "Sagaria, please do not die. I have a plan. You must live, and when we make our escape from the City of Attila, you must come back with me to my lands."

She smiled. "I would like to hear your plan, but it is not wise for you to be here."

"Please do not die," I repeated. And then I began to tell her my vision, which of course required that I tell her of my daughter and her nurse and much more. On and on I talked, for I felt that as long as she smiled, as long as I had her attention, she would not die. "I love you like a sister," I said in conclusion. "My brothers will love you too, as will all the Franks and the Burgundians. You have only to wait for the salve to work."

"And you have only to wait for Attila's death," she whispered.

"But what is this?" I cried. "You must listen to what I am telling you. You must think of the future I have planned for you. You must cling to that."

"I love you too, sister," she said, or so I thought, for in truth her voice was weaker yet and her lips hardly moved.

I was losing her. I did not know what to do. When she turned her gaze away from me, I got to my feet and rushed from her hut. Outdoors, I tried to move slowly, so as not to attract attention. I walked to the food tent, my thought now being that if I could feed her, I could keep her alive. But the line was long, and I stood impatiently for as long as I could. When I could stand it no longer, I left the line and rushed back to her hut.

To my surprise, a young Hun girl of perhaps ten years jumped up in front of me as if she had been caught in some devious activity. "I heard her moaning," the girl cried. "But now the moaning has ceased."

I pushed the girl aside. Sagaria's beautiful, almond-shaped eyes were open but lifeless. There was a faint smile on her lips. I fell to my knees and bent over her. I could hear the girl babbling behind me. I grabbed Sagaria's wrist. It was, as I knew it must be, cold and pulseless. The girl was still carrying on behind me, and as I could think of nothing but that I must be alone with my friend, I cried, "Go for help. This woman is dying."

The girl was gone in an instant, before I saw my error. Now I should have to leave before others arrived. My heart was pounding wildly. I ran my fingers over Sagaria's flawless face and closed her eyes. It occurred to me all at once that I should search for her letters, that she would want me to have them. I tore my gaze from her face and scanned the hut, but I could make no sense of any of the objects my eye fell on. I got up on one knee, prepared to run, but my fingers found her face again and I could stir myself no further. I touched her cheek, her smile, her long white neck. Then my fingers found her chain and ceased their frantic motion. Thinking of nothing and of many things at once, I seized the chain and jerked it once. It broke in two and fell into my hand. Then I ran.

In the days that followed I went to the food tent only once a day, when it was nearly dark and the Thuets were preparing to leave. As a result, there were many times when there was not enough left for me to fill myself, but I preferred that than to risk being seen by the Hun child and pointed out as the woman who had run away like a thief with the chain of a dead woman. And, too, I avoided passing Eara's hut. Now my imprisonment was self-imposed, and for the first time since my coming to the City of Attila, I was glad there was no one to care what had become of me, for I wanted only to dream of Sagaria and of what might have been.

I was on my way back from the food tent one evening when I heard thunder, and as the sky was clear and full of stars, I knew the Huns were returning. I stopped where I was, up on a knoll not far from my hut, and listened. In the distance, I could see the villagers who were still about, running for the safety of their huts. But I was mesmerized and could not move. In no time the Huns were entering the village, shouting frantically and carrying their torches high over their heads, heading for Attila's gates. I saw a horseman break off from the throng and ride in my direction, and thinking that it must be Edeco, I fell to my knees involuntarily, weeping with joy. But when the rider came closer, I saw that he was too thick and low on his horse to be Edeco, that he was, in fact, one of the men whom I had often found posted outside my hut. He approached shouting and with his whip flying threateningly over his head. I found my feet and ran for shelter.

The next afternoon, I prepared to leave for Attila's hall, but when the guard who was without saw me at the curtain, he ordered me back inside. The Huns' wild ride into the city had assured me that the campaign had not gone well, and now I took the guard's charge as further proof that Attila was dead. Satisfied to think that our plot—mine and Edeco's—had worked, I blew out the taper and sat on a skin in the center of the hut and tried not to think of Edeco and what might have become of him. Instead, I attempted to imagine the scene going on in Attila's hall, the surviving officers and Attila's sons, free to argue at last, fighting amongst themselves as to what to do now and when to inform the villagers that their leader was gone. When the blood began to flow in the chaos that I believed would follow, I would, I promised myself, find a way to leave, to learn about Edeco and to locate his sons.

A day passed, and my wild speculations, which had kept me up all the night before, were interrupted by the guard's voice shouting into my doorway, "Woman, should not you have left by now for the palace?" The bolt that ran through my body could not have been greater if someone had plunged a blade into it. I responded with a profound groan, and then I gasped for air, for there seemed to be none of it left in the hut. With my mind a blank now, I combed my hair and readied myself to serve Attila. And as I reached for Sagaria's chain, which I had managed to repair and which I had filled with Eara's poison, I vowed to see to it that Attila should not live another day.

I carried myself toward Attila's palisade as if on legs made of wood and with no thought save the one—that I was on my way to slay Attila. I passed villagers and horsemen as I neared the gates, but I saw them only peripherally. The only image I saw clearly was that of my fingers on the green stone—concealed now in my robe—twisting the green stone over Attila's cup or bowl of meat—only that and nothing more—until my blind eye fell on Edeco and regained its sight.

He was sitting on his horse conversing with some others but glancing about so that I knew he had been keeping an eye out for me. As soon as he saw me, he pulled up his horse and detached himself from the group. As he approached, he yelled, "You had better hurry along, woman." But when he reached me, he bent low over his horse and whispered hastily, "Attila has set a trap for you. In a moment you will see a sight which would otherwise bring you to your knees. You must not yield. He will be watching." Then he turned and rode back to the others.

As I passed the group, I heard one of the men say, "I wonder that you should be so stern with one of Attila's wives."

"They are not married yet," Edeco countered.

Then another said, "Perhaps Edeco is jealous."

Edeco responded, "Bah! Me, jealous?" and all the others laughed.

It surprised me that I should have taken this in, for my legs, once wooden, were stone now, and my mind was equally insipid. I felt myself trembling, but when I looked down, I saw that my hands were dangling motionlessly at my sides. I turned into the courtyard and went slowly past the men who had gathered near the gate. There was no jubilation among them. I approached the line of tents which belonged to Attila's wives but saw none of the women themselves sitting outside them drinking from their golden goblets. I glanced up and saw, beyond the tents and the riders left between myself and the hall, that Attila was standing on the threshold, watching me. I lowered my head and kept walking, one absurdly heavy foot after the other. I was breathing through my mouth, panting really, and I concentrated on breathing more regularly. My father's words came to me from nowhere: *We shall have music. And we shall sing of events that tear our hearts asunder.* I glanced to my right in time to see Hereca, Ellac's mother, closing the silk curtain from behind which she had been looking out. *We shall have music,* I said to myself.

I glanced at the hall and saw that poles had been erected again at either side of Attila's door. And as before, there was one head atop of each of them. I looked at my feet and was pleased to note that they were still moving. I stole a quick breath and looked up again, at the faces of Attila's victims, and among them, the faces of my brothers. *We shall have music,* I repeated to myself. I forced my eye to travel to each head in turn and to linger on none of them. *And we shall sing of events that tear our hearts asunder.* I was so intent on my father's words, on the motion of my feet and the regularity of my breathing, that I forgot about Attila, and when I stepped up into the hall, I collided with him. I gasped, and muttering an apology, stepped back down and prostrated myself. When I got to my feet again, he was still there, still blocking my entrance. Our eyes met. He smiled his sneer-like smile. I smiled back. Then he moved aside, and smiling still—smiling madly, smiling stone and flint and granite, smiling so hard that I thought I should never be able to cast off the absurd and hideous thing that had taken hold of my face—I joined the other servants.

If Attila made a speech that night, I did not hear it. If he knocked Ellac over a table or shouted at his officers, I had no sense of it. When I went to fetch Attila's cup, Eara stepped forward and snatched it from me. And later, Eara brought him his tray as well. Other than that, I had no knowledge of events.

I had rid myself of my grotesque grin, but Father's words were still pounding in my head, corresponding now to the rhythm of the guard's horse pacing outside my hut. Now I wished to drive the words away—for they seemed to be steering me toward madness—but they played on in spite of my efforts, senselessly. I did not realize that someone had come with my tray until I saw it in the place where nothing had been before. Then my eye fell on my taper, and preferring darkness to light, I blew it out. There was an interruption in the rhythm outside, so that I knew that one guard had come to replace the other. Then the rhythm began again, but as the new guard was riding slower and covering a greater distance, I had to adjust the words that tramped through my head accordingly.

Gudrun's Tapestry

"Gudrun," a voice called out.

I crawled to the doorway and pulled the curtain aside. I did not have the wits to wonder how Edeco had managed to acquire a shift at my hut. "You betrayed me," I whispered. Had I more strength, had my accusation come during a lapse in Father's words rather than right on top of them, I would have screamed it so that it touched the sky and bounded back again, so that even Attila, living still when he should have been long dead, might have heard. Edeco rode past me and turned. When he passed a second time, I sprang to my feet, leapt out of the doorway and struck at him frantically.

He passed and turned. "Gudrun," he said, "go back in. We have come too far to take a chance on spoiling things now."

His words made no sense, but the calmness in his delivery infuriated me. When he passed again, I flew out at him once more, striking his horse inadvertently as well as him. Neither had any reaction. Feeling defeated by Edeco's refusal to strike me back, to cut me down, to end my life and the absurd parade of senseless words dancing in my head, I went back in and closed the curtain behind me. Then I began to cry.

The tears brought some relief, for the sound of my own sobs engaged me and at length I grew calm. There was a narrow gap between the closed curtain and the frame around it, and, putting my eye to it, I said, "It could only have been you."

Edeco answered, "It is true that I told Attila that you had a brother called Gunner. My orders back then were to tell him everything you said, no matter how seemingly trivial. It is true that I was playing you back then, showing you some affection so that you might forget yourself and provide just that sort of information. But I told him, too, that you had said that this Gunner was not a brother in blood and that personally I did not make much of it. But Attila was unsettled over it for a time, and as my affection for you became genuine, which was not long after, I made it a point to undo the wrong I had done . . . on the off chance that you did have such a brother and thus had lied about everything.

"Oh, Gudrun, you cannot know the things I invented, the traps I swore I set for you after that. And as I swore, too, that you averted each and every one of them, Attila finally came to believe that your motive in coming to the City of Attila was neither more nor less than what you had stated. Still, when you first went into his service, all the other servants had strict orders to watch your every move, to report your every transgression. That was why I was so adamant about your behavior in the hall. I risked much, having him take you on . . . . But the others gave him only good reports. And he was pleased, and I was—"

"Tell me about my brothers," I demanded.

Edeco's head jerked up, as if he were surprised to hear me, as if, having been interrupted in the midst his speech, he had lost his drift of thought entirely. He sighed and rode past once more. When he turned, he began again, speaking slowly, choosing his words carefully, so that I was reminded of Attila's speeches. "Some few days before we departed, Attila called a meeting between ourselves and the Franks, whom, you will recall, he had decided to aid once he had marched on the Romans. And in the midst of the discussion that followed, Attila said to the leader, 'Did you ever hear of a Thuet called Gunner who is known for his songs?' The leader replied immediately, saying there was a Burgundian called Gunner who was known for such. Then Attila asked whether this Gunner had a sister, and the leader said he did and that her name was Gudrun. My heart stopped beating in that instant, Gudrun, for you had told me your real name only the night before. And I saw then all at once how you had used the Burgundians in the tale that you told when you first arrived—not because they had stolen the war sword from your Sigurd as you said, but because you thought by doing so to steer me farthest from the truth. And then I remembered that we had laid waste to the Burgundians some years ago. And it all came so clear to me that I could not think how Attila could fail to realize as well. And though I was relieved when he turned our discussion back to the campaign, I was startled too.

"Later I realized that your name was the crucial thing. Without knowing your name, the Frank's disclosure confirmed your story rather than contradicting it. Still, I was thankful that Attila had a good many other things on his mind, and when our meeting ended, I felt certain that the matter was forgotten. But later yet, when Attila and I were alone, he asked me whether I thought there might be any connection between you and the Burgundian Gunner. And I told him, as I saw no harm in it now, that he was likely the brother of the woman whom your Sigurd had married—a man you had never met—and that the Gunner you referred to, the one whose songs stirred you so, was likely from a different tribe altogether. I told him, too, that I had heard it said that Gunner was a common enough name among Thuets. Again, he seemed satisfied.

"I do not know what went wrong, Gudrun. Perhaps he saw me pale when he first questioned the Franks. Or perhaps when he questioned me later, I wrung my hands or gave way to some other nervous habit. Anyway, later, when we were out fighting the Romans and the Thuets in the field, it came to Attila's ears that there were Burgundians about and that the leaders among them, brothers, were called Gunner and Hagen. And he turned to me then, and with a wild gleam in his black eye, he confided that he would like to have the heads of these two Burgundian brothers so that he could be satisfied for once and for all that there was no connection between them and the woman who had brought him the gift of the war sword. I told him that in my opinion we had best concentrate on all our enemies and not seek to single out any two of them. But he cast me a look which was rife with suspicion and shouted, 'Go and get their heads yourself.'" Edeco paused.

I felt my knees buckling and then my body sinking to the ground. "Go on," I whispered.

Edeco paced in silence for some moments more. "You see, Gudrun," he said then, "I was being put to the test too. I had no choice but—" He broke off and hung his head.

All during his speech, Edeco had been riding back and forth. Watching him—and I had watched his every step—I felt calm and empty, as if someone had wrenched my entrails out, leaving me an empty shell. I was glad for the dark, glad I could not see Edeco's face. Edeco had killed them and I had pretended not to know them. We had both passed Attila's tests. And for what? I pulled Sagaria's gem out of my robe and rubbed it over my lips.

"One of the prisoners we had taken identified them, and I found them easily enough. Gunner fought me valiantly, in silence at first, but when he saw whose sword his clashed with, he cried, 'So it is come to this, Thuet against Thuet.' And even as I was plunging my blade into his flesh with Attila looking on at some distance, I answered, 'Thuet against Thuet for now, but perhaps not always. There is a woman among us who strives to find a way to cut Attila down so that Thuets and Thuets can be brothers again.' He fell back smiling, Gudrun, on my honor. I had no chance to bring peace to your other brother, for while I was fighting him, Orestes appeared out of nowhere and finished him off."

Edeco paced in silence, and I clung to the constancy of his motion. He passed me perhaps twenty times more before he spoke again. "I realize that now is not the proper time to tell you about the battle, but as I may not have another opportunity, I will do so. I will make it brief, though there were many details I had hoped to discuss with you. Try to take in what I say. You can make sense of it later—when you feel more yourself." He waited, as if for some objection, and then went on.

"We marched along the Rhine and many cities fell to us. Attila was very pleased and certain that we would return victorious. But when we reached Orleans, we were driven back by an army as great as any I have ever seen—Romans, Franks, Burgundians, Visigoths . . . . Yes, Gudrun, the Visigoths, the life-long enemies of Aetius, marched with him against us.

"There was much blood spilt on both sides, but still it seemed we were the stronger force. It was during this time that your brothers . . . were killed. Not long after that, Theodoric, the Visigoth king, was slain. And then the Visigoths went wild with rage and became stronger than men who have long been at battle can possibly be. By the end of the day of Theodoric's death, Attila began to speak of the possibility of defeat—with great nettle at first, but then, later, with resignation. When night fell, he had us make a circle with our wagons, and those of us who are dearest to him went in with him. He told us to prepare ourselves for death. We were surrounded by the enemy, and he believed we would eventually be starved out. As for himself, he had a funeral pyre prepared from some of our saddles. His plan was to light it and throw himself on it first thing in the morning so that none of his enemies would have the satisfaction of cutting him down. Then he spoke so eloquently of his life and all that he had done with it that some men cried. And when dawn was nigh, he encouraged each of us to speak of our love for him, so that while we were frantic for our own hides we were forced to invent reasons why we cherished his.

"But when the sun began to rise, we looked out from among the wagons and found that the Visigoths and the Franks had withdrawn and that the Romans had removed themselves to a greater distance. Aetius must have found a way to turn the Thuets for home, and now it was clear that he was inviting us to retreat as well. Why Aetius should have permitted this, I can only wonder. Perhaps he believed that he could find a way to turn his generosity to a greater advantage in the future. I suggested to Attila that Aetius's mind was perhaps swayed by the power of the war sword, for my own thoughts then were on your future. If Attila has heretofore believed that the war sword was responsible for his good fortune, I said to myself, might he not blame it, and thus Gudrun, now for the bad?

"Being allowed to retreat is a worse disgrace than to go down fighting. But as Attila likes his life as well as any man, he had us prepare to leave. All that long march home, Attila spoke not a single word to anyone. And when we neared the city gates, we had more bad news. As you know, Attila promised Theodosius that he would let go of the lands south of the Danube.

Gudrun's Tapestry

But when Theodosius died and Marcian took his place, Attila reclaimed them. When we left to march, Attila left a good many men behind to watch over those lands. The messenger had come to inform us that Marcian's troops had wiped out most of our forces there and reclaimed the lands for the Eastern Empire. The wonder of it is that Marcian's troops did not ride here and take the city as well!

"Attila heard this news and then he ordered a guard to ride up to your hut and make sure you were within. I tell you, Gudrun, it frightened me more than I can say to see that his mind would jump to you the instant after he learned that his defeat was even greater than he had imagined. Then, with his eyes on me, he ordered the rest of us to refrain from having anything to do with you under any circumstance until after you had come to the hall and seen the heads of our few victims erected outside it. It was a boon for us that you were late in coming. Attila's favorite men had already gone in by then. And as I had an order to carry out for him, which I am certain he invented to keep me away, I was not expected. The men you saw me conversing with tonight when I gave you the warning were too far back, I think, to have heard his order. In any case, they made no mention of it when they saw me speak to you. Attila, who sent for me later, has already informed me that he was satisfied by your response—and that confidence leads me to believe that he is no longer suspicious of me, either.

"What he will do now, I cannot guess. Nor do I know whether he still intends to marry you. In the meantime, you can be certain that I will do everything in my power to convince him that there are fortunes yet to be gained by the war sword and from the woman who brought it to him—for I would rather see you married to him than disregarded . . . or dead.

"I have said all that I wanted to say, Gudrun. The guard whose shift I took—a man who owed me a favor, for I saved his life on the field—should be returning shortly. Sleep now. You will need your strength in the days to come. You must never enter Attila's hall—or his bed, if it comes to that—with a long face and swollen eyes. You must continue to appear unmoved by the sight in the courtyard. We have come too near to our purpose to make any mistakes."

As if he thought that I might make some response, Edeco paced on for a time. Then he pulled up his horse and rode off.

I continued to sit just behind the curtain with my eye fixed on the night.

SAPAUDIA

CHAPTER 16

I had thought my spirit dead during the time when I believed that I had lost Sigurd's love, but now I know it was only tainted then. It was a weak, black, useless thing to be sure, but still it subsisted. True death came to my spirit when Guthorm came into the bower wielding the sword that had been his birth gift, a sword he had never as much as lifted before. That was the time of true death—though I did not know it until later. For at the moment of my spirit's passing, I was caught somewhere between sleep and wakefulness, and I lacked the wherewithal even to detect whether Guthorm's hurling of the sword and Sigurd's hurling it back again were real events or a part of the dream I felt myself to be verging on. I screamed, yes, but even my anguish seemed illusory. I was more a spectator watching, listening from the gray abyss that we are made to glide through when mindfulness is behind us and sleep is fast approaching. And when I stopped screaming and grew calm, I saw, I suppose, that there was safety within that eerie gorge—that the real and the unreal need not be divided there—and thus I stayed there, dreaming, dead to life or living in death, for a very long time.

All of this is not to say that I became a stranger to my surroundings, for there were moments when I was aware. But again, I took all that I saw and heard to be a part of my dream. Torches were lit in the hall very soon after the tragedy, that I know for certain. I suppose Hagen lit them. And someone came to me—again, probably Hagen—and embraced me long. As far as I know, I did not respond to this embrace. Nor did I hear the words that accompanied it. I merely felt the speaker's utterances hot against my ear. And then there was a great commotion in the hall, cries and raised voices and footsteps wending in every direction, but I paid them no heed either. More light came—daylight, I think—and with it, more footsteps and voices. I sensed a crowd around me in the bower, but I have no recollection of looking up into their faces.

Gudrun's Tapestry

Then darkness came and then light again, and I was carried into the hall where I saw the two corpses lying side by side, each covered over with a white cloth. I was aware of being surrounded by women, who made me sit beside the corpses. One said, "We have come to cut their nails so that their enemies will not make curses on them." And later, another said, "She must be made to cry." Then one of the women lifted the cloth on the smaller corpse and I saw Guthorm's face. I remember thinking, Ah, how sweet and round his face is, how sweetly he sleeps. Then someone took my chin in her palm and turned my head gently toward the larger corpse. I felt the eyes of the women on me, eager for what, I did not know. Someone snapped back the cloth covering Sigurd's face. I saw that his lips were, as always, curled at the corners, and I thought, *His dreams must be carrying him away to some sweet place. If only I could join him there.* And all at once Sigurd and I were walking together in the clearing by the rock-horse, surrounded by birches and sunlight. I saw Guthorm in the distance, and I was about to point him out to Sigurd when I heard a loud shriek, and then I was back in the hall again and Brunhild was flying in my direction. She pushed aside the women surrounding me and threw herself on Sigurd's corpse. She held his face in her hands and covered it with kisses. I was happy, in my senseless state, to see that he did not respond. Then she lay her head on his chest and wailed. The women gathered around and tried to tear her from him. I longed to say to them, *Let her be, she loved him too,* but no words emerged from my mouth, and I was pleased on this account too, for it confirmed to me that I was dreaming still.

In spite of her assailants, Brunhild continued to cling to Sigurd. Between sobs she cried, "Forgive me, forgive me. I was born motherless, fatherless. My name I gave myself. I had no home. No food. I stole from the peasants, and when I could not, I feasted on leaves and berries like a beast. I had no one, nothing. I slept in barns in the Winter and under the stars when it was warm. I lived for you, for your coming. And then you came, as I knew you would, and swore your love for me. You swore I should never be alone again. It was you. Only you. And now I will follow you, whether it be to Hel or Valhalla—"

Brunhild broke off abruptly. The fingers of the women who would bear her away retreated, and a hush fell over the hall. I looked up and saw Gunner approaching. His aspect was fierce. His lips were pulled back so that his teeth were bared. He took Brunhild's long hair in his hand and wound it round and round his fingers. Then he yanked, and then Brunhild was gone. There was a thud, then a whimper. Someone's hand came to rest on my shoulder, but Gunner turned toward me next, and the hand withdrew at once.

225

Gunner took hold of my arms and jerked me to my feet. He shouted for the others to leave us. There was a swish of robes, then silence. Moments passed before he spoke. Or perhaps moments passed before I began to hear him. "From the beginning she hinted," he said. "She tormented me. Do you hear me, Gudrun? Your eyes are glazed over. You must hear. You must forgive. The women are saying you are likely to . . . and if you should die without forgiving me . . . then the gods will never . . . . Oh, Gudrun, hear me. At night, she looked into my eyes by the light of our candle and said to me, 'Ah, but that these were Sigurd's eyes, Sigurd's lips.' Then she laughed and said she was jesting, that I made my envy so clear to her that she could not help but . . . so that I did not know what to think. It was not for the gold, Gudrun. You must believe that. She made me to think that the blood-bond had been broken. She knew I was jealous from the start, and it amused her to see . . . . I thought I should go mad with jealousy—I loved her that much. It was not so much the gold as . . . . And I lied, Gudrun. I knew he would have no part in it unless I asked her directly. I told him I had. I felt I had no choice. The gods wanted me to act. The storm . . . . But then, once he had pledged his loyalty to my aim, I began to have second thoughts. I am a weak man. I feared what would happen to me if it turned out that he had not . . . what the gods would do . . . . And thus I was loathe to . . . to do the deed myself. I coached Guthorm. I had no way to know whether or not he would . . . . But I believed that if the gods wanted the deed carried out, they would find a way. Hagen was against it of course, but I told him I'd had a dream, and that the gods appeared to me . . . . Perhaps I did dream . . . . I cannot be sure anymore. My thoughts and my dreams were . . . are . . . all of one. Guthorm fell asleep. I took it to be a sign that I was wrong, that I had misinterpreted. But I played out my charade with him, Sigurd, anyway, as I had planned it. I believed that he, if thus incited, might confirm what she had only . . . . And his reaction did seem to confirm . . . . Alone in our bower, I told her. I was desperate that she should comprehend how far her intimations had driven me. I told her everything. But still I could not bring myself to ask her outright. 'Why not awaken Guthorm and go through with it?' she said. I answered, once I had recovered from the impact of her words, 'Because you have not yet convinced me . . . .' She laughed then. I threatened to kill her. Her reaction had pushed the moment to a climax. I had to know. And laughing still, laughing in my face to see how crazed her insinuations made me, she told me that I had been right, that they had . . . more details than a man can bear to hear. And all the while her laughter . . . .

"My blood boiled. You are a woman. You cannot understand these things. I was full of hatred, full of . . . . I went into the hall. Guthorm was vomiting . . . . Mother sitting up with him. I went back to the bower. I paced. I heard you get up. I saw you helping. I waited, seething . . . until you had gone and Mother was asleep again. Then I tiptoed into the hall and brought Guthorm his sword. I prayed to the gods to make their decision. Guthorm awoke. I signaled him to be quiet. I had made him earlier to think that hurling the sword at Sigurd would be a game. I had promised him honey. I could see that he remembered. He had vomited up the wolf and the snake, yes, but some of their essence must have remained, for that boy, that half-wit whom I loved as much as anyone . . . ." Gunner broke off sobbing and let go of one of my arms to cover his face. The arm he clung to hurt, and the pain seemed more authentic than the words I dreamed he said.

"He went off to the bower without my saying a word," Gunner moaned. "I should have said to myself then, The blood-bond has been broken; there is no reason to send the boy. But that did not occur to me. My mind was void of logic, void of all . . . but hatred, jealousy, the image of them together, laughing at me, conspiring . . . .

"I rushed back into the bower and told her that I had set Guthorm on him. She appeared shocked. 'Take my life too, then,' she cried. And the gods know I would have, but then I heard the screams . . . .

"'He is dead,' I said, half to myself. She began to tremble. 'Fool!' she screamed. 'The blood-bond was never broken. Sigurd lay his sword between us that night in the cave.' Her eyes were like torches, burning through me. Then the fire went out of them. She reached for me. She touched my face as if she pitied me. And so comforted was I by her gesture, so great was my need for comfort, that I took her in my arms. But when she saw me soften, she pushed me away and began to laugh again, high-pitched hysterical laughter. My hands found her throat. She was gasping, laughing. Hagen came in. He spoke. I could not hear. He shouted. 'Guthorm is dead!' Guthorm was dead. Guthorm was dead . . . . The blood-bond had not been broken and Guthorm was dead."

Gunner lowered me gently to the floor. He stood above me with his hands spread over his face, heaving, gasping, pulling at his fleshy skin. I thought to tell him that there was no sword between them on that night, but I could not speak. I closed my eyes. I continued to hear him sobbing for a time, and then I drifted away into darkness, thinking, *I must tell Gunner, I must tell Gunner.* But the darkness became absolute. And then I could not remember what truth it was that I must tell.

Then we were all outside. I do not know whether this was the same day or one after. As in a real dream, events seemed to occur separately, isolated from those that came before or went after. Surely other things happened in between, other words were said to me, but of these I have no recollection. Most of the time my dream was a dream of darkness, of shadows and whispers which made no sense.

We were standing at the edge of the forest, in the same place where the slaughtering had taken place. I could feel myself supported on either side, but I did not look to see who held me. There was much sobbing and wailing. Before me, a great funeral pyre had been made of peat and branches. On top of it lay Guthorm, his once-used sword across his chest. Someone stepped forward with a torch and lit the pyre. Screams went up with the flames. I recognized Mother's among them, from somewhere behind me. I wanted to turn, but I had no power to do so. My gaze was fastened to the fire. It burned blue and gold and white and red. And when the wind changed, it seemed to reach out to those of us who had gathered to watch it. There was a collective gasp, and I was dragged back a pace. I was aware of a burning sensation deep within me, and I believed the fire had found me after all. I wished to sit, but the men who held me, my brothers, surely, made no move to release me.

One funeral seemed to follow on the heels of the other, but as the second took place on Frankish lands, this could not have been the case. I remember nothing of the journey, but I suppose I sat in the oxcart with Sigurd's corpse at my side. There was no wind on the day of the second funeral, and the flames rose straight to the sky. There were men holding me up again, and there were more men holding back what I took, at first, to be some wild beast who sought to break into the clearing. But when the beast broke free of its wardens, I saw that it was only Brunhild. Screaming wildly, she ran to the pyre, her golden hair itself a flame. Then one of the men holding me released me so suddenly that I half fell. He rushed to the pyre behind Brunhild with his arms outstretched, but he was too late. Brunhild's screams rose up with the smoke. Then they ceased. The man who stood before the pyre—Gunner, surely, though I did not recognize him at the time—dropped his head so low that it seemed it would fall from his shoulders.

Now a very long time passed during which I was not aware of my surroundings at all. I had, I suppose, fallen deeper into my abyss, into a place where even true dream images evaded me. If the sun shone, I failed to see it. If there were people around me eating and sleeping, I took no note of them. I had no fears. I had no memories. I was outside time and dead to circumstance.

And then, all at once, I was aware of a stinging sensation on my face, and I opened my eyes and saw an old man staring at me, his face not more than a hand's length from my own. His expression was soft, unguarded, a contradiction, I thought, to the fact that he had just slapped me hard. His hair was white and clumps of it stuck out in stiff points on either side of his head. As I blinked at him, he began to chuckle.

"Chero! Sunhild!" he called.

Two women appeared. They froze when they saw me, their expressions rapturous.

"Good work," cried the younger of the two as she clapped her hands together. She was very stout, and her high-pitched voice made her obesity all the more apparent. Her small gray eyes were nearly lost in her heavy face. Her thick, dull, straw-colored hair fell untidily all about her shoulders. She was dressed in a coarse colorless robe, dirty at the hem. She came closer, and I noted that she smelled. The old man fell back to make room for her. She sank to her knees before me and touched my face. Her rough fingers slid down my cheek, across my lips, under my chin, down the length of my nose. "Do you know me?" she asked, a finger lingering on my bottom lip. I made no attempt to answer. "You must try to speak now," she said, blinking her eyes as if to hold back some emotion.

Now the other woman came forward. "Let me, Sunhild," she said. Sunhild made a space for her, but unlike the girl and the old man, Chero did not kneel. She bent over me and lifted my chin so that I was forced to look up at her. Her eyes were a darker version of Sunhild's, gray with yellowish streaks running through them. And she, too, was large, though not as large as Sunhild. Her face was squarish, and her cheekbones were high and prominent. Her fingers were not as rough as Sunhild's, but her touch was not as gentle either. She smiled at me. "We must not rush her," she said to the others. "She will come around when she is ready. It is enough that she is awake. How did you do it, Gripner?"

Ah, Gripner, I thought. The older of the two women would be Gripner's wife then, and the younger, their daughter. I had met his wife and daughter once many years ago, at Worms. But I knew these things as one knows things in a dream. And I expected at any moment that these people would vanish, as all the others had, and that then I would find myself alone again in the eerie safety of my abyss.

"I slapped her," Gripner said. He chuckled. "Good and hard. I should have done it long ago."

Sunhild gasped. "You cannot mean it, Father!" She reached past her mother to caress me again, her big cow face full of alarm and sympathy. But Chero seized her wrist.

"You did well," Chero told Gripner. "But now I will take charge. I think that best. I have a plan. No one is to see her unless I say so. Do you understand that, Sunhild?"

Sunhild lowered her massive head and added one more chin to the two I had already taken account of. Her mass of dry hair fell forward from her shoulders. Gripner began to laugh again. "You are a hard woman, Chero," he declared. Chero smiled as if she had been flattered. Gripner got up slowly, holding his back in a manner which indicated that it pained him. He went away chuckling softly.

Now Chero turned her gaze on Sunhild, and she, too, got up, though reluctantly, and went away. I followed her huge figure with my eyes. Then I took stock of my surroundings. I was in a bower smaller than my own. It was cluttered with distaffs and piles of cloth and wooden vessels and rolled mattresses. It was a rolled mattress against which I was leaning. "You must rest now," Chero said. "Tonight we will begin our work."

I closed my eyes obediently and immediately returned to my abyss. But when Chero returned later, I was propelled from it just as quickly. My dream, I sensed even then, was coming to an end. Chero had a bowl of milk in her hand, and when she saw my eyes open, she bade me to drink from it. As I neglected to lift my hands for it, she placed one of her hands behind my head and with the other, she held the bowl to my mouth. I drank. Then I became aware of a wailing coming from the hall. I moved my head from side to side to see beyond Chero. She looked over her shoulder. "It is the little one," she said turning back to me. "Sunhild," she cried, "bring in the child."

Sunhild entered smiling, the child all but lost in her heavy embrace. Chero moved aside and Sunhild sat the child down before me. She regarded me curiously for a moment, and then she began to smile, though her face was still wet with tears. She was a lovely, fat baby with large, round eyes, the bluish-gray color of dusk. Her cheeks were so full that when she turned her head to smile at Chero, her little nose all but disappeared. Her mouth was curled in a way that seemed familiar to me. I felt an immediate connection to her, an intimacy. Sunhild said, "She looks like Sigurd, does she not?"

I stared at Sunhild. She was still smiling, but there were tears in her eyes. Though I did not understand her sadness, I felt it, and I made an attempt to place a comforting hand on hers. But my hand was stiff and feeble, and it fell short of its goal and plopped back onto my lap. Sunhild, who had been watching its progress, threw her arms around my neck and began to cry more loudly.

"Hush," warned Chero. "You will frighten her."

Sunhild withdrew. The baby began to laugh. Sunhild wiped her tears away and laughed too. Then she put her arms out to the child. I was afraid she would take her away, but when she got hold of her, she lifted the child up and placed her on my lap. My hands found their power immediately. I caressed the child. She clung to me, cooing. I held her tighter, thinking I must find a way to take her back with me, into my abyss, when I went.

"You will hurt her," Chero cried, pulling the child out of my grip. And sure enough, the child looked at me accusingly and began to cry again. She put her arms out to Sunhild, and Sunhild, whose expression was openly apologetic, took her from Chero. "Take her away now, Sunhild," Chero said.

Sunhild hesitated, but Chero narrowed her eyes. Sunhild's eyes widened in response. Then she turned and left the bower.

Chero regarded me for a long time, with her arms folded under her bosom. Her gaze was steady, thoughtful, purposeful. Her squarish face now resembled a man's more than a woman's. "The child has no name," she began. "We have been waiting all this time for you to give her one. You have been with us now for twice the span of her age. She has gone nameless long enough. What will you call her?"

When I did not respond, Chero began to move about the room distractedly. She stopped near a pile of cloths and bent to examine it. "I should have made Gripner give her a name," she mumbled as she extracted a cloth from the center of the pile. "I should have insisted. A child should be named as soon as it is decided that it should live. It is bad luck to leave a child nameless for long. The evil spirits love nameless things. But Gripner never listens. He sprinkled her with the water and smeared the honey on her lips, but would not name her. What does he know about such matters? I should have insisted."

She turned and tossed the cloth to me. It fell onto my lap. "You have responsibilities," she said. "You must find your tongue. It has not been easy for Sunhild and me, what with caring for you and the child as well. We had to hold the child to your breast so that she could be suckled. Your milk was barely enough. We had to start her on goat's milk early on. She might have died. And you—like a baby yourself! We had to feed you, dress you, clean you, keep you warm. And throughout it all, you slept. You slept like a baby, without a notion of what was going on around you. Even when you bore the child, you slept. Think of it. You screamed as other women scream, but you never as much as opened your eyes. You never looked on your child. She's more Sunhild's than yours in that sense. Sunhild's the one who bathes her, who feeds her. Poor Sunhild, who will likely never have a child of her own. She loves you and the child better than she loves herself. She never tired of watching you sleep. So many evenings holding your dead, white hand in hers, singing to you, talking to you, praying for you . . . . Think of it, Gudrun. Do you even know where you are? Do you remember anything?"

Chero threw her hands up. She turned on one foot and went to the wall against which the wooden vessels were lined up. She reached into one and extracted a needle and several colored threads. She held them out to me. "We have no idle hands here," she said. "Take up the needle and thread it. Surely you remember how to embroider."

Kneeling, she sighed and turned one of my hands palm up. "Child, I do not mean to be so . . . ." she began. Then she pressed her lips together so that her face became stern again. She threaded the needle quickly and placed it in my hand. Then she took the cloth from my lap and placed one corner in my other hand. She sighed again and got to her feet. "You are to begin tonight," she said loudly. "Do you understand? When Sunhild and I come in to make you ready for sleep, I will inspect your work. If it does not satisfy, out with you. I will send you away first thing in the morning, out into the wind and the snow without so much as a loaf of bread." She narrowed her eyes the way she had narrowed them at Sunhild earlier.

As soon as she was gone, I closed my eyes. But I sat for a long time, the needle in one hand and the cloth in the other, before blackness finally came. And again, it was short-lived. I heard voices, then footsteps, and then I was aware of people nearby. I kept my eyes closed and pretended to be asleep. I felt my fingers being uncurled and their contents removed. Sunhild said, "She has done nothing."

"I did not think she would," Chero responded.

"You spoke to her harshly."

"We have tried other approaches. Look how well it worked for your father."

"When he slapped her?"

"Aye, indeed, when he slapped her."

"It does not seem right to me."

Gudrun's Tapestry

"Life is harsh, Sunhild. She must see that and choose to enter back into it anyway. Otherwise her return, if it comes, will only be temporary."

They worked in silence after that, unrolling the mattresses and spreading them out. Then they put their hands on me, on my shoulders and ankles, and lifted me onto one of the mattresses as easily as if I were a child. They covered me over with rugs.

When Chero had gone, Sunhild took hold of my mattress and yanked it until she had moved it where she wanted it. Now we were very close together, for when her voice came, I could feel her breath brush my cheek. "Sweet dreams, sister," she said in her little girl voice. She fumbled with her rugs. When she had settled herself, she whispered, "Father says that you will be well soon and that then you will want to go away to live with your own people. He has already sent a messenger to say that you awoke today and held your daughter in your arms. I waited a long time for this day to come, sweet sister, to look into your eyes, but now I wish it had not come so soon. Oh, I do not mean that . . . . It is just that . . . . I cannot bear it. I simply cannot bear it. You are ours now. You must not return. I was so lonely before you came. And the child . . . . Oh, I cannot bear it. The gods forgive me, but this I cannot bear." She began to cry softly into her mattress.

I smiled and felt myself drifting into a dream of her face. But then the face became that of another, a bright, flawless face as different from Sunhild's as two faces can be. The beautiful woman in my dream backed away from me. I saw that there was a pool behind her. She dove into it. I kept my eyes fastened to the surface, waiting for her to emerge, but it was Gunner who emerged, triumphant with the war sword in his hand. Then he was gone and I heard Sunhild crying again. Suddenly I was afraid. I freed my hand from the rugs that covered me and felt along the edge of her mattress. I found her shoulder. She stopped crying immediately. She snatched my hand and pulled it to her lips. She kissed it wildly, a hundred times, a thousand times. I squeezed her hand to let her know I loved her, too.

I awoke the next morning to find my hand still in Sunhild's. She was facing me, breathing heavily through her mouth with the flesh of her cheek bunched up against her nose so that only one nostril was exposed. I found myself greedy for her company, her voice and her smile, and I slipped my hand out of hers and touched the tip of her nose. She did not stir. I wiggled her nose gently with my finger. Her mouth closed and her jaw began to rotate as if she were chewing something. Then her eyes popped open, and with that came the smile I had been longing for. She sat up at once, and throwing her rugs aside, she bent over and embraced me. Her weight was too much for me. I laughed and pushed her away. "Are you well?" she cried.

I nodded. I felt well enough. She called out to her mother, and Chero came rushing in. She had the child on her hip. "Gudrun is better!" Sunhild exclaimed. "She woke me up. She held my hand last night."

Chero scrutinized my face. "Let me hear it from your own mouth," she said.

I opened my mouth to speak, but the sound that came out was no more than a grunt.

"You are not trying hard enough," Chero said.

Sunhild grabbed hold of the hem of her mother's robe. "But she is. Can you not see it? Oh, I beg you, do not be so harsh with her. Look how she struggles. She is helpless. Her voice is locked away. She has gone too long without using it. It will come back in good time."

"Perhaps," Chero said, looking at me from an angle. "But she must come into the hall and eat at the table properly today. That, at least, will be something."

Anxious to please, I tried immediately to raise myself, but I found that my legs were as useless as my voice. Sunhild got up and took hold of my arms. She was a strong girl, and in a moment I was up on my feet. But for all her tugging, I could not seem to get my feet to move. Then one of my ankles buckled and I fell against her. Gently, she lowered me back down to the mattress. Chero grabbed one of the rolled mattresses with her free hand and stuck it between the wall and my back so that I could sit.

"It is too soon," Sunhild cried, her eyes brimming with tears. "You said yourself only yesterday that she should not be rushed. She can eat in here a little longer. I will bring her food. I will work with her. I will massage her feet. I will make her move her legs. You will see how quickly she will learn from me."

Chero sighed. Then she closed her eyes and nodded reluctantly. She was about to depart when Sunhild whispered, "Leave us the child." Chero wrapped her arm around the child protectively. "She will not hurt her. I will watch. Look at her. Her eyes never leave the child. She longs for her. Please, Mother."

Chero looked from Sunhild to me. Then she sat the child down before me and pointed a finger at Sunhild. "If any harm should come to Sigurd's child . . . ." she warned. Then she sighed again and went out.

With Sunhild's help, I lifted the child onto my lap. Happily, she showed no sign of fear. I stroked her fine hair and breathed deeply of her scent. Her eye fell on one of the colored threads which Sunhild and Chero had overlooked the night before. When she began to squirm, I released her, and she crawled away in pursuit of it. "Go ahead, little one," Sunhild said gently. "Pick it up if you like."

The child picked up the thread and held it before her face. Then she crawled to Sunhild and held it out for her to inspect. "Pretty," Sunhild said. "Now go and show it to your mother." Sunhild pointed to me. The child followed her finger. She crawled over and held the thread so close to my face that I could not focus on it. I lifted her and held her against me. I kissed her head, her nose, her eyes, her mouth. Sigurd's child. I kissed her ears and her neck. And in the smile that rose to her face, I saw him, Sigurd, smiling. And all at once I knew that Sigurd was gone, and Guthorm too. Both gone, both dead—just as it had happened in my dream. I handed the child back to Sunhild and began to weep. My child had come into the world without my noticing. The tears would not stop. They rolled down my face and moistened my robe.

Chero came in. When she saw me, she put aside the food bowl she had been carrying and rushed to my side and wrapped her arms around me. "Cry all you want," she whispered. Over her shoulder I saw Gripner appear in the doorway, squinting his eyes. He nodded encouragingly. Through my burning tears, I sought out Sunhild's face. She was crying, too. When Chero released me, Sunhild took her place. And all the time Gripner remained in the doorway, nodding and smiling sympathetically. And so it went. My healing had begun.

Whenever I cried after that—and I cried often—there was always someone there to console me. Chero, no longer harsh—or at least no harsher than was her way—spoke gently to me then, encouraging me to visualize my grief, to see it as a flock of birds which would soon take wing and leave me in peace. Even the child, who spent more and more time playing at my side in the bower, learned to hold me when the tears began. In imitation of Sunhild and Chero, she rubbed her small hand on my back, rocked with me, her little face buried in my bosom. Gripner alone never took a turn holding me, but he came often to stand by my side, sometimes with his stiff, aged hand on my head.

When I was not crying for Sigurd and Guthorm, I worked with Sunhild. She made me move my limbs in various ways for long periods of time. No matter how discouraged I became, she remained cheerful and confident that I would soon learn to walk again. And if my slow progress, a constant contradiction to her confidence, ever disheartened her, she never let on. She was nothing but patient. She seemed to have no thought beyond my well-being and that of the child. And how I marveled at her selflessness, so vast, so genuine. And many times I promised myself that when I was well again, I would find a way to emulate her.

In the evenings, I embroidered on the long, colorless cloth. It was Chero's request that I should embroider my own history, right up to my marriage and Sigurd's and Guthorm's deaths. In the beginning, I had no bent for such a project. My embroidery skills had never been good, and I found it tedious to stitch the little figures the way that Chero showed me. Nor could I imagine how, one day, I would bring myself to stitch the bodies of my loved ones, high upon their funeral pyres, engulfed by flames. But I was so slow about my task, that day seemed very far off indeed. And furthermore, I would not have dared to disappoint Chero after all that she had done for me. And thus did my unskilled fingers set about their task.

To frame the events that I desired to portray, I made for each a square, the width of my hand, with my threads. I determined in advance that this would afford me one hundred squares in which to work—four rows of twenty-five each running along the length of the fabric. Then into each square I stitched events as I imagined them. I stitched first my ancestors coming down from the north and crossing the great river in search of fertile lands on which to begin a new and better life. I stitched them plowing, building, praying, and gathering about their hearths to raise their drinking horns to the gods and share their dreams for a prosperous and peaceful future. Then I stitched the Romans coming to take the many by force to be their slaves or to fight in their armies. I stitched the Burgundians who remained behind, making their new home at Worms and looking to Gundahar, their king, the brother of my father, for consolation and protection.

All this and more I stitched. And by the time I had used up some twenty squares and twice as many nights, a strange thing happened to me. The stories my fingers told were the stories I had heard all my life, from the mouths of my father and my brothers and our freemen. And always I had heard them with interest and sympathy. But now, as I lingered over each event in my work, these stories began to become real for me in a new way. It was as if, when I took up my cloth, colorless no longer, I was not one person but two. And while one stitched, tirelessly now, in quick time, and with a skill I had never thought to acquire, the other lived in each little square, took part in each battle, held her hand over the quiet heart of each still-warm Burgundian whose life-blood had been spilt for his people. I heard the war cries now, the horses charging, the clash of blades, the screams of the women and children. I felt their pain—our pain—our anguish, our anger, our fears. By the time I got to the square that was to depict my father, I felt less his daughter than his peer. Likewise, as I stitched my mother, so young and vibrant and indifferent back then to the black veil that hung over the future, I felt her desire to put my father's mind at ease as if it were my own. And when they married, this solemn, saddened, thoughtful man and this carefree girl half his age, I was there. I was there to see my brothers come into the world, first Gunner, then Hagen. Even at my own birth did I seem to stand watching, feeling the blend of pleasure and pain as my mother experienced it, hearing the voice of the old woman who brought me forth saying, "A girl this time," seeing my father's initial disappointment vanish when he saw my mother's slow smile come to her face.

I was there at Gundahar's side, not as the child I had actually been but as I was now, as I stitched his attempt to take Belgica and Aetius's coming forth with his armies to check him, to punish him for wanting what all men want—a stronghold of his own, lands of his own, a life for his people. I was there to see the Huns marching to Worms at Aetius's beckon to put an end to my people for good. I was there for the battles that ensued, the burning halls, the executions, the blood, the grief, the shattered dreams. I was there for Gundahar's death, and there with my father, among his men, as I stitched him negotiating with Aetius to spare the lives of the few Burgundian survivors. His great effort to conceal his hatred for his enemies from the general to whom he made his appeal was my effort too. His feigned humility was mine. His shrouded rage was mine. Mine was his grief at his brother's passing. I felt it here, deep in my heart—and my heart grew heavy and full again. And little by little there came into my body a new spirit to replace the one that had died. And this new spirit was so unlike the other that it made me giddy sometimes to think that such a thing had taken up within me, for this was a collective thing, the spirit of all the Burgundian hopes and fears together. It came trickling in with the rhythm of my fingers, filling the void that had been the result of my loved ones' deaths. It sated me. It made me feel very old—yet ageless and outside time. It made me feel wizened. I imagined I was beginning to understand something of sweet Sunhild's selflessness. She, too, was filled with a collective spirit, the spirit of her folk and her past. But for her this occupation was unconscious, while for me it was a learned thing which more than likely would have evaded me altogether had not my suffering, my death in life, prepared me for it.

And thus, by the time I got to my own more personal history, my own sorrows diminished somewhat. It was with pride now that I showed my work to Chero each night—though it was evident that she failed to see what was happening to me, that the events I stitched now represented the ancestral memory which I had acquired in stitching them. She complimented me on my little figures, prettier and more animated than ever, but she remained obsessed with finding a way to free my tongue. For her, only such an outward manifestation of my healing would suffice. Looking over my shoulder, she would ask me, "Who is this child? What is this man doing? Whose blood flows here?" And when I only stared back at her dumbly, amazed to realize that she had failed to see that I was the child and the man, that it was my blood which flowed forth, she would sigh and go away full of concern for my well-being.

Sunhild and Gripner, on the other hand, did not seem bothered at all by my silence. And I cannot say that it bothered me much either, for I learned to watch and listen more carefully as a result. Now, when I sat at the table in the hall (for I had, by then, regained full use of my limbs), I needed only to hear one word from Gripner or Chero to know what they were truly thinking. And sometimes no words were needed at all. My silence mirrored a peaceful place within me. And in that place the thoughts and needs of others seemed to flow in effortlessly. I knew, for instance, even before Sunhild did, the times when Chero was beginning to be annoyed with Sunhild's childish chatter, and then I would take Sunhild's hand and lead her from the hall. I knew, too, when Gripner was feeling aged and useless, and then I would go to him and sit at his side. Sometimes he would ask to see my tapestry, and in spite of his poor eyesight, he would find the squares depicting Sigurd's ride into the high mountains and stare at them for a long time. And I sensed then that he was waiting for an opportunity to speak to me alone about these events in Sigurd's life. But it was some time before he did so, for with Gripner nearly blind and his back always a source of pain to him, he seldom left the hall. And Chero, having Sunhild and a handful of servants to do the work that had to be done outdoors, was content to stay indoors caring for him.

Other than my anxiety about Gripner and the words that he would one day say to me, this was the most peaceful time in my life. I did not have Sigurd and Guthorm anymore, but I had my memories of them. I had Sunhild and my daughter to console me when memories were not enough. At about the time I learned to walk again, my daughter learned to walk too. And as Gripner's lands were full of meadows and quiet streams, Sunhild and my child and I spent much of our time walking and marveling at the beauty of the world. Sunhild was like a child herself, then. Sometimes she reminded me of Guthorm. There was not a flower or a cloud that escaped her attention. And she would do most anything to get my child and me to laugh, for she loved the sound of laughter better than anything else in the world. On all fours she would imitate the cows or the sheep that my child never tired of pointing out to us. And then my child was never content until she could climb onto Sunhild's back. As Sunhild's back was broad, I would have to hold my child in place as Sunhild began to move like the animal she sought to portray. And when Sunhild began to move too quickly for me, we would all three go tumbling into the high meadow grasses, laughing and happy enough to be in one another's company.

Sometimes we would walk down to the place where Sigurd's ashes were buried. Sunhild was solemn then. With my child between us and our hands locked behind her back, Sunhild would tell me of the adventures that she and Sigurd had shared as children. There was something familiar about some of her stories, and I came to realize that Sigurd had told them to me long, long ago, in the days before the siege. In this way Sunhild reawakened my earliest memories of Sigurd. And my love for her doubled when I realized that Sigurd had loved her as much as I did. I felt I could stay on Gripner's lands forever, listening to Sunhild and the words that my child was learning to utter. When I recalled that my mother and brothers were waiting for me to come home, I grew sad and hoped, like Sunhild, that it would still be some time until I was that much recovered.

But one evening in the late Spring, all this came to an end. We had finished eating early, and Sunhild and I, seeing that there was still plenty of light, decided to take our embroidery outdoors. By this time my tapestry was nearly complete, and as I did not know whether my Frankish family knew all the details surrounding Sigurd's death, it had been a while since I had volunteered to show my work to any of them. Still, I imagined that someone, Chero most likely, had peeked at it anyway when I was not about, for after I had embroidered Sigurd and Brunhild lying together in the cave, no one asked to see it anymore.

I had stitched myself eavesdropping on my brothers in the forest, my reaction to their words, and my going to Brunhild to make the bargain with her (though the picture of this last event was insufficient to represent the words that passed between us). I had stitched the weddings, and Sigurd's rejection of Brunhild up in the clearing north of the bathing pit. I had stitched, too, the night that Sigurd confessed to me his involvement with Brunhild. Here, to make the scene sensible, above my portrait of Sigurd and me speaking together in the bower, in a little circle, I duplicated the events in the square that showed Sigurd and Brunhild in the cave. In the square that followed, I had stitched Sigurd crying, for though I know that men are loathe to be thought capable of tears, I felt that Sigurd's remorse was an important part of my story and should not be left to speculation. In the next square, I had stitched Gunner and Brunhild in their bower, and again, by adding a little circle above Brunhild's head in which I depicted the cave, though not its occupants, I was able to suggest that Brunhild had hinted of the event which Sigurd, and Brunhild, earlier, had told to me. In the next square, Gunner and Hagen were riding out into the forest with Guthorm. And then, in the next, there was poor Guthorm, vomiting evil things, and, finally, him hurling the sword and Sigurd hurling it back again. Then I had only five squares left. In the first of these five, I stitched myself, oblivious to the people and events around me. To depict my state, I rendered my eyes pupil-less. In the next two, I stitched the two funerals, with Brunhild heaving herself onto the pyre in the second one. In the background of both, I stood among the others with my eyes blank. In the next, I stitched the birth of my child as I imagined it. Now there was only one square left. And as Sunhild and I sat on the rocks outside Gripner's hall, I began to stitch myself and Sunhild stitching. Though my eyes were lowered in the little scene, and thus my pupils not visible, the expression on my face confirmed that I had found tranquillity on Gripner's lands. Beyond us, I stitched Gripner's hall, but not its walls, and thus was I able to depict Gripner and Chero within, and my child asleep in her cradle near the hearth. My tapestry was complete. I sighed and whispered, "It is done."

"Done already?" Sunhild asked. Then she jumped down from her rock, careless of her own embroidery, crying "You spoke! You spoke!"

Aye, I had, though until Sunhild exclaimed, I had not realized it myself. And as I considered the words I had said, I saw that they were as much a comment on my life as I had known it as they were a comment on the status of my tapestry. I rolled up my work and got down from the rock to retrieve Sunhild's. When I handed it to her, I saw that she had not yet decided whether to rejoice or despair. She was dancing from side to side, her eyes wide and her mouth opened. But I took her hand, and she said nothing. As we began to walk up to the hall, Sunhild finally decided on an attitude and began to cry. I squeezed her hand and pulled her along.

The door being up, we entered unannounced. Chero and Gripner, who were sitting at the table in positions uncannily similar to the ones in which I had only just depicted them, ceased their conversation abruptly so that I knew they had been talking about me. Sunhild, who was calm now, said flatly, "Gudrun is cured."

Chero straightened and dropped her hands into her lap. Gripner smiled.

"It is true," I said. "You cured me, the three of you, with your kindness and your love."

Chero got up slowly and approached me, her trembling fingers extended as if I were an apparition which she felt compelled to touch before it vanished from her sight. I took her hand and kissed it. Then I went past her, to the table, and unrolled my tapestry before Gripner. Sunhild and Chero moved to stand behind him. Gripner's aged finger began to move slowly over the last row of squares, the ones I had not yet shown to anyone. It came to rest on the square that depicted Sigurd and Brunhild lying in each other's arms in the dark cave. Gripner bent his head low so as to compensate for his poor eyesight. When he had made out the picture, he sat up again and turned to look at Chero. Her face had reddened and her eyes glistened with tears. Still, she had no response other than to nod at Gripner.

Now Gripner's finger came to rest on the square that showed my brothers conspiring in the forest while I hid among the trees. It lingered there a moment and then moved to the next square, the one that showed me prostrate and tearing at my hair, overcome with grief at what I had just overheard. Gripner considered this square long and hard, but decorous as he was, he refrained from questioning me about it. His finger moved again, now to the square that showed Brunhild and me conversing by the stream, and again he considered it carefully.

"Aye," I said, "Brunhild told me about their night together here, when we bathed together in the river," and I showed them where to look. "Her reason for coming to our lands was not to marry Gunner but in the hope that this incident might repeat itself. And as I thought it likely that it would, and as I needed her help, I went to her to say that I would suffer Sigurd's infidelities on the condition that she make certain that Gunner never learned that the blood-bond between himself and Sigurd had already been broken. My decision was a poor one, for as you will note farther down, Sigurd had already decided that he no longer desired Brunhild's love. If I had not gone to her, if I had not made her to think that it would all be so easy, perhaps Sigurd would still be alive today. It is important to me that you know all this."

"Gripner suspected it," Chero mumbled.

"Do not hold yourself to blame," Gripner said, raising one brow.

"Your offering her what she could not have does not change the fact that she could not have it. Sigurd loved you. You could not have changed that."

Ah, but I could have, I thought, though I did not say so to Gripner.

His finger moved quickly over the next few squares. When he got to the one depicting Sigurd's death, he withdrew his hand entirely and sat for a moment with his eyes closed. Then he rolled up the tapestry. He was about to lay it aside, but Sunhild snatched it from his hand. She carried it over to the hearth and opened it up anew. In a moment, Chero joined her. Though their backs were to me, I could hear them whispering, speculating.

"And now?" Gripner asked softly.

I turned to face him. "And now I must leave. I must make peace with my brothers."

"They have been concerned about you. Many times during your illness they sent messengers to ask whether they might come, but always Chero and I thought it best—"

"You thought wisely."

Gripner stretched his neck to see past me. I turned too. Sunhild and Chero were wrapped in each other's arms now, sobbing softly, the tapestry still laid out before them. "Sit," Gripner whispered. I sat. He glanced once more at Chero and Sunhild. Then, satisfied that they would remain preoccupied for some time, he whispered, "I do not like to speak of your future in front of them. They love you dearly, and their greatest wish is that your life will now be one of peace and tranquillity. But I have had glimpses, and I feel I must tell you the things I have seen."

I laughed. "Is my future so bleak then?"

He shook his head. "I have had only glimpses, as I said. But there is one thing I know for certain. You will take up the war sword."

"Sigurd's sword? The sword of the gods?" In my mind's eye I saw the thing as I had seen it last, flickering maliciously from its place on the wall the night of Sigurd's death.

"Gunner's now."

"But you cannot mean it."

"I pray you be still and listen. We have little time to speak of these matters. Your future and the future of the war sword are linked. Gunner had it with him when he came to bring us Sigurd's corpse and to tell us how he had died—and I knew. You will have the opportunity to make good use of it, this I know, too. How, I cannot say. This you must discover yourself."

"But Gripner, this is laughable. Am I to believe that I am to cut off my hair and don the animal skins of the warrior? Look at me. I am little more than skin and bones since—"

Gripner leaned forward so that his face was very close to mine. "I am looking at you. And I see that in your diminished form you have become twice the woman you once were. You know this too. Still, you must be careful. The sword is cursed."

I reached across the table and seized his hand. "Oh, Gripner, Father, tell me everything you know. Was it the curse that brought about my dear Sigurd's death?"

"Child, I know so little. When I was a younger man . . . but I am old now, and often uncertain. My glimpses of the past and the future are entangled with my glimpses of the demons an old man is prone to see when his death is near at hand."

"No, Gripner. You imagine—"

"I know what I know. But let us not speak of that now." He glanced again at Sunhild and Chero. "See how they console each other? In a moment they will have done with their crying, and then they will rejoin us. And there are still things I would say to you about the sword and Sigurd, too."

"Then tell me quickly. I must know the truth."

Gripner dropped his eyes from mine and his bottom lip began to stretch and tremble. In a moment he gained control over his emotion and brought his gaze back up to meet mine. "He was a son to me," he began. "I loved him dearly."

"I know you did."

"I told him not to go. I told him that the gold was cursed and that in retrieving it, he would be changed—for what man is not changed when he gives himself over to greed? I told him that under its influence, he would do things he had thought himself incapable of. I regret to tell you all this, but you must be made to understand the power of the curse."

"Go on then. I can bear it."

"I told him what I had foreseen, that his connection with the gold would bring about an early death. If Gunner had not killed him, someone else would have, for, under the influence of the curse, he betrayed everyone who crossed his path, as you well know. He was only himself again after he had buried the bulk of the gold and given the war sword away."

"But Gunner has had it for some seasons now, and he still lives."

Gripner's eyes widened. Indeed, they seemed to glow. "Can you truly say that he lives? He has lost his wife, his brother, and, in his mind, his sister as well. When he was here for Sigurd's funeral, he was a broken man. When I refused to take the gold, he begged me to take his life as Sigurd's man-price. And when my messenger returned from him last, he informed me that the war sword was covered over with dust the depth of a man's finger, as was his harp. Gunner does not live, Gudrun. His life ended along with Sigurd's and Guthorm's."

I heard Gripner's words with one ear. My mind was still fastened on Sigurd. "So," I said, "Sigurd had believed in the power of the curse even as he sought to persuade me otherwise. I see. Then you are saying that Sigurd chose a short life as the keeper of the hoard over a long life of love and happiness with me. But why, Gripner? Why should Sigurd have made such a choice?"

"Regan was determined to recover the gold. He spoke of little else. He knew where it was hidden. And as often as I told Sigurd of the horrors I foresaw in connection with the gold, Regan told him otherwise. Regan told him that the getting of the gold and the killing of the dragon would make him a great man—the greatest man who had ever lived. That all men through all ages would know his name and sing his praises. In the end, Regan won his ear."

"Forgive me, but could you not have sent Regan away when you saw that he would corrupt your brother's son?"

"Sigurd's father granted Regan his own lands north of here years ago. It was not in my power to send him from them. And besides, it was Sigmund's wish that Sigurd's instruction on the ways of life be by Regan. Sigurd was always so vulnerable. My brother's hope was that some of Regan's cunning might rub off on him."

I shook my head. "He chose death over me. Forgive me, Gripner, but I cannot seem to drive my mind from it."

"Child, he chose greatness, and death was its consequence. It was greatness he saw in his mind's eye—glory, power, immortality—when he considered his quest. His death he refused to consider. He believed somehow that his greatness would enable him to overcome it."

"Then, Gripner, I know what I must do. I know what my life's work will be. If you say I must take up the war sword, why then, so be it—though unused or not, I cannot think how I will get it away from Gunner. But I will have a second pursuit as well. I have already resolved to bequeath my tapestry to you. But I will make another, and one day, when the Burgundians are a kingdom again, it will hang in the king's hall where all men will know that Sigurd—"

"Aye, Gudrun, you will tell Sigurd's story again within the context of your own, that you can be sure of." His eyes twinkled and he smiled warmly. "But it will not be by the stitch. Nor will you be young anymore when you find yourself with the leisure for the telling of it. But our moment dims and I stray from my intent. Gudrun, my child, Sigurd's account of his quest was not entirely true. When you tell it next, you must tell it truly. And though truly told it will diminish his greatness some, it may help your listeners to understand that it is an error to choose greatness over life. For when a man lives for greatness, he often forgets that he is still a man, and he no longer likes to abide by the laws that once governed him, that govern all—"

"There was no dragon after all, was there? I suspected this, and I think my brothers did too. Oh, it is too much to think that Sigurd should have lied—"

"No dragon, Gudrun? Did I say there was no dragon? There was a dragon. I saw no image of him, but I felt Sigurd's disdain for him, his struggle, here." Gripner made a fist and struck his heart. "If only it had been the dragon . . . ."

"But what then?"

Gripner lowered his head. I reached across the table and touched my fingertips to his crown. He straightened slowly and took my hand in his. In his soft, pale eyes I saw what pain our discussion was costing him. "In what manner was his story untrue?" I urged. "He wanted me to know. He tried to tell me once, but I would not hear him then."

"I believe he killed Regan."

"You cannot mean that!"

"The image is clear to me. I see it over and over—when I am dreaming and when I am not."

"But he loved the dwarf."

"Aye, he loved him well. Regan must have betrayed him somehow. Perhaps Regan decided that he wanted the gold for himself after all. I do not know. No one will ever know."

I looked aside. "And so it was Regan's heart . . . ."

"Aye. Regan's."

I slipped my hand out of Gripner's. "I can hardly believe this."

"Nor could I. But remember, Sigurd was not himself. He had, by then, the gold, and the gold is cursed. The gold changed Sigurd. I saw this clearly when he returned to us. And his remorse over his transformation was great. That I can tell you. He was downtrodden, not at all what you would expect from a man who had just performed such a feat. He avoided me—I suppose because he knew I knew. He went off into the forest condemning himself for his errors. This I know. I saw images. I saw him prostrate on the forest floor, crying, beating his fists on his head."

"And so now the gold is in my brother's hands—and had been before Sigurd's death. I thank you, Gripner, for telling me all this. You have provided me with the means to forgive Gunner—a thing I thought myself unable to do in spite of my obligations." All at once I remembered the words that Gunner had said to me in the hall after Sigurd's death. He did not yet know, after all this time, that Brunhild had lied to him in the end, when she retracted her story about the cave. So great was my urge to tell him the truth that I began to lift from the bench on which I was seated.

"You must get the gold away from him," Gripner said. "Or at least the war sword. I feel the curse culminates in that one piece."

"Aye, Gripner, for his sake if for nothing else. And there are words I must say to him, too, words which I was obligated to tell him sooner. But what will become of me? Will I too die or kill or worse?"

"You are stronger than the curse. But you must appear weak to Gunner and make him think that if he refuses to give you the sword that you will likely return to your stupor."

"But—"

Gripner's eyes drifted away. He held up his finger to keep me from speaking. "No more. They rise."

I turned to see Chero helping Sunhild to her feet. I turned back to Gripner hastily and whispered, "But how shall I use the sword? I must know."

"You need only to have it fall into the hands of your enemies—"

"But how? Who?"

"You will know when you know. No more."

Chero and Sunhild approached. Chero wiped her tears from her face with the back of her hand. "We have spoken," she said to me. "We understand that you and the child will have to leave us soon. We want you to know that though our hearts are broken, we will do nothing to detain you. We will send you off with our best wishes for your peace and happiness." Chero turned to Sunhild who was slumping beside her, pouting and staring at her feet. "We wish her peace and happiness, do we not, Sunhild?" Sunhild nodded grudgingly, without looking up.

I got up from the bench and went to stand before them. "You have given me my life back," I began. "There are no words—"

"No words are necessary," Sunhild mumbled ceremoniously.

I turned to look at Gripner. He nodded encouragingly so that I knew that he knew what I would say next. "Chero, Sunhild, after all that you have done for me, I have no right to ask for more, but there is one favor I would have you grant me."

"Anything," Sunhild mumbled. I could see that she was close to fresh tears.

"You are right to think that I must leave soon. In fact, I should like to do so as early as tomorrow, if that is possible."

Sunhild let out a cry, but Chero struck her lightly with the back of her hand and nodded for me to go on.

"But the work I must do will be complicated, for my first task is to make peace with my brothers. The child's presence will only complicate matters more. I wish to leave her here. When I come back for her, I will have made my peace, and I will be able to stay with you again for a time."

Sunhild lifted her head. Her astonished smile came slowly. Then she grabbed her mother and sobbed against her bosom.

I glanced at Gripner. He was smiling at me as if to confirm that my decision had been the correct one. For me, it was the only one. Although the idea of leaving my child behind was appalling, I would no sooner have her come in contact with the gold—the war sword—than I would abandon her in some strange forest. Sunhild, who had known her longer, loved her longer, would make a fitting mother. And when the time came for me to take her away, I would take Sunhild, too. We three would have two homes—and my child, two mothers.

A wave of exhaustion came over me. Thinking that I must lie down and rethink Gripner's words, I looked toward the bower. But Chero noticed and cried, "Wait. You still have not given the child a name. Should we take it upon ourselves then . . . ?"

"Forgive me," I said. "I have known for some time what she is to be called, but until tonight, I had no tongue to say it."

"Say it now," Chero urged.

"She shall be called after my sister. Her name is Sunhilda."

Sunhild gasped and stepped forward to throw her heavy arms around my neck.

Safe in her embrace, I felt small and weak and full of fear for what would come. How much easier, I thought, to stay with my Frankish family, Sigurd's family, and watch my daughter grow. I freed myself gently from

Sunhild's grip. "I must lie down now," I said. "I have many things to think about tonight."

Gripner said, "Go, child. I will send one of the servants tonight to round up your escorts for your journey. I will have them here before dawn if you like."

"How well you know my mind, Gripner, Father," I answered. And I ran off without looking at their faces again.

THE CITY OF ATTILA

CHAPTER 17

Perhaps the heads of his victims only served to remind Attila of his defeat. Or perhaps the flies that swarmed around them unsettled him. In any event, the heads were gone when I next went to the hall. And in the days that followed, I found myself hoping to encounter Edeco in the courtyard so that I could ask him what had become of them. The matter was all important to me. But as I had no opportunity to speak to Edeco alone, I went on dreaming of my brothers' heads night after night—sometimes out on the plain beyond the City of Attila with maggots groveling across their cheeks and vultures working at their eyes, and sometimes floating in the dark of my hut with their swollen, black tongues flickering and their protruding, dead eyes full of grief and accusation.

There was only one other matter on my mind. Once I saw Eara walking ahead of me in the courtyard and I ran to catch up with her before she entered the hall. "I envy you now that you have been given the privilege of serving Attila each night," I said to the old woman. "I wonder did I do something to upset him."

Eara looked at me with penetrating eyes. "I asked to be permitted to serve," she answered curtly. "I fancied you were under some strain, and I feared that you might err in some way."

"Did you say that to Attila?" I asked, amazed that Eara had seen through me.

"No," she answered, and she hurried away before I could find the words to convince her that I must be the one to serve Attila, for I had set my mind so rigidly on emptying the contents of Sagaria's gem into his wine cup that sometimes I awoke wondering whether the deed had already been accomplished.

I had only one small pleasure to counterbalance my grief, and that was the privilege of witnessing Attila's decline. He spoke to no one now; even his speeches, which had been a prelude to every meal, were abandoned. And where he had always appeared to be indifferent to his surroundings, now he seemed to be in a kind of stupor from which he could not awaken. His fingers took an eternity to get from his bowl to his mouth, and more often than not, half his meat remained when the meal was over. And all the time his eyes were hard and unfocused, so that I thought he must yet reside out in the field—in that moment when the sun's first rays betrayed that his enemies had withdrawn and made a fool of him. His officers and his sons, noting his disposition, spoke in whispers, if they dared to speak at all, and even Ernac knew better than to attempt to speak to Attila directly. He lost weight; his skin—once sanguine—paled, and he showed no interest anymore in his wives. He was sinking, and had I not come to hate him with a passion which made my former feeling seem like mere distaste, I might have said to myself, *The war sword has finally begun to do its work. I have only to wait and let events unfold.*

One night, when Spring was close at hand again, Ernac said to his brothers, "I suspect that Aetius loves our father still."

Attila, who seemed to be sleeping only the moment before, glared at the boy. "Never let me hear you speak of Aetius and his love for Attila," he snarled.

Ernac gasped to find himself the victim of his father's wrath, and then his face hardened so that it was clear that he was close to tears. He lowered his head and set about playing with his food.

But Attila continued to stare at him.

This brief exchange disturbed me, for I recalled how a seemingly candid remark had once stirred my father from his lethargy. And sure enough, the next evening, Attila passed his wine cup around and made his first speech in many nights. "Perhaps we have taken this matter of Aetius and his Thuets too seriously," he said. "We have lost men, yes, but their sons are coming of age and anxious, I have no doubt, to fight for Attila. My guess is that Aetius thinks we feel indebted to him now. Perhaps we should send him a letter and say that is what we feel." His men and his sons perked their ears to hear more, but there was no more that night. On the next, however, he spoke to his men at length on the matter of the Western Empire. And not long after, they marched again.

This time, I did not speculate on what might or might not happen to Attila or Edeco. It sufficed to know that they were gone and, also, that Attila had left enough guards behind (there were plenty of men too badly wounded from the last battle to march) so that one was always posted outside my hut,

Gudrun's Tapestry

for I had no desire to leave it. Now that I did not feel compelled to spend my time measuring my hatred for Attila and examining the image of my fingers at work over his cup, I was free at last to mourn for my brothers in earnest. And mourn I did, for my brothers and for all the other Burgundians who had likely died along with them. And how strange it came to seem that my conspiracy, meant to bring Attila down, should have had for its result their deaths. My mind went cloudy when I thought of it, and I could not seem to recall the sequence of events which had brought about such a dire result. I felt certain of one thing only: I had made a grave mistake in coming to Pannonia; the Burgundians would have fared far better had I stayed at home and raised my child. I thought of the old days, and of how my going to Brunhild had its part in Sigurd's death, and I felt myself more cursed than the war sword. And as I sat, day after day and night after night, as rigidly as Attila had sat during his brief moment of distress, I considered taking my life so as to put an end to the curse within me. The only thing that kept me from doing so was the memory of Sagaria. Truly, I did not like to do a thing of which I knew my friend would disapprove. That is how much I loved her. Of course I knew that Sagaria would not approve of my killing Attila either, when the time came, but that there was no hope for. If I were to heed the words which I seemed to hear Sagaria saying during the fleeting moments when I was able to sleep, then my purpose in coming to Pannonia would all have been in vain—as would my own sufferings and my brothers' deaths. Only by killing Attila could I justify all that had gone before, and thus, when Sagaria drifted unbidden into my dreams, I bade the young Roman hold her judgment and her tongue.

One evening it was the young Hun again who came in with my dinner. I moved my mouth to greet the girl, for I had not seen her in some time, but in the end, I did not manage it. The Hun stood looking down on me with so much pity in her eye that I thought my heart should break anew. Then she smiled all at once, and after glancing behind her to be certain that the guard was not riding near the open doorway, she said, "I have some news. A messenger came today to say that Attila will soon return."

I could see by her look, which was one of encouragement and expectation, that the Hun had volunteered this information solely to comfort me, thinking, as I had once given her cause to think, that I was interested in events concerning Attila and his men. I forced myself to smile. Indeed, I should have been happy enough, for Attila had not been gone long enough to wage war on anyone, let alone the Western Empire. But I had no feeling on the matter one way or another. The only thing it meant for me was that now I would have to cease my mourning and begin training my mind again on the poison and its descent into Attila's cup.

They marched into the city at night, quietly this time, and once again without any celebration to mark their entry. And thus I was surprised when I went to the hall the evening following and found Attila looking satisfied with himself and his officers. I was surprised, too, when my careless eye fell on Edeco, to find that my disdain for him was not at all diminished. So as to please Sagaria in one respect at least, I had made some effort to forgive him, for he could not have done otherwise.

Though I made no attempt to listen that night, I happened to be near when Attila said to his men, "Let Aetius and Valentinian think that it was the words of their Pope that turned us back. We saved many lives by getting out before the plague flourished. The plague is our ally. It will work on our behalf now and take as many lives as we would have . . . but at no risk to ourselves. Attila is content to wait. And when the plague has finished its work, when the living are wandering among the dead, counting them up and grieving over their number, we will march again. It is all very clear to me now. I had a dream last night wherein I saw it all at work. As soon as the plague is over, I will make Honoria my wife and claim my right to half the Western Empire. In the meantime, we will march on the Eastern Empire. After the way I played into the hands of the Pope, making such sweet promises to him, Aetius would not dare to come to Marcian's aid."

Attila chuckled and nodded at his men. And though I had seen a few of them exchange amazed looks between themselves while Attila had been speaking, his men chuckled and nodded back. Then Attila sat forward suddenly, his face rigid and his fist held ready to strike his breast. "I am Attila!" he roared. "The war sword was sent to me for a reason. Me. Not Valentinian. Not Marcian. Let no man forget that." He dropped his fist and stared down at his tray. When he looked up again, his features had softened. "Now eat and go," he said softly. "I have my letter to Marcian to compose tonight." Then he shifted his tray and began to poke at his meat. But a moment later, with his mouth stuffed full, he added, "Let no one here speak a word of this until I say so."

Perhaps unconsciously, Orestes turned to look at Eara and me; we were pouring at the table just behind him.

Attila swallowed his mouthful hastily and laughed, saying, "Do you concern yourself with the loyalty of my sister and the one who will soon be my wife, Orestes?"

Gudrun's Tapestry

Involuntarily, I looked up at Eara and found her looking back at me. So, I thought, Eara is Attila's sister. And all at once I realized that she hated him as much as I did.

One afternoon I heard a voice outside my hut saying to the guard, "You need not come again. She marries Attila tonight."

I sat up promptly, thinking that I must have been dreaming, and waited for my head to clear. In a moment, the curtain was pulled open and Edeco stood at the threshold with his mouth open as if he had so many things to say that he did not know where to begin. "I heard," I said to save him the trouble of repeating himself.

He turned to watch the guard ride off. Then he cried, "You must hurry. My orders were to tell your guard to bring you to the bath house to prepare. But Attila is meeting with his sons now, almost all of whom will be riding with us tomorrow when we leave to march on the Eastern Empire. I am taking the chance that no one will say to him, 'I see it was Edeco who brought the Thuet to the bath house,' for no one heard his order but me."

I jumped to my feet, crying, "Fool. How dare you risk reviving his suspicions now!"

"Gudrun," Edeco began, "I only desired to bring you the news myself, to say a few words to you before—"

"Did you imagine that I would be pleased to have your company?"

Edeco's eyes hardened. "My mistake," he said stiffly. "But it is too late for it now, Gudrun. Hurry along."

"And never say my name again," I snapped.

Edeco lifted his head higher. "Forgive me. As soon as we reach the bath house, I will assign a guard to take over. I only thought—"

"Enough," I said, and I went out of the hut before him.

I was walking so briskly that Edeco had to rush to mount his horse and take his place behind me. When he had caught up, I cried over my shoulder, "You will not be marching tomorrow. By tomorrow Attila will be dead." I smiled when I heard him gasp.

"What can you be thinking?" he asked. "We tried, we failed. Now you will marry him. There will be plenty of time in the future to—"

"To conspire again with you, Edeco? You make me laugh. Your heart is what it has always been, a vessel for two opposing passions." I began to walk faster.

"Wait, Gu . . . Ildico," Edeco called, bringing up his horse. "We must speak about this. I must know what your plan is. You cannot possibly think

253

that you can overpower him. You need only seem to be reaching for the war sword, and in the next instant, your head will be rolling on the floor."

"We Burgundians are used to losing our heads," I answered dryly. I was sorry now that I had bothered to disclose my ambition to him.

"And even if you did manage it," Edeco was saying, "you would never escape alive. Not a night goes by when his guards are not posted outside the palace. And furthermore, there is no reason to act. We are weak. The Eastern Empire is strong. Let these events take care of themselves."

Edeco went on in this vein, loudly at first, and then softly as we went through the village.

But I had an idea, and I had stopped listening to his tirade so as to consider it. When we reached Onegesius's gates, I took advantage of their screeching to say to Edeco, "Can you get Ernac away tonight?"

He stared at me incredulously. A guard came to take his horse, and we entered the tunnel that led to the world without. There was no one about. "Can you?" I asked again.

"I have no reason to."

"You have. This is likely the last request that I shall ever—"

"It is not possible. I am to ride tonight to meet with some of the leaders of the tribes outside the city to make certain they are well prepared. It is my guess that Attila wishes to spare me the pain of watching you become his wife. And it will be painful, Gudrun, because—"

I cut him off. "All the better. Surely Ernac would be pleased to be asked to ride at your side."

"My sons ride with me."

"Ask Ernac, too."

"But, I—"

"Now fetch me a guard," I said, and I turned into the tunnel that led to the bath house.

"I must know your plan," Edeco whispered, hurrying behind.

I reached the door and extended my arm as if to lift it myself. "Go," I commanded. I turned from him, and in a moment I heard him retreating. I bent my head and pulled off the chain, for if anyone were to recognize it, it would be here, where Sagaria, too, must have come regularly to bathe. I heard footsteps behind me and glanced over my shoulder to make sure that it was the guard.

All the usual attendants were within. They greeted me, as they had learned to do over the years, and stood back, as they knew I liked, while I undid my broaches and slipped out of my robe. I slid the chain from one hand to the other so that now it was enclosed along with my other trinkets. Then I placed the lot against the wall in a heap. Hoping to keep the attentions of the attendants and the guard on me, I made my way to the pool chattering, asking one woman whether the water was warm today and another whether she had slept well, for I thought, I said, that she looked tired. While the second woman answered, enumerating all the tasks she had to see to in the course of a day, I slid into the pool and bathed quickly. When the woman had finished with her catalog, I turned to the guard and cried, "Can you not turn your back?" He laughed and went on staring. "Monster," I cried as I climbed out of the pool. "Has no one told you that I am to marry Attila tonight?"

His expression sobered at once, and he looked to the attendants for confirmation. They nodded and chuckled as they wrapped me in drying cloths, and the guard, whose mouth was still agape, turned aside. One of the women came toward me with a pale silk robe. And when I saw another moving to collect my broaches and other trinkets, I dodged out from under the drying and swooped them up myself. "We must hurry," I cried. "I could not bear it if Attila were upset with me on our wedding day. I have waited far too long for this."

I slipped the chain into one hand and held the broaches and the rest of it out to the attendant with the other. The robe was lowered over my head. "It is not likely that he would expect you so early," my attendant commented. The woman with the broaches added, "It seems to me that I remember someone saying that Attila's new wives are first brought to the old ones to be advised."

"Ah," I answered. I was dressed and ready to go. No one had seen the chain. The guard, who was standing now with his back to me, was so far lost in his own thoughts that I had to tap him on the shoulder to inform him that the time had come to lead me out. As I walked in front of him, I slipped the chain over my head and the gem into the neck of my robe. But whereas the gem's bulge had never been noticeable beneath the fabric of my looser, coarser garments, it protruded now prominently under the silk one. I moved the gem to the back, so that my hair fell over the bulge. Now it only looked as if I were wearing a short chain, and as many of the Hun women wore such things, I had no reason to think that anyone would notice it.

Edeco was outside, talking to the guards at the gate. My own guard, still dumb-founded, approached him timidly to ask what he should do with me next. Edeco answered, "Take her into the courtyard, to Hereca's tent."

Hereca, who was waiting outside, looked me over carefully as I approached. I looked her over, too. I had never seen her this close before, and with the sun ablaze in the west, I saw how old and wrinkled Ellac's mother was. I glanced at the hall. There were, as always, several guards on horseback before it. As the door was still down, I assumed that Attila was still meeting with his sons.

"So, Attila has decided to marry you," Hereca said.

"So it seems," I answered flatly.

Hereca walked all around me. When she came before me again, she said, "I cannot think what he sees in you."

"I might say the same of you," I replied.

My boldness surprised me as much as it did Hereca. I considered it for a moment and concluded that such an attitude must be common among folk who are prepared to die. I had many important things to think about, and I did not want to spend my last moments sparring with Hereca. I saw Edeco ride past and join the guards at Attila's door. I looked away from him.

"You are impudent," Hereca said. "You were brought to me so that I might instruct you on how to behave tonight in Attila's bower, but—"

"I have no need of your instruction."

Hereca smiled and glanced at the men at Attila's door. "Oh, yes. I had forgotten. You were once Edeco's lover. Some say you still are."

"Do they?"

Hereca began to circle me again. "Now, if I were to go about asking questions, I could probably find someone willing to say to Attila that he saw you with Edeco just last night."

I laughed. "That would be a difficult task, Hereca, as there was a guard posted outside my door last night."

Unperturbed, Hereca turned to look at Edeco again. "A handsome man, is he not?" she asked.

"Aye, but nothing compared to Attila," I answered blandly.

Hereca stepped back and raised her voice slightly. "I might have given you some useful advice," she whined. "But as you are so stubborn and impudent, you will have to do without it. And should Attila come to me in the morning before he marches and ask how it is that I failed to instruct you properly, I will be sure to tell him that I tried, but that your eyes were all for Edeco."

Unable to fetter my smile, I answered, "I doubt he will say that to you in the morning."

"I wonder," Hereca said. Then she shot one more look at Edeco and marched into her tent.

Gudrun's Tapestry

I sat down on the rug that was spread out at the entrance to the tent, eager to concentrate on my plan. But my mind was full of distractions now, and I could not seem to remember the carefully detailed strategy I had designed when I had first learned that Attila was still intent on making me his wife. Instead, my entire life seemed to want to erupt before me. I closed my eyes and let the visions come. I saw their faces—Sigurd's, Guthorm's, Hagen's, Sagaria's, Brunhild's—all dead, and all because I had failed them somehow. Then I saw the faces of my mother and Sunhild and Sunhilda, and I bade them each a silent farewell. And then I seemed to feel a burning sensation on the backs my eyelids, and I said to myself, *It is nothing but the sunlight at work on my eyes.* But I was facing east, and the sun had begun its descent behind me. The sensation became light and the light divided and became two fiery orbs, and I wondered whether these might not be Wodan's eyes. Thinking that perhaps he had found me in this godless land after all, I prayed hastily, *Oh, Wodan, all-father, if only you had not abandoned me since my coming here. What mistakes I have made without you to guide me! But you are here now, and I beg you not to leave until you have heard my petitions. Guide me now, Wodan. Lend me your wisdom, your cunning. If this is the thing I was born to do, then be at my side when I do it. Guide my fingers. Let me not err in this one account.*

And then the two orbs burst into new flame, so that now I fancied that they had not been Wodan's eyes after all. And thinking that it was perhaps Thunor who had come to hear my last words, I prayed, *Thunor, how many times have I praised you for leading my father to Valhalla? Requite me now and lead me to the task that will make of Thuets and Thuets brothers once more, free men who minister unto themselves. If not for me, then do it, I beg you, for my father, whom you proved you loved when you marked his passing with your bolts and bellows. Oh, Wodan, Oh, Thunor, hear me, I beg you, though I am surrounded by enemies and must speak your praises inwardly.*

My eyes popped open and I found myself looking at Edeco. I was horrified to see that he was hanging back from the conversation with the others on horseback near Attila's door so as to stare at me with his eyes full of longing and remorse. It seemed to me that no man could look at him and fail to realize that we had been conspirators and more. I shot him a look and closed my eyes again, but now Wodan or Thunor was gone. I saw only an orange glow floating over a darkness that put me in mind of Sagaria's eyes. And I had such a sense that my sweet friend was with me again just then, that I began to pray to her: *Sagaria, my beautiful, peaceable friend! Had you lived, perhaps I would not be here now, plotting Attila's death. Perhaps you would have swayed me against my purpose and we would have stolen away together. We might have climbed into the food wagons and had the Thuets cover us over with the scraps of the Huns. We might have gotten past the guards and set off to fetch my daughter and the dear friend in whose charge I left her. How could you let yourself die, Sagaria? You knew so much, yet you failed to note how sorely I needed you, how hungry I was for your wisdom. Why do you come to me now, when my mind is set and my fingers are readied and the only thing left is the deed itself? Are you looking down at me from your heaven, Sagaria? Is your Jesus at your side? It seems to me that I hear your voices beckoning,* Do not take the life of your enemy. *Or do I only imagine? I have suffered too long now and too thoroughly; my mind is not my own anymore.*

I do not know myself anymore, Sagaria. I thought on your words many a night, and I hoped by recalling them to find myself able to forgive Edeco. But I find it no easier to forgive him than I can Attila or myself. And thus it pleases me to think that I shall soon be dead, for my heart is already as cold as ice . . . though there are times when I think I see my daughter's eyes, and in them Sigurd's. Oh, but if I could live to see those eyes again. Hear me, Wodan, Thunor, Balder, Loke, Frig, Frey. Aid me in my quest. Pray with me, Sagaria. I loved you so well. Say you love me yet. Let me live to see my daughter's face again. Wodan, Thunor, Balder, Sagaria, come altogether and guide my hand, and then let me live long enough to describe its motion to my child. Or better yet, carry out the task yourselves—not tomorrow when he marches, but now, today, as I sit here lost in your essence. Let his heart fail him before he reaches his couch. Let his lungs give way before he steps down from his bower. Show me some sign that you hear me. Do not force me to do the thing that will make my friend an enemy and myself a corpse. Truly, I do not want to die.

I was startled out of my reverie by a sensation along my upper arm. I opened my eyes and saw Edeco looming over me from up on his horse. The thing on my arm was his riding whip. He held it there so tenuously that it was a wonder that I had felt it at all. Suddenly, I found myself longing to embrace him, longing to cry into his broad shoulder. He must have seen the fear in my eyes, for with a flash of his, he indicated the entrance to Hereca's tent. In his officious voice he said, "The time has come, Ildico."

The serving women were already within, and it was strange for me to think that I was not to join them. Attila, whose heart had not failed him, whose lungs had not given way, was already spread out on his red couch. I stared at him a moment, hoping childishly that the gods and Sagaria had heard my pleas and would act as I looked on. But Attila only looked at me indifferently, and thus I bowed my head and quickly prostrated myself. Then I moved to stand near the bower, in the spot where I had seen so many of Attila's wives stand, and waited for my table to be brought to me. Soon I was joined by Hereca and two of Attila's other wives. Our table was brought and we sat down around it.

I was very calm now. I felt foolish for having attempted to conjure up the gods out of my last frivolous impulse for life. They were too far away to have heard me, and, in the end, I had bared my soul to no one.

The hall filled up quickly. Except for Edeco, all Attila's officers were there. Except for Ernac, all Attila's sons were present, too. I smiled. My strategy, which had evaded me earlier in favor of my folly, returned now, and I remembered that I had embellished it by adding a scheme so evil that even the self-possessed Attila would likely become unhinged in whatever time would be left him between his drinking of the poison and his succumbing to it.

Attila received his plain wooden cup from Eara's hand and made a toast to victory and to his new bride. I lowered my head humbly then, but I could not help but smile, and I was smiling still when the cup came round to me. I sipped and carried it back to Attila—not awkwardly, as I had carried him his cup on my first day in his service, but with confidence and pleasure. And when I pressed it into his hand, I lifted my face so as to show him my conviction and let him make of it what he would. His eyes became slits then, and he looked at me with loathing. But he said nothing. When I returned to my seat, I found that his gaze, which was still on me, had changed to one of intrigue. In all the time that I had served him, he had never looked at me that way before, and I determined to use his new posture to my advantage.

"You are bold," Hereca whispered. I ignored her and raised my head so that Attila could see my smile over the heads of all the others who sat at the tables between us. Eara brought Attila his tray and conversations from the various tables ensued. Attila's three wives spoke in whispers amongst themselves, mostly about the wives who were not present. Zerco was brought in, and in no time the hall was filled with laughter. Eara came over to my table with a wine jug, and when she saw that my goblet was still untouched, she cried merrily, "Drink up. A bride should always drink a good deal on her wedding night, as should her husband." But when I caught her eye, her smile vanished and she nodded once, solemnly. I lifted my goblet and drained it, and then I held it up to be filled again. And when Eara came around again later, I was quick to lift my goblet once more.

Several times during the course of the meal did I look up and find Attila staring at me, and I thought I saw some desire in the steady, black gleam of his gaze. Each time I answered his look with a smile, and once I even lifted my goblet to salute him. He brought his own cup to his lips then, and we sipped simultaneously. *How ugly he is,* I thought. *Even his smile is a fierce, hideous thing.*

I heard Hereca whisper to the others, "Do you see how bold she is?" And later she whispered to me, "Attila is drunk now, but later he will make you pay for your boldness."

I kept my eyes on Attila and made no response.

At length Attila raised his hand and said to his men, "Tomorrow, then. Prepare yourselves," and the conversation and laughter were instantly replaced with the sound of chairs being scraped along the wooden floor boards.

I turned to one of Attila's wives—not Hereca—and whispered, "But when will we have the wedding ceremony?"

The woman whispered back, "You have had it." And she got up and hurried out with the others.

I waited to be gripped by the fear of the events that would follow, but still I felt only calm and conviction—and a little drunk. It was as if my frantic prayers had somehow liberated me from that part of myself that was linked to life. *So, I am to go out like this,* I mused, with a smile on my face and a demeanor that has long been foreign to me to mark my demise. And I was satisfied.

I looked up from my musings to find Attila stretching his neck to see me beyond the servants who were clearing away the tables between us, his wooden cup still in his hand. I felt confident that he would take it into the bower, that my confidence itself would ensure it. My table was removed, and with it my goblet. In a moment most of the servants were leaving and only Eara and the other old woman were left, busy at the long table emptying the scraps into a barrel. And a short time after that, they were leaving, too.

Now there was nothing but space between Attila and me. Keeping his eyes on me, he lifted his wine cup and drained it. I got to my feet slowly, saying, "Husband, let me get us more to drink." I took his cup from his extended hand as I passed him and went with it to the long table. I could feel him watching me. The goblets, all wiped clean now, were set out in a row in front of the wine jugs. I reached for one, but then changed my mind and took a wooden cup like Attila's for myself. *Tonight,* I mused, *We will be equals—in simplicity and cunning alike.* I set the two cups down side by side and filled them. I was about to reach for the venomous gem when I felt Attila's breath on my neck. *No matter,* I said to myself. *When the time is right, I will know it.* I turned with the two full cups and smiled at him, charmingly, I hoped. He smiled back, and then he went to the door.

This took a moment, for of course he had his sword in hand, and he had to balance it between his knees while he lowered and bolted the door. His back was to me, and had I been holding one cup instead of two, I might have done my work then. But again, my confidence persisted, and I was satisfied to wait.

When he had finished at the door, Attila went to the bower and held the curtain back to allow me entrance. I saw his bed, a thick mattress up on a frame of gold, and a table on which there were several tapers and a bowl of dates. He went past me and laid his sword down on the table. I placed the two cups in front of it. As I was turning from them, he grabbed me and began to kiss me roughly. In spite of the promise that I had made to myself to feign affection for him, my reaction was to push him away. He stepped back and stared at me incredulously.

To countermand my mindless display, I whispered, "We have all night."

But he only continued to glare at me with his lips stretched and his teeth exposed and his small dark eyes darting from my eyes to my mouth.

Suddenly I was afraid. I touched my lips and found my fingertips bloodied. While I was still staring at my fingers, unsure what to do next, he grabbed my hand and stuck my fingers into his mouth and sucked away the blood. And all the time he watched me, so that I could see that he was defying me, daring me to confirm my reluctance.

I forced myself to smile, to seem pleased and aroused, and when I saw his defiance quit his eyes, I began to grow calm again. And when I had my fingers back from his mouth, I put them to my lips and bloodied them again. Then I turned from him and smeared my blood along the blade of the war sword. I found it brought me pleasure to touch the evil thing after so long, and, too, some of the reckless spirit I'd had when it was mine. I turned back to Attila. His little black eyes were glowing; my bold act had caught hold of his imagination. "When the gods led me to the war sword," I whispered, "they instructed me in this manner. You shall have victory, Attila. You shall soon be ruler over all the world."

His hideous smile throbbed on his face. He put his hands on my shoulders and began to move me toward the bed. But I removed his hands gently and said, "In good time, my husband. We have yet to drink our wedding toast. I am a Thuet, after all, and on Thuet lands, the bride and groom drink a toast together before the marriage is consummated. Go lie down and let me wait on you, as I have learned to do so well. Let me bring you your wine, and then the knowledge of other Thuet ways of which you may not know. I promise you, you will not be disappointed."

"Would you dare to order Attila about?" he cried, but his tone was playful, and I could see that he was delighted with this game. Still, he stood in place for a moment with his head cocked as if he were questioning himself on some matter. Then he reached past me and retrieved the war sword. Chuckling to himself, he moved off toward the bed with it. I turned immediately to the table and brought the gem around to the front of my robe. I was about to lift it out when Attila cried, "Bring me the dates, wife."

He was lying on his back on the bed. Since I could not see the sword, I assumed that he had put it down on the floor on the far side. Hoping that he would not notice the bulge now at the front of my robe, I carried the bowl of dates over and lowered it onto his chest. He grabbed my hand as it was retreating, and I smiled down on him until he released it. Then I went back to the table and began to blow out the tapers one by one.

"No," he said.

I hesitated and then blew out one more so that now only one was left burning. "One will suffice, husband," I said. I glanced at him again. He was eating his dates, watching me contentedly. I undid my broaches and let my robe fall to the floor. I slid the chain off my head and stepped out of my robe and in front of the two cups. Then, very quickly, as I had done it in my mind a hundred times, a thousand times, I emptied the contents of the gem into one of them. As I was turning, I noticed that in my haste I had spilled some of the white powder, but there was nothing to be done for it. I handed Attila his cup. With his eyes locked on mine, he drained it. I took it from him and set in down on the floor, along with my own cup. It was over. I could hardly believe it. Now I had only to wait for him to die—and, as I had resolved earlier, to make certain that his death would be as vexatious as my life in the City of Attila had been.

I climbed onto the bed laughing.

He laughed too, heartily, and I realized that I had only heard him laugh once or twice before. His laughter was gruff and vulgar, and it made me want to laugh more. He popped a date into his mouth and tore the meat from the pit profanely, with his mouth opened and his teeth exposed and his jaw working exaggeratedly. Then he turned his head aside and spit the pit across the room.

I laughed, for how could I do otherwise?

And thinking that I found his profanity amusing, he popped another date into his mouth and began the process again.

But now I began to be concerned that the poison might have its impact while he was still laughing—and worse, thinking that I enjoyed his bawdy display. "Where was Ernac tonight?" I asked all at once.

Still sucking on the pit, he answered, "I am waiting to become knowledgeable in the ways of Thuets. If you disappoint me, I will kill you. Let us speak of my sons later."

"I know where he was," I whispered. His eyes grew large in response to my sudden change of expression, and the movement of his mouth slowed some. I leaned over him. I had planned to drag out my fabrication, but now I was afraid to take the time. "Edeco said he would take him with him to the Hun camps, did he not?"

Now his mouth ceased its vulgar rotation entirely, but it stayed open, the date pit held between his teeth.

I removed the bowl of dates from his chest and began to massage him there. "Edeco tells me everything," I went on. "And he follows my orders as well."

Attila's hands came up around my neck, but it was no matter to me. I was ready to die, and I would rather it be by Attila than by his guards in the morning.

"Tonight, for instance, I ordered him to take Ernac out on the plain and cut out his heart." I shivered to hear myself say the words.

Attila bolted up. His hands began working harder around my neck, and surely they would have succeeded at their task, but he gagged just then, and I used his easing off to catch my breath and say more. "I am a Burgundian, Attila," I cried. "My brothers were Gunner and Hagen, the men whose heads you bade Edeco to sever from their bodies."

I stopped and stared at him, for it seemed he was already past making sense of my words. He had let go of me entirely now and was holding his own neck. He was gasping for breath, coughing and choking and gasping for air. I made to slip off the bed and watch him die at a distance, but his hand shot out and grabbed hold of my hair. He forced my head down onto his heaving chest and croaked, "You lie!"

"You are poisoned, Attila. And Ernac is dead. The Empire is finished.

Bring me down with you if you have the strength for it, or leave me for the guards. I do not care which. I have done the thing I came to do."

He gasped and choked and tried to reach my neck, but his hand kept slipping from its target. Then he fell back on the bed and gasped and choked some more. I jumped off the bed. Attila's eyes grew so large that I thought they would fly out of his head, and as he struggled to take in one last breath, he lunged at me. There was a thump as his body hit the floor—and nothing more.

I knelt beside him and listened to the silence for a long time. Then I fancied I heard a ringing in my ears. I was weak, and it took a great effort for me to stand again. I dressed slowly. There was a basket in one corner, and without bothering to examine its contents, I dropped Sagaria's chain into it. Then I dusted the powder I had spilled on the table onto the floor.

I felt I must keep moving, for Attila was dead and there was nothing left to consider but my own demise at the hands of the guards in the morning. The courage had all gone out of me, and I wondered how I had managed to accomplish such a thing. I said to myself, *I should be happy; now is a time to rejoice.* But I felt only the need to be active and to quell the ringing in my ears.

I went to the corpse and turned it over. As if he were hankering yet after that one last breath, his eyes still bulged. His skin was pale now, and there was a stream of blood running out of one side of his mouth. I wiped it off with the hem of my robe, and remembering the blood on the war sword, wiped that too. I returned the war sword to the table, but then I thought better about it and replaced in on the floor at the side of the bed. I tried to lift Attila onto the bed, but he was too heavy. There was an ornate bench at the foot of the bed, and this I dragged around to the side and maneuvered it between the bed and the corpse. I managed to get his legs up on it, and then, by lifting him under the arms and using my foot to slide the bench, his rump. Then I heaved his upper body onto the bed, and after that, the rest of him. I pushed and pulled until he was centered, lying on his back just as he had been. I closed his eyes and wiped at his mouth once more. I removed his shoes and set them down in front of the two wine cups. I blew out the taper and stood in the middle of the room wondering whether there was anything I had overlooked. There was nothing. I stretched out on the floor and let my thoughts take me where they would.

I awoke to the sound of banging and voices shouting for Attila. Even so, it was some moments before I knew where I was and what had happened. I got to my knees and studied Attila's corpse. The banging persisted, and I wondered whether it would benefit me to go to the door and unbolt it. Before I could decide, there was a crash, and then the sound of rushing feet.

I lowered my head to Attila's chest and began to weep.

"Father!" a voice cried. I turned in time to see Ernac swooning to the floor. The others rushed in behind him, gasping and shouting with disbelief. Someone grabbed me and jerked me to my feet.

"What happened here?" Edeco shouted.

"Attila is dead," I whispered. But I saw by the glint in his eye that Edeco would have me say more. "We were talking, discussing the campaign, and all at once he began to cry out as if he were in pain." I burst into fresh tears.

"Could you not save him?" someone shouted.

I saw through my tears that it was Onegesius. His face was drained of color. "I tried," I cried. "I pounded on his chest, for I thought it was his heart that had given out, but it did no good."

Ellac stepped forward from the throng and grabbed my hair. Then, pushing me toward a guard, he cried, "Seize her! She has killed Attila!"

The guard, who was moaning uncontrollably, reached for me, but Edeco shot an arm out between them and shouted, "She could not have done it. There are no wounds."

"She did it, I say," Ellac shouted back. "There were guards outside all night. Had she not, she would have called for help."

"There was nothing to be done," I cried. "He died in my arms, and I held him to my breast all night and wept—"

"You lie!" Ellac barked. "You killed him! You smothered him! Guard!"

"Wait," Edeco shouted. "Look at her. Look how she weeps." He took my chin in his hand roughly and jerked my head toward the crowd. "I know this woman well. She had no reason to kill Attila. When I told her he planned to marry her, she fell to her knees and cried for joy." Ellac opened his mouth to protest, but before he could speak, Edeco drew his short sword and held it over his head. "Look at you," he shouted. "All of you, weeping like women. Forget the Thuet. Now is not the time for us to concern ourselves with her. Our leader is gone from us. Gone forever. The man who was born to rule the world is dead. Let no man mourn him womanishly."

Tears sprang to Edeco's eyes so suddenly that I thought they must be genuine. Then, with his lips pressed tightly together, he lowered his sword and drew its blade across his cheek, from his ear to his chin, nearly along the same scar that had marked him as a Hun subject from birth. He held his bloodied sword over Attila and whooped and howled so loudly that it drowned out the sobbing and moaning of the others. In an instant, others set about following his example, and when their faces were bloodied, they fought one another to hold their own reddened blades over Attila's corpse. Then the greater number of wildly howling men went running out of the bower shouting, "Attila is dead! Our leader is gone from us!"

Edeco grabbed the wrist of one of the guards before he could follow and said, "Take her back to her hut. Let no man enter until after we have buried Attila. Then we will decide her fate."

"I have already decided it," Ellac growled.

"Perhaps it is not your decision to make," Edeco responded.

The two stared at each other while the guard who had taken hold of me waited to see what would happen. Then Ellac, whose face was the only one yet unbloodied, said to the guard, "Take her out of my sight."

Even from my hut I could hear the madness surging as word of Attila's death spread through the village. Roar after roar of grief went up like so many funeral pyres bursting into flame. I could hear the women screaming, and I imagined that they were tearing at their hair and their faces, not because they loved Attila but because they feared what would become of them if it were thought that they did not.

It was late when I heard Edeco's voice, but it seemed to me that no time had passed at all. "Ride off to your hut now," he said to the guard outside my door. "As soon as I am done here, I will meet you there, for there is something else I would have you do before we join the others." I uncurled myself, but Edeco did not enter. I heard him ride off, and then there was a banging in the distance, but I did not have the strength to get up to see what he was about. There was silence, and then more banging.

I forced myself to sit up when Edeco finally returned and entered. His face was swollen almost beyond recognition and caked with dried blood. In one hand he held a battle-ax. "Where did you get it?" he asked, his eyes gleaming against his grotesque flesh. Having been rendered nearly senseless by the chaos I had set into motion, I could only stare at him. "Where did you get the poison?" he repeated.

"Are you not pleased that he is dead?"

Edeco's lips stretched and quivered. He lifted his face to the roof and moaned. When he had lowered it again, he cried, "You must go now. I have made it all ready for you. Look." He grabbed my arm roughly and pulled me to feet and then to the door. My eye fell on the sun descending beyond the Western palisade. It was a wonder to me that I was still alive to look at it. He steered me around to the back of the hut, and I saw immediately that one plank of wood had been hacked away from the palisade. "Go through there," Edeco said, his gaze set rigidly on the narrow opening. "And then through the one beyond it. The village is empty. They have all gone to watch the funeral just outside the city gates. No one will see you. There is a horse waiting. But you must ride fast. And you must ride east first for many days, for they will be searching for you in the other direction. Attila's sons are already fighting amongst themselves. When I saw them last they were arguing over the war sword. Ellac says it should go to him now as he is he eldest. Ernac insists it be buried with his father, that its power was meant for him alone. The only thing they all agree on is that a new leader should not be chosen until after the funeral—and that only because each knows that he is less than capable, and yet none is prepared to step aside to make way for his brother. Most likely the Empire will be divided among them. And divided it will fall. You have succeeded, Gudrun. You have killed the greatest man who ever lived."

Too weary to be stirred by his emotion, I mumbled, "I shall never find my way home."

"You should have thought of that when you left the evidence behind," Edeco shouted. "You should have thought of that when you set out to—"

"But what evidence did I leave?" I asked.

He stared at me incredulously. "I went to his bower only moments ago, to stare at the place where he breathed his last and to consider my part in it," he said. "There were two guards there, and as I was looking on, one noticed the two wine cups at the side of the bed behind Attila's shoes. 'What is this?' he said, seeing that one was full and the other empty. Then he lifted the full one to his lips and tasted it. He fell down dead within moments. I would have killed the other guard then, but I heard someone coming in behind me. It was Onegesius. I said to him, as I had to, 'It seems the Thuet killed our leader after all. He was poisoned.' And he said to me and the guard who was witness, 'Say nothing of this until after the funeral. I would not have

Attila's funeral befouled by such a scandal. Killed by a woman, a Thuet! When the funeral is over, we will kill her, and no one need ever know the truth.'"

I stared at him in amazement. "But it is not possible. Only one cup was poisoned, and that he . . . ." But even as I said these words, I saw Attila again, sucking vulgarly on the date pit, sucking, laughing, playing with the pit between his teeth—and then gasping when I told him the lie that I had invented so that he should not die in peace. "You must come with me," I cried. "You dismissed the guard here. Onegesius will learn of it and—"

"The guard I dismissed will not live long enough to tell Onegesius anything. This ax is his. It will seem as if you got it away from him, and fearing the wrath of Attila's sons, that he killed himself."

"Spare his life and leave with me, I beg you. We can live in peace on my brothers' lands. I have a daughter. I will teach you to be a Thuet again. I will help you to forget your part in this, for I can see that it troubles you now that it is done."

"Would you have me plant wheat and herd sheep, Gudrun? Men who have long gotten their luxuries freely do not bend so easily. I must stay here. Here I can prepare my sons for the vision you once foresaw."

With my only thought being that Edeco must flee with me, I opened my mouth to declare that the vision had been a lie. But then Edeco added, "That is the only thing left to me now. If not for that, then all the rest has been in vain."

I closed my mouth abruptly, but Edeco continued to stare at me as if he were defying me to disagree. His knuckles were white around the handle of the ax. "Your Odoacer will prosper," I whispered at last, and some of the tension went out of Edeco's face. But when I stood on my toes and kissed his bloodied cheek, his agonized expression returned again, and he lifted his chin high and looked away from me. I lingered a moment.

Then I hurried past him, out of the hut. When I reached the opening in the first palisade, I stopped and turned to look back at him. And it seemed to me that I had never seen such a terrible sight as that of the Thuet with the Hunnish scars and the bloodied face and the rigid eyes that refused to look back at me. I began to run. And I prayed that the gods, who perhaps had ears for my voice after all, would comfort Edeco and bring his sons their just reward.

Epilogue

It took Gudrun a full year, but eventually she found her way back to her people. And by that time there was not a Thuet alive who had not heard that the Hunnish Empire, having been divided equally among Attila's sons, had lost its force and begun to crumble.

Although she missed Edeco sorely and speculated often on what might have been between them, the next several years of Gudrun's life were a great pleasure. Along with Sunhild and her mother, she raised her daughter on Burgundian lands. In her absence, Hagen and Gunner had both married and produced five offspring between them, and Gudrun's belief that the Burgundians would prosper yet was renewed. Likewise, in her absence, the knowledge of writing had come to some of her people, and Gudrun made fast work of acquainting herself with it. She died peacefully not long after completing her account of Sigurd's death, her recovery from it at the hands of the Franks and her imprisonment in the City of Attila.

Unfortunately, her death occurred some years before Edeco's Odoacer marched into the Empire and made himself the first barbarian king of the Western Empire—an event which marked the end of the already declining Roman Empire.

Author's Note

Gudrun's Tapestry is based on the "Sigurth" and "Guthrun" lays, as they appear in the *Poetic Edda*, and on the history of the Germanic and Hun tribes during the reign of Attila the Hun. While there were many instances where the legend and the history were close enough to be combined, where there were not, I took the liberty of creating the links that I imagined.